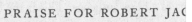

"Robert Jackson Bennett deserves a huge audience. This is the book that will earn it for him. A story that draws you in, brilliant world building, and oh my God, Sigrud. You guys are going to love Sigrud."

—Brent Weeks,
New York Times bestselling author of *The Way of Shadows*

"Smart and sardonic, with wry echoes from classic tales mixed up in an inventive, winning narrative. [Bennett is] a master of the genre."

—*Kirkus*

"An excellent spy story wrapped in a vivid imaginary world."

—*Library Journal* (starred)

"A rich, layered, thoughtful story, full of gods and magic and characters that feel unflinchingly *true*. . . . Every once in a while I read a book that's so well done, I find myself wanting to punch the author in the face out of pure envy. Congratulations, Mr. Bennett—you just made the face-punching list!"

—Jim C. Hines,
Hugo Award–winning author of *Libriomancer*

"Alien and human at the same time, Bennett's world is engrossing and fascinating. The pacing kept me reading far later than was healthy."

—Mur Lafferty,
Campbell Award–winning author of *Playing for Keeps*

CITY OF BLADES

a novel

ROBERT JACKSON BENNETT

B\D\W\Y
BROADWAY BOOKS
NEW YORK

Copyright © 2016 by Robert Jackson Bennett

Published in the United States by Broadway Books, an imprint of the Crown Publishing Group, a division of Penguin Random House LLC, New York.
www.crownpublishing.com

BROADWAY BOOKS and its logo, B \ D \ W \ Y, are trademarks of Penguin Random House LLC.

Library of Congress Cataloging-in-Publication Data
Bennett, Robert Jackson, 1984–
City of blades : a novel / Robert Jackson Bennett. — First edition.
Sequel to: City of stairs.
I. Title.
PS3602.E66455C57 2016
813'.6—dc23
2015020205

ISBN 978-0-553-41971-9
eBook ISBN 978-0-553-41972-6

Printed in the United States of America

Book design by Lauren Dong
Cover design by Christopher Brand
Cover illustration by Sam Weber

First Edition

*To Sir Terry, who wrote words upon my heart
and to Nana, who was a never-ending fountain of books*

CITY OF BLADES

He said to them:
  "Life is death and death is life.
  To shed blood is to behold this holiest of transitions, the interwoven
mesh of the world,
    The flow from shrieking life to rot and ash.
    For those who wage Her wars, who become Her swords,
    She will deem you shriven and holiest of holies.
    And you shall forever reside beside Her in the City of Blades."

And he sang:

"Come across the waters, children,
To whitest shores and quiet pilgrims,
Long dark awaits
In Voortya's shadow."

—EXCERPT FROM "OF THE GREAT MOTHER VOORTYA
ATOP THE TEETH OF THE WORLD," CA. 556

1.

make it matter

Somewhere around mile three on the trek up the hill Pitry Suturashni decides he would not describe the Javrati sun as "warm and relaxing," as all the travel advertisements say. Nor would he opt to call the breezes here "a cool caress upon the neck." And he certainly would not call the forests "fragrant and exotic." In fact, as Pitry uselessly mops his brow for the twentieth time, he decides he would rather describe the sun as "a hellish inferno," the breezes as "absolutely nonexistent," and the forests as "full of things with far too many teeth and a great desire to apply them to the human body."

He almost cries with relief when he sees the little tavern at the top of the hill. He hitches up his satchel and totters over to the shoddy building. He's not surprised to see it is almost deserted, save for the owner and two of the man's friends, because life is quiet and slow here on the resort island of Javrat.

Pitry begs them for a glass of water, and the owner, exuding contempt, slowly complies. Pitry gives him a few drekels, which somehow makes the man even more contemptuous.

"I was wondering," Pitry says, "if you could help me."

"I've already helped you," the owner says. He gestures to the water.

"Well, yes, you did do that, and I thank you for it. But I am trying to find someone. A friend."

The owner and his two comrades watch him, their expressions stony and inscrutable.

"I am looking for my aunt," says Pitry. "She moved here after an accident in Ghaladesh, and I am here to give her the dispensation from the settlement, which took some time."

One of the owner's friends—a young man with a formidable unibrow—casts his eye over Pitry's satchel. "You're here carrying money?"

"Ah, well, no," says Pitry, trying wildly to think up more of his improvised cover story. *Of all the things Shara taught me,* he wonders, *why did she never teach me to lie?* "Only the checking account and instructions for the dispensation."

"So a *way* to get money," says the other friend, whose mouth is lost in an abundance of ill-kept beard.

"Anyway, my *aunt,*" says Pitry, "is about so high"—he holds out a hand—"about fifty or so, and is very . . . how shall I put this . . . solid."

"Fat?" suggests the owner.

"No, no! No, no, no, not really. She is"—he curls his arm, suggesting a formidable bicep that is, in his case, absent—"solid. She, ah, is also one-handed."

All three of them say, "*Aaah*," and glance at one another, as if to say—*Ugh. Her.*

"I take it you are familiar with her," says Pitry.

The mood among the three men blackens so much that the air almost grows opaque.

"I understand she might have purchased property around here," Pitry says.

"She bought the beach cottage on the other side of the hill," says the owner.

"Oh, how lovely," says Pitry.

"And now she won't let us hunt on her property anymore," says the bearded man.

"Oh, how sad," says Pitry.

"She won't let us look for seagull eggs on the cliffs there anymore. She won't let us shoot the wild pigs. She acts as if she *owns* the place."

"But it sounds, a bit, like she does," Pitry says. "If she bought it and everything, I mean."

"That's beside the point," says the man with the beard. "It was my uncle Ramesh's before it was ever hers."

"Well, I . . . I will have to have a talk with her about that," Pitry says. "I'll do that now, I think. Right now. I believe you said she was on the other side of the hill, ah, that way . . . ?" He points in a westerly direction. The men do not nod, but he feels a flicker in their surliness that makes him think he's right.

"Thank you," says Pitry. "Thank you again." He shuffles backward, smiling nervously. The men keep glaring at him, though he notices the unibrow is staring at his satchel. "Th-Thank you," he mutters as he slips out the door.

***

Pitry regrets not defining the phrase "other side of the hill" more precisely. As he marches along the wandering paths, it increasingly feels like this hill keeps producing other sides out of nowhere for him, none of which bear any sign of civilization.

At last he hears the dull roar of the ocean, and he spies a small, crumbling white cottage nestled up against the rocks along the beach. "Finally," he sighs, and he trots off toward it.

The forest pushes him down, down, until he's wandering a narrow thread of path with the forest brooding over his left shoulder and a rambling, intimidating drop-off on his right. He wanders along this stretch of road for a few yards before he hears something over the waves: a rustling in the forest.

The man with the unibrow from the tavern steps out of the forest and onto the path, about twenty yards in front of him. He's holding a pitchfork, which he keeps pointed directly at Pitry.

"Oh, ah . . . Hello again," says Pitry.

More rustling behind him. Pitry turns and sees the man with the beard has stepped out of the forest and onto the path about twenty yards behind him, brandishing an axe.

"Oh . . . well," says Pitry. He glances down the ravine on his right, which ends in what looks like a very angry patch of sea. "Well. Here we all are again. Um."

"The money," says the unibrow.

"The what?"

"The *money!*" barks the unibrow. "Give us the money!"

"Right." Pitry nods, pulls out his wallet, and takes out about seventy drekels. "Right. I know how this goes. H-Here you go." He holds out the handful of money.

"No!" says the unibrow.

"No?"

"No! Give us the *real* money!"

"The bag," says the bearded man. "The bag!"

"Give us the bag!"

"Give us the bag of money!" shouts the bearded man.

Pitry looks back and forth between the two of them, feeling as if he's in an echo chamber. "B-b-but it doesn't have any money," he says, smiling madly. "Look! Look!" He fumbles to open it and shows them it is full of files.

"But you know how to *get* it," says the unibrow.

"I do?"

"You have a bank account," says the unibrow. "You have an account number. That account is full of money."

"Full of it!" shouts the bearded man.

Pitry now deeply regrets the flimsy cover story he made up on the spot. "Well . . . You . . . I don't . . . I don't . . ."

"You *know* how to—"

But then the man with the unibrow stops speaking and instead makes a very high-pitched, ear-rattling sound, a sound so strange Pitry almost wonders if it's a bird call of some kind.

"I know how to what?" says Pitry.

The unibrow collapses, still making that odd sound, and Pitry sees that there is something shining redly just above his knee that was definitely not there before: the tip of a bolt. The man then rolls over, and Pitry sees the rest of a bolt protruding from the back of his leg.

A woman stands on the path a few dozen feet beyond the shrieking man with the unibrow. Pitry sees one dark, thin eye glaring at him along the sights of an absolutely massive bolt-shot, which is pointed directly at his chest. Her hair is dark gray, silver at the temples, and her brown, scarred shoulders gleam in the sun. The hand she uses to steady the bolt-shot—her left—is a prosthetic, dark oak wood from mid-forearm down.

"Pitry," she says, "get the fuck down."

"Right, right," Pitry says mildly, and he stoops to lie down on the path.

"It hurts!" cries the man with the unibrow. "Oh, by the seas, it hurts!"

"Pain's a good sign, really," she says. "It means you still have a brain to feel it with. Count your blessings, Ranjesha."

The unibrow shrieks again in response. The man with the beard is now shining with sweat. He stares at the woman, then at Pitry, and glances at the forest to his left.

"No," says the woman. "Drop the axe, Gurudas."

The axe falls to the ground with a thud. The woman takes a few steps forward, the point of the loaded bolt hardly moving one inch.

"This is kind of a sticky situation, isn't it, Gurudas?" she says. "I told you two that if I caught either of you on my property again I'd expose a goodly amount of your innards to the fresh sea air. And I hate breaking promises. That's what the whole of civilized society is founded upon, isn't it—promises?"

The bearded man says, "I . . . I—"

"But I've also heard rumors, Gurudas," she says, taking another step forward, "that you and your friend there used to lure tourists out here and rob them blind. Being as you have such a fluid interpretation of property, I'm not surprised you thought you could keep pulling your trick on land that I now own. But I just don't have it in me to tolerate that kind of bullshit. So. Am I going to have to put a few inches of bolt in you, Gurudas? Will that communicate the message that you need to hear?"

The bearded man just stares.

"I asked you a damn question," snaps the woman. "Where do I need to shoot you to free up your tongue, son?"

"N-No!" says the bearded man. "No, I don't . . . I don't want to get shot."

"Well, you do have a funny way of following that dream," says the woman, "since the second your foot falls on my property, the opposite is most likely to happen."

There's a pause. The man with the unibrow whimpers again.

"Pitry," says the woman.

"Yes?" says Pitry. As he's still facedown on the path, the word generates a lot of dust.

"Do you think you can get up and step over that idiot bleeding all over my road?"

Pitry stands, dusts himself off, and gingerly steps over the man with the unibrow, pausing to whisper, "Excuse me."

"Gurudas?" asks the woman.

"Y-yes?" says the bearded man.

"Are you competent enough to come down here and pick up your friend and get his dumb ass back to your brother's shitshack of a tavern?"

The bearded man thinks about it. "Yes."

"Good. Do it. Now. And if I ever see either of you again, I won't be so generous with where I stick you."

The bearded man, careful to keep his hands visible, slowly walks down the path and gathers up his friend. The two of them hobble back down the path, though once they're about fifty yards away the man with the unibrow turns his head and bellows, "Fuck you, Mulaghesh! Fuck you and your mone—"

He shrieks as a bolt goes skittering across the rocks inches beside his feet, making him jump, which must be very painful considering the first bolt is still lodged above his knee. She reloads and keeps the sights on them until the bearded man has dragged his screaming friend out of sight.

Pitry says, "Gener—"

"Shut up," she says.

She waits a little longer, not moving. After two minutes she relaxes, checks her bolt-shot, and sighs. She turns and looks him up and down.

"Damn it all, Pitry . . ." says General Turyin Mulaghesh. "What in the *hells* are you doing here?"

***

Pitry was not sure what to expect of Turyin Mulaghesh's living quarters, but he hardly anticipated the graveyard of wine bottles and filthy plates he meets when he steps through the door. There is also an abundance of threatening things: bolts, bolt-shots, swords, knives, and in one corner, a massive rifling—a firearm with a rifled barrel. It's a new innovation that's only just become commercially affordable, thanks to the recent increased production of gunpowder. The military, Pitry knows, possesses far more superior versions.

The worst of it all, though, is the smell: it seems General Turyin Mulaghesh has taken up fishing, but has yet to work out how to adequately dispose of the bones.

"Yeah, the smell," says Mulaghesh. "I know about the smell. I just get used to it. Between the ocean and the house, it all smells alike."

Pitry fervently disagrees, but is smart enough to not say so. "Thank you for rescuing me."

"Don't mention it. It's a symbiotic relationship: those two excel at being idiots, and I excel at shooting idiots. Everyone gets what they want."

"How did you know to be there?"

"I heard a rumor some Ghaladeshi was walking around the beaches asking for me, claiming he had a lot of money to hand off. One vendor at the market likes me, so he let me know." She shakes her head as she sets a bottle of wine on the kitchen counter. "*Money*, Pitry. You should have just hung a 'Please rob my stupid ass' sign on your forehead."

"Yes, I realize now it was not . . . wise."

"I thought I'd keep a lookout, and saw you walking up the hill to Haque's bar. Then I saw you leave, and Gurudas and his friend follow. It didn't take me long to work out what was about to happen. You *are* welcome, though. That was the most fun I've had in a while." She produces a bottle of tea and a bottle of weak wine, and, to Pitry's amusement, goes about arranging a drink tray, a traditional gesture of welcome in Saypur with its own subtle messages: taking the tea would be an indication of business and social distance, and taking the wine would be an indication of intimacy and relaxation. Pitry watches her motions: she's become quite used to doing everything more or less one-handed.

She places the tray in front of Pitry. He bows slightly and selects the open bottle of tea. "My apologies," he says. "Though I would be most grateful for the wine, General, I'm afraid I am here on business from the prime minister."

"Yes," says Mulaghesh, who opts for the wine. "I figured as much. There's only one thing could possibly put Pitry Suturashni in my backyard, and that's Shara Komayd's say-so. So what's the prime minister want? Does she want to drag me back into the military council? I quit about as loud as anyone could ever quit. I thought it was pretty final."

"This is true," Pitry says. "The sound of your resignation still echoes through Ghaladesh."

"Shit, Pitry. That was downright poetic."

"Thank you. I stole the line from Shara."

"Of course you did."

"I am, actually, *not* here to convince you to return to the military council. They found a substitute for your position."

"Mm," says Mulaghesh. "Gawali?"

Pitry nods.

"I thought as much. By the seas, that woman kisses so much ass it's a miracle she can find the breath to talk. How the hells she made general in the first place, I'll never know."

"A solid point," says Pitry. "But the real purpose of my visit is to share some information with you about your . . . pension."

Mulaghesh chokes on her wine and bends double, coughing. "My *what?*" she says, standing back up. "My *pension?*"

Pitry nods, cringing.

"What the hell's wrong with it?" she asks.

"Well . . . You have heard, perhaps, of what is called the 'duration of servitude'?"

"It sounds familiar. . . ."

"The basic gist of it is that, when an officer of the Saypuri Military is promoted to a new rank," Pitry says as he begins digging in his satchel, "their pay is automatically increased, but they must serve in that rank for a set duration of time before receiving the pension level associated with that rank. This was because twenty or some-odd years ago we had a series of officers get to a rank, and then promptly quit so they could live off the enhanced pension."

"Wait. Yeah, I know all this. The rank of general requires four years of servitude, right? I was almost positive I was well past that. . . ."

"You *have* served as a general for more than four years," says Pitry, "but the duration of servitude begins when your paperwork is *processed*. And as you were stationed in the polis of Bulikov at the time of your promotion, the paperwork would have been processed there—but a good deal of Bulikov was destroyed as, um, you are well aware. This meant they were quite delayed with, well, anything and everything."

"Okay. So. How long did it take Bulikov to process my paperwork?"

"There was a delay of a little under two months."

"Meaning my duration of servitude was . . ."

Pitry produces a piece of paper and runs a finger down it as he searches for the precise amount. "Three years, ten months, and seventeen days."

"Shit."

"Yes."

"*Shit!*"

"Yes. As your duration of servitude is not completed, when the fiscal year ends, your pension will revert to that of previous rank—that of colonel."

"And how much is that?"

Pitry puts the piece of paper on the desk, slides it over to her, and points to one figure.

"*Shit!*"

"Yes."

"Damn . . . I was going to buy a boat." She shakes her head. "Now I'm not even sure if I'll be able to afford all this!" She waves her hand at her cottage.

Pitry glances around at the dark, crumbling cottage, which in some places is absolutely swarming with flies. "Ah, yes. Such a pity."

"So what? Are you just here to tell me I'm getting the rug pulled out from under me, I'm off, see you later? Is there no option to, I don't know, appeal?"

"Well, this is actually a common occurrence. Some officers are forced to retire early due to their health, family, and so on. In these instances, the military council has the option of voting to ignore the remaining time, and award the pension anyway. Being as you, ah, did not leave on the best of terms, they have *not* opted to do that."

"Those fuckers," snarls Mulaghesh.

"Yes. But, we do have an option of recourse. When the officer in question has shown exemplary service to Saypur, they are often assigned to go on what I believe is magnanimously called the 'touring shuffle.'"

"Aw, *hells*. I remember this. I serve out the remainder of my time wandering around the Continent 'reviewing fortifications.' Is that it?"

"That is it exactly," says Pitry. "Administrative responsibilities only. No active or combat duty whatsoever. The prime minister has arranged it so that this opportunity is now being extended to you."

Mulaghesh taps her wooden hand against the tabletop. While her attention's elsewhere Pitry glances at the prosthetic limb: it is strapped to a hinge at her elbow, which then buckles around her still-considerable bicep. She's wrapped her upper arm with a cotton sleeve, presumably to avoid chafing, and he can see more of what looks like a harness wrapped around her torso. It's clearly an extensive and complicated mechanism, and probably none too comfortable, which can't help General Mulaghesh's famously choleric moods.

"Eyes, Pitry," says Mulaghesh calmly. "Or have you not been in a woman's presence for a while?"

Startled, Pitry resumes staring into the piece of paper on the table.

Mulaghesh is still for a long time. "Pitry, can I ask you something?"

"Certainly."

"You are aware that I just shot a man?"

"I . . . am aware."

"And you are aware that I shot him because he was on my property, and he was being an idiot."

"I believe you have articulated this, yes."

"So, why should I not do the same to you?"

"I . . . I beg your pa——"

"Pitry, you are a member of the prime minister's personal staff," says Mulaghesh. "You're not her chief of staff or anything, but you're not just some damn clerk. And Shara Komayd would not send a member of her personal damn staff all the way out to Javrat to tell me my pension's getting reevaluated. That's why they invented the postal service. So why don't you stop dancing around and tell me what's *really* going on?"

Pitry takes a slow breath and nods. "It is quite possible that . . . that if you were to do this touring shuffle, it would provide an excellent cover story for another operation."

"Ah. I see." Mulaghesh screws up her mouth and loudly sucks her teeth. "And *who* would be performing this operation?"

Pitry stares very hard at the paper on the counter, as if somewhere in its figures he might stumble upon instructions on how to escape this awkward situation.

"Pitry?"

"You, General," he says. "This operation would be performed by you."

"Yeah," says Mulaghesh. "Shit."

✱✱✱

"I mean, damn it all, Pitry," snarls Mulaghesh. Her wooden hand makes a *thunk* as she brings both hands down on the countertop. "That's some dirty pool right there, holding an officer's pension hostage to make them go off and get themselves shot."

"I am sympathetic to your position, General. But the nature of the oper—"

"I *retired*, damn it. I *resigned*. I said I was done, that I'd done what I needed to do, thanks, leave me alone. Can't I just be left alone? Mm? Is that so much to ask?"

"Well, the prime minister did suggest," says Pitry slowly, "that this might be just the thing you need."

"I *need*? What the hells does Shara know about what I *need*? What could I possibly need?"

Again, she waves her hand at her cottage, and again, Pitry looks at the reeking, filthy home, with carpets tacked up against the windows and one kitchen cabinet door askew, and the counters littered with wine bottles and fish bones and tangled, dirty clothes. Finally he looks at Mulaghesh herself, and thinks only one thing:

General Turyin Mulaghesh looks like shit. She's obviously still in tremendous shape for a woman her age, but it's been a long while since she bathed, there are rings under her eyes, and the clothes she's been wearing are in desperate need of a wash. This is a far cry from the officer he once knew, the woman whose uniform was so starched you could almost carve wood with the cuffs, the woman whose glance was so bright and piercing you almost wanted to check yourself for bruises after she looked at you.

Pitry has seen someone in such a state before: when a friend of his went through a rough divorce. But he can't imagine what Mulaghesh divorced herself from, except, of course, the Saypuri Military.

But though this explains *some* of what he's witnessing, Mulaghesh's complete and utter fall from grace is still confusing to him: because no one—not the press, not the military council, not Parliament itself—has any idea why Mulaghesh resigned in the first place. Almost a year ago now she telegraphed the *Continental Herald* fifteen words: "I, General Turyin Mulaghesh, resign from my position on the Saypuri Military Council, effective immediately." And in one instant, her retirement papers were submitted, and she was gone. As with so many of Mulaghesh's actions, what she did is inconceivable to any ambitious, motivated Saypuri: how could someone just *walk away* from the position of vice-chairman of the Saypuri Military Council? The vice-chairman almost always becomes chief of armed forces, the second most powerful person in the world after the prime minister. People pored through her interactions in the weeks before her resignation, but no one could find any hint of what could have pushed her over the edge.

"So this is what Shara's become?" Mulaghesh says. "She's a blackmailer? She's blackmailing me into doing this?"

"Not at all. You have the option of just doing the touring shuffle and not engaging in the operation. Or, you could forgo the shuffle and accept a colonel's pay."

"So what's the operation?"

"I am told we are unable to reveal that until you have fully signed on."

Mulaghesh laughs lowly. "So I can't figure out what I'm buying until I've bought it. Great. Why in hells would I want to do this?"

"Well . . . I think she hoped that her personal ask might suffice. . . ."

Mulaghesh gives him a flat, stony stare.

"But in the eventuality that it did not, she did ask me to give you this." He reaches into his satchel and holds out an envelope.

Mulaghesh glances at it. "What's that?"

"I've no idea. The prime minister wrote and sealed this herself."

Mulaghesh takes it, opens it, and reads the letter. Pitry can see pen strokes through the paper. Though he can't read the writing, it looks to be no more than three words.

Mulaghesh stares at this letter with large, hollow eyes, and her hand begins to shake. She crumples up the letter and stares into space.

"Damn it," she says softly. "How in the hells did she know."

Pitry watches her. A fly lands on her shoulder, a second on her neck. She doesn't notice.

"You wouldn't have sent that if you hadn't meant it, would you," she murmurs. She sighs and shakes her head. "*Damn.*"

"I take it," Pitry says, "that you are considering the operation?"

Mulaghesh glares at him.

"Just asking," he says.

"Well. What *can* you tell me about this operation?"

"Very little. I know it is on the Continent. I do know that it concerns a subject lots of people are paying attention to, including some very powerful people in Ghaladesh, some of whom are not wholly benign toward the prime minister's agendas."

"Hence the cover story you're giving me. I remember when we used to do this stuff to dupe *other* nations, not our *own*. Sign of the times, I suppose."

"Things do continue to worsen in Ghaladesh," Pitry admits. "The press likes to describe Shara as 'embattled.' We're still suffering from the last round of elections. Her efforts to reconstruct the Continent continue to be enormously unpopular in Saypur."

"Imagine that," Mulaghesh says. "I still remember the parties when she got elected. They all thought we were about to start our Golden Age."

"The voting public remains quite fickle. And for some, it's easy to forget that the Battle of Bulikov took place only five years ago."

Mulaghesh pulls her prosthetic arm in closer, as if it pains her. Pitry feels like the temperature in the room has just dropped ten degrees. Suddenly she looks a great deal more like the commander Pitry saw that day, when the god spoke from the sky and the buildings burned and Mulaghesh bellowed at her soldiers to man the fortifications.

"*I* haven't forgotten," she says coldly.

Pitry coughs. "Ah, no. I don't suppose you would have."

Mulaghesh stares off into space for a few seconds more, lost in thought. "All right," she says, her voice unnervingly calm. "I'll do it."

"You will?"

"Sure. Why not." She places the balled-up note on the kitchen counter and smiles at him. His skin crawls: it is the not-quite-sane smile he's seen before on the faces of soldiers who have seen a lot of combat. "What's the worst that can happen?"

"I . . . I'm sure the prime minister will be delighted," says Pitry.

"So what *is* the operation?"

"Well, like I said, you won't know until you've fully signed on. . . ."

"I just said *yes*, damn it all."

"And you won't be considered fully signed on until you're on the boat."

Mulaghesh shuts her eyes. "Oh, for the love of . . ."

Pitry slides one file out of the satchel and hands it to her. "Here are your instructions for your transportation. Please make note of the date and time. I believe I will be rejoining you for at least part of your trip, so I expect I will see you again in three weeks."

"Hurrah." Mulaghesh takes the file. Her shoulders slump a little. "If wisdom comes with age, why do I keep making so many bad decisions, Pitry?"

"I . . . don't think I feel qualified to answer that question."

"Well. At least you're honest."

"Might I ask for a favor, ma'am? I need to return to Ghaladesh for some final preparations, but, considering today's events, I . . ." He glances at her various armaments.

"Would like something to defend yourself with on the road back to port?"

"I mistakenly assumed Javrat would be civilized."

Mulaghesh snorts. "So did I. Let me dig you up something that'll look scary but you can't hurt yourself with."

"I did receive *some* basic training when I first joined the Bulikov Embassy."

"I know," says Mulaghesh. "That's what I'm afraid of. You probably learned just enough to be a danger to your own damn self."

Pitry bows as she marches off into the recesses of her home. He realizes that he has never seen Mulaghesh walk another way: it's as if her feet know only how to march.

When she's gone he snatches the balled-up piece of paper on the counter. This is, of course, a grievous violation of his position, not to mention a betrayal of Shara's trust in him. *I am such a terrible spy,* he thinks, before remembering that he's not actually a spy at all, which makes him feel a little less guilty.

He stares at the words on the letter in confusion. "Huh?" he says.

"What was that?" says Mulaghesh's voice from the next room.

"N-Nothing!" Pitry balls the letter back up and replaces it.

Mulaghesh returns carrying a very long machete. "I have no idea what the original owner used this for," she says. "Maybe hacking up teak. But if it can cut lukewarm butter now, I'll be surprised." She hands it over and walks him to her door. "So, three weeks, huh?"

"That is correct."

"Then that's three weeks to eat as much decent food as I can," says Mulaghesh. "Unless the Continent suddenly figured out how to make dumplings and rice right. And, ugh . . ." Her hand goes to her stomach. "I thought for so long my belly would never have to deal with cabbage again. . . ."

Pitry bids her good-bye and walks back up the hill. He glances back once, surveying her bland, unhappy little cottage, the sands around it winking with empty bottles and broken glass. Though he's never been involved in an operation—besides Bulikov, which he feels doesn't count—he can't help but be a little concerned about how all this is starting. And he's not sure why a letter containing only the words *"Make it matter"* could have any impact on whether it starts at all.

I have trudged through fire and death to come and ask you this: Can we not be better? Can we not do better? Are we so complacent in our comfortable lives that we can no longer even dream of hope, true hope—not simply hope for Saypur, but for humanity itself?

Our ancestors were legends who remade the world. Are we willing to be so small-minded with our brief time upon these shores?

—PARLIAMENTARY ADDRESS BY PRIME MINISTER
ASHARA KOMAYD, 1721

2.

a ReLiaBLe oLδ HoRSe

She awakes in the night and tries not to scream. The scream rattles around in her throat, a hot bubble of air swelling up inside of her, and she flails around trying to find purchase on something, anything, her right hand twisting the bedsheets into a knot and the balls of her bare feet pressed against the stone wall. She pushes and strains as her brain insists she's still there, she's still at the embassy and it's still five years ago, her arm trapped under the rubble and the sky thick with smoke, the whole world ruined and gone in an instant. She's still turning over on the street, still glimpsing the young soldier facedown on the concrete, a dew drop of blood in his ear that swells and swells until it brims over, and a trickle of red weaves down his smooth cheek, the cheek of a boy.

Mulaghesh listens for the waves. She knows the waves are there. She knows where she is. She just has to find something to hold on to.

Finally she hears them: soft and steady, the gentle rise and fall as the waters scrape the sand on the shore, just a few hundred feet beyond her little cottage.

You're in Javrat, she tells herself. *You know that. You're not in Bulikov. All of that happened long ago. Just listen to the waves. . . .*

She tries to remember how to relax. She tells each system of muscles to stop, just *stop* already, and she finally goes limp. It's then that the pain seeps into her as every muscle remembers it's been straining to the point of breaking.

She takes a breath and moves her arms and legs to see if she's strained or sprained anything. She aches, but she seems to be all right.

She glances at her alarm clock. It's not even midnight yet. But she knows she'll get no more sleep tonight.

Oh, well, she thinks. *Only four hours to wait.* She does not look forward to waiting on the docks for the ship to come in. She finds she doesn't want to see people, or perhaps to be seen by them.

Her gaze moves to the object to the right of the alarm clock: a human hand rendered in dark oak wood, frozen in mid-clutch. The artisan who made it for her said it would help her hold things, and while this is true, Turyin Mulaghesh has always found its pose slightly disconcerting: there is something painful about it, like the hand is so tense in its desire to grasp something that it can hardly move its fingers.

Groaning as her stomach muscles protest, Mulaghesh sits up, takes the false hand and its harness, shoulders her way into its well-worn straps, and gently affixes the prosthetic to where her arm ends a few inches above the wrist. She wraps the soft cotton sleeve around her upper arm, then takes the four leather belts at the false hand's end, ties them over the sleeve, buckles them, and draws them taut.

She spends some time with the belts, tightening them, loosening them, adjusting them. It always takes time for everything to fit into the right place. She knows it'll never be perfect.

In the dark, General Turyin Mulaghesh tries to make herself whole.

***

Mulaghesh squints as the passenger vessel *Kaypee* slowly approaches the dock, a blinding knife of white on the dark tablecloth of the sea. It takes some time for her eyes to decipher that it is not moving incredibly slowly but is simply incredibly large—nearly eight hundred feet long. She sourly reflects that once her country reserved such effort and industry for warfare, yet now in its eighth decade of hegemony, Saypur deigns to put her vast resources toward decadent indulgences.

But the ship is probably not the true source of Mulaghesh's ire: there on the boarding dock, she is surrounded by families with shrieking babies and sulky teens, doe-eyed lovers still tangled in one another's arms, and elderly couples emitting a beatific, contented glow as they stare out at the sea.

Mulaghesh seems to be the one person who hasn't been reinvigorated by her stay on Javrat. Whereas everyone else is loose and open in their light, tropical clothing, Mulaghesh's appearance is decidedly contained: her graying hair is pulled back in a taut bun, and she wears her immense gray military greatcoat, which conceals most of her false hand. The one tropical influence she allows is a pair of blue-tinted sunglasses, but their chief purpose is to conceal her puffy, hungover eyes.

From behind the dark lenses she watches the young families, the fathers gawky and long-legged in their too-short shorts, the children awkward, mumbly, desperately earnest. She watches, envious, as the young lovers caress one another.

When did such opportunities become closed to me? she thinks as she watches their clear faces, bereft of scars or kinks in their noses, or their smooth shoulders, which have clearly never borne the weight of a pack. She shifts her left sleeve so it covers more of her false hand. *When did I get so old? When did I get so fucking old?*

She's startled by a sharp whistle and sees that she's been so lost in thought she completely ignored the ship's arrival. She picks up her bag and tries her hardest to not think about the journey back to the Continent, the land where she fought a war in her youth, wasted decades of her life in bureaucracy, and lost a hand, all in the shadow of that nation's dead gods.

***

To call the *Kaypee* sumptuous would be an understatement, but Mulaghesh has no eye for its latticed ceilings or expansive decks. Instead she marches straight to her cabin—not one of the nicer ones by a long shot—and waits for evening. She sleeps all the way through the ship's departure, nestled down in the folds of her greatcoat. She forgot how comfortable it is, and as her shoulders and arms lose themselves in its fabric she is reminded of long rests outdoors, in the cold and the rain and the mud, memories that would be unpleasant for most but have gained a somewhat rosy hue for Mulaghesh.

How sad it is, she thinks as she dozes, *that on a luxury passenger ship I am cheered most by memories of miserable soldiering.*

The sky is purpled and hazy through her porthole when she wakes. She checks her watch, confirms it's 1600, rises, and winds her way down to the Tohmay reception room.

An attendant out front politely inquires which company she should be listed under. "Thivani Industries," she says. He checks the list, nods, and opens the door for her with a smile. Mulaghesh enters and walks down the narrow hallway until she enters the final chamber. Like the rest of the ship, it is ridiculously luxurious—*How much did they spend on my damn ticket?*—though, to her regret, the bar is deserted. The only person in the room sits at a table before a row of glass doors that look out on the wide, dark sea.

Pitry Suturashni hears her coming, stands, and smiles. His face is a pale green color, and there's a stench of vomit about him. "Welcome! General. I'm glad you could make it."

***

"I'm going to assume," says Mulaghesh, "that the only reason I'm on *this* ship is because it was the first available."

"You are correct in thinking that, though you are a valued resource, we would not normally opt for such transportation." Pitry hiccups and places the back of his hand to his mouth.

"You need me to get a bucket?"

Pitry shakes his head, though he has to think about it. "As . . . unpatriotic it might be for a Saypuri, I admit my seamanship is not . . . terribly accomplished."

"Shara had a terribly sensitive stomach, I recall," Mulaghesh says as she sits. "You just had to show that girl a picture of a boat to make her paint the walls with her breakfast." Pitry's shading grows more unpleasant. "This ship's bound, I note, for Ahanashtan. Is that where the operation is?"

"No," says Pitry. "You will be taking a ship from Ahanashtan to your final destination. Though Shara has given me strict instructions that she would prefer to tell you about that herself."

"Herself?" asks Mulaghesh. She glances around the room. "Is she . . . here?"

Pitry reaches down and picks up a leather satchel from beside his chair. He pulls out a small wooden box and places it on the table in front of them.

"What, is Shara in there?" asks Mulaghesh.

"In a way," says Pitry. He slides a panel from the side of the box, revealing a brass tube that he rotates out so it points toward Mulaghesh. Then he slides the top panel away, revealing a small, oily black disc in the center of the box. Pitry finds a small lever on the side of the box and cranks it for about twenty seconds. Then he hits a button and the box begins to hiss.

"Oh, what fresh hell is this," says Mulaghesh. "Another contraption?"

"One of the Department of Reconstruction's interesting new projects," says Pitry, with a slightly hurt tone.

"The DOR never found a functioning thing it couldn't fuck up," says Mulaghesh. "I dread what would happen if they tried to reinvent the toilet."

Pitry sighs again, takes a file from the satchel, and hands it to her. It has a fat, red wax seal on the front. Mulaghesh notes that the seal has no insignia or symbol. *So whatever's in it*, thinks Mulaghesh, *certainly didn't come from any of the normal authorities.*

"Crack it open when she tells you to," says Pitry.

"She?"

Then a voice rises up from somewhere in the box's hissing, soft and somewhat sad, and sounding much, much older than when Mulaghesh last heard it: "Hello, Turyin."

"Damn," says Mulaghesh, surprised. "*Shara?*"

"She can't hear you," says Pitry. "It's a recording. It captures sound, just like telephones transport it."

Mulaghesh squints at the box. "Where does it keep it?"

"Well, it's . . . The sound's carved, I suppose, into that little black disc bit. . . . At least, I *think* it is. They had a bunch of graphs when they explained it to me. . . . Anyway, I'll leave you to it."

"Pitry," says Shara's crackly, ghostly voice, "if you're still there, you can leave us now."

"See what I mean?" says Pitry. He smiles again and slips out the door to the balcony, leaving Mulaghesh alone with the box and the file.

***

"I hope you're well, Turyin," says Shara's voice. "And I hope your time in Javrat has been comfortable. I apologize for approaching you with this task, but . . . everything aligned far too well for me not to make the ask. It's been ten months, and you are still a general of prestige who has slipped from the public eye. And you also have good reason to be on the Continent, touring nearly anything you like, and everyone will believe it's solely to earn out your pension—your country doing you a favor before it puts, how shall we say, a reliable old horse out to pasture."

"Shit," says Mulaghesh. "Don't pull your punches. . . ."

"It is, of course, unusual to appoint a general of your stature to such fieldwork," says Shara's voice, "but even more than all the reasons I have listed, I believe that you are *personally* suited to this task for a number of reasons which I hope will soon become clear.

"I'll explain now. This message cannot be replayed, so listen closely."

Mulaghesh leans in until her ear is almost right next to the brass tube.

"Two years ago, a discovery was made on the Continent: one of our installations stumbled across a curious, powdery ore along the mountainous western coastline. This material went unremarked upon until, as part of an experiment, a team in the regional governor's office tried to pass an electric current through it.

"What they discovered is that this material conducts electricity in a manner *heretofore unseen*. If you are unaware, no conductor is perfect—whether it is copper or steel, some electricity is lost along the way. But with this material, none is lost. *None*. And . . . some recent reports suggest that it possesses properties far, *far* stranger than that. . . ." A pause. "But I am not sure whether or not to trust these accounts. I will leave it up to you to judge when you arrive."

Something about that unsettles Mulaghesh. It's something in Shara's voice, as if to repeat aloud what she'd been told would make it all a little more real, and thus a little more disturbing.

"If we use this material to its fullest potential, then it would be nothing short of revolutionary for Saypur *and* the Continent—which could desperately use power and heating. Powerful industrial factions are very keen to make that happen right now. However, I have not allowed it to be processed on any larger scale. My primary concern is that our scientists and engineers are unable to determine exactly *how* this material does what it does. Normal conductors they understand: this they most certainly do not. And I am most distrustful of what we cannot explain, as you can understand."

Mulaghesh grimaces, because she absolutely does. If this material possesses astonishing properties, and if those properties can't be explained, then it's possible those properties are *miraculous:* the product or direct creation of one of the ancient Continental Divinities. Between the actions of Shara and her great-grandfather, the much-revered Kaj of Saypur, nearly all of the original Continental Divinities *should* be dead, and all their miraculous items completely dead and nonfunctional with them. *So if this stuff is miraculous,* thinks Mulaghesh, *then maybe yet another Divinity isn't as dead as we'd like it to be.*

"You are probably now thinking, correctly, that I am concerned this material may be Divine in nature," says Shara's voice. "This will probably cause you to wonder why I am sending *you* to investigate rather than someone from the Ministry of Foreign Affairs, someone whose field of study is all things Divine and miraculous."

"That would be correct," mutters Mulaghesh.

"The simple answer to this is that we did. Eight months ago. And after three months of studying this material, she vanished. Disappeared. Without a single trace."

Mulaghesh cocks an eyebrow. "Hmph."

"Her name was Sumitra Choudhry," says Shara's voice. "Her file is in the dossier Pitry has provided to you. As I said, she studied this material for three months, operating out of the Saypuri Military installation in the region. Her communications back became erratic, and then one day Choudhry was simply gone. Quite abruptly. Our forces in the region searched for her and found nothing. They did not suspect any . . . *unusual* foul play." There is a clink of glass, a *bloop* of gushing liquid—is she pouring a glass of water?—and the sound of a sip. "And I say unusual, because this material was discovered in Voortyashtan. And this is where you are bound."

"Ah, shit!" shouts Mulaghesh. "*Shit!* Are you fucking *kidding* me?"

Another sip.

Shara's voice says, "I will give you a moment to compose yourself."

***

Mulaghesh then says a lot of things to the little box. Mostly she tells it the things she's going to do to Shara when she gets back to Ghaladesh, *if* she gets back to Ghaladesh, because isn't there a one in three chance of her being murdered or drowning or dying of the plague in fucking *Voortyashtan,* ass-end of the universe, armpit of the world?

And this is where Shara has sent her: to the worst possible hinterlands on the globe, the military outpost you get shipped to only if you sleep with or kill the wrong person.

". . . don't even care if they throw me in prison!" Mulaghesh shouts at the box. "I don't care if they draw and quarter me! I'll do it to you in broad daylight, and the hells with your fancy titles!"

Another contemplative sip of water comes from the box.

"You rip me out of Javrat and stick me on a boat to *Voortyashtan* without even telling me?" says Mulaghesh. "That is bad form, *bad* form right there! Low character!"

Another sip.

Mulaghesh buries her face in her hand. "Damn it all. . . . What am I going to *do*?"

"I hope you're calming down now," says Shara's voice primly.

"Fuck you!" says Mulaghesh.

"And I think you may be somewhat relieved when I tell you that the military installation in question is our regional governor's quarters, Fort Thinadeshi. So, you will be in what is, I hope, a tightly controlled region. As you know, the fortress is located just outside of Voortyashtan proper, the urban area, so it will be a little more . . . *civilized* than the rest of the region."

"That's not saying mu—"

"This may not be saying much," says Shara's voice. "We will also be providing you with a contact, someone who can help you acclimate to the situation in Voortyashtan. Pitry will have more on that."

Mulaghesh sighs.

"I need someone on the ground that I can trust, Turyin. I must have someone ascertain whether there is any reason to believe this new material has any Divine origins, as well as what happened to Choudhry."

"What else do you want me to do, capture the sky in a damn beer glass?"

"You may prove uniquely suited to this," Shara's voice says. "Because the new regional governor of the Voortyashtan polis is General Lalith Biswal."

The name is like a hammer upside Mulaghesh's head. She sits in shock, staring at the little box.

"No," she whispers.

"As you both fought together in the Summer of Black Rivers," continues Shara's voice calmly, ignorant of Mulaghesh's distress, "I am hoping you will have some leeway with him, where most operatives would not."

His face flashes before Mulaghesh's eyes: young, dark-eyed, smeared in mud, watching her from the shadow of a trench as the sky pissed rain down their necks. Though she knows he must be close to sixty-five by now, this is how she'll always remember him.

"No, no, no," whispers Mulaghesh.

"And Biswal being about as brass as you are, I think he may be sympathetic to your cover story. He's a veteran of the military's petty bureaucracy and has seen many comrades go on the touring shuffle."

Mulaghesh just stares at the little box on the desk. *What vast sin did I commit,* she wonders, *to be damned to a fate such as this?*

"There is also the matter of the harbor," says Shara's voice. "As you are aware, Saypur is cooperating with Voortyashtan and the United Dreyling States to try to create a second functioning international port on the Continent. This should not, I hope, influence your mission in any significant way—but it is not an easy project, and tensions are running high in the region."

"Great," says Mulaghesh.

Shara then summarizes some communication channels Mulaghesh can use to report back, codexes and tradecraft methods that will be provided to her. "However, this is only to be done in *extreme* situations," says Shara's voice. "Due to recent . . . political pressures, if the nature of this operation were to come to light, it could turn out very badly. As such, I will have to be much more hands-off with you than either of us would likely prefer. But I have every confidence in you to navigate any obstacles."

"Ah, shit."

"I want to thank you for accepting this operation, Turyin," says Shara. "I can think of no one else I'd rather have in Voortyashtan. And I want to thank you for returning to me, even if it's for this one operation. I will not claim that I completely understand why you resigned, but sometimes I think I do."

You obviously do, thinks Mulaghesh, *otherwise you would not have sent that letter.*

"Thank you again for your support, and your friendship, Turyin

Mulaghesh. Your country honors you for the service you have given it—service in the past, present, and future. Good luck."

A hiss, a click, and the voice fades away.

***

The door to the Tohmay reception room cracks open. Pitry, who has been staring over the balcony at the moonlit sea with his hands behind his back, glances back and does a double take as Mulaghesh emerges carrying a crystal tumbler full of what looks like very expensive liquor. "Wh-Where did you get that?"

"Helped myself to the bar."

"But . . . But we'll have to *pay* for tha—"

"Did you know?"

"Did I know what?"

"That Shara was sending me off to damned *Voortyashtan*?"

Pitry hesitates. "Well, I . . . I was *somewhat* aware you wou—"

"Fucking hells," says Mulaghesh. She quaffs the liquor, then winds up and hurls the tumbler over the edge of the balcony. Pitry watches as what must be a forty- or fifty-drekel glass disappears into the ocean with a *plook*! "Of all the places in the world to send me sniffing up the Divine! As if I'd ever *want* to. Haven't I seen enough of all of that? When am I allowed to rest?"

"But you'll be among familiar company, won't you? General Biswal will be there; he's an old comrade. Which is not to say that your heroic days are necessarily *behind* you, of course. . . ."

Mulaghesh's face goes blank, losing all of its cynical swagger, and she stares out at the sea. Though Mulaghesh has not seemed pleased with this mission so far, this is the first time Pitry's seen her genuinely afraid.

"He wasn't my comrade, Pitry," she says. "He was my commanding officer. I thought he was dead, frankly. I hadn't heard wind of him for years. How did he get appointed to regional governor of Voortyashtan?"

"Because the last one was assassinated," says Pitry, "and no one else would take the job."

"Ah."

"They thought he was the right man for the position, though. I understand General Biswal has a . . . a history of making do in contested territories."

"That's one way of putting it," Mulaghesh says.

Pitry glances at her. "What was it like?"

"What, the Summer of Black Rivers?"

"Yes."

There's a long pause.

"Do you remember much of the Battle of Bulikov, Pitry?" she asks softly.

"I . . . I do."

"Do you ever want to see something like that again?"

"It is, perhaps, cowardly of me to say so, but . . . No. No, I do not."

"Smart choice. Well. I will put it this way: what Biswal and I did to the Continent during the Summer of Black Rivers makes the Battle of Bulikov look like spilled milk."

Pitry is quiet. Mulaghesh stares out at the sea, running the index finger of her right hand up and down the knuckle of her wooden left thumb.

"Get out of here, Pitry," says Mulaghesh. "I want to be alone right now."

"Yes, ma'am," he says, and steps back through the door.

Saypur proudly claims that because it was a colony with no Divine assistance, it was forced to think for itself. We claim that because we were forced to innovate or die, we had no choice but to innovate.

This is somewhat true. But it is the notes of Vallaicha Thinadeshi that allow us keen insight into Saypur's sudden technological advances—many of which originate with the forgotten Continental saint Torya.

From a smattering of mentions in Bulikov's records of executions we can confirm Torya was a Taalvashtani saint who spent most of his life in Saypur, being sent there in 1455. As followers of the builder Divinity Taalhavras, Taalvashtanis were architects, engineers, designers, and machinists—people who tinkered with the rude materials of mortal life as well as the Divine miracles that supported so much of it.

Torya grew so bored with his work on his Saypuri estate that he often pestered his servants to feed him distractions, treating them as puzzles and problems. Some of his creations involved wheeled shoes that allowed his servants to race up and down his lengthy hallways, as well as a stove that used convection to cook bread twice as fast.

As far as we can tell, he did this solely as a cure for his boredom—not out of any charity.

It was his Saypuri valet who realized the opportunity Torya presented. Over a series of months the valet fed him a variety of large-scale problems for him to solve, and Torya became so involved in his work that in 1457 he felt obliged to create a series of rules for the mortal world: laws of mathematics and physics that applied to reality without any Divine intervention, as well as some innovations that could easily exploit these rules. As Torya had access to countless Divine devices with spectacular properties, he was able to establish these rules both quickly and accurately.

This soon proved revolutionary. The valet secreted out copies of Torya's writings and had them sent all over the country. Within a decade Saypuris were farming with irrigation, building structures *faster and better than ever before. But it was the creation of a small steam-powered loom in 1474 that brought unwelcome attention, for the Saypuri who created it lived in a Voortyashtani colony—and Voortyashtanis understood the nature of power and knowledge far more than the Taalvashtanis did.*

The Voortyashtanis realized someone had taught the Saypuris these methods, and quickly traced the information back to Saint Torya. The Voortyashtanis then executed every slave and servant who had come in contact with Torya's estate, and petitioned Bulikov not only for Torya to be defrocked, but also executed. They won their petition, and Torya was brutally disemboweled in 1475 for crimes against the Continent's colonies.

But the Voortyashtanis' victory was not complete: Torya's laws persisted and were worked upon in secret. When the Kaj himself created his mysterious weaponry to slay the Divinities in 1636, a copy of Torya's laws was one of his most heavily used references. And in the 1640s, when Vallaicha Thinadeshi began the great technological revolution that would secure Saypur's place in the world, none of it would have been possible without the work of Saint Torya, performed just under two hundred years earlier.

Saypur, being a proud nation, would not like to admit that a Continental contributed so much to the foundation of their technological achievements. But we forget another lesson of history when we do so: a slave will use any tool to escape their slavery, even those of their masters.

— DR. EFREM PANGYUI, "THE SUDDEN HEGEMONY"

3.

PROGRESS

First the rain—the screaming, awful rain. The slap of the downpour is so stunning that Mulaghesh, who's spent the latter part of her trip cloistered in her cabin aboard the Dreyling cargo ship

Hjemdal, is almost stupefied by such brutal weather, and it makes her rethink the desire she's had for the last two weeks: to get the hells off of this chain of boats and set her feet on dry land.

But not this land, she thinks. *Not any land that exists under weather like this.* . . .

She shields her eyes, walks out on deck, and looks.

She is faced with the wide, expansive mouth of a river—the Solda River, of course, whose waters once passed through Bulikov, the very city where she was stationed for nearly two decades. On each side of the river mouth are two vast, ragged peaks that slowly recede down to the waters in a rambling jangle of sharp, broken, blade-like stones. *No wonder they call it the city of blades,* she thinks. It all looks like rubble, as if the cliffs surrounding the city have been steadily collapsing—yet amidst the stones about the peaks are lights, streams of smoke, and thousands of glimmering windows.

"So that's the city of Voortyashtan," she says grimly. "Well. It lives up to expectations."

Then she sees the harbor. Or, rather, what will one day be the harbor—maybe.

"Holy shit," she says.

The main issue with reconstructing the Continent—the underlying aim of nearly all of Shara Komayd's legislation—is one of access. There has only ever been one functioning international harbor on the Continent in modern history: Ahanashtan, which has always been Saypur's key foothold on the Continent. But if you're trying to bring aid and support to the entirety of the Continent, having only one way in and one way out makes it quite difficult.

Yet as the Continent's climate changed—growing steadily colder with no Divinities to miraculously warm the weather—there became only one remaining decent warm-water port: Voortyashtan. Which happens to sit on the mouth of the Solda River, which, if brought under control, would give the entire world access to the inner recesses of the Continent.

And long ago, Voortyashtan did once possess a harbor. In fact, back in the days of the Divinities, it was far, far larger and busier than any harbor the contemporary powers could ever aspire to. But it was put to unspeakable, monstrous purposes—purposes that make modern Saypuris shiver to think of even today.

"Every obstacle," Shara used to say (before her own career became mired in its own obstacles), "is always an opportunity." Would it not be a tremendous symbolic victory, she asked, if Saypur built a new harbor in Voortyashtan and put it to good use? Wouldn't they all sleep a little better at night knowing Voortyashtan, that most backward and dangerous of cities, was slowly being modernized, led along like a mule is led by a dangling turnip?

So it was decided that the Department of Reconstruction, with the approval of the polis of Voortyashtan, would reconstruct its ancient harbor, thus bringing swift aid to the other half of the Continent, and probably making Voortyashtan the second-richest polis on the Continent in the meantime.

But as to who would do the actual work—that was another issue. Saypur, being a naval nation, naturally had a dozen contractors and companies willing to do the job—but for Saypuri prices, all of which were astronomically high. For a while it seemed the harbor would never be built without some outrageous financing miracle, but then the newly founded United Dreyling States—having overthrown the corrupt Dreyling Republics a mere three years ago, and desperate for income—came forward with a series of bids so low that Saypur wondered if the Dreylings were using slave labor. But in the end, the Southern Dreyling Company—or SDC, as many prefer—finally captured the prize and signed the contracts.

Though from what Mulaghesh last heard, the construction of the harbor has so far proven to be more difficult than anyone anticipated. She remembers hearing about how some tremendous wreckage from the Blink blocked up much of the Solda River's mouth and would have to be removed. And if she recalls, all of SDC's most brilliant engineers were still scratching their heads over it.

Yet now, just outside the Solda Bay, she sees that they seem to be making headway. Remarkable headway, in fact.

In the mouth of the bay is a forest of dredging cranes, each 150 feet high, all in lines radiating outward from the shore. Some of the cranes are building other cranes, reaching farther and farther out to sea, while the ones closer to the shore are deconstructing the cranes at the back. It's a brilliant, confusing, impressive mess of construction work, and for a moment Mulaghesh wonders if these mechanisms are here to repair the ruined mess of Voortyashtan or if they're here to tear it down. The shore behind the cranes is awash with activity: tiny timber structures and makeshift piers all fueling the work taking place in the bay, reforging this ruined metropolis into what could one day be the trade capital of the western coast of the Continent.

But where's the wreckage the cranes are supposed to be hauling away? From what Mulaghesh can see, the Solda Bay is wide and clear.

"We'll have to cut a sharp turn here, ma'am," says the captain of the *Hjemdal*. "Might wish to hold on tight."

"Cut around what?" says Mulaghesh. "It damned well looks like we're in open seas to me, Captain."

"Stand on the port side and look down, ma'am," says the captain, "and you might catch a glimpse of it."

Mulaghesh does so, holding tight to the railing.

The ship veers beneath her. Dark water washes up the hull. She sees nothing, but then . . .

There is a disturbance in the current a few dozen feet out: the surface of the water is rippled where it ought to be smooth. She squints, and sees something down below. . . .

Something white. Something wide and smooth and pale, just below the surface of the water. As the *Hjemdal* cruises by she spies the faint outline of an aperture in this white surface below the water—a long, thin gap, pointed at the top and flat at the bottom. As they near she sees molding lining the gap, and a shutter hanging off of one ancient, rusted hinge.

Then she understands: *It's a window.*

"That . . . That was a building," she says aloud, looking back. "There was . . . There was a building under the water back there."

"Welcome to *old* Voortyashtan," the captain says with false cheer, waving at the mouth of the Solda. "Though you can't see much of it these days. It's moved, y'see, about three hundred feet. Vertically, straight *down*." He grins and laughs wickedly.

"It's under*water*?" she asks. "Wait . . . The wreckage that's blocking the Solda is the *city itself*? How have I never heard of this?"

"Because someone would have to survive to tell you," he says. "This here bay is practically a minefield, ma'am—hence why we won't be going much farther—and once you make it ashore, and you're among those wild Continentals, why . . . I'm not sure if your odds improve any." He stops when he spies a small cutter making its way through the forest of cranes. "Ah, here's your escort, ma'am. I've no doubt you and them'll have plenty to chat about."

***

The cutter zips across the bay, ripped back and forth by the howling winds. Mulaghesh shields her eyes from the gales as they draw close. The area's not totally bereft of civilization, she sees: farther down the west coast stands a tall, beautiful lighthouse, its slow, revolving beam lancing out to dance over the waters. Beside it is a large, colorful wood-and-stone structure that feels very out of place amid dark, dreary Voortyashtan. Large banners festoon the stairs leading up to it, each embroidered with the letters "SDC."

"They're certainly setting up shop, aren't they," mutters Mulaghesh.

The cutter pulls up to a pier just east of the lighthouse, which is deserted except for one person, who stands at its end with a flick of glowing cigarette ash suspended in their shadow. Besides this, all she can spy is their thick, sealskin coat with its hood up, wrapped tight about their face.

Mulaghesh awkwardly descends the rope ladder to the pier, forced to compensate for her false hand. The figure at the end of the pier waves to her.

She remembers what Pitry said as the *Hjemdal* shipped out: *We've secured you a source, who will contact you when you arrive.*

She asked: *Who is it?*

The best possible resource, the chief technology officer of the whole of SDC. They should know absolutely everything about what's going on in Voortyashtan. Though now that she thinks about it, Mulaghesh realizes he never actually told her the CTO's name.

Mulaghesh walks down the pier, her bag slung across her shoulders. "Are you here for me?" she shouts to the figure.

The figure just waves again. As Mulaghesh comes closer she sees another SDC badge on their breast, though this is of a bright yellow color with a gear insignia below, suggesting something different.

"Thank you for meeting me here," says Mulaghesh as she approaches. "But it won't mean much if I drown to death in this rai—"

She stops as the figure pushes back their hood.

She expected to see some dour, red-faced, glowering Dreyling, a foreman or dockworker with an abundance of scars and burst blood vessels and a receding hairline. What she did *not* expect to see is an intimidatingly beautiful Dreyling woman in her mid-thirties, with high cheekbones, bright blond hair, and glacial blue eyes set behind a pair of austere spectacles. She's tall, over six feet, which means she towers over Mulaghesh. The woman takes a massive drag from her cigarette, flicks it into the sea—it sizzles angrily, begrudging its abandonment—and smiles at Mulaghesh.

And Mulaghesh sees many things in that smile. She sees charm, wit, and a roiling sea of cleverness; she sees a sharp, diamond-hard attention, recording everything that's witnessed; but what Mulaghesh sees most in that broad, white smile is an unshakable, concrete confidence that its owner is at any given moment the smartest person in the room.

The woman says, "Welcome, General, to the polis of Voortyashtan. I hope our crew treated you well?"

Mulaghesh stares into the woman's face. There is something familiar about her that she can't quite place. . . .

In her mind, Mulaghesh removes one of the young woman's eyes, adds a brutal latticework of scars, and replaces her charming smile with a look of implacable, lethal menace.

"By all the hells," says Mulaghesh. "If you're not the kin of Sigrud je Harkvaldsson, then I am a dead fucking dog."

The charming smile evaporates. The young woman looks at Mulaghesh, astonished, but instantly recovers: she gives a delighted laugh, though her eyes can't quite match it.

"You have a head for faces, General!" she says. "You are correct. I am Signe Harkvaldsson, chief technology officer of the Southern Dreyling Company. And you, of course, would be the famous general Turyin Mulaghesh."

"If you say so. You know, I feel like someone could have *told* me it'd be Sigrud's daughter I was meeting here. Why couldn't they get me someone at the military base?"

"Because that's where Sumitra Choudhry disappeared from," says Signe coolly. "And I don't particularly think your minister trusts everyone there right now."

Mulaghesh glances over her shoulder. "Why don't we find someplace else to discuss this?"

"Certainly. I've arranged for you to stay with us at the SDC construction headquarters, just outside of the city." She points in the other direction, toward the SDC building beside the lighthouse. It's about a thousand times more hospitable-looking than Voortyashtan.

"That works fine for me."

"Excellent! Then please follow me. The train to the SDC headquarters is waiting for us."

"You have a train just for your headquarters?"

"More for the work on the bay itself. We can't ship resources to the river mouth—we're here to specifically *amend* that situation. So we ship them to an easier spot, outside of the city, and use a train to bring them here."

"All to build a harbor for the Continent," says Mulaghesh. "Seems like it'd be easier to just make a new one somewhere else."

"But this isn't just a *harbor*, General. It's a gateway to the Continent itself!" She points to the two peaks above the Solda River. "Past those gates—or what's left of them—lies a water passage granting access to nearly the whole of the Continent! And no one's been able to

use it in *decades*! Yet soon, in a matter of months, we'll be able to"—
she opens the door to the train's sole passenger car—"well, throw the
gates back open."

Mulaghesh glances back at the peaks. "You keep calling them
gates. Why?"

Signe smiles. "That's a very interesting question. Come aboard,
and I'll tell you."

***

The tattered cityscape of Voortyashtan slides by as the train picks up,
replaced by tall white cliffs. Signe lights another cigarette—her fifth
so far, Mulaghesh gauges. There's something distinctly mercantile
about the Dreyling woman: her hair is tied back and parted in a fashion Mulaghesh knows is now quite chic in Ghaladesh, and she wears
a close-cut, collarless black jacket with a flap that hides all buttons,
paired with slim, dark trousers and glossy black boots. A tremendous
gray scarf sits in piles around her neck, going right up to her chin.
Mulaghesh feels Signe would fit right in at some high meeting of a
company board, spitting out numbers and calmly allaying the fears
of stockholders. *Which is probably exactly what she does,* Mulaghesh
reminds herself.

But her hands are an anomaly: when Signe removed her gloves
Mulaghesh expected to see smooth, soft, perfectly manicured digits.
But instead her hands are hard, callous, cracked things suggesting
years of brutal labor, and they're smudged and smeared with black
ink, as if she's been handling cheap newspapers all day.

Mulaghesh shivers as a draft snakes into the train car.

"Late winter," says Signe. "It's quite harsh here, as it is for the
rest of the Continent. But Voortyashtan sits on the Great Western
Current, ensuring its waters will never freeze over. Otherwise, we
wouldn't be here."

"What a pity that would be."

"Perhaps so. It does bring with it a great deal of moisture. Did
you know, for instance, that Voortyashtan is the flood capital of the
world?"

"Another charming trait to recommend it. As if its history wasn't enough."

"True. What do you know about Voortya, General?"

"I know she's dead."

"*Besides* that."

"I know I *like* that she's dead."

Signe rolls her eyes. Smoke pours from her nostrils.

"Fine," says Mulaghesh. "I know she was the Continental Divinity of war and death. I know she was terrifying. And I know her sentinels once essentially controlled the known world, shipping out of this very bay by the thousands."

"By the *hundreds* of thousands," Signe says. "If not more. And you are correct that she was the Divinity of war and death, but she was also the Divinity of the sea—something many forget. Likely because her martial exploits are . . . much more memorable."

"If by that you mean her sentinels killed and maimed and tortured Saypuris by the millions, yeah. That's pretty memorable, for us. Maybe a little too memorable."

"True. But what many forget is that, as the Divinity of the sea, most of her domain was *built* on the sea. The original Voortyashtan, as we understand it, was one giant, floating city, constructed on many docks and plinths, or perhaps floating on the sea itself. Either way, we've gleaned from its current position that, whatever its methods of support, they were definitely *miraculous*."

"You mean because it's at the bottom of the bay." This part of the story is familiar to Mulaghesh: there's hardly a part of the Continent that wasn't devastated when the Divinities were killed by the Kaj, which caused all the miracles that supported the Continent's way of life to abruptly vanish—an event known as "the Blink." If the original city of Voortyashtan was allowed to float on the ocean by miraculous means, that would definitely explain why it's currently playing home to the fish of the North Sea.

"Correct." Signe flashes her cunning smile. *How the hells does she keep her teeth so white*, Mulaghesh thinks, irritated, *if she smokes so much?* "What you see now of the city was *not* the city. Just the entrance portion of the Voortyashtan of old. Those two peaks east of the city aren't mountains, General—they're the frame of a *door*."

Mulaghesh chews her cigarillo. "So modern Voortyashtan is built on ruins of the old city's *gates?*"

"Correct. And the original city now clogs up the Solda, causing massive seasonal flooding downriver and preventing one of the grandest rivers in the world from becoming a passageway of incredibly lucrative trade."

Mulaghesh laughs wickedly. "So your job here is to give the whole of the Continent an enema, is that it?"

This doesn't even put a dent in Signe's smile. "That is one way of putting it, yes."

"And you actually think you'll make this rendition of the schedule?"

"Oh, well . . . In truth, my current calculations suggest we'll beat the latest iteration of the dredging deadline by nearly three months."

Mulaghesh stares at her, mouth open. "You . . . You think you'll *beat* it?"

"Yes," says Signe mildly.

"You'll *beat* this deadline that keeps getting pushed back *years?*"

"Yes."

"And you're not being completely and utterly *mad?*"

"Not to my knowledge, no."

"How do you think you could possibly manage this?"

"I don't begrudge you your skepticism," says Signe. "For years, SDC struggled with figuring out how to dredge the bay, how to rectify this decades-old damage done by sustained catastrophes. But eventually our engineering staff came up with a solution: modular component processing."

"What?"

Signe smiles, and Mulaghesh realizes she's just given the expected reaction in Signe's little presentation. "We can't work from the outside in of the Solda Bay—there's a whole undersea city between us and, well, the city. So we decided to work from the inside out. We broke down the two main pieces of equipment—a crane, and a cargo ship—into their most basic components. Simple, cheap, functional components requiring the least amount of effort to put together and take apart. Then we made a small landing depot a few miles from Voortyashtan where we could get to shore"—she motions out the window toward the approaching lighthouse—"and built track that would allow us to ship the components closer to the bay. Once we could get the components to the mouth of the Solda, and once we got our first two cranes built, the game was over."

Signe takes a nonchalant puff from her cigarette. Mulaghesh studies her, waits, and finally asks, "How was it over with just two cranes?"

"Why, get two cranes in the right places, and you can do anything. First they built ships and piers. Then they built four more cranes farther out in the sea, one on either side of each of them. Then those four cranes hauled up rubble, loaded up the ships, and built eight more cranes out into the sea, one on either side of each of *them*. Then the eight new cranes hauled up rubble, loaded up the new ships, and built sixteen new cranes . . . and then thirty-two, and sixty-four, and so on, and so on. This is a gross simplification, but you get the idea."

Mulaghesh looks at the forest of cranes out the window. "So all that out there took . . ."

"The state of the project, as you see it today, took just under twenty months to produce."

"Are you *serious?*"

"Yes," says Signe, with a very slight pout of vanity. "We're told the Solda has already stopped flooding downstream—something your old station of Bulikov will be glad of. And one day, very soon, parts of the Continent that were once completely isolated and cut off will now be linked. Pretty soon the rejuvenation of the Continent will truly begin."

"Whose brilliant idea was all this?"

"Oh, why, the credit belongs to a variety of teams, as each component and each step in the process required incredible oversight and planning, and—"

"It was you, wasn't it."

Signe pauses just long enough to satisfy modesty. "I had the idea on a . . . somewhat grand, abstract scale. I *did* formulate the modular process and oversee its sourcing and detailing, yes. And portions of the arm design are mine. Though there were countless other SDC teams that played their part."

"I guess you don't get to be chief technology officer for nothing."

"Who can say? My position is the first in the company's history. We've never had a CTO before me."

"So . . . how exactly does a member of the Dreyling royal family come to have a hand in all this?"

Signe blinks, confused. "Dreyling royal family?"

"Your daddy is, unless I'm forgetting, the heir to the Dreyling throne?"

Signe exhales slowly through her nostrils and taps her cigarette ash into the ashtray in the armrest. "The United Dreyling States are a free democracy now. We no longer cater to a monarchy, or to the pirate kings like we did back during the Republic days."

"Even if that monarchy was originally yours?"

Her eyes glitter. "It is not *mine,* General. It was *never* mine. And that has nothing to do with the harbor."

"So you're saying your father has nothing to do with your position here?"

Signe pinches out the end of her cigarette with her thumb and forefinger, her skin hissing as it touches the ash, though her face registers no pain. *Those calluses run deep,* thinks Mulaghesh. "My father, General," Signe says slowly, "has terribly little to do with anything significant happening these days, as far as I can tell. And if you want his opinion on the matter, I suggest you find someone who would know more than I do. Or, moreover, someone who would *care* to know."

Signe looks up as the train comes to a halt. The white shaft of the lighthouse hovers above them. Signe's composure immediately returns, the clever smile blooming back on her pretty face. "Ah! We're here. Allow me to take you to dinner. I know it's late, but I'm sure you're starving." Without another word, she strides off the passenger car, leaving Mulaghesh to struggle with her bags.

***

Mulaghesh and Signe dine in the private dining room just below the control rooms for the lighthouse. It's clear this is reserved for the upper echelons of the company: Signe had to use multiple keys just to get to this part of the building. Their server—a Dreyling boy with a wispy half-beard—enters and exits through a secret panel door beside the bookcase in the corner. Everything about the room is designed for privacy, a place to hold conversations and do the real work once the formal meetings are done, though it feels like an extremely upscale whalers' inn: everything is dark, ornate wood, and most of the walls are covered in the bones of unsettling sea creatures, some with harpoon barbs still lodged in them.

"One way to keep a skilled workforce," Signe explained to her when they entered, "is to give them every creature comfort. These men have come out to the end of the world to risk their lives—so even if they are hard laborers and seamen, we give them the best chefs, the best entertainment, and the best accommodations money can buy."

But Mulaghesh also notes that the accommodations are quite permanent. One wouldn't build such a site if you weren't intent on staying here for a while. And if they truly expect to get the harbor ready in a matter of months, then what comes after?

From this angle she can see Fort Thinadeshi: a dark, squatting, massive installation on the cliffs just north of the lighthouse. Its most immense cannons are pointed at the city, threatening to rain death down on them at any second. She wonders how the Voortyashtanis must feel with those cannons pointed at them day and night.

"You're briefed on the situation?" asks Mulaghesh quietly.

Signe picks up her napkin and delicately dabs at the corner of her mouth. "Sumitra Choudhry. Yes."

"So," says Mulaghesh. "What can you tell me about her?"

"She came here a half a year ago. Sent to investigate some discovery made just on the outskirts of the fort."

"Do you know what discovery that was?"

"No. When I volunteered to be your contact here they made it very clear that, for me, this was a need-to-know situation, and I did not need to know *that*." She sniffs. "Anyway. At first Choudhry stayed up at the fortress, but then she started coming down and asking questions of my employees. I chose to handle it for the company. She seemed quite . . . disturbed."

"Disturbed?"

"Yes. I wondered if she was slightly mad. Bit loopy in the head, if I may say so. At some point in time she had suffered a head injury," says Signe, gesturing to her left brow, "a white bandage here, so I wondered if that was it, but I wasn't sure."

"How'd she get injured?"

"I'm afraid she didn't say, General. She asked us a lot about geomorphology—the way land is formed. I suppose that because we were doing all this work on the bay, she thought we would know something. But we're just fixing damages done a few decades ago, not millions of years." She points out the window to an area just west of the fortress. "People would see her wandering the cliffs with a lantern at night, looking out to sea. I'm told she looked like a painting— the maiden awaiting the return of her beloved, or whatever. Like I said, we thought she was mad."

"Then what happened?"

"Well, then one day we got word she was just . . . gone. I heard rumors it took the fort some time to even realize she was AWOL— that's how odd her movements were. They conducted searches out as far as they could, but found nothing. And that, quite seriously, is all I know."

"Would any of your employees know anything more?"

"Possibly. Why? Would you like to talk to each and every one of them? How much time do you have, General?"

"I was thinking you might have an alert you can send out. A notice to all SDC employees to come forward if they ever had any contact with Choudhry."

"Well . . . we do have a system somewhat like that, but it's usually reserved for emergencies, an—"

"If you can put that alert through I'll be quite grateful, CTO Harkvaldsson." Mulaghesh studiously ignores Signe's irritation. "But what I find most curious right now is—why you?"

"Why me what?"

"Why are you the one to help me, of all people? You're not involved with anything at the fortress. And I'm surprised SDC can spare their CTO to help out on a clandestine military operation."

"Oh, they can't. Not really. Though we did just go through one of the more difficult crane sitings, so that does make it a little easier. Less burdens upon my back."

"So why you?"

"I'm familiar with the country, the culture," says Signe. "I was raised just outside of this polis, after all."

"You were?"

"Yes," says Signe. She kneads her napkin in between her finger and thumb. "I'm a Dreyling, certainly. But after the coup we couldn't stay in the Dreyling Shores. There were plenty of people who wished to see me and my family dead. So we had to hide away somewhere. Voortyashtan was closest, and the least likely place for anyone to look."

"What did you do when you got here?"

"Survive, mostly. And little more than that." She smiles, and there's a touch of bitterness to it. "So, after thirty years here, I know the culture. I know the people. I know the geography, and I know the history. And I have resources that you can't get at the fortress without raising questions."

"But you don't actually want to help," says Mulaghesh.

"Does anyone actually *want* to help in a clandestine investigation?"

"Saypur says, 'Dance,' you say, 'How many turns?' Is that it?"

"Hm . . . True enough," Signe says acidly. "Your nation does have mine by the delicates, as one might say. But there is also the matter of your reputation."

"My reputation? And what reputation is that?"

"General Mulaghesh," she says, "you are, whether you like it or not, something of a celebrity. You're not only associated with the prime minister of Saypur, you are also associated with the death of two Divinities. And you're *also* associated with an unimaginable amount of destruction and devastation done to the city of Bulikov, damage that city still hasn't fully recovered from—if it ever can."

"*I* couldn't have helped that!"

"Possibly. But, nevertheless, your reputation is such that your very presence in this city makes me wary. It also makes a lot of *investors* wary. Voortyashtan is an old friend of violence. The concern is that you, as innocuous as your cover story may be, could be a catalyst."

"So what? They think I'm going to show up and blow up the city?"

"You forget that these people have cannons pointed at them day and night," says Signe. "And although you might have developed a reputation as something of a cautious taskmaster in Bulikov, there are still many rumors surrounding what you did *before* your stint as governor." Signe smiles so wide Mulaghesh can see her molars. "None of it's confirmed, of course—but you and General Biswal have some kind of special connection to the capture of Bulikov during the Summer of Black Rivers, don't you?"

Mulaghesh says nothing.

"Continentals fear you, General," Signe says. "They fear Biswal, especially. And they fear those cannons. And now you're all in the same place. I think their concerns are quite valid—don't you? So it's wise that *someone* has to keep an eye on you. It might as well be me."

I do not envy Lalith Biswal. He made what was likely the most difficult choice of his career, if not the whole of the Summer, and I believe no matter what he chose he knew he and his soldiers would be punished for it—if they survived, which he surely thought unlikely.

Perhaps history will one day be a better judge of him than you or I shall be. For though the Yellow March was likely the very thing that turned the tide during the Summer of Black Rivers, such was its nature that we cannot ever acknowledge that it actually happened.

—LETTER FROM CHIEF OF ARMED FORCES GENERAL
ADHI NOOR TO PRIME MINISTER ASHARA KOMAYD, 1722

4.

the black room

Mulaghesh sits at the window of her spacious room, staring out. The view is gorgeous—Voortyashtan is like a wall of fireflies below her—but she cannot bring herself to enjoy it. Not after that conversation.

Just what in the hells have I gotten myself into?

She walks back to her bags, rummages about, and takes out something wrapped in an old scarf.

Mulaghesh is not an eager neophile, but she knows efficiency when she sees it, which is why, unlike many commanders her age, she took the time to train in firearms. Her favorite is this particularly vicious little piece of technology: a short, thick, snubby little contraption called a "carousel," which earned its name because of its cyclic design of five little barrels each containing one shot, rotating to the next with each squeeze of the trigger. The carousel is much easier for a person with one hand to load and unload than most other weapon systems, as you just need to pop off the empty barrel cylinder and pop on a full set. She hasn't used it on a live

48 ROBERT JACKSON BENNETT

target yet, and frankly hopes she never has to, but she places it on her nightstand, just in case.

She lies down on the bed. Tomorrow, she's decided, she'll go to the last place Choudhry was seen: Fort Thinadeshi.

She shuts her eyes and tries to listen to the waves outside.

Don't forget where you are. Don't forget where you are.

***

Mulaghesh wakes at 0500, grabs a portfolio for notes, commandeers one of the few telephones in the SDC headquarters, and phones Fort Thinadeshi. The tinny voice of an on-call sergeant answers, surprised: they expected her, but not this soon. She's in luck, though, as General Biswal is present at the fortress, having returned from a tour of other installations in the region, and can indeed make time on his calendar for her. "Provided the car can make it down to you in time, General," adds the sergeant.

"Why wouldn't it?"

"Well, there's really only one road down to the city from the fortress, and it's a little . . . variable in quality. It's the only road in the city that will tolerate an automobile, but even then it's a stretch."

"So don't bring any cups brimming with hot tea, is that what you're saying?"

"That's about the cut of it."

"Great."

When the auto arrives it's hard to believe there's a functional vehicle underneath all the mud and moss and sprays of gravel, which stick to the sides like barnacles on a ship. She's happy she wore her fatigues rather than her dress uniform. "Holy hells," she says when the driver hops out. "I damned well hope the wheels stay on."

Then she looks at the driver and does a double take. He's a young man, short but fit with a well-trimmed beard. He would be considered quite handsome were it not for his rather weak chin. But there's something familiar in his face, especially in the way he's grinning at her.

He gives a sharp salute. "Morning, General. Ready for the trip up?"

"I know you," she says, stepping closer. Then in a flash, she has it. "Damn. Sergeant Major Pandey, isn't it? From Bulikov. Is that you?"

His grin practically glows, pleased and proud. "It is, ma'am. Happy to see you again."

She remembers him a little more than some of the other soldiers she had under her command in Bulikov: he was captain of the barracks rowing team, which practiced in the summer on the Solda, much to the displeasure of the Bulikovians. And she remembers he was a wickedly talented swordsman, sparring with a liquid grace that even Mulaghesh, who was no slow hand with a blade herself, found remarkable.

"You went and got yourself all grown up, I see," she says. "What in the hells are you doing all the way up here?"

"Mostly driving, ma'am," Pandey says. "Turns out there aren't too many soldiers up here knowledgeable with automobiles, so I've been stuck with this noble duty."

Instinctively she looks Pandey over, checking his arms and legs for a sign of injury, his cheeks for any hint of malnourishment, his teeth for any sign of scurvy. *He's not yours anymore,* she thinks. *He's Biswal's now—or, perhaps, he's his own.* "Well, I hope you've honed your skills. I need to get up the cliffs and quick, but I'd like to do it in one piece."

Pandey throws open her door. "The road is a vasha string, General," he says, referring to the Saypuri instrument, "and the auto my bow. I'll give you a grand performance."

"If you can drive half as well as you can talk, Pandey," she says, climbing in, "I expect I'll be fine."

Ten minutes later Mulaghesh watches out the window as Voortyashtan lurches by, the auto pitching and yawing like a boat in a storm. She spies tents and yurts and ditches and alleys, makeshift structures that can hardly bear the brunt of the wind. Standing throughout this disordered sprawl are tall, curious stone formations, tottering, misshapen cairns that run in lines along the Solda. Something about the cairns disturbs her, but it's difficult for her to say what.

"It's like a damned refugee camp," says Mulaghesh.

"It would be similar, General," says Pandey. He points at one of the cairns. "Were it not for those."

"What do you mean?" She looks closer at one as they drive underneath it. It's much taller than she'd anticipated, twenty or thirty feet, but she spies the suggestion of human features on the bulbous top of one towering cairn: the shallow dimples of eyes, the soft bulge of what could be a nose. She examines the others in the distance, searching for the divots of shadow at their tops, and sees the same.

"Statues," says Mulaghesh. "They're *statues*, aren't they?"

"They were, once," says Pandey. "Rumor has it they guarded the Solda, greeting those who floated down to the old city, passing through the gates." He nods at the two peaks along the river. "The change in climate's been none too kind to them."

She imagines what they might have once been: tall, human figures dotting the shores, perhaps splendid and regal, now beaten and twisted into something barely recognizable, staring down forever at a missing city. "What must it be like, living in the shadows of these things?"

They come to the clifftops. Fort Thinadeshi broods on the horizon like a storm cloud, immense and dark and gleaming wetly, so covered with cannons that it resembles a vast porcupine. "I suppose the shtanis are used to living with threats hanging over their shoulders, General," says Pandey.

"Shtanis?"

"Oh. Um. It's what we call the locals here, ma'am."

Mulaghesh frowns. The word puts a bad taste in her mouth, or perhaps it's the sight of the fortress looming ahead.

As they approach the first perimeter of fences, Mulaghesh looks northwest of the fortress and sees a curious installation not more than two miles from the fort's walls. The structure looks bland and benign, a dull, small concrete creation, but it's got twice as many fences and watchtowers as the rest of the fortress's perimeters.

"What in the hells is *that?*" she says. "That's a damned truckload of wire sitting around it, whatever it is."

"I believe they're considering expansion, General," says Pandey. "Or so I'm told. Haven't made much progress, though, or so it seems."

She nods pleasantly, fully aware that this is a cover story—though she can't tell if Pandey knows that. That little gray button of a building, she suspects, must be the extraction point for whatever ore they discovered out here.

"What brought you here, Pandey?" she asks. "After Bulikov you could have gone anywhere."

"Well, when General Biswal took command here, I couldn't re-sist. He was your old commander, wasn't he? It was an education serving under you, ma'am. I suppose I wished to continue it."

"Why's that?"

"Well . . ." Pandey struggles for the words. "It seems like there are only a few of the true old heroes still serving today. When they retire, so much history will be forgotten with them."

Mulaghesh looks out the window toward the fir-dotted hills, stark and looming under the gray skies, and tries not to think of the first time she saw countryside like this. "What a pity that will be."

***

Fort Thinadeshi—named after the famed innovator Vallaicha Thinadeshi—is one of the oldest military installations on the Continent, half coastal fortress, half military base. Sporting an immense coastal battery, precipitous battlements, tangles of wire fences, and a sprawling barracks, there is something both grimly majestic and crudely improvised about Fort Thinadeshi, all things for all situations, for all situations are found and met here in Voortyashtan. *What a grand and noble mess it is,* thinks Mulaghesh as the auto putters through a gate, the dark walls towering over her.

She imagines what Sumitra Choudhry would have thought of it. She thinks back to when she read Choudhry's files aboard the *Kaypee* with Pitry. The girl served eighteen months in the Saypuri Military, a common practice undertaken to improve one's odds of Ministry recruitment. During her time in uniform she received a Silver Star and a Golden Stroke for "Distinguished Service" during an "altercation" when a Continental charged a checkpoint.

Mulaghesh was experienced enough to parse through these neutral phrases. *She shot and killed someone,* she said aloud, *when someone really needed her to do it.* She glanced at the Silver Star notation. *And she got injured doing it.*

Yes, Pitry said. *Took a bolt to the left shoulder when a Continental charged a checkpoint, just above the collarbone. Nearly killed her. But she managed to get the shot off after she'd been injured.*

She pulled off a killshot after *being critically injured? She's either a hard case or lucky.*

From what I've heard of her, General, he said mildly, *I rather think it's the former.*

They park and Pandey leads her into the headquarters, whose interiors are dank and tomb-like, yawning hallways and tiny, tunnel-like stairways. This part of Thinadeshi, she realizes, was built mere years after the Kaj took the Continent, and is so out of date it's almost mind-boggling. As someone who's been part of the planning and construction of multiple installations, the many glaring flaws—this staircase too tight for evacuation, those windows too large and exposed—come leaping out to her, almost causing her to cringe.

"Where are we going?" asks Mulaghesh as they climb up a winding staircase. "I thought Biswal was here."

"He is, ma'am," says Pandey. "He's in the nest, just above us."

"The what?"

"The nest. The crow's nest, sorry. General Biswal is, as he puts it, a visual thinker, so he likes a view."

Mulaghesh is about to ask him to please clarify his damned self when gray light comes spilling in from above, and they emerge into a rounded, glass-walled room like something you'd find at the top of a lighthouse. She glances to the side and has a moment of vertigo when she realizes how high up they are, the battlements sprawling out three hundred feet below her.

"General Biswal," says Pandey. "General Mulaghesh."

Mulaghesh looks around. She realizes this chamber—which must be the topmost spire of Fort Thinadeshi—has been converted into something like a makeshift office, with a small desk facing east. Stuck on the windows before the desk are numerous maps of the region, many of which she finds familiar. The wall of colors and images confounds her eyes so much that it takes her a minute to realize there's someone seated at the desk, wearing a bright orange headcloth.

He grunts and slowly swivels in his chair, turning to look at them. Mulaghesh's world seems to spin around her.

He is not the man she remembers. There's some remaining suggestion of the broad-shouldered, powerfully built man he was once, but he's got more around the middle now, his carefully manicured beard is now bone white, and small, delicate little spectacles now balance atop his nose.

But his eyes are still the same: still pale, pale gray and somewhat deep-set, as if viewing the world from deep within himself.

General Lalith Biswal smiles—a somewhat forced gesture—and stands. "By the seas," he says. "By all the *seas*, Turyin! Turyin, is it really you? How many years has it been? Are you *really* somewhere in that old woman's body?"

"I could ask the same of you," says Mulaghesh. "I remember now why I don't catch up with my former colleagues. They remind me of how damn old I've gotten."

He shakes her hand and his grip is the same, the fingers of a person meant either to build things or break them. Then, to her surprise, he gently pulls her into an embrace—a gesture of affection she's never witnessed from him before.

"I don't care," says Biswal. "I wish I'd seen you more often." He holds her by the arms and stares into her face, like a father reviewing a child home from boarding school. "It helps me fight the feeling that I'm a fiddly old man wondering if the past ever really happened."

Mulaghesh tries to return his affection, but it's difficult: her left arm hurts, and her right one is making a fist, something she can't stop. He somehow smells the same: a masculine but not unpleasant musk, dashed with the scent of juniper berries and pine. Yet the faintest ghost of this aroma brings a thousand memories with it: the smell of smoke, ash, rain, animal dung, rotten food, and putrid meat, and with the scents come the sounds, the distant screaming and the mutter of the flames.

Don't forget where you are, thinks Mulaghesh. *Don't forget where you are.*

Biswal releases her. "Sergeant Major Pandey, you're dismissed. It's not appropriate for the young to witness the commiseration of the old." He smiles brightly at Mulaghesh. "How about some tea? After all, up here is the farthest we can get from the problems of this unsightly shithole."

* * *

"As the wise man says," Biswal says, pouring her a cup, "when the shepherd lies down with his goats, he finds himself listening to them. And soon, who are the shepherds and who are the goats?"

The wind rattles the windows. Mulaghesh tries to tell herself that the swaying sensation she's feeling is her imagination. She definitely doesn't want to believe that the tower they're in is actually moving. "You think of the Voortyashtanis as goats?" says Mulaghesh, watching steam languidly massage the brim of her cup.

"No," says Biswal, pouring his own. "I think that's giving them too much credit." His voice hasn't changed: it's still low and husky, like the low groan of a ship's timbers. He still talks the same way, too, like he's reluctant to speak but determined to carefully say his piece. Having a conversation with him was always like having a conversation with a bulldozer, slow and indomitable.

"So what's the situation?"

"It's simple on the surface. Minister Komayd wants to build a harbor, yes? Open up the Solda, change the Continent forever, yes?"

"Yeah?"

"The problem is, this plays into local politics, if I can even use such a civilized term. Old rivalries, perhaps." He points to the maps on the glass wall. One features color-coded regions along the Solda and up in the highlands. "There are two types of Voortyashtanis here, Turyin. Those that live in the highlands and those that live along the river. The ones along the river are rich and fat and happy. They have the best pastures and charge everyone an arm and a leg to cross the Solda. Those in the highlands, well. They have it tough, they always have, and they've always fought for better land."

"So?"

"You have the reasonable response. So? So what does this backwater nonsense have to do with the harbor? Who cares about these bumpkins? Well, unfortunately, if we want the harbor to work, we're going to have to live with these people. And if we open up the waters, who will we disturb?"

Mulaghesh grimaces and nods. "Ah."

"Yes. The river tribes wish to acquire new lands in order to relocate their settlements and farmland. The only decent land available, however, belongs to the highland tribes—in fact, it's the only arable land they possess. So this leaves the highland clans very upset. The sort of upset that makes you raid military rail shipments, steal a bunch of riflings and explosives, and go to war. The sort of upset that makes you pillage and burn settlements along territorial boundaries. The sort of upset that makes you put a bullet through the face of the previous commander of this damned region. That kind of upset."

"That's pretty fucking upset."

"You have no idea," he says. "I've been here about a year and a quarter now, and I've got upcoming negotiations with the tribal leaders to try and get them to stop killing one another. Not to mention us. My hopes are not high. Good choice wearing your fatigues, by the way. Don't distinguish yourself as an officer at all, if you can help it. Thinadeshi seems secure, but it's still a combat outpost. There are lots of hidden people in the hills all too happy to reward your decorum with a bullet."

"So that's how you came to be here? The previous commander got shot, so they came to you?"

Biswal deflates a little. "No. Not quite. I was teaching. Military history, at Abhishek Academy. The shelf, in other words."

Mulaghesh nods. "The shelf" is the military term for a state of disuse, when a soldier, operative, or officer is not dismissed but set aside and, likely, forgotten. One can get on the shelf for any reason: some fall out of favor politically, some screw up an operation or make some fatal career flaw. . . . Still others just get old. Very few go to the shelf voluntarily—yet this is precisely what Mulaghesh herself attempted to do. *And I couldn't even get that right. . . .*

"No one else wanted the job, so they gave me another look," says Biswal. "I should have known that if they were willing to give it to me, I shouldn't take it. This is a daunting task, and the number of souls on my shoulder weighs heavily."

Mulaghesh glances at a map on the wall detailing the installations throughout Voortyashtan. "How many?"

"Seven thousand here in Thinadeshi. Four thousand in Fort Hadji, where the rails see a lot of action—just north of the highlands, you see. Thirty-five hundred at Fort Lok. More at the border with Jukoshtan. All in all, I find myself commander of twenty-three thousand soldiers here in Voortyashtan, Turyin. A lot, but not as many as we need."

"No?"

"No. We're spread too thin. My predecessor tried to disrupt the insurgents' bastions in the mountains, and that was a miserable failure. Cost him his life. For now, the military council's orders are strictly to *hold on.* Fortify. Protect the harbor. As if it needs it. The Dreylings practically have their own army down there. They've even got a damned minigun."

"Really." Mulaghesh makes a note of this.

"And somehow all the shtanis manage to have firearms, too." He gives the carousel in her holster the briefest of glances. "I hate them, Turyin. I hate these damned new guns, which suddenly seem to be everywhere."

"I never figured you for a technophobe," says Mulaghesh.

"I'm not," he growls. "But these things make it damned easy to kill a man. With bolts, ammunition is so much more of a hassle. Too much wind and you can't use them at all. Short-ranged, too. With ri-flings . . . Overnight, we've gone from bolt-action to fully automatic and beyond. Dying has gotten a whole lot easier all over the world."

"We've always been able to make them," says Mulaghesh. "We were just never able to scale up production before."

"Then perhaps we should have left them on the factory floor," says Biswal. "Are you a convert, Turyin?"

"If you can't fight the future, you might as well learn the ropes quick as you can. Especially if you've got to climb them with a handi-cap." She holds up her prosthetic left hand.

"Ah." His eyes sadden. "I'd heard about that. I'm so sorry for what you went through."

"And both of us know it wasn't much. I'm alive. That's more than most get."

"Yes. That is true. You always did have a head for priorities, Turyin. It surprised me when I heard you'd walked out on the job. Why *did* you leave?"

She gives a neutral shrug. "They wanted me to be something I wasn't."

"Ah. A politician, then?"

"Something like that."

"And now you're here on the shuffle," says Biswal. "I don't think *anyone's* ever done the touring shuffle in Voortyashtan. Why did they send you here?"

"I pissed on a lot of important shoes when I left," says Mulaghesh. "They could've just waved the discrepancy off, but they didn't. I don't think they even wanted to give me the opportunity to get it taken care of, really. I think maybe they sent me up hoping I'd get buried here."

Biswal's eyes dim and crinkle. "Yes. I . . . I wonder that, too. Perhaps they're just trying to mop us up. Me and you, still being alive—we inconvenience them, don't we?"

She hesitates. She feels nauseous. She hasn't discussed this with anyone in over ten years, and she never wanted to break the subject open like this, with the very man who led them all way back when.

She wanted to forget. She did a good job of it. It's downright obnoxious of the world to remind her that the Yellow March actually happened.

To her relief, they're interrupted by the sound of steps behind them. Mulaghesh turns to see a Saypuri soldier of about forty mounting the stairs, and from the chevrons on her uniform she's a captain, first class. But there is an unmistakable air of lethality about this woman that Mulaghesh finds striking: everything about her posture and bearing—jaw set forward, shoulders square, legs spread wide—seems intended to either take or deal damage. Her hair is tied back so tightly it seems to stretch the skin on her forehead, which has a curious whitish streak in the middle. It's a large scar, like she's had almost all of her scalp peeled off in some injury. This does nothing to affect her stony, still gaze, though: Mulaghesh only has to glance at her to see that this is a soldier who's seen a great deal of combat, probably the messy kind.

Once she's at the top of the steps, the captain swivels on her heel and smartly salutes. "General Mulaghesh. It's an honor to have you here at Thinadeshi."

"Ah, you found me, Nadar," says Biswal.

"When you're at Thinadeshi, General, you're almost always in the nest." She glances around disapprovingly. "*Against* my advice."

"Turyin, this is Captain Kiran Nadar, commander of Fort Thinadeshi. Nadar doesn't admire my makeshift office here. She thinks the shtanis are dangerous and could take advantage of it. But on the contrary, the reason I'm up here is *because* I know they're dangerous." He gazes east, at the ragged, pink peaks of the Tarsil Mountains. "Where else can I get a better look at what we have to deal with?"

"I'm guessing this is something of an artifact," says Mulaghesh, standing and looking around at the little room. "Built before artillery and small arms had quite the reach they do now."

"Correct," says Nadar. "And since we lost our last commander to a sharpshooter—may he find peace in his slumber—it makes me nervous that General Biswal chooses to take his tea up here."

"Perhaps I enjoy spending time in the portions of this fortress," says Biswal, "which were built when we had clearer aims about what we wished to accomplish here."

Nadar lowers her gaze. There's an awkward beat.

"It's one hell of a place," offers Mulaghesh. The words seem to die miserably in the air.

"No doubt you're familiar with more modern installations, General," says Nadar, with a touch of wounded pride. "But here, we're forced to make do with what we have."

"Some of it looks damned modern, though." Mulaghesh walks to the west side of the spire, which looks toward the ocean and the cliffs. But before the cliffs is the bland little structure she saw on the way up here, lined with miles of razor wire. "What in all the hells is that?"

"A halted attempt at expansion, General," says Nadar smoothly.

"Expansion?"

"Yes, General."

Mulaghesh looks at her. "No, it isn't."

Nadar's confident expression wilts. Biswal glances back and forth between the two of them, his face inscrutable.

"I've seen expansions before, Captain," says Mulaghesh. "Lots of them. And that's not one. More to the point, I spent a lot of time reviewing requests and proposals to try to expand Fort Thinadeshi. None of them broke ground. Which that out there obviously has."

Nadar looks to Biswal, who looks back at her as if to say, *I told you so.* Nadar frowns, nettled, and says, "With all due respect, General— and I think this is something you expected—this is an intelligence compartment that I don't believe you're read into."

"Maybe, Captain." Then, casually, "Is this that thing about the metal?"

Nadar looks like she's been slapped. "The . . . The metal?"

"Yeah. The metal you found around here."

"How . . . You . . ." Nadar struggles to control her reactions. "How was it that you came to be, ah, informed about this, General?"

"I'd seen reports on something about it back when I was on the council." This is a lie, but since very few ever know what powerful people see and do, it's an easy one to believe. "I suppose that was before it got formally compartmentalized, though. I thought it was just some curiosity. But if it's big enough for compartmentalization, and for you all to build that out there for it . . . it must be pretty damn curious indeed."

There's a long silence.

Biswal leans back in his chair and chuckles. "The years have been kind to your mind, Turyin. You're a sight cleverer than I remember."

"I'll take that as a compliment, sir," says Mulaghesh.

"General Biswal," says Nadar, now quite flushed, "I . . . I do not consider the intelligence orders we have regarding our affairs here to be anything to laugh at. If there has been a breach of this compartment we need t—"

"I recall once hearing a young captain very tactfully tell me," says Biswal, "that one can both respect and obey Ghaladesh while remembering that it is over a thousand miles away."

Nadar's flush deepens. "This is still an alarming revelation. Even if it *is* General Mulaghesh who's aware of the situation here. My concern is that, if she knows, someone else could. That poses a serious security breach."

"You're right to be worried," says Biswal. "But this breach didn't happen on *our* end—something I'll happily tell Ghaladesh. Perhaps we ought to be grateful to General Mulaghesh for making us aware of the breach in the first place."

"I'm just here on the touring shuffle," Mulaghesh says. "I don't wish to be an intrusion."

"You aren't," says Biswal. "This *project* is an intrusion. It's wise to seek your discretion, though—and the best way to be discreet is to know exactly what it is we need to be discreet about. Captain Nadar, will you please read General Mulaghesh into this compartment and give her the full briefing on Operation Arc Lightning?"

Nadar makes a face as if she's just been asked to swallow a spoonful of some very foul medicine.

"I don't wish to waste any more time discussing this absurd diversion," says Biswal quietly, holding up his hands. "Please, Nadar. Show her the most recent eccentricity our nation has chosen to spend money on, rather than more walls, more soldiers, and more support."

"With all due respect, General," says Nadar, "this flies in the face of proce—"

She stops talking as a round of small *pops* echoes across the battlements. Mulaghesh looks up, alarmed. "Is that gunfire?"

Neither Biswal nor Nadar seem surprised. Biswal checks his watch. "Ah. I'd forgotten what time it is."

"What the hells is that? It sounded like a volley."

"Well, it was, in a way." Biswal takes out a spyglass and walks to the walls. He glasses a yard to the east, behind walls and walls of wire fencing. "Just another daily duty of Fort Thinadeshi."

He hands Mulaghesh the spyglass. It takes her only a moment to find it, and though it's hazy with gunsmoke the scene is quite clear.

Nine Saypuri soldiers with riflings stand at one end of the yard; at the other is a tall, earthen berm with dark, stained soil at its bottom. There's something lying there in the dirt, limp and crumpled, and two Saypuri soldiers run forward and drag it away, leaving behind a streak of red mud.

"They surprised a checkpoint," says Biswal beside her. "Shot two of the guards there. We only captured them by pure coincidence—a returning patrol happened upon them."

The two soldiers drag in a filthy, cowering Continental man, his face almost completely obscured with bruises. They put a blindfold on him and stand him up before the berm. The crotch of his pants blooms dark with urine.

"You're *executing* them?" says Mulaghesh.

"Yes," says Biswal. "This is not Bulikov, Turyin. There is no order of law here, beyond tribal law. The only courts here are military courts. And the fortress's prison is tiny and old. We can't keep people there indefinitely."

She watches as the supervisor of the rifling squad shouts orders. The nine soldiers lift their riflings.

"In Voortyashtan," says Biswal, "we make do with what we can."

The yard fills with gunsmoke. The Continental man topples over. It takes a little bit longer for the sound of the gunshots to drift up to them.

She lowers the spyglass and slowly hands it back to Biswal.

"Perhaps you can now understand," says Biswal, "that I have much more important things to care about than any secret science experiments. Captain Nadar—please show General Mulaghesh the laboratories. Perhaps before she retires she can inform the council what a ridiculous burden this all is. And once you've done so, report back to me on the status of the eastern perimeter. We still have real work to do."

***

Nadar is still composing herself at the foot of the stairs when Mulaghesh gets there. Nadar coughs. "I apologize for that, General. That must have been uncomfortable."

"I'll say," says Mulaghesh darkly. She oversaw executions of her own in Bulikov, of course, but they were far more ceremonial affairs, attended and supervised by civilian officials. What she just witnessed felt as mundane as taking out the day's trash.

"The thing is, I agree with him," says Nadar. She begins walking down the hall, and Mulaghesh follows. "Operation Arc Lightning places a great burden on us when we need it least."

"But?"

"But, Biswal has . . . little patience for any issue that isn't actively posing a threat."

"When your predecessor got shot in combat, I can see why a clandestine mining operation might not top your list of priorities."

"General Raajhaa . . . Yes, he was a great leader, General. He was much admired. His loss changed many minds about what we're doing here." She shakes herself and begins taking a long staircase down. "How much do you know about Arc Lightning, General?"

"I know it's a metal. I know it's in the ground. That's about the run of it. I didn't even realize it'd gotten a fancy code name yet."

"I see. And how much do you know about electrical engineering?"

"Nothing. Maybe less than nothing."

"Well, that'll make this easier," says Nadar. "It'll mean fewer questions."

They walk down the hallway to the lab doors. The ceilings here are covered with pipes and tubes, all sighing or squeaking or softly bubbling.

"You are probably aware that electrification promises to be the next great step for our nation," says Nadar.

"I read about it in the papers from time to time. I thought Vallaicha Thinadeshi had tried it before and failed."

"True, but she only made small inroads. Yet now, as you might've seen in Ghaladesh, entire homes and buildings run off of it."

"Yes," says Mulaghesh, who's honestly never really cared for electrical light. It somehow seems to bring out the flaws in the human face.

"The main issue right now is transmission," says Nadar. "We have coal, we have dams. But scaling up transmission to match Saypur's industries . . . that's proving difficult." She throws open a wooden door on the other side of the hallway. Inside is a pristine white laboratory featuring all kinds of complicated equipment: pumps and processors and something that has an inordinate amount of tubing. Four attendants are perched over glass dishes containing various amounts of gray, unimpressive powder. They look up, startled.

"Lieutenant Prathda," says Nadar. One of the attendants stands up straight and salutes. "This is General Mulaghesh. I'm giving her a tour of the facilities. Why don't you give her the technical rundown of what we're doing here?"

Prathda—a gangly, odd peacock of a man—paces over and salutes Mulaghesh directly. "Certainly, General. An honor to have you with us. How technical would you like me to be?"

"Just give her the general rundown," says Nadar. "And no charts this time, Lieutenant."

"I see," says Prathda. He bites his lip. "But, Captain, I did some additional production work on one, and I think this chart *really* clarifies how—"

"*No* charts, Lieutenant," says Nadar forcefully. "Just the five-minute tour."

"Certainly, Captain." Then he thinks for a moment and says, "A demonstration would probably be simplest." He turns to his attendants. "Please get me the components for the Aamdi test, if you could." One of the attendants leaps up and digs underneath the counter until she produces a very large lightbulb that's more than two feet long, a bulky battery, and two sets of thick cables. "Thank you," says Prathda, and he picks them up and carries them to a dense door with a sign reading TESTING ROOM FOUR. "This way, General," he calls over his shoulder.

Mulaghesh follows, but Nadar hangs back. "I've seen this show, General," she explains. "I'll, ah, hang out here in the hallway, if that's all right."

Concerned, Mulaghesh walks into the testing room. "Please shut that door securely," Prathda says. "Thank you, General."

She notices the door has a layer of steel on the interior, like a blast door. "Uh . . . Is there anything we need to be, uh, shielded from?"

"I assure you, it's all quite safe. Now, we have here two very ordinary components—a bulb, and a battery. The battery is large and has a very large charge, and the bulb is from a high-powered street lamp in Ghaladesh—so its capacity for taking in electricity and putting out light is very, very high. Am I clear?"

Mulaghesh grunts.

"Excellent. Now, *these* cables are of common copper—the sort of copper that is currently being used in most electrical practices. If I apply them to the battery's connectors like so . . . And then, of course, to the lightbulb's base . . ." The bulb, lying on its side on the counter, flickers with a faint yellow light, which grows as Prathda adjusts the cables until it's a flat, somewhat decent source of light in this rather dark room.

"Right," says Prathda. He removes the cables, killing the light. "It functions, carrying the charge to and from the bulb. However, there is considerable loss—hence why the bulb does not glow particularly brightly. But *these* cables"——he holds the two other cables up so that Mulaghesh can see that they're flagged red—"are an alloy, mixing copper with a very recently discovered element."

"And what is this new element?"

"It's something that was found nearby in Voortyashtan, totally by accident," says Prathda, fixing the cables to the battery. "We were originally helping SDC source the materials for the harbor. The harbor project, it was thought, would likely need a large amount of stone, so we considered siting a quarry near the fortress. Our engineers went digging, and found . . . this. A seam of ore the likes of which has never been discovered before." Prathda looks up, smiling beatifically. "Are you ready, General?"

Mulaghesh nods.

He touches the cables to the bulb's base.

And then . . .

Mulaghesh's eyes interpret what is happening as an explosion, but one that is silent and pristine. She fights the impulse to dive to the floor—she imagines the cough and shriek of shells, the rumble of nearby blasts—and keeps watching.

The bulb fills up with a white, white hot light, a bursting, blinding eruption of pure incandescence that's so intense Mulaghesh can almost feel it on her skin. It's so bright it's like the light is shooting back into her head and out the other side, and she cries out and looks away as the walls themselves begin to glow, reflecting this terrible light.

There's a *pow!* as the filament in the bulb gives out. Mulaghesh shouts, "Fucking hells!" and holds up her portfolio to shield herself from the shattered glass—but it doesn't come. She slowly lowers it. The bulb is whole but dark, the interior of its glass scarred and smoky. Prathda has his face turned away as well, but when he looks back at her he has a dazed smile, as if having just swallowed some wonderful drug.

"Amazing, isn't it?" he says. "We call it *thinadeskite*. After the engineer, you see."

***

"This bulb," says Prathda, unceremoniously dumping it in a trash can, "should have been capable of handling 110 kilomundes. It's an electrical term. Enough to light up a goodish portion of your average city park, I should say. So the fact that the thinadeskite was able to blow that out is . . . significant. However, we did use a very *refined* portion of thinadeskite in these cables. If you would, General—I have a few more interesting things to show you."

He walks out the door without looking back. She starts to follow, then stops and picks up the battery. It's warm. She turns it over and sees a label on its bottom reading 90 KM. KM standing for kilomundes, presumably, a terminology she's never heard of before, but then she's no scientist.

"Hm," she says. She replaces the battery and follows.

Nadar stands outside with a smile on her face. "Still have your eyebrows, General?"

"I kind of wish we'd gone with the charts," says Mulaghesh.

"Trust me," says Nadar, "you don't."

"As you can see, its conductivity is *staggering*," Prathda is saying as he walks ahead. "Simply *staggering*. The Department of Reconstruction is *very* interested in this, as are countless industry representatives, though we've only been allowed to give them very limited reports, of course. Just think of every power need of all of Ghaladesh, met by one centralized little plant—or even distributed plants! Imagine miles and miles of wiring and cabling, made of thinadeskite! Imagine a whole factory powered by a piece of wire no thicker than your finger!"

"It certainly is a lot to think about," says Mulaghesh. They pass by a window looking into a strange laboratory with lots of microscopes. Lots of lenses, lots of bulbs, lots of wire, lots of refining. She takes a careful look at the raw material itself in one glass tank: it looks a little like ordinary graphite to her. "How does the stuff work?"

Prathda coughs, suddenly awkward. "Well, that is a subject of some controversy. There are a lot of *theories*. The right one is currently being determined."

"You don't know?"

"We're working on it. We think it *might* be an alteration to a commonly found dielectric compound, or it might have something to do with oscillations in the spin of certain subnuc—"

"You don't know."

"Um. No. We don't. Not yet, anyway."

Mulaghesh knew all that, of course. But it's quite something to see Prathda collapse so quickly.

"Prathda and the rest of our science department here are working away on that," says Nadar.

"Sure, but that must put a kink in your production plans," says Mulaghesh. "You can't build a completely new power system out of shit no one understands."

"It's true that, like any good scientist, we need to be thorough," says Prathda. "And we are trying to be. I know what Ghaladesh is concerned about, and"—he shakes his head, laughing in frustration— "and we have confirmed, repeatedly—repeatedly!—that it is of *no* concern: they are worried that this material is Divine, somehow."

"I guess I can see why they'd be concerned about that," says Mulaghesh, as if she'd only just heard the idea.

"But, it *cannot* be. Not only because the Divinity of these lands, Voortya, is most certainly, *undeniably* dead—Saypur would not be a free state if the Kaj had not struck her down at the very start of the War, of course—but also because we have conducted numerous tests endorsed by the Ministry of Foreign Affairs itself to ascertain the Divine nature of a substance or event, and each test has come back irrefutably *negative*. The Ministry's *own* tests!"

"Okay, but . . . to be clear, thinade . . . What is it, again?"

"Thinadeskite."

"Right. Beyond the conductivity, thinadeskite doesn't do anything else inexplicable, right?"

"Well. That . . . depends on your definition of inexplicable."

"I would define it," says Mulaghesh, "as something you do not know how to explain."

He pauses. She watches as his eyes search the upper left corner of the room: a habit, she's learned in her time, of someone trying to navigate a difficult truth.

What Mulaghesh really wants to do right now is, as it is delicately expressed in reports, "apply the full measure of her authority"—that is, get right up in Prathda's face and chew him out at maximum volume until he's good and rattled. This is often the simplest way of dealing with a soldier tiptoeing around a hard truth, she's found; and it's definitely what she would do if she were in Bulikov with the full backing of the polis governor's office.

But she doesn't do that. Mulaghesh forcibly reminds herself that she is not in command here, and she isn't here to clean house, to take command, to report back to any oversight committee on the workings of Fort Thinadeshi. She's not here to be a commander, but an operative, a spy. And these people think her to be no more than a tourist, someone here for a month or two before saying farewell and sailing off into obscurity.

A molar on the right side of her jaw *pops* as she grinds her teeth. *I cannot think of someone more ill-suited to this task.*

She asks herself—what would Shara do?

She'd keep him on the hook and string his dumb ass along.

So instead of physically assaulting Prathda and bellowing questions at him, she slowly asks, "Would it have something to do with how your 110 kilomundes bulb got blown out by a 90 kilomundes battery—20 kilomundes *less* than what I'm guessing is the full capacity of the bulb?"

Prathda looks at her with the face of someone who is slowly realizing that this person is much smarter than he gave them credit for. Captain Nadar tenses up slightly, surprised at this turn in the discussion.

"Does thinadeskite *conduct* electricity, Prathda," Mulaghesh asks, "or does it *generate* it?"

He thinks for a long time. "We . . . haven't determined that yet."

"Okay."

"But in a refined state, it . . . amplifies the charge. Considerably."

Mulaghesh is silent. Prathda shifts on his feet, uncomfortable.

"Should that be possible?" she asks.

"Well. No."

***

"This subject area," says Nadar, "is a little . . . sensitive, General."

"I can understand that," says Mulaghesh. "I don't like the impossible more than anyone else does."

"It does defy our current understanding of physics," Prathda admits. "Electricity cannot just come from *nowhere*. It has to be generated from some phenomenon. But our understanding of physics is changing all the time. We learn new things every day," he says as he leads them back through the labs. "This is the goal of Arc Lightning. Science is like a glacier: slow and indomitable. But it will get to where it's going."

"Thank you for that eloquent speech, Prathda," says Nadar curtly. "And for the tour. Very informative, as always."

Prathda bows expansively, thanks them both, and returns to his work.

"He's a nice enough guy," says Nadar as they exit. "But it's hard to get top-grade scientific talent out here."

"I see. So until we can verify exactly how thinadeskite does what it does, it's not hitting any factory floors."

"Correct, General. And we have all kinds of industry muck-a-mucks clawing at our backs to get their own people in here to run their own tests. But I'm not playing babysitter for a bunch of damned tweedy *civilians*." Nadar says the word with a surprising amount of disdain. "We have enough problems here. We don't need academics or scientists getting gutted or shot on our back door as well. Not to mention the security risks that poses, letting industry get their say in military matters."

"Any security issues with Arc Lightning?"

"No serious ones, at least."

"Serious ones?"

"Well. Truth be told, there was one odd incident a few months back that now seems to have been somewhat harmless. Some of our operations crew noticed signs that someone had started a fire in one of the branches. Not as sabotage, it seems, because there's not much to burn down in a tunnel underground, but . . . Something like the ruins of a campfire. A very small one."

"That is odd." Mulaghesh makes a note of it.

"Yes, I went and looked myself. It looked as though whoever had done it had been burning just . . . well, plants, I suppose. Leaves. Some cloth. Things like that. As if someone had camped out down there, trying to escape the rain, perhaps."

"How long ago was this?"

"Oh, months . . . Probably four or five months ago. We checked the fences, checked the security checkpoints, checked the tunnels, but found no sign of forced entry or tampering. It was strange, but it's never happened again. It's weak tea in comparison to the other issues pressing on us."

"If you could have your way, Captain—what would you do with this project?"

Nadar blinks. Her heavy, dark eyes flick back and forth over the floor. "If I can speak freely, General?"

"You may."

"I'd mothball this. Shut it down. Now's not the time to play scientists."

"And what would you do instead?"

Her response is immediate: "Arm and train the river clans, and coordinate with them to drive the highlanders out of the Tarsil Mountains entirely."

"No more negotiations, then?"

Nadar scoffs. "It's just a front. The highland tribes use the talks to stall just long enough until they can make their next move. They disassociate themselves from any conflict, of course. 'That wasn't us who did it, just people who happen to fervently agree with us—and how can we control them?' Very convenient."

"I see." Mulaghesh clears her throat. "One last thing, Captain . . ."

"Yes?"

"I know you said that you'd used tests to confirm that this material was *not* Divine . . . but when they sent me here, I saw a record of a Ministry of Foreign Affairs representative coming here to do some additional tests."

Nadar's face darkens.

"But," says Mulaghesh, "there was some kind of note that she went AWOL. Is that correct?"

Nadar thinks for a long time, her mouth working. "This, too," she says finally, "is probably something that can be explained with a simple demonstration."

***

She leads Mulaghesh to a small dormitory hallway. "This wing is for senior officers," she explains, "as well as a few technicians and guests." She comes to one room door and sorts through a ponderous ring of keys, procured from a maintenance worker. "We still haven't cleaned it up, under my orders. I had a feeling someone would want to come looking for her." She unlocks the door. "Though I suspect, General, you'll want to just glance and move on until your pension's earned out . . . with all due respect, of course."

She pushes the door open.

Mulaghesh's mouth twists as she looks into the room. "By the seas . . ."

Sumitra Choudhry, it seems, did a lot of redecorating before her disappearance: all the furniture has been removed except for a mattress, and a four-foot-wide black stripe with oddly fuzzy edges runs along the bare white walls. Mulaghesh notes that the stripe goes from about waist-height to shoulder-height . . . and as she looks closer she sees that it is not one solid stripe but *writing*, endless scribblings overlaid on one another until they become a dense, black fog, thousands and thousands of words running along the walls. Above and below this stripe, on the ceiling and on the floors, are drawings and sketches that leap out of the wandering black ribbon to stretch across the corners, until nearly three-quarters of the room is covered in black ink.

"She did all this?" asks Mulaghesh.

Nadar nods. Some of the writings must have needed censoring, for they've had whole bottles of black ink dumped out onto them, concealing their message. The ink has dripped down the walls in thin, tapered lines, reminding Mulaghesh of icicles running along a roof edge. In the center of the black-smeared floor is the bare, gray mattress.

"So," says Mulaghesh. "She went mad."

"So I would conclude, General," says Nadar.

Mulaghesh walks in. The ink has puddled so thickly on the floor that it's dried and cracked, like the parched ground of some waste-land. Some of the ink must have dried while Choudhry was still here, for Mulaghesh can see numerous tiny carvings of faces gouged into the calcified ink.

She stands in the center of Choudhry's old mattress—which is nearly as ink-stained as the rest of the room—and looks around. *It's as if she painted her own nightmare,* she thinks, *and crawled inside.*

The paintings and drawings have a handful of similarities. There are a lot of images of people holding hands, many of them standing on what looks like water. In some, one person—somewhat female looking—is wounding themselves, cutting off their arm or maybe their hand, while a second woman looks on in horror. There are countless images of weapons: swords, daggers, spears, arrows. Some drawings are less clear: one set in the corner looks like four chicken wings on kebab sticks, though there's something disgustingly strange about them.

But one sketch is strangely arresting to Mulaghesh: it is a land-scape, quite well done in comparison to some of the other drawings, depicting a shoreline on which many people kneel, heads bowed. Rising behind them is a tower, and though the outline is done in black ink, somehow it's been drawn so that Mulaghesh feels the tower is purest white, reflecting the light of a cold winter moon.

"What happened?" says Mulaghesh.

"She came here about half a year ago to research the thinadeskite. Her efforts yielded the same results as ours—nothing. Nothing Divine about it. But then her research got a little . . . extracurricular. She started leaving the fort, going out to the city and some of the countryside. She stopped visiting the labs completely. She spent some time at the harbor, I am told. We thought it was odd, and I worried she was a security risk, though if you can't trust a Ministry officer . . ." She sighs. "But we never ventured into her room here. She was a Ministry officer, after all. So we didn't know how bad she'd gotten. Then one day, she never came back. We conducted a search, and found this. I've no idea what happened to her. But then, she did disappear right when another spate of fighting broke out."

Mulaghesh steps on the mattress and slowly looks around. "And she left no paperwork trails? Nothing in your labs or in the fort that she was unusually fixated on?"

"She stopped coming to the labs mere weeks after arriving," says Nadar. "Soon she was like a ghost. We rarely saw her, and she rarely engaged with us. Though some patrols mentioned she was sometimes seen walking the cliffs, holding a lantern. But that could have been anyone, General."

"What sorts of tests did she run?"

Nadar runs through a litany of tests Mulaghesh hasn't ever heard of, things involving lily petals and graveyard mud and silver coins. "What's more," says Nadar, "she went beyond the thinadeskite itself, and started testing the *fort*. The stones in the walls, the dirt, the trees . . . She tested all of this region, practically, for any trace of the Divine—and found *nothing*. It was like living with a madwoman."

"Who was the last person to see her alive?"

"That's difficult to say, because we aren't totally sure when she disappeared. We had some reports of a Saypuri woman being sighted on the shore down in Voortyashtan, but no one could confirm if it was Choudhry or not. That's the last hint of her movements that I have."

Mulaghesh makes a note of this. "And is there any cause for this?"

"Cause?"

"Any, I don't know . . . abuse or injury or trauma that could have given her this break from reality?"

"She did receive some kind of wound at some point. . . . A head trauma, though she made up several stories about how she got it."

"Is that the reason for her behavior?"

"I doubt it. Her change was much more gradual."

"Then what?"

"General . . ." Nadar sighs and smiles weakly at her. "If you figure it out, you'd be the first. But this place puts pressure on a mind. A lot of awful things happened here. A lot are still happening. And if I can speak freely, General . . ." She glances around the room. "This shit frankly gives me the heebie-jeebies."

Mulaghesh can certainly see why. She tries to memorize everything she's seeing, all the sketches, all the strange glyphs. She tries to make some copies in her portfolio, but they feel clumsy and crude. *I wish Shara was here,* she thinks. *She knows about everything Divine. Or I wish I knew a Voortyashtani to ask about this. . . .*

She then realizes that she does—or, rather, she knows a Dreyling who grew up in Voortyashtan.

She grimaces. Playing with Signe Harkvaldsson, she feels, is playing with fire.

Then she notices a stack of papers lying in the corner. She walks over, picks them up, and does a double take.

"What the hells?" she mutters.

Mulaghesh knows Choudhry graduated with top honors from the Fadhuri Academy with a discipline in history—so why was she reading about a historical subject every schoolchild in Saypur knows backward and forward?

Mulaghesh stares down at the painting of Vallaicha Thinadeshi, perhaps the most famous woman in Saypuri history, and the person Fort Thinadeshi is named after.

***

When Mulaghesh was in school—which was so long ago that she doesn't even want to think about it—there were two kinds of kids: those that worshipped the Kaj and those that worshipped Thinadeshi. Most flocked to the Kaj: the man was, in a way, the savior of Saypur, a brilliant martial leader who freed them from bondage.

But what children eventually realized was that the Kaj never came *back:* he died on the Continent, less than a year after his final victory. He never saw the founding of Saypur. He never had any idea that their country could ever happen. He didn't build; he only destroyed.

Which was where Vallaicha Thinadeshi came in. As the Continent had relied on Saypur to provide a huge amount of resources *without* Divine assistance for hundreds of years, Saypuris had been forced to grow pretty canny about engineering and planning. And Vallaicha Thinadeshi proved to be the canniest: when Saypur was finally founded in 1648, she led the effort to build roads, develop irrigation and farming, and set up urban planning practices that could deal with the millions of Saypuri slaves suddenly set free. Saypur's sudden freedom wasn't easy, but it would have been a hell of a lot harder if Vallaicha Thinadeshi hadn't been there to get the right things in the right places.

But she didn't stop at that: she was also an innovative genius. It was Thinadeshi and her cadre of engineers who developed the railways and the telegraph systems. Her protégé had been the one to bring running water to Ghaladesh. And when Saypur opted to continue occupying the Continent in 1650, and "reconstruct," it had been Vallaicha Thinadeshi who sailed over and brought railways to the Continent—though Mulaghesh now knows this was chiefly so Saypur could quickly move troops throughout the polises, as they did not trust the Continent to remain passive.

It's this era of Thinadeshi's life that's endured, this image of her as adventurer and inventor, braving strange, hostile lands and bringing enlightenment with her. Mulaghesh knows the image is only somewhat true: Thinadeshi brought her family on her travels, and lost two children to plague, something she never forgave herself for. But perhaps the most mystifying and fixating thing about Thinadeshi's life is how it ended. And it is this subject that Choudhry was apparently reading about.

Mulaghesh reads.

By 1661, Thinadeshi had brought railways and some basic infrastructure to every Continental polis except one—Voortyashtan. She finally ventured into Voortyashtan in order to, as one journalist put it, "bind the most monstrous Continental state beneath the noble steel of the Saypuri rails," but it was during this expedition that Vallaicha Thinadeshi suddenly and inexplicably disappeared. Her scouting team searched for her and questioned the locals, but found no sign of Thinadeshi anywhere. It was as though she simply vanished. After months of searching they returned to Ghaladesh, and the country mourned the loss of a national hero.

Mulaghesh flips back to look at the painting of Thinadeshi: proud, regal, fearless, aristocratically thin and brown from the sun.

And both she and Choudhry, she reminds herself, *vanished without a trace in this place, over sixty years apart.*

"Any other interesting reading habits?" says Mulaghesh.

"It's all we found," says Nadar. "We think she burned the rest, though we're not sure when. Or why."

There's one final page to the stack of papers, a sketch of something Mulaghesh's eyes can't quite interpret: it looks like a black hand holding a sword blade, but the hand has been fashioned to become the hilt. It's a severed hand, she realizes, the severed wrist of the hand serving as the grip and pommel, with the clutching fingers acting as the blade's cross-guard.

Below this sketch of the sword are two smaller sketches, one of the sword blade alone, the other of the disturbing hand-hilt. Below this is a note, torn out from some other publication:

The blade and hilt of Voortya each had individual meaning to Voortyashtanis. The blade was attack, assault, aggression, but the hilt, fashioned out of the severed hand of the son of Saint Zhurgut, was a symbol of sacrifice. Together the two pieces were emblematic of the joy of warfare as well as the devotion and cost warfare required.

Together they balanced, becoming the warrior spirit, both taking and giving, dominating and submitting.

—EP

Mulaghesh doesn't have to think hard to realize whose initials "EP" are. *Efrem Pangyui,* she thinks. *You still haunt me to this day. . . .*

Mulaghesh looks up at the sound of a door slamming outside, followed by the patter of sprinting footsteps in the hall. Sergeant Major Pandey appears at the open door, panting. "Captain Nadar . . . I'm sorry, I've been looking all over for you, ma'am."

"Yes?" says Nadar. "What is it, Pandey? What's the matter?"

"It's . . . It's, ah, happened again, Captain."

"What has?"

Pandey frowns as he tries to think of how to phrase this. He says, "Another family north of here."

Nadar goes terribly still. Slowly she turns to Mulaghesh and says, "Will you excuse us?"

"Certainly."

Nadar and Pandey exit and stand in the hall, quietly conferring. Mulaghesh grabs Choudhry's notes and stuffs them in her portfolio, but she makes sure to tilt her head toward the door, listening. She can't catch any clear words—the one she can make out over and over again is "victim" or "victims"—but when she glances out Nadar's face is pale and her mouth is pulled tight in distaste.

Mulaghesh sticks her head out the door. Pandey is nervously watching Nadar, waiting for an answer but too frightened to ask further. Mulaghesh walks over to them. "Something up?"

Nadar shakes her head, furious. "Fucking shtanis . . ."

"Eh?"

"I apologize, General. There's . . . A report just came in about an attack. A family on an isolated farm north of here. Four of them. Town called Poshok." She pauses. "We are told it's quite gruesome."

"I see. So. What are you going to do?"

Nadar sighs. "There's an upcoming meeting of clan leaders that will surely feature a lot of difficult negotiation."

"Biswal mentioned that."

"Right. And this is the *last* thing we need, especially if it was one clan killing another."

"So. What are you going to do?"

"Ride out there and look at it. Try and find the perpetrators, and put them on the gallows or in the ground. The faster this dies, the better."

"Want me to come along?" asks Mulaghesh.

Nadar looks at her, surprised. "You'd want to do that, ma'am?"

"Really, I'm here to do whatever needs doing," she says. "I might have dealt with a few things like this as polis governor. And, frankly, I think Biswal would prefer it if I wasn't up under his feet. Besides, you're all busy. I'm not."

"I'm . . . I'm told the scene is quite upsetting, General," Nadar says.

"I've dealt with my share of upsetting scenes," says Mulaghesh. "Odds are this won't be anything I haven't seen before."

Nadar considers her words very carefully. "I'm . . . not so sure of that."

Saypur may boast a formidable navy and claim control of nearly all the trade routes of all the seas, but even if our navy were twice as large as it is today it would still not hold a candle to the naval forces of ancient Voortyashtan.

But their might was not derived from the number of ships they commanded, nor the number of warriors that manned the ships— though both of these were immense. Rather, each individual ship, no matter its size, possessed incredibly destructive powers. For though it is true that Voortyashtani sentinels armed themselves with naught but a sword and waded into battle with no shield, records indicate that their relationship with their swords was one loaded with unusual Divine properties.

A Voortyashtani sword was considered an extension of its warrior's soul, a piece of their heart: the two were linked on an almost metaphysical level. Most formidably, a warrior's sword always returned to the hands of its owner, which meant that when hurled across battlefields or even the open seas, it would inevitably come speeding back to the hand that threw it, no matter what the sword struck or encountered.

As Voortyashtani blades were extraordinarily large and sharp weapons, and the sentinels possessed superhuman strength, this meant that one sentinel essentially wielded as much destructive power as a modern-day cannon. If records of naval battles are to be believed— and they are so numerous and consistent, one must assume that one can—a tiny Voortyashtani cutter with only a handful of sentinels aboard could easily sink a Saypuri dreadnought.

Understandably, the relationship between a warrior's soul and its blade carried enormous spiritual importance for Voortyashtanis. If the warrior survived for long enough it was said that the sword would become the vessel of their soul, and their body would become simply a tool for wielding it. There are even some stories of common Continentals wielding a Voortyashtani blade and becoming possessed *by the previous owner, undergoing a grotesque transformation to do so. There is not much evidence found to substantiate these claims, however, and this myth may simply be an exaggeration of Voortya's relationship to her warriors: she asked them to be weapons for her, and weapons are what they willingly became.*

—DR. EFREM PANGYUI, "THE CONTINENTAL EMPIRE"

5.

components

It's midafternoon by the time they start out, twenty of them on horseback with Nadar in the lead. It's been a while since Mulaghesh went anywhere on horseback, and her ass and crotch start reminding her of this almost immediately as they compensate for her handicap—handling the reins one-handed isn't always easy—but the country roads won't tolerate an auto.

The ride north is quiet and somber. The firs on either side are close and dripping with moisture. Low clouds veil the distant Tarsil Mountains, turning their bright pink hue to a muddy brown before obscuring them entirely.

Not for the first time that day Mulaghesh wonders if she knows exactly what in all the hells she's doing. She's not at all sure if impetuously hopping onto an expedition north to what's apparently a brutal murder scene will benefit her investigation into Choudhry and the thinadeskite.

She supposes it *could*. She imagines Shara saying something like, *A good operative plays every angle, insinuates themselves into everyone's good graces, and learns every story they can.*

That seems like something Shara would say, Mulaghesh thinks. *So maybe this isn't that bad of an idea.*

But another thing Shara might say, though, would be, *A good operative doesn't waste everyone's fucking time.* Which Mulaghesh just might be doing here.

Curious forms emerge from the mist as they ride: tall, smooth standing stones, placed in patterns that couldn't be coincidental. Then a fallen arch or causeway, white stones stained green by the mold and moisture. A mile later they encounter half of a tower, vivisected by some unknown catastrophe, its bricks scattered over the hills like broken teeth. Relics and remnants of a culture that collapsed long ago.

The last is the most startling. The sight must be a familiar one, because only Mulaghesh reacts as it comes into view: at the top of a distant hill sit two giant stone feet, perhaps eighty feet long and fifty feet high, truncated at the ankles. The feet are bare and stand on a massive marble plinth that sits uneven on the loam, like the soil below could no longer suffer the weight of whatever huge figure once stood there. But no matter how Mulaghesh searches she sees no more of the statue: no distant stone shoulder or marble hand, shattered and moldering on the nearby hills. No blank white visage half-submerged in the loam, cracked and corroded.

She looks back at the feet and the plinth as they ride on. "Do I want to know what that was?" she asks.

Nadar says, "I know I don't."

***

Mulaghesh smells it before she sees it: soft, wet wood burning somewhere nearby. Pandey consults the report he received—"Directions are a devilish bastard here, General," he breathlessly confides—and points down one of the narrow country roads. They round a copse of firs, and Mulaghesh sees a narrow tendril of dark smoke threading its way into the late-afternoon sky.

They ride up in silence. The farmhouse is a low structure with a large porch, dark smoke streaming out from somewhere at its back. But there's something in front of the porch that's hard to comprehend: six totems, perhaps, or maybe decorations, pale white and placed on stakes. Yet they seem to tremble strangely, like the light around them is fluttering.

I don't like this, thinks Mulaghesh.

As they ride closer they spy a hint of a breast on one of the totems, and on another a wisp of chest hair, and soon it's apparent that the reason the air seems to tremble is because it's positively swarming with black flies.

"Oh, by the *seas*," says Nadar, disgusted.

They are human torsos, or rather halves of human torsos, vivisected from collar to crotch, with each half placed on a stake. The body cavities are open and exposed, the organs within withered and black. The heads, arms, and legs have been neatly shorn off and placed in piles in between the stakes as if they were no more than kindling. It is, despite the viscera and stink, a curiously neat presentation, carefully and thoughtfully done, as if these corpses were vegetables to be washed and peeled for dinner.

As the sight comes into view many of the soldiers hang back, appalled. Nadar senses the change in disposition, turns, and says, "Secure the area. Pandey, search the woods for signs of any passage. You and you, stay here and guard the gate. Stop anyone you see nearby for any reason." Then she turns back to the grisly scene, muttering, "Fucking shtanis . . ."

"Are you good to look closer?" asks Mulaghesh.

Nadar glares at her defiantly. "Yes."

Mulaghesh rides forward and Nadar follows, looking fainter and fainter with each step. Soon the horses begin to resist, disturbed by the scent.

"How could they . . . How could they *do* this?" asks Nadar.

"Carefully, it looks like," says Mulaghesh, waving away flies and circling the bodies. "They managed to part the sternum and the spine, even. That's not easy to do—though the spinal column seems to have been a more difficult tas—"

Nadar turns her head and vomits onto the grass. Her horse whickers, startled.

"Do you need some water?" asks Mulaghesh.

"How can you just *look* at them?" says Nadar, spitting and wiping her eyes.

"It's the worst I've seen, yes," says Mulaghesh grimly, looking at the closest body. "But not by a lot." She looks at the severed heads on the ground. A family, Pandey said—a wife and two sons, both adolescents. Their faces, blue and distorted, have the dull, stupid look of the dead, as if they've just been asked a difficult question.

Mulaghesh dismounts, waves more flies aside, and steps closer to the corpses. There are no wounds on them besides their mutilations, no stab wounds or slashes or bullet holes. One of the sons has some kind of ugly rash on his ribs, but that's clearly not fatal. Though she doesn't search the pile of limbs on the ground much—even she has her limits—she doesn't see any damage there, either. "Either they were poisoned or suffocated or something," she says aloud, "or the wounds they suffered were the killing blows."

"As in, they had their heads struck from their shoulders?" says Nadar.

"Maybe." She looks at half of a truncated neck, which is already withered and gray. "It's a smooth cut. Done either all at once, in one blow, or done slowly. Tricky to do, either way. People aren't liable to stand still for such a thing. The boy has some kind of skin infection, something nasty. . . . But I'm not sure if that means anything."

"Would you . . . Would you get *away* from there?" says Nadar. "You are absolutely *crawling* with flies."

Mulaghesh wades out of the throng of buzzing insects. "Pandey said there were four."

"What?"

"The initial report. He said it was a family of four. Where's the fourth?"

The two of them ride around to the back of the farmhouse and find the fourth body lying in a patch of clover by the fence, facedown. It's a man of about forty, from what Mulaghesh can see, but he shows no sign of mutilation or even harm. Mulaghesh dismounts again, looks him up and down, then squats, grasps him one-handed, and flips him over.

His still, white face stares up. Though he's now discolored and crawling with beetles—she grimaces as something dark and scuttling dashes out of his mouth to hide in his shirt collar—she sees no slashes, cuts, or injuries of any kind on him. His throat, however, bears a strange tattoo, a band of green ink that resembles a braid, completely encircling his neck.

"So this is the dad, I guess," she says.

"I guess," says Nadar. She dismounts as well, though it's clear she doesn't want to.

"What's this tattoo here?"

"Tattoo?" Nadar's face darkens as she looks at it. "*Shit.*"

"What is it?"

"It's a tribal tattoo. All the tribes have them. Once you've passed all the tests and are sworn into the tribe, they give you this mark, a ring around the neck. The symbolism implies that the only way to leave the tribe—"

"Is to lose your head," says Mulaghesh.

"Right. All the tribes have different colors, patterns. This one is the Orskova tribe, a river clan. So this will piss off some important people, probably."

Mulaghesh looks up at the farmhouse, whose back side is smoldering, and suddenly this is all too familiar: the smoking farmhouse; the wet, cold grass; the whine of the flies; and the smell of corpses. . . .

Mulaghesh shakes herself. She stands and walks over, examining the crude wooden structure. Part of the back door has collapsed, like someone drove a truck into it. This must have broken open the hearth, which started the fire. "Lucky it's wet," she says aloud. "Otherwise we'd have a forest fire." She looks back at Nadar. "You know what this is, don't you?"

"I do?" says Nadar.

"Shorn of limbs, with the torsos vivisected and placed on stakes . . ."

Nadar thinks about it. Then her eyes spring wide. "Oh, by the seas . . ."

"Yeah. This is what Voortyashtani sentinels used to do to Saypuri slaves who rebelled or tried to escape. Breaking them down into components, I think is what they called it. Proving that we weren't really humans in their eyes: just devices, instruments, easily taken apart. Then they put the bodies on display for everyone to see. You're unlikely to resist slavery with something like that out your bedroom window." She shakes her head. "I've read accounts of it happening, but . . . I've never seen someone try to duplicate it."

Nadar and Mulaghesh lead their horses back around to the front of the farmhouse. "So you think it's a message?" asks Nadar.

"This is your region, your backyard," says Mulaghesh. "You tell me."

"I do. He's Orskova, and this is disputed territory among the tribes. Maybe this is an insult, or warning—betray us, and we'll treat you like Saypuris."

"Seems likely." Mulaghesh brushes a fly off of her face. "This is going to fuck up your negotiations something fierce, isn't it."

Nadar groans and rubs her eyes. "Oh, definitely. Biswal and Rada will have a merry time trying to get the damned tribes to stop trying to murder one another after this abomination."

"Rada?"

"Rada Smolisk. She's the polis governor here."

"Rada Smo . . ." Mulaghesh's mouth opens as she realizes what Nadar's suggesting. "That name . . . You mean the polis governor is a damned *Continental*?"

"Oh, yes," says Nadar. "It's one of the Ministry programs, trying to get more Continentals involved in governing themselves. Unlike other programs, though, this one turned out quite well. Rada's a good sort. She's a bit of a shrinking violet, but she's a highly accomplished doctor. Goes all over the place fixing people up, even comes up to the fort to work on the wounded. She's well liked."

"I've never heard of such a thing in my life! A Continental, as a polis governor!"

Nadar smirks. "I thought you were part of the minister's cadre, General. Isn't she quite the progressive?"

"There's progressive and then there's stark fucking barmy." She shakes herself and tries to focus. "You said this had happened before?"

"What? Oh. Right. Yes, once, seven months ago. It was a couple, though, not a family, and the murder wasn't nearly as . . . ornate as this."

"No body parts on stakes?"

"No. From the patrol's reading of the scene, a man killed his wife, removed her head and limbs. He didn't get to vivisecting the torso, though. We found him dead in the same room in their little hut. The wolves had been at him."

They begin walking back to the front yard. "No sign of foul play in his death?"

"Like I said, the wolves had been at him. But no. We thought he'd been drunk when he did it, maybe died of alcohol poisoning. Or had a heart attack. That scene wasn't nearly as fresh as this one is—they'd been there for a while. We thought it was an isolated event. All kinds of horrible things happen here. But this . . ."

"Yeah," says Mulaghesh. "It's a trend now. Maybe the first one was a warning, too; they just didn't complete the job the way they wanted to. They got sloppy. But now they've learned. They know how to do it right."

Nadar looks off into the dark trees. "So it'll happen again."

"Probably, yeah. Unless you can find the person or, more likely, people who did this."

"You think there's more than one?"

"It's tough, killing a whole family. Kids run. Someone comes at you with a knife, maybe. Best to bring some helping hands. Though I wouldn't rule out poison or suffocation. Start a fire, choke them in their sleep. That's one way they could do it alone, I suppose."

"How do you know all this?"

"I just know." She clucks her tongue and shakes her head. "They don't mutilate the men, though. The rest are fair game. It's damn odd."

There's a shout from the lane outside. Nadar and Mulaghesh remount and ride over to find Pandey and three other soldiers grouped at where the trees run along the road. "What is it?" asks Nadar.

"We found something, ma'am," says Pandey. He points at the trees. "It's like a deer blind, in a way."

Nadar and Mulaghesh dismount again—Mulaghesh's thighs are

already complaining—and squat to see. There between two trees are dozens of fir cuttings, carefully arranged to make a crude wall.

Nadar parts the wall a bit with one hand and peers inside. "Needles have been cleared away," she says softly. "Like someone sat here for a long time. Good eye, soldier."

Mulaghesh stands and lines herself up with the blind. Its line of sight peers right through the fence to the side of the farmhouse, giving a clear view of anything that might be happening in the front or the back.

"They watched," she says quietly. "Watched and waited until the time was right."

***

It's late evening by the time they return to the city proper. Mulaghesh is exhausted, and the muscles in her lower back feel like they can hardly keep her upright. "I'll send a messenger to notify the Orskovas," says Nadar as the gates to Fort Thinadeshi open, "as they'll probably want to be the ones who'll dispose of the bodies."

"What's the next step for you, Captain?" asks Mulaghesh.

"Send a patrol to start canvassing the area in the morning," says Nadar. "Ask questions, see what looks suspicious. That's as good a place to start as any. Will you be staying here tonight, General?"

"No, I think it'd be wiser to stay in the city," says Mulaghesh. "Two generals under one roof . . . I don't want to step on any toes."

"And I assume that SDC's goosedown beds, ample fireplaces, and top-line chefs have nothing to do with your decision," says Nadar. Her voice is surprisingly cold.

"It's been a long day, Captain," says Mulaghesh sharply, "and you've seen some disturbing shit. So I'm willing to give you a pass this one time, Nadar. But just the one."

"I apologize, General. You have been most helpful in your assessment of the scene back there. Pandey can drive you back down, if you'd like. I'm afraid the rest of us have a busy night ahead." She salutes, Mulaghesh returns it, and she trots inside Thinadeshi headquarters. Mulaghesh watches her go, reading her subtext loud and clear: *You make motions like you want to help, but at the end of the day, you're still on vacation.*

"Whatever," mutters Mulaghesh, walking to the auto. "I've got work to do, too."

Pandey salutes. "Back to the lighthouse, General?"

"No, not tonight," she says, climbing in. "Let's go to the harbor works instead." She flips through her portfolio, staring at the copies of Choudhry's strange, disturbing drawings. "I've got someone I need to talk to."

***

The first place Mulaghesh goes to find Signe is the SDC front desk, where she's met by a thickset man who glances at a schedule, says "Dock D4," and points in a somewhat northeasterly direction. Mulaghesh treks to Dock D4, only to be informed upon arrival that Signe has moved on to Prep Station 3, a fenced-off portion of the SDC construction yards. But when she arrives there the foremen tell Mulaghesh she's missed Signe by twenty minutes; and while they don't know her schedule, they *think* she was headed for the Tower Test Assembly Yard—whatever the hells *that* is.

Mulaghesh, huffing and puffing, trots back in the direction of the SDC headquarters, thinking that Signe must be under the impression that there are actually seventy-two hours in a day: there's no other explanation why a sane human being would ever schedule their work in such a manner.

As she runs she looks to the edges, the shadows, searching the workers. Dreylings are commonly thought of as pirates and savage seamen by most of the civilized world—and Mulaghesh knows that this reputation is not unearned—but industrialization seems to suit those working here for SDC. Their sealskin coats are all color-coded and smartly arranged, their construction helmets festooned with badges and stickers signaling which areas they're approved to enter. These people are here to do work, and they mean to do it well.

But some are . . . different. She spies some of the workers lurking in the shadows, watchful creatures with what are obviously riflings and scatter guns hidden in their coats. She even spots something downright disturbing on the top of a watchtower above the train tracks: a PK-512, a stationary, fully automatic, six-barreled turret capable of spitting out an incredible amount of destruction per second. She takes careful note of the hulking pile of machinery and its massive barrel set: it's like a scaled-up version of the carousel currently holstered at her side. She remembers seeing one of those during a demonstration just a few years ago and recalls how it shredded a quarter-inch-thick steel plate like it was paper.

Biswal was right, thinks Mulaghesh. *They've got a private army here.*

She finally catches up to Signe, who is being pursued by a flock of anxious Dreylings like a mother duck pursued by her ducklings. As she nears she hears Signe rattling off instructions, and at the conclusion of each order a man peels himself away from her entourage and goes sprinting off through the construction yards. ". . . Dock G7 is currently undergoing maintenance, so we'll need to reroute all shipments to H3 until 1200 next Thursday. Repeat, *next* Thursday. Tower 5 is being assembled, but when it's finished, it should be able to provide stabilization for Tower 34, which is having trouble finding purchase. Tower 34 needs to be fully operational by 1000 hours Sunday in order for us to do the lift—we *have* to get that obstruction cleared if we want to get started on the western delta. How are we on diesel?"

"Tanker's due in tomorrow."

"What time?"

"Oh-nine-hundred hours."

"Not good enough. Escalate."

"Yes, ma'am."

On and on and on. Signe winnows down her entourage until only three men are left. One of them is obviously her bodyguard, though from his uniform he's somewhat high-ranking. He spots Mulaghesh coming, glances at the carousel holstered at her hip, and twitches slightly—almost certainly undoing a clasp on some hidden holster.

Signe glances at her. "Oh. Ah! Hello, General. How was the fortress? Illuminating, I trust?"

"Something like that," says Mulaghesh. She watches the body-guard closely—he's a lean, lupine sort of Dreyling. His hair is so short it's hard to tell what's hair and what's stubble.

"Allow me to introduce you both," says Signe. "This is my chief of security, Lem."

Mulaghesh smiles thinly. "Evening, Lem."

Lem just nods. His glower doesn't change one bit.

"I have some matters to discuss with you," says Mulaghesh.

"Absolutely," says Signe, checking off something on a clipboard with a surprising amount of vindication. "I would be more than happy to chat with you. However, I'm reviewing a new tower assembly process that might significantly accelerate a crucial stage in our process."

"Okay . . . So?"

"So . . ." Signe points ahead to a line of thick iron walls, nearly twenty feet tall, riddled with riveted seams. The only visible entrance is a very threatening door with a multistep locking system. It looks like something built to withstand an armed assault, though its roof is a series of canvas tarps, stretched out to give it shelter from the rain. "So, you will not be able to accompany me, I'm afraid. That's the tower test assembly yard. There are quite a few very, *very* valuable patents hidden behind those walls, and it wouldn't do to keep the door open too wide, if you understand me."

"You're worried about me being an industrial spy?"

"I wouldn't normally, but . . . A Saypuri general, eager for retire-ment, looking for a way to carve out a nest egg . . . Maybe I'm para-noid, but paranoia has, in my experience, rarely harmed, and usually helped."

"Thanks for the kind assessment. So when the hells can I talk to you?"

"Mm . . . After this, I'll be headed back over to Dock G7, so . . . tomorrow?"

"You can't talk until *tomorrow*?"

"It *is* a busy evening," says Signe. One of her aides hands her a clipboard, which she casts an eye over. "I believe I can give you an hour tomorrow evening. Say, 1900, in the board club."

"The fancy place we ate at? Fine. Just one more question. When do you sleep?"

"Lem?" says Signe.

"Yes, ma'am?"

"When is my next scheduled sleep?"

He consults a ledger-sized notepad. "Eleven hundred tomorrow, ma'am."

Signe smiles at Mulaghesh. "Well. There you go. I do have *some* information for you as well, General—some that needn't wait. I put out the alert you requested, notifying all employees to come forward if Sumitra Choudhry had approached any of them. And it turns out she did. She asked one of our medics as to whether or not Voortyashtan had an apothecary—a place where one can purchase all manner of—"

"I know what an apothecary is," says Mulaghesh. She makes a note of this in her portfolio. "Did she say why?"

"She didn't, I'm afraid. But our medic told me she was quite eager to buy something. What, she wouldn't say. Look for the shop with the green door on Andrus Street."

"Wait, the streets have *names* here? I didn't even notice."

"They're written in the curbs at corners," says Signe. They approach yet another checkpoint—this one at the door to the tower test assembly yard—and Mulaghesh hangs back, eyeing the Dreyling guard with the rifling slung over his back. "They use fish bones to spell them out. Anyway, here's hoping more of my workers come forward with something about Miss Choudhry. Maybe one of them will know something more useful to you."

Mulaghesh continues taking notes. The giant iron door in the wall swings open. Signe walks through, head buried in her clipboard and whispering notes to herself. She doesn't even look back as the door swings shut with a tremendous clang.

***

The shop on Andrus Street is really more of a hut, featuring animal-skin walls with seams tightly stitched shut with tendon. The door is a dangling wooden slat painted dull green, its paint cracking. It offers absolutely no insulation against the chilly drafts.

Mulaghesh walks up, knocks three times. Someone inside calls, "Come in!"

She pushes the door aside and finds she is inside of a labyrinth of messy shelves, all curling around her, a cyclone rendered in wood. All the shelves are filled with bottles and jars, most holding black-ened and shriveled things that might have once been organic. Others hold seeds, powders, the cores of strange fruits. It takes Mulaghesh a moment to focus on a desk at the other end of the hut, where a small man who's just as shrunken and withered as his wares is smil-ing at her.

"Hello, ma'am," says the little man, "how are you?" His eyes widen, then narrow when he sees her Saypuri uniform. "Beautiful evening, isn't it?"

"I guess."

"What can I help you with?" asks the little man. He nods at her arm. "Need a pain poultice for that? I get a lot of sailors from the harbor works here missing all kinds of their bits. I know my way around a stump or two, that I do."

Mulaghesh pauses, trying to figure out how offended she is by this statement. "No, I—"

"Having women's issues, then?" He grins. His teeth are like peb-bles laced with black lichen. "A lady your age—do you feel the heats upon you? Not an issue at all. I have a—"

"Do you have any poultices that work on a fractured eye socket?" she asks. "Because you're going to need them if you persist in this line of salesmanship."

He blinks. "Oh. All right."

"I'm not here to buy. I have some questions about someone who came here a while ago."

The little man whistles. "Well, that particular subject matter can be tricky. Very tricksome indeed, unfortunately."

"Why's that?"

"Well, it would not be in the interest of my clients or my business if I were to go blabbing about what they buy here." And then, as if an afterthought: "It'd also be a mite bit dishonest, too, I suppose."

"This would have been a Saypuri," says Mulaghesh. "A Saypuri woman, like me. Would this be a different situation, then?"

"I'm offended that you would think me being a Continental would prejudice me against a Saypuri enough to compromise my honesty," says the little man. "It's a hurtsome thing to think, honestly."

Sighing, Mulaghesh slaps a twenty-drekel note down on the table. The little man pockets it in a flash. "Right," he says brightly. "So. This Saypuri woman."

"She would have come in several months ago, at least."

"That's as I thought. You're in luck. We very, *very* rarely get any Saypuri women in here, so I think I remember the one you're talking about. Short? Bandage here?" He points to his brow. "Acted like she'd been shut up in a room all day?"

"Sounds like the one."

"Mmm. Yes, I remember her. Very strange person, she was."

"What makes you say that?"

"The way she acted," he says, as if her question was powerfully stupid. "The way she looked at things. I take a pellet of drangla weed every morning—it helps me notice things about people." He taps the edge of his right eye with a dirt-encrusted finger. "Helps me glimpse the edges of their secret selves. Not easy to make, but I have it reasonably pri—"

Mulaghesh loudly cracks her knuckles against her jaw, bending each finger.

"Right, right. Well. This girl, she made me think of someone who'd come out of hiding, and was counting the seconds until they could sneak away again. She bought some very strange things, too— things I hardly ever sell." He tilts his head back, eyes closed, thinks, and says, "Rosemary. Pine needles. Dried worms. Grave dust. Dried frog eggs. And bone powder."

"That's an impressive memory."

"Stems from a concoction I make." He sniffs. "Which I, ah, would never be interested in selling you."

"Smart move."

"Of course, it *did* help that she came back and bought those same ingredients over and over again. Each time in larger quantities, too."

Mulaghesh makes a note of all this. "And I suppose you wouldn't know," she says, "exactly what all this could be used for."

The little man scratches his head theatrically. "Mm, I might have once known, but the thought escapes me now. . . ."

Mulaghesh puts another twenty-drekel note on the table.

The little man snatches it up. "Well, the *reason* I never sell any of those items anymore is that their primary use doesn't *exist* anymore. In that their primary purpose used to be Divine."

"I see," says Mulaghesh.

"Yes. They were popular reagents for performing some of the more mundane miracles, with the sole exception being the frog eggs, as those were more top-tier, I suppose you could say. All of the ingredients she bought were Voortyashtani-oriented: rosemary and pine needles, for their evergreen nature; dried worms, for their regenerative properties; grave dust and powdered bone, for their finality; and frog eggs, for their capacity for metamorphosis. All of these things, you see, deal with the threshold dividing life from death."

"The domain of Voortya," says Mulaghesh.

"Uh, yes," he says, somewhat nervous to be so candidly discussing the sacred.

"And what exact miracle do you think someone would try to accomplish with these reagents?" she asks.

"That I can't say. All the specific stuff was banned when Saypur enforced the Worldly Regulations. They took all those books and packed them away somewhere. I only know the general stuff, which wasn't quite so illegal."

"Do you know anyone who *might* know what miracle they could be used for?"

"Well . . ." He scratches his chin. "Komayd did roll back a whole lot of the Worldly Regulations when *she* took the crown, but so far it hasn't trickled down to us little fellers yet. The only folk who might know are the highlanders."

"Like, the tribes?"

"Them's the ones. They're old traditionalists, they are. They wouldn't have forgotten a thing like that. Though it's a bit hard to just sit down and have tea with them."

Mulaghesh makes another note of this. "What do you have in the way of sleeping aids?"

"Oh, well . . . that depends on the sleep you need. Do you have trouble falling asleep? Or *staying* asleep?"

"Staying," says Mulaghesh, rubbing her left arm.

"And what kind of sleep do you seek, ma'am? Light? Dreamy? Or deep?"

"Deep," she says immediately. "No dreams, if you can."

He looks at her, and there's a curious shine to his eye that makes her think that maybe he wasn't lying about the drangla weed. "Is it sleep you want to find?" he asks quietly. "Or dreams you wish to *escape?*"

She looks at him hard. "The latter."

He reviews his shelves, then takes down a small glass jar filled with tiny brown dots. "Nickletop mushroom caps," he says, "have a distinctly soporific effect—they make you sleepy, I mean, ma'am. Gets stronger when you steam 'em." He carefully pours some of them into a tin and affixes the cap. "Sometimes used to put horses asleep before surgery. What this means, ma'am, is *don't* take too much of 'em. Cut one in half, and put it below your tongue before bed. You can brew it in tea, too, but the effects take longer. And *don't* lick your fingers or prepare any food without washing your hands. Or, ah, engage in any manual intimacy. A dusting of nickletop will render any man's trouser eel worthless for hours."

"Now *that* I'll keep in mind." She takes the little tin, pops the cap open, and looks inside. The mushroom caps look like tiny, flaky brown pearls. "Any side effects?"

"Just the one on your purse," he says. "Thirty drekels, please."

She grouses for a moment—thirty drekels would be enough for a steak dinner, if there was any beef to speak of around here—but she forks it over. She needs sleep more than she needs money.

***

Back in her room at the SDC headquarters Mulaghesh massages her arm, pulls the carousel from its holster, and sets it on her nightstand. Then she sits on the edge of her bed, alone in her sumptuous room, listening to the wind and the sea bickering outside her window.

The images of the farmhouse swirl about in her mind: bodies ravaged beyond recognition, the black smoke unscrolling from the tips of the dark trees, a human form half-concealed by a clump of clover.

She tries to tell herself that she's just disturbed, as anyone would be. She just strolled through the scene of a brutal mass murder and abominable desecration—that's why her heart is beating so fast. It has nothing to do with the fact that these sights, however grisly, are somewhat familiar to her.

She rummages through her coat, pulls out the little tin of nickletop mushrooms, and taps out one of the dark little buttons. She uses her combat knife to cut it in half and examines the tiny, crumpled half-circle balanced on her index finger. After a second's hesitation she opens her mouth, sticks it under her tongue—it tastes of wood and wool—and lies down on the bed.

The effects are almost instantaneous. She feels woozy, like her brain is waterlogged, and everything is suddenly incredibly heavy. It's as if her bones are so dense they're about to fall through her flesh and through the bottom of the bed.

She remembers what Biswal said to her: *It helps me fight the feeling that I'm a fiddly old man wondering if the past ever really happened.* . . .

Her lids grow heavy. The nickletop might keep her from dreaming, but it's helpless to keep her from remembering so much in the few fleeting minutes before sleep.

***

If you were to bring up the Yellow March in Saypur these days, chances are you'd get a variety of reactions, none of them positive: there'd be a lot of sighs and eye-rolling—*not this again*—and perhaps a snicker or two. Among the more patriotic quarters such a mention would likely evoke outright hostility: you could be booted from the premises, or even struck in the face.

This is because, in Saypur, all talk of the Yellow March has long been considered either a smear campaign or a paranoid delusion, a dangerous or ludicrous conspiracy theory that only crackpots and the unpatriotic would ever entertain.

Everyone respectable agrees that the Summer of Black Rivers (called such even though it lasted nearly three years) was one of Saypur's greatest triumphs. It was the war that defined Saypur's modern national identity, so who would dare besmirch its reputation? Those Saypuris who wish to appear thoughtful will concede that, yes, there might have been *some*thing that inspired the wild tale of the Yellow March—war is war, after all, and full of horrors—but it was certainly far short of the events the conspiracy theorists detail.

But Mulaghesh knows it was no conspiracy. Because she remembers. Even though it was almost forty years ago, she remembers.

The Kaj captured the Continent in 1642, and Saypur pulled off the Great Censoring just eight years later, scouring the Continent of all of its sacred images and art. Shortly after that Saypur plunked down the Worldly Regulations, hoping—in futility—that outlawing mention or acknowledgment of the Divine would mean it would no longer affect modern life. Saypur was pretty strict about the WR for most of the Continent, but they tended to tiptoe around Bulikov: even in its postwar, decimated state, it was still a massive metropolis, and it still wielded a lot of power by sheer population. So, to a certain extent, the WR were enforced in Bulikov in name only, so that Saypur could remain unchallenged and keep the remainder of the Continent in check.

Up until 1681, that is. By then Saypur had built up its military and started to flex its muscles, and it was decided Ghaladesh could no longer tolerate such lax control over the Continent's central city. A litany of severe laws were passed and the crackdowns began. Things escalated—first a protest, then a riot, and then municipal buildings were occupied and the clerks there held hostage—until by '85 Bulikov was in a full-fledged revolt: the Bulikovian Uprising, they called it. And what started out as an uprising quickly evolved into an outright war.

It was to be the world's first taste of modern warfare, of battle bereft of Divine intervention. Saypur had just scaled up its production of bolt-shots and other mechanized weaponry to the extent that common infantry could utilize them, and its forces were fresh and eager to fight, keen to prove to their old repressors that Saypur deserved to be a world power. But the Continent had numbers and territory on its side, and despite General Prandah's claims that this would be a "lightning-fast war, a lot of noise followed by a long silence," and the vigorous public campaign that all hostilities would merely last a summer—hence the name, which stuck—soon both Saypuri and Continental forces found themselves dug in two hundred miles east of Bulikov on the banks of the Luzhkov River, with no indication that either could break through the other's fortifications.

Enter Captain Lalith Biswal, then twenty-three years old, a careful, bookish student of what few non-Divine wars could be studied. And, under his command in Yellow Company, a sixteen-year-old Turyin Mulaghesh who had run away from home, lied about her age, enlisted, and gotten her stupid ass promoted to sergeant without even realizing what was going on.

It was during the fifth Battle of the Luzhkov when Captain Biswal and Yellow Company were dispatched in an ambitious flanking maneuver, marching upstream, floating the river, and attacking the Continental positions from the north. It should have worked perfectly and caused massive disruptions in the Continentals' lines . . . or it would have if the Continentals hadn't been aware of the pending attack, right down to the minute it started.

The Saypuri attack was routed both quickly and brutally. The skiffs that had been used to float across the Luzhkov were captured and burned, leaving Yellow Company stranded on the wrong side of the river. All order and discipline collapsed, and the Continentals drove them mercilessly north, away from the battle and the Saypuri lines.

Yellow Company retreated through the night, a rambling, uncoordinated rush through the Continental countryside, pursued by forces far more knowledgeable about the territory than they were. The woods were filled with screams, sprinting horses, distant firelight. When the sun came up, the ragged Saypuri soldiers looked around and realized they did not recognize where they were.

They had never seen this particular set of hills before. Their scouts reported settlements nearby, but not fortifications: they were simple farms.

It took Biswal a moment to realize: "We're past their fortifications," he said, sitting atop his horse. "By the seas, we're *behind* them!" Though Yellow Company could not have known, the Continental brigade that'd been dispatched to pursue them had been distracted by a full-frontal assault by General Prandah's forces far to the south. Which meant Yellow Company no longer had any pursuers, no one to push them out of Continental territory.

It should not have happened. But it did.

Mulaghesh still remembers the evening of that first day, when Biswal approached her and took her aside. The mist gathering on the hills, the moaning and weeping from the scattered troops. Fires were forbidden—the smoke would give them away—so all of them clutched their arms and legs and shivered, eating dried meats. This had not been intended to be a far-ranging mission, so they had very few provisions, and many of those had been lost in the retreat.

He led her to a small forest clearing. "Lieutenant Pankaj died of wounds this morning," he said.

"I'm sorry, sir."

"Thank you, Sergeant. Though I've heard a lot of sorries today. The word's losing meaning." He sighed. "We can't find Niranjan, or Kapil, *or* Ram. Which means that I've lost nearly all of my officers overnight. I don't have powers of promotion, but you're more or less going to have to be my lieutenant, Mulaghesh, so that's what I'm going to call you. And if we live to get busted down for that, I'll be grateful."

"Yes, sir."

"You're young, but I've watched you fight. You're not stupid, and other soldiers listen to you. That's a valuable thing."

"Thank you, sir."

Biswal turned to watch the hills. "So. It seems like we have three choices. We can return south, survey the enemy's position, and try and flank them again when the time's right, carrying out our original orders. Or, we can go east, try and ford the Luzhkov, circumvent the enemy's position, and rejoin Prandah." He paused.

"And our third choice?"

He looked at her, his pale eyes sharp. "What do you think our odds are of pulling either of those two options off, Lieutenant?"

"Minimal, sir."

"And why's that?"

"The Continentals aren't stupid. At some point they'll realize we're still here. If they aren't in pursuit by now, they'll be ready for us to return. They'll watch the river. That's what they'll expect." She glanced, side-eyed, at the ragged, wounded soldiers sitting below the pines. "And I don't think we're in any shape for serious combat, sir. We don't have any supplies. I'm not sure if we can last more than a handful of days."

"I agree." He looked at the hills surrounding them again.

"Sir?"

"Yes?"

"You mentioned a third option, sir."

"I did." He sucked his teeth. "Do you know what keeps the Continental forces on their feet, Lieutenant? What keeps their fortifications so firm?"

She was smart enough by then to know not to answer a superior officer's rhetorical questions. "I don't, sir."

"Farms," said Biswal. He walked to a tree, leaned against it, and watched a tiny hamlet nestled in a distant valley. "Food and farms. We're in the middle of the breadbasket of the Continent, Mulaghesh. By complete and total accident, sure, but here we are." He paused. "And there are lots of ways to win a war. A war isn't between armies, it's between nations." He pursed his lips, sighed, shook his head. "But by the seas, what a way to fight."

"Are you suggesting we . . ."

He looked over his shoulder at her. "Go on, Lieutenant."

"Are you suggesting that we make war upon the civilians here?"

"I'm saying one option is we destroy their farms, their infrastructure, their irrigation systems. Take what we need to survive, destroy the rest, then move to the next town, and do it again. We'd cut right through all of the Continentals' supply lines. But it's a damn bastard thing to do, that I'll say."

He looked at her, and she somehow understood that he wanted her to judge him, to say something, perhaps to approve. And what lay unspoken between them was the knowledge that they now made war in the nation of those who once enslaved them.

All Mulaghesh could manage was, "We're dying, sir."

He nodded. "Yes."

"We're starving."

"Yes."

"I think we're going to die here no matter what we do."

He was silent. Then: "Yes. I agree."

"My conclusion, if I might be so bold to give it, sir, is we might as well try and do our part," she said quietly. "With as much time as we have left."

He nodded and stared off into the distance, lost in thought. Then: "Gather as many troops as you can. Comb the forest, comb the hills—*carefully*. Round up the survivors. Tomorrow morning, we're going to move." He took out his spyglass and watched the little hamlet in the valley. "We'll approach from the southwest, through the forest. It'll be slow going, but we'll want to surprise them. And damn it, Mulaghesh . . ." He ripped away his spyglass and held it tightly in his hands, as if imagining choking someone, and she understood how furious all this made him. "If . . . If we're going to do this, we're going to do this *right*. We'll do it *peaceably*. We'll be organized, disciplined. No casualties, unless we can't avoid them. I will *not* condone the shedding of innocent blood, even if it is Continental. Certainly not women or children. We are soldiers, not raiders, with strategic goals. Is that clear?"

"Perfectly, sir."

"Do you think we can achieve that?"

"Yes, sir."

"Then you have your orders, Lieutenant. Dismissed."

She saluted and trotted away through the woods.

***

Lying upon the bed in the SDC headquarters, head swilling with the fog of nickletop, Mulaghesh looks back on that moment and thinks, *What wild promises we make in order to justify the worst of decisions.*

Yet even as her body grows leaden and numb, one last thought persists, nagging at her.

Something she saw today isn't right.

She remembers the corpses from the farmhouse that afternoon, and thinks, *I've seen those bodies before. I've seen something like that before.*

She tells herself: *Bodies in the Continental wilderness. Certainly. I know that sight well.*

Yet still: *No. No. I saw those bodies just recently. I saw that sight just today,* before *I went to that farmhouse. . . .*

And she realizes that she's right.

Mulaghesh attempts to sit up, but her body won't obey. She lurches forward with one arm outstretched, grasping for her portfolio, but succeeds only in knocking it off her nightstand. Then darkness closes in on her.

Don't lose that thought. Don't lose that thought. . . .

***

When she wakes in the morning she feels like her eyes are made of drying mud. It takes a disconcertingly long time for her to make some basic connections—*Where am I? Why does my arm hurt? What in hells is wrong with my head?*—and an even longer time for her to find the energy to sit up and rub her face.

"No side effects," she mutters. "Fucking bullshit." Everything hurts: her back, her legs, her arms. It's a miracle she didn't overdose and kill herself.

Suddenly, she remembers.

"Holy *shit*," she says. She grabs her portfolio and sprints out the door.

It takes twenty minutes for an SDC telephone to open up—apparently some major construction work is going on upshore—and even longer for the on-call sergeant to get Captain Nadar on the phone.

"What?" says Nadar's voice, not even bothering to try to be cordial. "What is it? Who is this?"

"It's General Mulaghesh. Listen, I realized something about those bodies the other day."

"Oh." Nadar clears her throat, affecting a more formal tone. "Yes, General?"

"We'd seen them before. Both of us had. That very day, as a matter of fact. We saw them before we ever went to that farmhouse."

A long pause.

"What?" says Nadar, bewildered.

"I made some copies of the sketches in Choudhry's room," says Mulaghesh, flipping through her portfolio. "And in one corner was something I couldn't make sense of. They looked like, like little chicken wings on kebab sticks or something like that. But that's not what they were. It was a drawing of *human bodies*. Bodies mutilated just like the ones we saw yesterday!"

The Dreyling foreman on the phone next to her slowly turns to stare at her over his shoulder, bug-eyed.

"What are you suggesting, General?" says Nadar.

"I'm suggesting that Sumitra Choudhry drew the murder scene we saw yesterday *months before it actually happened*. She predicted it, somehow!"

"What? How could that be?"

"I don't know. But I know what I'm looking at."

"But Choudhry was mad. . . . Couldn't it just be a coincidence?"

"I feel like drawing ritually mutilated torsos and then *seeing* ritually mutilated torsos is a pretty damned unlikely coincidence, even for a madwoman."

The Dreyling foreman is now sweating heavily and stretching out his phone's cord to its fullest extent as he inches away from her.

"So what are you proposing?" says Nadar.

"You probably don't have time for this, but I do," says Mulaghesh. "I want to ride up to where the first murder took place and check it out. If there's a chance Choudhry was involved in this, we need to look into it."

"The first murder took place deep in disputed territory, General. It's not safe."

"Neither am I. I can handle myself."

"I admire your confidence, General, but—if it turns out that you can't?"

"Well, you all are getting pretty handy at boxing up dead generals. I expect you could handle me in your sleep."

Nadar sighs. "I'll talk to Pandey and have him make preparations for you."

"Excellent," says Mulaghesh. "I appreciate your cooperation, Captain Nadar."

"Always happy to help, General," says Nadar, though she pauses just long enough to make it clear the reverse is true.

✳✳✳

Later that day Mulaghesh—armed and provisioned in case she gets lost—sets out into the countryside, taking the same road they took yesterday, north of Fort Thinadeshi. But at one creek she makes a hard right toward the Tarsil Mountains, which swell up in the distance, forming a towering pink-and-green wall.

She consults the map again. The village she's looking for is called

Ghevalyev, deep in the woods along one of the many creeks in this area. Everything she sees is covered in damp, soft green moss—tree branches, stones, even the road itself. Eventually Mulaghesh wonders if she, too, would find herself covered in moss if she didn't keep moving. But after a few miles the lumps of moss take on some more organized shapes, and she realizes that underneath the greenery are walls, fences, and gates—civilization, in other words.

She checks the map. "I must be here," she says, surprised. "Huh." She checks the rest of the original report, which Pandey included with the map. There's not much on this first incident—they thought it was a clear and simple case of murder at the time, albeit a particularly gruesome example—but there is a note that the man found dead at the scene was the village charcoal maker.

She keeps riding until yurts and huts emerge from the firs ahead. A small boy of about eleven sits by the road, filthy and malnourished, surrounded by an absolute swarm of tiny goats. Both the boy and the goats stare at her with the same expression: curious but utterly lacking in intelligence.

Mulaghesh looks at him. "This Ghevalyev?" she asks.

He stares at her, openmouthed. She can't tell if he's impressed or if his face just does that.

"I understand there was a charcoal maker here until a few months ago," she says. "Know where he would be?"

The boy just stares at her. Then there's a voice from the yurt behind him: "Vim, the only damned *reason* I asked you to be out there in the *first* place is to *keep*. The *goats*. Out*side*." There's a frantic *baa*-ing, and a tiny goat scurries out the front flat of the yurt, springing away down the muddy road. "Now there's shit all over the floor and it stole some of the turni—"

A big barrel-chested man exits the yurt and does a double take when he sees Mulaghesh sitting on her horse. "Oh," he says. She watches carefully as his eyes take in her weapons: carousel, rifling, and sword. His look is much too watchful for her liking. "How can I . . . uh, help you?"

Mulaghesh smiles widely. "Good morning," she says, her words ringing with forced cheer. "I'm General Turyin Mulaghesh of the Saypuri Military."

"A general?" he says, surprised. "Here?"

"Seems to be so."

"Oh. Well. My name is Drozhkin," says the man. "And this is Vim." He nudges the boy with the toe of his leather shoe. The boy, unsurprisingly, doesn't react.

"Good morning to both of you," she says. "I'm told there was a charcoal maker in this village once."

"*Was* and *once* are the right words to use," he says. "Mad bastard's dead."

"Mad?"

"Oh, yes. Mad as a hare in a collapsing tunnel. But most charcoal makers are. Part of the trade."

"Why's that?"

"*Why?*" he says, as if the question is absurd. "Because he had to spend days awake making sure the whole forest didn't burn down. Poor bastard had to invent himself a one-legged stool to sit on. If he fell asleep then it'd tip and he'd fall on his ass. No surprise he murdered his wife. I'd go mad, too, if I had to stay awake that long."

"I suppose you'd be surprised if I told you we actually don't think he murdered her anymore," says Mulaghesh.

" 'We' being"—his eyes trail over her uniform—"you." The word drips with many unspoken sentiments, chief among them: *And why would we care what you think?*

"A family was killed southwest of here in nearly the same fashion. Four of them."

"A whole *family?*" His face pales a little. "Zhurgut's tears . . . What an abomination. So there is a killer, then?"

"Did anyone actually see him kill his wife?"

"No one wants to live next to a charcoal maker. But I heard a rumor Gozha said she saw . . . something. The night they died."

"Gozha?"

"An old woman. Mushroom peddler. Also mad. Might be why she went to see Bohdan, so they could have something to talk about."

Mulaghesh scribbles furiously. "And who's Bohdan?"

"Who? The charcoal maker, of course. Don't you know anything?"

"Apparently not," says Mulaghesh. "So Gozha says she saw something the night Bohdan the charcoal maker got killed. Is that about the cut of it?"

"She didn't *say* that," he says hastily. "I just heard she acted like she did. I don't have anything to do with this business. I'm . . . I'm not even sure I should be answering your questions. I mean . . ." He gestures to her. "Even this looks bad."

"Tell me where Bohdan and Gozha both live," she says, "and you won't have any more to answer."

∗∗∗

After twenty more minutes of riding along forest lanes, the trees begin to thin out, replaced by stumps. It doesn't take long to see why: up ahead is a filthy dirt clearing spotted with curious mounds of earth, almost like giant anthills or beehives, all reeking of cinder. Mulaghesh recognizes them as charcoal kilns: they'd make a pyramid of wood, cover it with earth, then set the exposed tip alight, letting it slowly smolder for days and days. And the maker would have to watch it carefully: if a log shifted the earth could collapse, allowing in too much air, and the pile of wood would go up in a flash—along with most of the forest, probably. *A filthy, miserable way to make a living,* she thinks to herself. *But at least it's a living. . . .*

She sees the living quarters up ahead, if it could even be called such: it's a misshapen wooden box of a structure, set atop a long dirt hill. Mulaghesh gets the impression that the charcoal maker didn't invest much effort in his home, as there was always a chance it could go up in flames. Perhaps it had burned down before, only to have him rebuild it.

Mulaghesh looks around the clearing. Then she ties up her horse, considers the angle of the home, and begins walking through the surrounding forest, trying to find the best angle where she can see both the front and the back of the house. . . .

It doesn't take long for her to find it: another blind, created from clippings from fir trees. These clippings have browned considerably by now, making it easier to spot, but when the blind was first made it would have been almost invisible—hence why the original investigation team never found it. That, and they didn't know to look.

Mulaghesh shoves the branches away. Again, she sees that whoever made it cleared the forest floor of needles. *Perhaps this mysterious observer,* thinks Mulaghesh, *possesses an unusually sensitive backside.* She looks around for some sign or spoor and finds nothing. As she starts to withdraw she pauses, stoops, and looks again.

Carved into the trunk of a tree is an unusual sign, but a familiar one to her: the crude image of a sword with the hilt made of a severed hand.

"The sword of Voortya," says Mulaghesh, touching it with two fingers.

She imagines this person, whoever they were, sitting behind this blind, carving this into the tree. . . . She gets the impression that this was not an act of reverence but rather boredom, just something to occupy the time. Someone patient, then, waiting a long time for the right opportunity.

She walks back to the hut on the dirt mound. It has no door—it's been torn off the hinges, somehow—so she walks in. It's the same on the inside as it is on the outside: just a simple wooden box built of scrap wood. The floor is wood slats, the ceiling patched over with skins. At first Mulaghesh thinks the floor looks unusually dark, but then she realizes it's stained—the residue of the blood of Bohdan's wife. To most people the stain would look unusually large, but Mulaghesh is quite aware that the human body possesses more blood than one would expect.

She looks around the depressing little shack. It's bereft of almost anything personalized or pleasant. The bed is just a raised fretwork of sticks covered in furs and skins, the fireplace a teetering stack of bricks. Mulaghesh can't imagine why someone would marry into such a life—but then, she knows not everyone has a choice.

As she walks around the shack she realizes her footsteps sound oddly . . . hollow. She bounces up and down on the balls of her feet and listens to the creak and moan of the floorboards. Then she squats and peers through two slats of wood. It's hard to tell, but it almost looks like there's some kind of a space down there. . . .

"He built it to escape a fire," says a voice from the door.

Mulaghesh snaps up, hand on her carousel, and pauses at the sight of the old woman at the doorway. The old woman, to her credit, hardly flinches: she's a brown, hard, wiry thing, like a human form carved from old, smoked wood. She's dressed in ratty furs and skins, her eyes dark and hard and glittering.

"Lady," says Mulaghesh, "I know there's no door, but there's still plenty of stuff to knock on."

"You're from the army," says the old woman. It's not a question. "An easterner."

"And you are?"

"I am Gozha."

"Ah." Mulaghesh relaxes, but only a little. "How is it you came to be here, Gozha? I have you on my list to visit. I have some questions for you."

"Drozhkin came to me to beg forgiveness." She steps inside. "He felt he had slighted me by telling you what I saw. Betrayed a neighbor, I suppose. That man . . . Nothing goes in his head that doesn't come out his mouth. I'm surprised his brains have stayed where they are."

"And what was it that you saw, ma'am?"

Gozha stands beside her, looking down at the stain on the floor. "He was not a bad man, Bohdan. Not smart, not lucky, but not bad."

"Is that so?"

"He built the cellar down there to hide in case of a fire, in case the whole house went up. He even built a pipe out the side of the dirt mound so they'd have air." She looks at Mulaghesh. "He loved her, you see. Wanted to protect her. He always had the doctor out here, checking on her, just in case. He fretted so. But . . . he wasn't smart—if she was hiding in the basement, and the house caught fire, why, she'd be trapped with it falling in on her. . . . Not one for deep thinking, Bohdan."

Mulaghesh stands up. "What happened here?"

"Why? What does it matter to you?"

"What's happened here has happened elsewhere. And it could happen again."

"Again. What does it matter to you?"

"They're getting better at it, I think. The last one was worse than this. The next one will be worse still."

"Again. Still. What does it matter to you?"

"Why *wouldn't* this matter to me?" says Mulaghesh.

"Why? You are an easterner, a Saypuri. We are Voortyashtanis. To you we are no better than pigs or goats—yes?"

"I've seen Voortyashtanis bleed and I've seen Saypuris bleed. It looks the same. I'd like to keep everyone's blood right where it is as much as I can."

"Glib pleasantries," says Gozha. "The sort of thing a diplomat claims before cutting your throat and making off with your daughter."

Mulaghesh looks her in the eye. "Do I *look* like a fucking diplomat?"

Gozha holds her gaze for a moment. She looks away. "I did not see the murders."

"Then what did you see?"

"Very little." She looks out the window. "I was just over there, in the trees. It was dark, late at night, but the moon was bright. I was leading my pony through the woods nearby. . . . She has a strong sense of smell, my little pony. And when she started acting up, I could tell what she smelled. I knew there was blood nearby." Gozha walks to the open door of the shack. "I came to the edge of the clearing to see, and I saw a woman standing there in the charcoal yard."

"Bohdan's wife?"

Gozha shakes her head. "No. This woman was shorter. I *think* she was short. Perhaps I only had eyes for what was standing at the door of the house. . . ."

"Which was what?"

"You'll think I'm mad."

"I've seen mad things. You can believe me."

Gozha tilts her head, thinking, and says in a dreamy voice, "I thought it was a scarecrow, at first. Not a real person, a real man. A picture of a man, arranged from . . . well. Made of things."

"Things?"

"Yes, things. Scraps, it seemed. Spikes. Rags and thorns. A man made of thorns, six or seven feet tall, dark and faceless. . . . And in his hands was a gleaming sword, silvery and bright. I didn't think he was real until he turned around and walked back in the house."

Silence.

Gozha turns around. "You don't believe me. You think I'm mad. Of course you do."

Mulaghesh thinks for a moment. "I don't. . . . Well. Hells. I don't know what to believe. He was wearing a suit? A suit of rags and . . . and thorns?"

"I don't know. I don't even know if he was a he. It was dark and hard to see. But he and the woman just looked at each other, seeming to speak quietly, before he went back inside."

"Tell me about this woman."

"Like I said, she was short, and wore a dark cloak. Purple or green, perhaps. She had it pulled tight over her head. I couldn't see her face or even her hands."

A careful one, then, to hide so much of herself. "What happened after the man in the thorn suit walked back into the house?"

"I had tied my pony up in the lane east of here. It began to whinny and whicker, frightened, and I worried the woman and the man of thorns would see me, so I snuck away. It wasn't until two days later that I heard that Bohdan and his wife were found dead."

"And you don't think Bohdan was in the thorn suit?"

"Bohdan was like a lot of men around here, easterner—he is lucky if he ate as a child. He was not, shall I say, broad of beam."

"Which the man in the suit was."

"He cut a fearsome figure, that thing," says Gozha quietly. "Like something from a nightmare." She looks at Mulaghesh. "You think these people killed Bohdan and his wife?"

"It seems likely, yes."

"Why? Why kill the charcoal maker of Ghevalyev? Who could possibly care about poor Bohdan?"

"I think that's the point," says Mulaghesh. "It's easier to harm those considered unimportant—a charcoal maker and his wife, or a family on a farm, out in the middle of nowhere."

"But why do it at all?"

"It sounds like . . . like some kind of ritual," says Mulaghesh. "A ceremony. The way the bodies are mutilated, the way the person doing it dresses. And someone watches, from a distance, needing to make sure it happens. . . ."

"Voortyashtanis have many ceremonies," says Gozha. "And surely they had more before the collapse, the Blink. But I never knew of this one."

"That's not to say it didn't exist," says Mulaghesh. "But what it's meant to do is beyond me."

Gozha begins to walk away. Then she stops at the door and says, "It feels strange to say this to an easterner. But I hope you catch these people." Her gaze sharpens. "We are not pigs or goats, General Mulaghesh."

"I know that."

"I hope the others who wear your uniform think the same as you."

Mulaghesh goes to the doorway and watches Gozha walk away through the forest. Then she looks up and tries to gauge the position of the sun in the sky. It's early afternoon. She needs to be back in the city by evening. If she misses her hour with Signe tonight, she'll probably die of old age waiting around for an opening again. She takes one last look around the shack.

She stops. Cocks her head. Then walks to the corner.

There's a trace of something silvery on the floor in the corner of the shack. Mulaghesh touches it with her fingertips and looks at them in the light.

It looks a little like graphite, soft and powdery.

"Ah, shit," says Mulaghesh. "It can't be. . . ." She looks around for the trapdoor, finds it, tears it open, and drops down to the earthen basement.

It's close, dark, and damp down here. She lights a match, sending warm, fluttering luminescence dancing over the dark walls. Bohdan stocked this room with the bare essentials, pots of water and skins for sleeping on. She looks up, guessing where she saw the residue, and walks to the corner.

The earthen floor glimmers at her feet. She squats to examine the loose pile of light, dusty ore collected in the corner, where it must've trickled through the cracks in the floor. She touches it with her fingers. It falls apart like powdered sugar.

She knows what it is. She saw mounds of it yesterday, after all.

"Thinadeskite," she whispers. "Well, I'll be fucking damned."

***

Nadar's eyes dance around Biswal's office as she thinks. "That's . . . not possible."

"I don't know how, either," says Mulaghesh. "I could be wrong— I'd *prefer* to be wrong. But I dumped out my water and put it in here so you could check to make sure." She holds her canteen out. "How long would it take for Prathda to confirm this is actually thinadeskite?"

Nadar takes it, still stunned and blinking as she tries to process this revelation. A dove flits by the windows of Biswal's crow's nest, glancing at these three strange creatures having a discussion at the top of the tower. "An hour at most," she says. "It's easy to identify."

"Then I suggest we start now," says Biswal. He sits staring eastward at the Tarsils, fingers steepled and deep in thought. "The security implications are . . . concerning."

"You're absolutely right, sir," says Nadar. There's a gleam of sweat around her temple. "To have such a substance appear in Voortyashtani hands . . ."

"And at the scene of a brutal murder," says Mulaghesh.

"And, if what you've said is correct," says Biswal, "a murder that a missing Ministry intelligence operative had some knowledge of."

"Maybe," says Mulaghesh. "There are a lot of maybes here. We still haven't worked out how Choudhry could have predicted the murders."

Biswal sits back in his chair, eyes fixed on the distant Solda. "There are no other verified or known sources of thinadeskite in this region. We're the only source. So somehow it got from here to *there*. Now I have to wonder what *else* might be getting from here to there, or vice versa—intelligence, resources, weapons. . . . Could someone have an operative or an informant in Fort Thinadeshi? Someone who could tell insurgents how to cut through the perimeters, throw open the gates, and work around the schedules of our patrols?"

"Determining this is a priority for me, sir," says Nadar. She looks pale. Mulaghesh isn't surprised: having a security breach take place under your watch is something your superiors aren't quick to forget.

"I'm glad to hear it. Have your most trusted people run the tests on what General Mulaghesh brought back," says Biswal. "Then do a thorough probe and reevaluation of the mining and research operations. We'll want to know what happens to the thinadeskite every step of the way, and who's involved. See if anyone squirms under the pressure. And have General Mulaghesh here check out the mines, too."

Mulaghesh's heart nearly sings. She was hoping Biswal would say that. If he didn't, she was going to have to ask for it herself, and requesting access to such a highly controlled site could be a considerable overreach of authority.

"Yes, sir," says Nadar. "I . . . I would like for my own investigators to get a look first, if that's possible."

Biswal looks to Mulaghesh. "Sure," she says. "I'm here to help, if I can. I've no talent for vacations. Make use of me if you can."

"We appreciate your assistance in this matter," says Biswal. "Without your attention we wouldn't have even known about this issue."

Mulaghesh keeps her face still as she nods, though she doesn't want his compliments. She doesn't need Nadar being more frustrated with her than she already is, and she knows the captain doesn't think of this as a "we" situation: this is Mulaghesh riding into Fort Thinadeshi and making everyone look bad, especially Nadar.

"It would take about four days for reevaluation, sir," says Nadar. "And that's a quick turnaround time."

"Four days . . . and on the fifth, we're talking to the tribal leaders." He rubs his brow, groaning slightly. "General Mulaghesh can take her tour that afternoon, then, I suppose. I've no doubt you and I will have plenty to occupy us by then, Nadar."

"We can make it work, sir."

Biswal nods at Nadar. "Good. Dismissed, Captain. Thank you." Nadar nods at him, then turns and trots down the stairwell.

"Take a seat, Turyin," says Biswal. He reaches down, pulls out two small glasses, and pours some plum wine. "You know, when I said I could give you some problems to handle, I didn't mean you needed to go out and find some new ones we didn't know about."

"You'd prefer I keep silent the next time?"

"Hells no. I just never figured you'd be one of those soldiers who spend their golden years banging around military halls, trying to find problems to fix."

"Let's watch it on the whole 'golden years' shit. And also, this is coming from a man who fought to take command here."

"Fair point." He slides a glass over, then picks up his own and holds it to his temple. He sighs. "But you're getting some impression of all the problems we're having here. All the problems I've inherited, in other words. And, if you can believe it, this new one isn't even the most alarming."

"I've got a feeling you're about to ask me to do something, Lalith."

"I do outrank you, remember." He smiles sardonically and taps the bars on his collar. Biswal is a third-class general of the Saypuri Military, whereas Mulaghesh is fourth-class, the lowest class one could possibly occupy while still possessing the rank of general. Mulaghesh is well aware that the only reason she has the rank at all is that Shara wanted her on the military council, which is forbidden to anyone below the rank of general. But then, nepotism is so rampant in Ghaladesh currently that there are more generals and colonels in service than there are captains and lieutenants.

"True," she says. She sips at her wine. It tastes like vinegar to her tongue. "I also know I don't want to be in your seat, so you can keep outranking me all you want."

He sighs. "You can say that again. When I brought up security breaches earlier, materials and resources mysteriously leaving the fortress . . . This wasn't the first time."

"I kind of got that impression."

"A year and a half ago a supply train traveling from Fort Hadj to Fort Lok was hit by highland insurgents. They dragged a bunch of logs up onto the track so the train had no choice but to stop. And this particular train was carrying a great deal of weapons, ammunition—and explosives."

"Shit."

"Yes. My predecessor waged a vigorous campaign in response and managed to recover most of the weapons and ammunition, and all of the explosives—or so he thought. This would be, as a note, the very campaign that he wound up dying in. But last month we did an inventory check, and we found fifteen pounds of the explosives we recovered aren't actually explosives at all. They're sand and clay. Mock-ups."

"*Shit.*"

"Yes. We don't know when the switch took place, unfortunately. Maybe when the insurgents first took possession of it. But now that you've found what you've found, maybe someone switched it here, at the fortress."

"You think that if someone helped secret thinadeskite out," says Mulaghesh, "they might have done the same for your explosives."

He nods, his steely gray eyes shining bright. "That's correct. And I worry enough about what happens outside these walls and wire. To have a rat amidst us . . ."

"So where do I come in? I don't want to horn in on Nadar's command here any more than I already have."

"I don't want you to, either," says Biswal. "Nadar is an exceptional officer in a difficult situation. No, I want you to talk to the CTO of SDC for me."

"Ah," says Mulaghesh. "Harkvaldsson. You're worried about the harbor."

"I am. Fifteen pounds of explosives in insurgent hands . . . That has me looking around, wondering exactly what's vulnerable. And there's a *lot* vulnerable down at the harbor. It wouldn't be the first time they tried. A sharpshooter once took a shot at our ambitious, young CTO a few months ago. He missed and the SDC guards mowed him down pretty quick—but still."

"Why not talk to her yourself?"

"We don't have the . . ." He grumbles and stares out the window. "Well. The easiest relationship. She asks for a lot. I say *no* a lot. It's a dance we do every time we meet. But I want her to respond to this threat adequately. It might help if the warning comes from someone else."

"I hardly deal with her any better," says Mulaghesh. "But I need to talk to her anyway. I'll take care of it."

"There's also the tribal leader meeting in five days," says Biswal. "They'll know all about the murders at Poshok by now. I want you to be there."

"What, to testify?"

"We don't have anything to testify on yet. No, I just want another set of eyes. You dealt with people like this in Bulikov. See if you spot anything squirrelly. Odds are someone in that room will be the person responsible for stealing those explosives—and possibly the thinadeskite, too."

"I'm not a mind reader, Lalith."

"But you're better than nothing. And nothing is what we have now." He stares glumly into his wineglass, then drains it. "Harkvaldsson sent us new forecasts. Three months until the harbor and rivers are dredged. Then two years until the harbor itself is a functioning port. She says the dredging is the hard part—they've been at it for years already. And from an engineering standpoint, that might be true. But I'm concerned about what comes after."

"After?"

"What's it going to cost to keep the peace? And how long are we going to be here?" He looks at her balefully. "Not all of us are lauded heroes such as you, Turyin. We don't get to hop from place to place. Some might be sailing out of that port soon. But I won't. I expect me and the rest of the troops here will be in Voortyashtan for a long, long time."

I was told she spoke, once, in younger days. I was told the other Divinities could see her face, her eyes, her smile, and she would talk to them, sometimes as a friend.

But no more. When I saw her there was only her queer, cold faceplate—how I hated its placid expression, a mockery of a face—and the never-ending silence of her eyeless gaze.

Empress of Graves, Queen of Grief, She Who Clove the Earth in Twain.

I hoped to never hear Voortya speak.

—MEMOIRS OF SAINT KIVREY, PRIEST AND
78TH WIFE-HUSBAND OF JUKOV, C. 982

6.

Rites and Rituals

Mulaghesh is in a cheerless mood when she walks into the SDC board club. She's done nothing here but find more questions, each one more troubling than the last. And while at first she worried over how Sumitra Choudhry could have known about the murders before they happened, now she keeps thinking about what Gozha said at the charcoal maker's shack. . . .

A short woman, thinks Mulaghesh. *Every inch of skin concealed.*

Choudhry came here eight months ago. The murders at Ghevalyev took place seven months ago. Then Choudhry disappeared two months later. The timing's right—Choudhry was in the region—though does anyone have any proof that Choudhry's not in Voortyashtan now, hiding out?

Let's not jump to conclusions, she thinks, shoving the door open. *Even if they seem so easy to get to.*

She sits, and the Dreyling boy with the wispy mustache slinks out of the secret door in the wall and places a platter before her:

fried biscuits, a variety of smoked or pickled fish, and some sort of dark green concoction that Mulaghesh isn't familiar with and doesn't wish to be.

She checks the clock on the wall. Just past 1900. Yet there's no Signe in sight.

She pulls out her portfolio and idly flips through the files she found in Choudhry's room. She stares at the painting of Vallaicha Thinadeshi, wondering what grave she lies in in this country.

"Why are you reading about Thinadeshi?" asks a voice over her shoulder.

"Huh?" She looks up to find Signe standing over her, clipboard nestled under her arm, a gray scarf piled around her neck, and a tiny porcelain thimble of ink-black coffee in her hand. "Oh, ah . . . Well. Choudhry was reading about her."

"Choudhry might have wanted a broad view of the region," says Signe, sitting, "but I didn't realize she wanted a view *that* broad. Thinadeshi disappeared here, what, fifty years ago?"

"Sixty some-odd, yeah."

"Well, *that* I could've chatted to her about. She was a childhood hero of mine, you know. The great engineer. And we had something in common, of course. . . ."

"And what was that?"

"Why, we both had a fucking miserable time here in Voortyashtan, didn't we?" She smiles briefly, then checks her watch, a complicated, sleek contraption. "We have a little over fifty minutes. What is it you'd like to discuss with me, General?"

"Well, now I have something new to talk with you about. Something . . . delicate."

"How delicate?"

"About as delicate as it gets." She begins to outline Biswal's briefing, but—as she expected—Signe doesn't let her get too far into it.

"A *bomb*?" says Signe, appalled.

Mulaghesh holds up a hand as she chews a fried biscuit. "Well, realistically, it's probably several bombs."

"*Several* bombs?"

"Fifteen pounds of explosives . . . That's quite a bang. Better to distribute it throughout your target. Or parcel it out and do a long, sustained, exhausting bombing campaign."

Signe is so horrified she's brought to her feet. "You . . . You can't be serious!"

"I am. Biswal is requesting you allocate your security forces appropriately."

"Requesting!" Signe hisses. "*Requesting!* How polite and considerate of him!"

"Sit down. And calm down. I'm about to say something that might ease your fears a little—but I still want to make sure you absolutely understand that this is a threat to be taken seriously."

"Does it look like I'm *not* taking it seriously?" shouts Signe. Mulaghesh has to admit, this is the most rattled she's seen Signe yet. *Threatening the harbor,* she thinks, *is like threatening her child.*

"Sit," says Mulaghesh forcefully. "Once I'm done you can go tell your chief of security. But I want you to hear this first."

Signe does so, her face pink with fury.

"Let's look at the timeline," says Mulaghesh. "A year and a half ago, the train gets raided. Biswal's predecessor wages an extensive campaign to recover what was lost and loses his life in the process. And now, just in the past days, we discover that the explosives that were recovered were fakes, and the real explosives are still out there."

"So?" says Signe.

"So whoever has the explosives hasn't done anything with them for over *a year and a half,*" says Mulaghesh. "That doesn't make sense. You steal something, you try and use it before the owner figures out it's stolen. You wait too long and then the owner starts investigating and trying to make sure you can't *ever* use it. Which is what we're doing now."

Signe lights a cigarette. "*So?*"

"So something doesn't add up. This isn't a 'lull your enemy into a false sense of security' situation. We've *been* in a false sense of security for months, and they didn't do anything. Just glancing at the timeline, it almost makes me think those explosives aren't in insurgent hands anymore. Haven't the tribes been warring with one another for months?"

"Of course."

"So you're telling me that for nearly a year, the insurgents found no opportunities to use fifteen pounds of high-impact explosives against the people they despise?"

"I suppose that's a good point. . . ."

"And why would they come after the harbor?" says Mulaghesh. "Everyone's squabbling over the money *you* and SDC are going to make everyone. It's not like *you've* done anything to piss off the highland tribes, have you?"

At that Signe's face does something interesting to Mulaghesh—nothing. Her mouth doesn't purse, her eyebrows don't wriggle, and her pupils don't move one jot. She barely seems to even breathe.

Then, finally, she takes a languid drag from her cigarette and says, "The very idea is ridiculous."

"Of course it is." Mulaghesh looks her over. Signe returns her gaze, her arctic blue eyes staring back coolly through the veil of smoke. "Go talk to your security people. You'll want to get started on this immediately. But when you're done, come back to me. We're not done here."

"Oh, aren't we?"

Signe wrinkles her nose as Mulaghesh stuffs half of a cured fish fillet into her mouth. "It was damned hard enough just getting you to sit down with me," says Mulaghesh. "I'm not letting you walk away without getting what I need."

***

Initially Mulaghesh is worried Signe won't come back. She can't blame her: a serious security threat isn't anything to joke about. But to her relief, Signe comes walking back into the room just as Mulaghesh finishes her plate.

"So," says Signe. "What is it that you wished to discuss with me?"

Mulaghesh wipes her mouth. "Voortya."

"What?"

"I want you to tell me about Voortya."

"Voortya? Why?"

She flips open her portfolio and slides it over to Signe. "Because that's what was on the walls of Choudhry's room. I'm no artist, but . . . It should give you a pretty solid impression of her situation."

Signe pages through the drawings, disturbed. "She, what . . . She drew these on the walls?"

"Yes," says Mulaghesh.

"Well . . . I *did* say she was peculiar. This sort of thing would get you arrested in a heartbeat before Komayd took office."

"But now you can talk about it," says Mulaghesh. "And you're Voortyashtani. Kind of. So. Talk."

Still transfixed by the pages, Signe produces her cigarette case, slips one out, strikes a match, and takes a drag. It's such a fluid motion Mulaghesh suspects she doesn't even realize she's doing it. "Hm. Well. It's interesting you've brought this to me now. It seems Miss Choudhry had been pestering more of my people than I thought. One of our surveyors read the alert I sent out and came forward. She'd approached him and been very friendly with him, though he never had any idea who she was—I actually think he was a little sweet on her. Though her being a Ministry intelligence officer, I suppose she would be skilled at manipulation. . . ."

Mulaghesh grunts, knowing this to be quite true.

"Anyway. She was asking my people about the geomorphological features of the shore, like I told you before. *But*, I didn't know why—yet it seems she discussed this with the surveyor."

"And?"

"Choudhry said she was looking for a *tomb* nearby, or at least some sign of one, a suggestion that such a thing had once existed. And he, of course, knew nothing of a tomb—but *I* do."

"Why would Choudhry care about a tomb?"

"That question is more complicated than you might think. It has a great deal to do with death, history, and the afterlife." She ashes her cigarette into her cooling thimble of coffee. "At the very start of the manifestations of the Divinities, Voortya was perhaps the most exceptional."

"Are you sure that's not just regional pride speaking?"

"Oh, no. I studied at Fadhuri. They corroborated that belief. Voortya was the first Divinity to mobilize her people for warfare on a massive, unprecedented scale. This isn't easy to do, as I'm sure you know. She was asking for her people to train for months, leave their homes, go to unfamiliar lands, and, very likely, perish. So she did something no Divinity had ever done before—she created an *afterlife*."

"Huh? I thought every Divinity had dozens of those. There were hundreds of various hells or heavens or purgatories you could wind up in, right?"

"Toward the end, sure, and Kolkan alone produced, oh, about forty hells for his various followers. But Voortya was the first, and, unlike all the other Divinities, the nature of her afterlife remained consistent for all one thousand three hundred years—or however much it was—of her reign. If you were a follower of Voortya—if you 'took up the sword' and shed blood for her, yours or someone else's, as she wasn't particularly picky about that sort of thing—then when you died, your soul would sail across the ocean to a white island, a city, where Voortya would gather all of her flock: the City of Blades."

"I thought Voortyashtan was the City of Blades," says Mulaghesh. "That's what everyone calls it."

"An old confusion," says Signe. "Traveling Voortyashtanis were prone to discussing their longing to go to the afterlife, describing this 'City of Blades.' They talked about it so much even the other Continentals began assuming they were describing their home city. The assumption stuck."

Mulaghesh grunts and makes a note of it.

"Once she'd assembled the most righteous and the most power-ful souls in the City of Blades, they would sail back across the ocean to the mortal realm, each returning to 'where their swords fell'— where they fell in battle, or so the story goes—and make war upon the whole of the world, bringing down the stars and the sun and the skies and the seas, until all of creation was utterly annihilated. They called it the Night of the Sea of Swords."

"Wait, wait," says Mulaghesh. "You can't tell me the other Divinities tolerated the threat of that?"

Signe shrugs. "Voortya's afterlife started well before the Divinities united. And when they finally did unite . . . Well, these things have momentum. It's tradition. You can't just stop tradition, even if the world changes around it. And Voortya and her followers took it very, very seriously. It was a pact, you see, a promise Voortya made between herself and those who loved her. That's another way Voortya is quite different from all the other Divinities—with the exception of Olvos, perhaps, no other Divinity brought themselves down to the level of their followers as she did, creating an agreement among equals. Or perhaps she gave herself to them, as if she'd made the afterlife *from* herself, pulled from her very body. It's a little unclear—but all Divine things usually are."

"So where does the tomb enter into this?"

"Well, theoretically, somewhere around here was a resting place for the Voortyashtani dead. All of them. Ever."

Mulaghesh whistles. "That'd have to be some tomb."

"One would assume. In *The Great Mother Voortya atop the Teeth of the World,* it's described as filling the whole of the center of the world. Maybe. Poets have a tendency to get somewhat hyperbolic, I find. But imagine finding *the* tomb belonging to a culture that more or less worshipped death! I expect that would be a huge, huge find for someone at all interested in the history of the Continent."

"But . . . why in the hells would Choudhry be looking for that?" asks Mulaghesh. "What does the tomb have to do with . . . well, anything?"

"Who can say? She did seem to go mad. *This* certainly suggests so." She gestures to the portfolio.

"And what could drive her mad?"

She exhales smoke through her nose. "This place . . . This place affects a weak mind, I think. People find themselves changed by it. Bulikov might have controlled the world, certainly, but it was Voortyashtan that made that happen. Without the support of Voortyashtani sentinels, the Divine Empire would have collapsed. Even though almost all of Voortyashtan is lost, I think . . . I think the stones and the hills remember."

That may be true, Mulaghesh thinks, but it seems unlikely that Choudhry would be a creature of a weak mind. Most of the Ministry intelligence officers she's encountered have been harder than a coffin nail, despite their cultured appearances. Trained for all kinds of torture and interrogation scenarios, certainly. And from her file, Sumitra Choudhry was as straight as a straight arrow could get, the sort of soldier any officer would love to have under their command.

What could an ancient tomb, she thinks, *have to do with Choudhry's real mission—thinadeskite?*

The obvious answer is that thinadeskite is mined from the ground, and tombs are underground . . . so perhaps the tomb could have affected or even *caused* the thinadeskite's existence? But though this is the obvious answer, wouldn't someone *notice* if they were mining directly into the walls of an ancient tomb? Especially the Saypuri Military, which still treats any whiff of the ancient Continent with extreme—and justified—paranoia.

And what possible interest could the tomb have held for Choudhry, anyway? Even if it was once Divine, shouldn't all of its Divine and miraculous qualities have ended when Voortya took a shot to the face back in the Night of the Red Sands? However wondrous it might have been, now it's certainly another damned hole in the ground.

"Is one officer worth all this?" asks Signe.

"Huh?"

"She's just one officer. Surely the Ministry has hundreds of them, thousands of them. Is it worth dragging in a general to chase her down?"

Mulaghesh slaps her portfolio closed. "We asked for servants, and she agreed. We asked her to come to the ends of the world for us, and she agreed. We asked her to risk her life for us, and she agreed. I don't care how many officers the Ministry has. She's worth it."

Signe raises her eyebrows, as if she didn't realize how sensitive the subject would be.

"Biswal mentioned a tribal sniper once took a shot at you," says Mulaghesh.

"Oh, that. Yes."

"You seem pretty blasé about it."

"He gave me quite a haircut," says Signe. She taps her ponytail. "I turned my head at the right moment—or, for him, the wrong one—and he clipped off about an inch or two. My security detail more or less shredded the little shack he was in, which contained a chicken coop. Feathers everywhere. Quite a scene."

"And was that worth it? You almost died. Is the harbor worth it?"

She nods, conceding the point. "Anything else you wish to ask me, General?"

At first Mulaghesh is about to say no, but then she gets an idea. "You certainly seem to know a lot about the Divine around here."

"It's difficult *not* to."

"Because you're Voortyashtani, right? Adopted, at least. What tribe did you live with?"

Signe pulls a face as if she's just asked her something deeply distasteful.

"What? It's not like I asked you your sexual preference or something."

"By the seas . . . I'm not sure if you could find a way to be cruder."

"What were you? Highland or river?"

Signe glares at her. "The Jaszlo tribe. Highland. They took us in."

Mulaghesh thinks back to what the apothecary salesman said. "Pretty traditional, then, yeah?"

"Very."

"So let me test your memory. If one were to have rosemary, pine needles, dried worms, grave dust, dried frog eggs, and bone powder . . . what Divine ritual would one be able to complete?"

There is a long pause as Signe considers it. For a moment Mulaghesh thinks she won't tell her, but then she says, "I believe the frog eggs give it away—those are the reagents one once used to complete the Window to the White Shores."

"The what?"

"The White Shores—the City of Blades itself. The rite would allow those that performed it to see across to the City of Blades and consult with their deceased friends and relatives."

"How would this rite work?"

"If memory serves, the components were placed in a sackcloth, which was then tied up with dried seaweed and set alight. But it doesn't work anymore, none of Voortya's miracles do. I've seen them tried. Why? What could that possibly have to do with anything?"

Instantly Mulaghesh remembers Nadar telling her in the laboratory: *Some of our operations crew noticed signs that someone had started a fire in one of the branches. . . . It looked as though whoever had done it had been burning just . . . well, plants, I suppose. Leaves. Some cloth. Things like that.*

Mulaghesh takes in a long, slow breath.

Choudhry snuck into the thinadeskite mines, she thinks. *And performed this rite down there.*

Which leaves the question: why? What did Choudhry think she could accomplish by going down to the mines and performing a Divine ritual that almost certainly wouldn't work anymore? If Voortya's miracles don't work anymore, certainly the afterlife she created is gone, too. And—perhaps more damning—*how* did Choudhry manage to bypass security to do it?

Thinadeskite shows up in a shack miles away from the mine, thinks Mulaghesh. *At the scene of a murder that Choudhry had some knowledge of. And now it seems Choudhry had some way of infiltrating the mines. . . .*

Suddenly things look quite bleak for the reputation of Sumitra Choudhry.

"Are you quite all right, General?" says Signe.

"No," says Mulaghesh huskily. "No, I certainly am not."

***

Over the next four days Mulaghesh's work grinds to a slow, creaking halt. She pores over the communications Choudhry sent to Ghaladesh and back. Mostly it's just requests for documents and references. She hauls out the codex of encryption keys and runs through any text of Choudhry's she can get her hands on. None of them produce anything, but she didn't expect them to: all of these messages would have been received by the Ministry, who would have done all this already, and then some.

If I were a Ministry operative, she thinks, *would I spy countless codes hidden in the margins? Would I know all the tradecraft about infiltrating the mines?* She has no idea, because she's a far cry from a Ministry officer. She's just a beat-up old military officer running into walls.

Mulaghesh spends her four days watching the SDC harbor works. Initially this was just an idle way to pass the time, checking to make sure Signe and her security people were reacting properly to the possible bomb threat. But as she watches them she notices something— something she's seen in combat drills before, when commanders didn't distribute their forces correctly.

She's fairly sure she's identified the most flagrant vulnerabilities in the harbor works so far: there's the fuel yard, which the whole harbor draws from in order to run; and then there are three manufacturing yards that see a lot of traffic, trucks and forklifts pouring in and out from the break of dawn until late at night. What they're manufacturing, she doesn't know—something for the cranes and the ships, she assumes—but hitting any of these four yards would probably cripple the harbor works.

Yet only a handful of new SDC guards are stationed at these three sites. No more than four to five more people, from what she can see—three at the main entrances and two performing surveillance. It's barely anything at all.

Instead the vast majority of any new security measures are stationed at Signe's test assembly yard, which is on the other side of the harbor works, far away from most of the construction. Mulaghesh spends two days, mornings and evenings, watching as over a dozen new security employees—thuggish-looking Dreylings with riflings

thrown over their backs—take up positions along all the lanes leading to the yard. Signe's security chief Lem is almost always with them,
glowering and scanning the streets, his hand close to his weapon.

On the evening before she has to attend Biswal's meeting of the
tribal leaders, Mulaghesh slinks through the harbor yard and finds
a hiding place among a stack of pallets. The SDC workers have seen
her with Signe, so most just accept her presence here; but seeing her
watching the door to the assembly yard with a spyglass pressed to her
eye would be another thing entirely.

For hours, there's nothing. Then she watches as Signe strides up,
clipboard in hand. Lem steps forward. They exchange a word or two.
She nervously flicks away a cigarette, stops in front of the door, and
checks something on her clipboard. She looks pale and ashen, like
she's eaten something foul.

She's anxious, thinks Mulaghesh. *No. She's* terrified. . . .

Signe turns back around and nods to the guard posted at the test
assembly yard door. He gives her a quick salute—a curious gesture,
for what's essentially a commercial operation—and he cranks a lever
somewhere in his checkpoint booth.

The door must function with some kind of mechanism, for it
slowly falls back. It's almost like a bank vault door, now that she's
watching, and beyond its threshold she sees . . .

A second door. Much like the first door.

Signe walks in, turns, and watches as the first door slowly, slowly
shuts. It's only when it's almost shut that she turns and begins to open
the second door.

They really, really don't want anyone knowing what's in there, she
thinks.

The first door slams shut with a faint *boom.*

Mulaghesh smirks. "Test assembly yard, my ass."

O, the things we kill for our dreams, forgetting all the while we shall wake up to find them naught but dust and ash!

What fools we are to pretend that when we walk to war we do not bring our loved ones with us.

If I had known the grief I'd bring upon myself, I would have been a toymaker instead.

—VALLAICHA THINADESHI AT THE FUNERAL OF HER
FOUR-YEAR-OLD SON, JUKOSHTAN, 1659

7.

out of the deeps

In the white citadel the goddess opens her eyes.

She knows what she'll see. She knows she'll see the huge, white, cavernous halls, the crenellated white columns, and the endless, twirling white staircases. She knows she'll see the cold white moonlight pouring in through the windows. And she knows if she goes to the windows she'll see the endless beaches beyond, the massive white statues, and hear the slow murmur of the sea.

She knows she'll see these sights because she has been in this white palace forever, since the dawn of time and all things.

She shakes herself. Her plate mail tinkles slightly with the motion. *This isn't true,* she tells herself. *You haven't* always *been here. . . . Don't you remember that?*

She wanders the white halls, her metal boots clinking on the white stone floor. She wanders for what could be hours, or perhaps days, she isn't sure. She sees no one, hears no one. She is alone here. Except for her, this enormous palace is utterly deserted.

At least, the *interior* is: what lies outside of the palace is an entirely different matter.

She can hear their thoughts even from far within the palace's depths. They toy at her mind, these pained desires and plaintive, wheedling pleas, begging for her attention, for her action. She tries to ignore them, to keep them out, but they speak so much and there are so *many* of them. . . .

Mother, Mother—give us what was promised to us. Give us what we need. Give us what we fought and died for. . . .

She finds herself walking up the stairways, perhaps to flee them— she isn't sure. She isn't sure of much these days. She has faint memories of how things were before, and she knows that, in some fashion, she *chose* to be here—but it gets quite difficult to remember sometimes.

She comes to a window. She hesitates—she doesn't want to see, she desperately doesn't want to—but she knows she needs to look. They're getting so much stronger that she can't quite help herself.

She walks to the window and looks out. She's high up, several hundreds of feet at least, looking down on a clutch of porcelain-white towers, shimmering and queerly organic, like sea sponges or lumps of coral. More disturbing are the statues, which stand among the towers and straddle the streets, massive figures that are only vaguely human, frozen in positions of combat: a raised blade, a thrusting spear.

These are not what disturb her the most. Because standing far below her, upon the shores of this island and along its many canals and in the streets, are . . .

Monsters. Abominations. Tall, horrific, glittering creatures with blank, primitive faces, their backs and shoulders covered in horns and tusks.

Their thoughts batter her mind like the winds of a hurricane upon a house:

Mother . . . Mother! Please, let us go! Please, give us what we were promised. . . .

She shuts her eyes and turns away. Some part of her knows that they were once human, that they became these things only because it was asked of them. But was it she who asked it of them? She can't quite remember.

She walks up the stairs to her throne room, and the great, hideous, red seat is waiting for her. It is like a living thing, in some ways: a creature she created, begging for her presence. To sit upon the red throne is to become more of herself.

It's not yours, she reminds herself. *Not really.* Yet some part of her remains unconvinced.

But to be near the throne makes her stronger, somehow, and it helps her remember. It helps her remember the very strange thing she saw the other day: she came across a window to another world, and inside that window were men. They didn't know she was there, that she was listening, listening as they described a mine they were building, a deep hole in the earth. . . . And she'd realized with sudden fury and disbelief what they were doing, whether they realized it or not.

As she remembers this, standing there before her great red throne, her fists clench, and she is filled with horror and rage and disgust.

After what *she* did for *them,* they would do this to her? They would make all of her sacrifices count for nothing?

She knows she must do something. She must act. But to do so might kill her.

Is it worth it?

She thinks about it.

Yes. Yes, it is.

She focuses, holds out her hand, and reaches for the sword.

The sword is always there. It is never truly gone, because since the day she picked it up it's been a part of her, or perhaps she's a part of *it,* for she knows deep down that it is really so much more than a sword: to grip the black handle and see the flickering blade is to bear witness to a thousand battles and a thousand murders and a thousand years of brutal conflict, to hear the shouts of thousands of armies and see the skies darkened with thousands of spears and arrows and watch the ground grow soft and dark with the blood of thousands of lives.

She holds the sword in the white tower. *You're me,* the sword whispers to her. *You're of me, and I'm of you.* . . .

This isn't true, she knows. She *thinks* it isn't true, at least. But she needs to believe it just a little longer. Cooperating with the sword lets her do so much. . . .

Including the ability to cross over to the land of the living, and wreak almost limitless destruction.

She takes a breath, shuts her eyes, and listens to the sword.

***

During Mulaghesh's seventeen-year tenure as polis governor of Bulikov, she oversaw 127 assemblies of the Bulikov City Fathers, 314 city hearings, 514 town hall meetings, and 1,073 Worldly Regulations trials for those who had dared acknowledge the Divinities under the surveillance of Saypur. She knows the exact number because after each one of these meetings—which sometimes lasted up to ten hours—she would go back to her offices, pull out her portfolio, and make a single, solitary tick mark on the very last page.

Just one. Because somehow making these little tick marks helped her compartmentalize all of her contempt and fury and frustration, bottling it all up and releasing it in that one tiny, contained motion, gouging the nib of the pen along the soft, vulnerable surface of the page. And she often had plenty to release, for another delightful feature of any meeting of civic-minded Bulikovians was the heaps and heaps of insults, scorn, and outright threats they hurled at her at the top of their lungs.

Yet as Mulaghesh watches the assembly of tribal leaders from the balconies of the Voortyashtani Galleries—the civic center of the city—she reflects that her stint in Bulikov was a leisurely stroll in comparison to this.

She watches, eyebrows raised, as an elderly, bearded man with a red band of a tattoo around his neck stands up from his bench, assumes a posture of deepest grief, and bellows, "I wish to lay deaths at the feet of the Orskova clan! I wish to hang the deaths of my tribe from their necks and their shoulders!" His comments are met with a chorus of boos and remarkably specific threats from about half the assembly.

Biswal, seated at the table at the front of the Galleries, rubs his temples. "Mr. Iska, you have been told twice now that the Laying of Deaths has been eliminated as a formal motion of the assembly. Please sit down."

"Then how shall the wrongdoers and murderers in this room with me know guilt?" shouts the man. "Shall the names of my brothers and sisters and children who have died wrongly be forgotten, and perish into ash?"

More boos and catcalls. Mulaghesh thins her eyes as she watches the tribal leaders. They are all skinny, haggard things, dressed in robes and furs, their necks brightly tattooed and covered with curious patterns. Some are women, she sees, which surprises her: Bulikov strictly forbade women from doing anything more than firing out children as quickly and efficiently as possible.

But then, she thinks, *Voortya probably wouldn't have tolerated that bullshit.*

"The persistence of the names of anyone," says Biswal wearily, "dead or alive, is no longer part of the charge of the assembly. That was decided three meetings ago. Now may we please move on to the primary item on our agenda?" He raises a piece of paper for the assembly to see. "The murders at the town of Poshok, which Fort Thinadeshi is asking for any assistance on."

"Murders committed by the Ternopyn clan!" shouts a woman at the back. "Butchers and thieves and liars!"

The Galleries fill up with bellowed accusations. Mulaghesh rolls her eyes. "Oh, for the love of . . ."

While Biswal deals with the commotion, Mulaghesh focuses on the unusual figure to his left: a small, mousy Continental woman of about thirty, with big dark eyes and a timid mouth, wearing clothes that look about three sizes too large for her. She sits hunched in a manner that suggests she wishes to fold up and disappear into the back of the chair. She scribbles madly on a large pad of paper as they talk, her fingers and wrists black with ink.

Biswal raises a hand in response to someone's question. "I believe we might need to check with Governor Smolisk on this issue. Rada, would you happen to have last month's minutes on hand?"

So that's the Continental governor, thinks Mulaghesh. She watches as Rada digs frantically through a sack behind her chair, produces a sheaf of papers, flips through them, and reads aloud, "Th-The representative in que-qu-question s-s-said at the t-t-time, and I qu-quote . . ." She takes a deep breath, and reads, " '*M-may all the sons and d-daughters of the Hadyarod clan be g-g-gutted as rabbits and d-die upon the f-flames.*' "

One of the tribal leaders crosses his arms triumphantly, as if his point has just been proven beyond a measure of a doubt.

"Thank you, Rada," says Biswal. "Though this threat, Mr. So-kola, was indeed uttered at the last assembly, the victims at Poshok were not gutted, nor burned, nor were they members of your clan, the Hadyarod clan—as you surely know. And if I recall, that exact curse has been used at nearly every assembly of the tribal leaders, sometimes more than once per meeting. At the moment, I am not convinced that it is an indication of guilt, and I would prefer if we adhere to ways you all can *cooperate* with our investigation, or volunteer more pertinent informa—"

Biswal's next words are drowned out by shouting. He sighs and looks to Rada, who shrugs in return and attempts to write down some of the more prominent shouts.

"This is a bit more energetic than most meetings," says a voice.

Mulaghesh, who's been slouching deep in her seat, looks up to see Signe standing above her. She's wearing her usual scarf, but has opted for a leather jacket today rather than the sealskin, though it too bears the SDC insignia. "Oh?"

"Yes. Even Brursk there is getting into it." She points at an obese man in a blue leather jerkin who is making a fist and screaming across the aisle at someone. "He's usually as placid as a cow."

"This doesn't seem like very placid company." She looks through their ranks again, trying to spy anything suspicious; but, in her opinion, the whole lot of them look like mad bombers. She can't imagine what Biswal wanted her to do here. "Do you come to these things often?"

"I try to. Don't let their tattoos and their crude threats fool you,

General—*some* of these people are quite clever, and smell change in the wind. The more powerful leaders imagine the harbor and all of its profits to be a pie, and themselves the only ones authorized to do the cutting. Hence why I'm here."

Something slowly clicks in Mulaghesh's head. "Is that why the SDC headquarters is so permanent looking?"

"I beg your pardon?"

"You keep claiming that the harbor will be done within two years. Why would you want to build something so permanent—unless you wanted to be here for a long, long while?"

"And what would you imagine us doing?"

"Taking your slice of the pie, of course," says Mulaghesh. "The harbor's a one-time deal. But if you're *the* shipping company on the Solda—by the seas, you'd make billions of drekels every year."

Signe smiles serenely. "Hm. You're no fool, General, I'll give you that. Though some of these damn tribes intend to milk us for all we're worth, threatening to give away portions of the shipping rights to other companies. . . . But they forget who it is who'll control the mouth of the Solda itself."

"I do wonder, CTO Harkvaldsson," says Mulaghesh, "if it's possible for you to even piss without some amount of skullduggery and plotting."

"Well, I also take it upon myself to be an ambassador for the harbor." She leans forward, listening. "Speaking of which . . ."

". . . murders were committed by no clansman!" a thin woman is shouting below. "Nor committed by any human hand! No Voortyashtani that we know did such a thing, this I assure you! This is a curse, a Divine retribution for the sacrilege being committed to our ancient ancestral home!"

"I assume, Mrs. Balakilya," says Biswal, "that you are referring to the harbor."

"The Dreylings and their great machines grind up the bones of our very culture!" cries the woman. "They awaken many things that lie sleeping! The Divine will not tolerate this insult, and we shall all pay the price!"

Biswal nods. "Thank you for your opinion on the matter, Mrs. Balakilya. But I do believe CTO Harkvaldsson is present in the balcony, so perhaps she'd like to comment."

All heads turn to Mulaghesh and Signe. Mulaghesh is used to being the focus of the ire of a crowd, but so many furious eyes make even her cringe a little. Yet one group of tribal leaders in the back— their necks dyed a soft yellow—stands and strikes a reverential pose, as if saluting them.

Or perhaps specifically saluting Signe, who stands at the railing and says in a loud, clear voice, "As I have testified to and even personally shown some of the assembly members, what the Southern Dreyling Company is hauling up from the floor of the Solda Bay is nothing more than rotting stone. We researched our undertaking carefully and concluded that no surviving architecture is present in the bay. What we drag up is sand and silt and rubble, and nothing more. If we were to find any artifact or item of cultural import, we would notify the assembly immediately."

"These are lies!" cries the thin woman—Balakilya—but again, the assembly dissolves into shouts.

"I assure you," says Signe calmly, "they are not."

Yet then there's one shout that rings out above the muttering: "*Who is that there?*"

Everyone stops, frowning, to see who's shouting. It proves to be a bowlegged man at the back with a ratty beard, and he leaps up onto his bench and flings a finger at Mulaghesh. "*Who is that beside you? Who is that with the wooden hand?*"

"Ah, shit," mutters Mulaghesh, sinking low in her chair.

Then someone else cries out: "It's the soldier who was there when Kolkan was slain!"

Balakilya screams triumphantly, "You see? Do you see? Why would Saypur bring the lieutenant of the god-killer if they did not fear the retribution from the Divine? Why would she be here if not to defend them against the vengeance of Voortya!"

"I . . . think I'm going to back out on this one," Mulaghesh says, standing. "I'm pretty sure my presence here isn't helping much."

"Leave now," says Signe, "and you'll only inspire more questions."

"She leaves because it's true!" shouts Balakilya, striding to stand in the central aisle. "She fears the truth, so she flees from it!"

"See?" says Signe.

"General Mulaghesh," says Biswal, looking up, "perhaps if you could spare a few words for—"

"She's come to murder whatever's left of our culture!" cries Balakilya.

"She's here to force us to bow to the whip of Saypur!" shouts another man.

"Oh, for the love of . . ." Mulaghesh walks to the railing. "You want to know why I'm here? Here of all places on this damned world?"

"Tell us!" shouts one of the men below. "Tell us!"

"Fine!" snarls Mulaghesh. *"I'm on vacation, you dumb sons of bitches!"*

A loud silence echoes over the Galleries. Mulaghesh turns and strides away. As she walks through the door she hears someone say, very quietly, "Did she say *vacation?*"

***

Mulaghesh sulks in the hallways of the Galleries as she waits for the assembly to end. The Galleries are a deeply strange place to her: the interior is like being inside the bones of a massive beached whale, its roof made of white, arcing ribs, topped with a line of vertebrae with spinous flowerings. The thunderous shouts from the assembly chamber begin to feel like the roar of water, and suddenly it's not so difficult to believe that she's trapped in the belly of some undersea leviathan.

Bored, she looks at the displays along the walls of the Galleries, which are curated like the walls of a museum. She strolls down the hallway, absently looking at each one—though she quickly sees these aren't just art pieces.

The first display is a massive, rounded standing stone that—according to the sign beside it—was carved by Saint Zhurgut himself during his "elevation." It looks to Mulaghesh as if the stone's been run through a sawmill: it's been hacked and slashed many, many times, yet never cracked. Whatever blade sank through this stone did so perfectly, like a knife through butter. The sign reads:

> *Upon gripping his blade forged by Voortya, Saint Zhurgut was el-*
> *evated, ascending into a state of pure warfare and battle, and this*
> *stone was his first test of power. Voortyashtani blades held many pur-*
> *poses beyond battle, however: stories suggest that the ancient Voortya-*
> *shtani swords could communicate, serving as conduits for thought and*
> *speech. Swords were such a way of life among this ancient polis that*
> *many records suggest that human and weapon were considered in-*
> *divisible. Regrettably, no Voortyashtani blades have survived to see*
> *modern times.*

"What a tragedy," mutters Mulaghesh. But she doesn't feel really disturbed until she looks at the next display.

She stops and stares. She's happy she's alone, for she feels she might make a scene.

The exhibit is completely empty except for a stone mask standing on a thin steel pole. Unlike many of the other displays this mask is not large, though it is perhaps slightly wider and taller than the average human face. It's also a little too round, as the normal human skull is somewhat oblong. But it's the face that is the most disturbing part: the eyeholes are small and set both too far apart and far too low, leaving a prodigious brow above them with a single ridge-like seam running through their middle. The seam ends in a tiny, insignificant point of a nose with no nostrils, and below that are two short rows of needle-like teeth, a bad parody of a human mouth. Around the edges of the mask are many small holes through which, presumably, one once threaded string to tie the mask onto one's face.

It's not the real thing. Mulaghesh knows it isn't. But she's seen an abundance of sketches and paintings, for these masks haunt Saypur to this day. These masks—the *real* ones, the ones made of steel and bone—were present in Saypuri life for hundreds and hundreds of years, right up until the Night of the Red Sands.

For wasn't every Saypuri terrified of waking up and finding such a face staring in through their window? Wasn't every road and every river and every port watched by those blank, staring eyes? Mulaghesh was told that the people (if they could even be called such things) that wore those masks would go by Saypuri slums at night while everyone slept, and toss in little metal tokens through the open windows, tiny coin-like baubles fashioned to resemble their headgear. The Saypuri slaves would then wake up and find these distorted, grinning skulls no bigger than the palm of their hand waiting on their floors or on their tables, and they would understand the unspoken message: *We were here. Walls mean nothing to us. Nothing can be kept from us.*

Mulaghesh, breathing hard, looks at the sign beside the display:

CLAY RE-CREATION OF A VOORTYASHTANI SENTINEL MASK.

There is nothing else. But of course there isn't: there is nothing more to say about such things.

"Not an original, of course," says Signe's voice.

Mulaghesh turns to see her walking down the hall in her quick, efficient pace. "It had fucking well better not be."

"They're wrapping up in there," says Signe. "Biswal and Rada should be out any time, if you're waiting." She stops and looks at the mask, then thinks and asks, "What do you see, General, when you look at it?"

"I see millions of my fellow citizens tortured and dead," says Mulaghesh.

Signe makes a small *hm* sound and nods, as if understanding her sentiment.

"Why? What do you see?"

"A culture that worshipped death," says Signe, "and particularly those who dealt it. Their ancestors, mostly. For instance, Voortyashtanis believed that if you picked up the sword of an ancient sentinel it would possess you, take you over—you'd become them, in essence, but cease being you."

"Sounds like a raw deal."

"Yes—to them, a sword was a vessel of the soul. To do such a thing would be to lose your soul entirely. But I'm told they only did it in desperate situations. They didn't only admire their ancestors, though. They also respected their foes, if they felt they were worthy. Hence why things went so smoothly just now, after your outburst."

"Huh? You mean I *helped* things in there?"

"Of course you did," says Signe. "Voortyashtanis respect those who have tested themselves in battle. You're not only a veteran, but you were in a battle against a *god*. They grudgingly admire you, General Mulaghesh. It put them on uneven footing. I thought that was why Biswal wanted you there in the first place?"

Mulaghesh cocks her head, turning this over. "Huh. You're probably right. Speaking of admiration . . . Why did that one group stand up when you spoke? Some of them looked like they were saluting you, in some way."

Signe is silent for a long while. "That would have been the highland Jaszlo tribe, General."

"Ah. Your old family, then?"

"They are not my family." Her voice is arctic. Not quite as cold as when Mulaghesh provoked her into talking about Sigrud, maybe, but close. "They hold to traditions that I no longer honor. But they gave us shelter when we needed it."

Mulaghesh looks Signe over carefully.

"What?" says Signe, irritated.

"You said they respected those who dealt death," says Mulaghesh. "And they seemed to respect you a whole lot in there, CTO Harkvaldsson."

Something in Signe's jaw flexes. Then she pulls out her beaming, perfect smile. "Have a good afternoon, General."

***

Mulaghesh waits for the tribal leaders to file out before entering the assembly chamber. Biswal and Rada are quietly conversing, reviewing the notes.

"You know, Lalith," says Mulaghesh as she approaches, "if you wanted me to put some scare in these people, you could have just asked."

Biswal looks up at her over his spectacles. "Some scare?"

"That's why you really wanted me here. To distract them, make them all hot and bothered. It's easier to herd sheep when they're skittish."

His eye gains the slightest of twinkles. "They *were* much easier to handle when they realized you were here, that's true. But if I'd asked you to come and be my celebrity guest, Turyin, I felt sure you'd turn me down."

"Probably true."

"You asked me to make use of you," says Biswal. "Which I did. I hope you won't hold it against me, but . . . the ends sometimes justify the means."

Something in Mulaghesh curdles at that. This isn't the first time she's heard him say that. Then she slowly realizes that little Rada Smolisk is staring at her with giant, shocked eyes.

Biswal glances at her and says, "I'm sorry, I haven't properly introduced you both yet. Governor Rada Smolisk, this is General Mulaghesh. Turyin, this is . . ."

Rada stands. Something in her posture makes her look even smaller when she's on her feet. "P-Polis Governor R-Rada Smolisk," she says. Her voice is almost less than an echo, and it's as though she has to dig each syllable out from some deep, difficult part of herself.

Mulaghesh smiles thinly. She doesn't like the idea of a Continental as polis governor—adders in charge of the chicken coop and all that—but she finds it hard to be worried by this small, shrinking creature. "Very nice to meet you, Governor."

The two of them look at Rada, expecting her to carry on in the pleasantries. But instead Rada gets a faraway look on her face, as if just remembering an awful nightmare she had last evening.

"Rada?" asks Biswal.

Rada snaps to attention. "G-General Mulaghesh, I'm s-sorry, but . . . I w-would like to s-say this while I h-huh-have the chance."

"Okay?"

She swallows and stares into the floor as she tries to assemble the words. "I—I am originally a n-native of B-Bulikov, and I—I was there in the B-Battle of Bulikov. And if it were n-not for you and y-your soldiers, I w-wou . . . Well. I most cer-certainly w-would have d-died."

"Uh, thank you," says Mulaghesh, surprised. This was about the last thing she expected to hear. "I appreciate the words, but we were just doing our jo—"

"M-my family's house c-collapsed," says Rada. "My wh-whole family d-d-d-perished. And I was tr-trapped in the ruins w-with them. For f-four days."

"By the seas, child, I . . ."

"It was your s-soldiers that found me. They d-dug me out. They didn't h-h-have to. There were th-thousands in n-need. But they d-did. They t-told me they had a p-p-policy of never leaving a-uh-anyone behind." Rada looks up. "I have al-always wanted to th-thank you for what y-you and y-your soldiers did."

"Your thanks are warmly received." Mulaghesh bows. "I'm happy to hear we were of service. But how, if I could ask, did you wind up in Voortyashtan?"

"I was a m-medical student at Bulikov University. A-after the battle, I w-went to Ghaladesh on a Ministry program. I'd become interested i-in humanitarian a-aid—as you c-can probably u-uhh-understand."

"Of course."

"Th-then news came th-they were tr-trying to escalate th-their w-work here in V-V-Vv . . ." Rada trails off, her face bright red. She sighs, surrendering. "In *this place*. They n-needed a new p-polis governor, one w-with a m-more humanitarian f-focus. I applied." Then she thinks and counts off on her fingers: "D-during my tenure here, w-we've reduced infant death by twenty-nine percent, maternal death by twenty-four percent, death by infectious disease by fourteen percent, child malnourishment by thirty-three percent, and I've personally performed seventy-three successful surgeries." She looks up from her fingers and glances around, dazed, as if just remembering where she is.

"Sounds like you've got a pretty good record going," says Mulaghesh. She notes Rada didn't stutter a bit while firing off those statistics.

"Thank you," she says meekly. Then she stoops and gathers up her papers. "I have to go and make formal copies of the m-m-minutes. I-I-eh-eh-*uh*, uhhh-i-it was a p-p-pleasure meeting you." She bows.

"A pleasure," says Mulaghesh, bowing back. She watches as Rada Smolisk scampers off, wondering if she was wrong to mistrust a Continental as polis governor. If anyone could have a desire to help Saypur reconstruct the Continent, it'd be a Bulikovian, someone who's witnessed the Continent's own gods wreak destruction on their very people.

"The girl is odd," says Biswal, watching her go. "As anyone who went through that would be. But she is a brilliant doctor. Much cleverer than a lot of the medics we have up at the fortress." He stops and looks around himself. "Now. What in the hells am I doing."

"Giving me access to the mines."

"Ah. That's right. Pandey and you seem to get along, so I've given him the proper clearances to take you on a tour of the facility. His auto is waiting outside, which you can take. I'll be going up to the fortress . . ." He sighs. "Well. Much later."

"More to clean up here?"

Biswal signs a report with unusual ferocity, nearly slicing the paper in half with the nub of his pen. "Always more. I was taught that peace is the absence of war. But I wonder if these days we've simply replaced conventional war with a war of paper. I'm not so sure which is better."

***

As Pandey drives her out to "the extraction site," as they call it, she watches the wire fences out the window, running along either side of the road with a threatening tangle of razor wire lining the tops. "Seven miles long," Pandey remarked when they first started out. "One hundred tons of aluminum, all stretched along the road. Though the fences are a little inconvenient now, as the road requires a lot of maintenance."

"So you knew this wasn't an expansion when you first brought me to the fort," says Mulaghesh. "As you claimed."

He coughs. "Ah, yes, ma'am. Cover stories and all that."

"Well. I'm pleased to find you could dupe me so thoroughly, Pandey."

"Always keen to impress, General."

She sees tall forms up ahead: towering lights, another fence. *Fences within walls, walls within fences,* she thinks. *It's almost as bad as Bulikov.* "We're here, ma'am," says Pandey.

They get out and approach the checkpoint. Another guard booth, another string of yellow and red warning signs. Pandey holds up their credentials, and the guards let them through.

"We call this the dock," says Pandey. One side of the concrete structure has a retractable aluminum door, which is open. They walk inside the concrete structure, which is really just three concrete walls, a tin roof, and some bare bulbs. The floor is iron, and Mulaghesh notices there's a seam running along it, forming a square.

Pandey walks to a small switch standing in the middle of the grated floor and says, "If you can, ma'am, please step closer."

Mulaghesh does so. As she does she sees Pandey is pale and ashen. "Something the matter, Pandey?"

"Ah . . . Well. Not too keen on the mines myself, ma'am."

"Why not? Do you have a problem with close, dark places?"

"Not that I'm aware of, ma'am. It's just . . ." He pauses. "Well. You'll see."

"See what?"

"I hesitate to give you the wrong impression, ma'am. If you're ready, ma'am . . ."

He flips a switch, and the floor drops out from underneath her. Well, not quite, but that's what it feels like: as she steadies herself, she realizes that the center of the floor is like an elevator of some kind, made to bring up huge quantities of material.

Exactly how much thinadeskite do they plan on mining here?

At first the walls of the elevator shaft are sheer, smooth concrete.

Then these begin to ripple and churn, turning into raw rock, dark granite with glinting silicates. Mulaghesh remembers Signe telling her about the tomb and inspects the shifting walls for any sign of architecture or civilization, but finds none. She cannot imagine there having ever been any ruin buried down here: it's all just curdled stone and shadows.

A large tunnel rises up to them, its ceiling lined with oil lanterns. The elevator comes to a sharp halt. Ten feet before them is a guard seated on a stool. He nods at them.

"And these, ma'am," says Pandey, "are the thinadeskite mines of Voortyashtan."

He and Mulaghesh pace forward, then stop as she looks at the tunnel walls. They are still dark granite, but the walls are riddled with holes, as if giant termites have been laboring here for decades.

"So . . . how does it work?" asks Mulaghesh.

"I suggest we start at an active branch, ma'am," says Pandey. "That'll probably be more informative."

They wind through the dark tunnels, ducking this way and that to avoid the dangling oil lamps. The air is cool and still, yet somehow Mulaghesh thinks she feels a breeze. She imagines the tunnels as the bronchi and alveoli of a giant lung, a vast underground mass of spongy tissue, gently flexing to push air through its endless corridors. . . .

"I can see why you said this place was unpleasant," she says. "There's something odd about it."

Pandey takes a sharp left. Mulaghesh hears a scraping and grinding up ahead. "Are you worried about it being Divine, ma'am? Like the Ministry is?"

"Well, yeah. Some. Can you imagine this stuff just naturally occurring?"

"Perhaps. Once when I was a child," says Pandey, "I was walking along a dry creek bed. I walked it many times in my youth, but that day I saw one of the creek bed walls had fallen in, General. And inside this wall, in all the loose earth piled there, were dozens and dozens of crystals. Quartz, of course. I didn't know that it was a commonly found thing, not then. I couldn't imagine something like this just *existing*. You know? It was beautiful and wonderful to me, because I didn't know any better. So now, faced with this strange stuff, I have to wonder if we just don't know any better."

"Maybe you have a point, Sergeant Major," says Mulaghesh. "Maybe."

"Imagine the first person to discover magnets. Or flint. Or milk! We Saypuris like to think we know so much about how the world works, ma'am, when in truth we're as ignorant as anyb—"

Another breeze.

The lights fade around her.

The temperature drops—no, it *plummets*. Then everything goes full dark.

Mulaghesh keeps moving forward, arms and legs pumping.

What's going on?

The ground is no longer hard stone, but soft.

Like moist grass . . .

A cold white light begins to seep through the darkness.

Mulaghesh squints and sees forms against the light, tall and thin.

Trees. It's impossible—this *can't* be happening—but she sees a small copse of trees ahead, the air heavy with mist and fog, the cold light of the moon shining through behind them. Pandey is nowhere to be found.

Somewhere there is the cheep of meadowlarks and wrens, and the soft sound of the ocean.

A stag slowly canters over the wet grass. A beautiful creature the color of pearl, its flanks shimmering in the moonlight. Its breath steams; its shanks are flecked with dark mud.

A young man emerges from the shadow of the trees. He is smeared with mud, the whites of his eyes bright against the earthen hues. Something in his hand glints: a small knife, made of bronze.

The stag looks at him, dark eyes watchful. It snorts, curious, distrustful. The young man extends his free hand to it. His palm is slick with something—honey.

She understands what will happen. No, it's like she *remembers:* it's like she's always known that the white stag will come and sniff the honey on his palm, and he will leap forward and bury the knife in the stag's neck, and he will ride it as it thrashes against him, leaking blood, and he will come back down to the waters from the cliffs anointed with steaming blood, fresh from his kill, and there he will face them, their helmets proud and regal and terrifying. . . .

She thinks: *How do I know this?*

An image slips into Mulaghesh's mind: seven Voortyashtani sentinels standing in a line, hands resting on the pommels of their massive swords, the vast, strange, twisting oceanopolis of Voortyashtan behind them—the Voortyashtan of old, like some sort of massive coral reef alight with candlelight. The sentinels will watch this blood-drenched young man, and he will kneel in the gravel before them, head bowed, and await their decree.

But for now, there is only the boy, and the stag, and the trees, and the soft moonlight.

How do I know these things?

The darkness fades.

The fluttering orange light of an oil lamp flares to life above her.

Pandey is saying: ". . . imagine how they figured out eggs. *I* didn't trust them, when I was a boy. I wanted no part of them."

Mulaghesh realizes she is still walking. She never stopped. She blinks and looks ahead, and sees only more tunnels and more oil lamps—certainly no trees.

"But I *do* eat eggs now, ma'am," Pandey adds. "Of course I do."

She looks down at herself—she seems to be the same. And it appears Pandey didn't notice anything. Did she imagine it all? She can't conceive how she could have: Mulaghesh does not consider herself a very imaginative person, but even so, a vision with so much depth and memory in it—the feel of the wet grass, the drip of the honey, the strange cityscape of ancient Voortyashtan—should be beyond even the most brilliant poet.

What in all the hells is going on?

"Here we are," says Pandey. He gestures ahead. Three Saypuri soldiers are grinding at the walls with what look like gas-powered drills, gunning their engines over and over as the wall dissolves and falls to a metal container at their feet. A few yards behind them is a massive wheelbarrow. Mulaghesh expected there to be a railcar, like a coal mine, but it looks like the thinadeskite mines aren't quite that established.

"Gentlemen," says Pandey, nodding to them. "The thinadeskite isn't really a solid ore, we've found. It's more like a particulate, ma'am, a dust found in the soft loam cavities. Very unusual. We hollow out the recesses, like you saw back there, and after that it's simply a matter of separating out the thinadeskite from the loam."

Mulaghesh is still attempting to control herself after the . . . What can she call it? A vision? She clears her throat. "How far do the mines go, Sergeant Major?"

"Quite far, ma'am," says Pandey. "The thinadeskite is somewhat erratically spread throughout the area. We use some specialized magnetized materials to detect it, though, and to separate it from the powdered loam."

"Mind if we keep looking?"

"Certainly, ma'am."

It's plain he thinks Mulaghesh will only see more stretches of blank, dull rock. Which she very well might, of course. But she's curious to see if she can spot any remnant of Choudhry visiting this place—and, now, to try to understand what just happened to her.

"How much thinadeskite has been mined so far?" asks Mulaghesh.

"About sixty tons."

"Sixty *tons?*"

"That's correct, General."

"They need to experiment with *that* much?"

"Oh, no," says Pandey. "That's for when the project gets approved.

Lieutenant Prathda believes that when the thinadeskite passes all its tests we'll start scaling up manufacturing capacities immediately. The thinadeskite is currently stored in a small warehouse facility at the fort. There it sits until Ghaladesh gives us the go-ahead, General."

"No security issues there, either?" asks Mulaghesh.

"Not that I'm aware of. We don't have many issues at the fort direc—"

Again, the light dies and the tunnel fades away.

No, thinks Mulaghesh.

There is the clatter of metal armor, the creak of leather.

Not again. This isn't real. . . .

The scent of jasmine and river water. The whisper and snicker of a nearby stream.

She sees soft daylight; tall, bright green grass massaged by gentle winds; and impossibly high trees.

She knows where she is immediately. She's in Saypur, of course. No other place in the world has such trees, such dense foliage. But though she recognizes it, it's again as if she *remembers* it, like she always knew these details.

Someone is walking through the grass. Though it is day—she knows it is day—the light is still indistinct enough that she can only make out the shape of the figure's head: it's oddly swollen, as if their skull is far too large. . . .

The light in the vision grows. She sees the frozen metal face, the fixed needle-teeth grin, the blank eyes. . . .

The Voortyashtani sentinel ripples with movement as it walks. It is difficult to tell if its armor is metal, or bone, or both. Spikes and spurs adorn the armor's shoulders, elbows, and knees, as if a forest of antlers is sprouting from its limbs. In some places the armor is held together by thick leather straps; in others it appears to have been grown, melded together over its wearer's body. It is covered in old stains, some brown, some red: blood, obviously, from some past slaughter.

She looks at the antler-like growths and understands immediately: *Their armor fed on bloodshed. That's how it grew around them, how it became so strong. And this one has fed its armor well.*

The sentinel cocks its head, listening, then continues on.

How do I know these things?

For all the ornamentation upon its armor, the sentinel's sword is clean and unadorned, a four-foot, slightly curved blade as thick as a cleaver. It must weigh over seventy pounds, but the sentinel carries it as if it's a switch of wood.

Another sentinel approaches from the stream. Both of them are huge, over six and a half feet tall. She remembers that all Continentals were much taller when they lived under the Divinities, as they were much healthier and well-fed. As the second sentinel nears it holds its sword aloft. The first sentinel does the same. And then . . .

It's difficult to say what happens next. Mulaghesh knows what is happening the same way she knows everything about this moment: it's as if it personally happened to her, long ago, and she's just now remembering it. But the sensation is so strange and so otherworldly that she could neither imagine nor truly express what it is.

The swords talk to one another.

This isn't *quite* true: it's more like the swords act as antennae for the two sentinels to speak. But they speak directly into one another's minds, with the second sentinel asking the first:

—*The escapees?*

The first answers:

—*Discovered two.*

—*Slain?*

The two sentinels—still using the strange connection between their swords—then share a memory: two Saypuri slaves, sprinting through the jungle, a mother and her son. The first sentinel, charging through the undergrowth, hacking whole trees out of its way. The child stumbles, the mother stops to help. The massive blade rises high, and then . . .

The memory acts as an answer:

—*Yes.*

The second sentinel says:

—Third cannot be far.

—No. Cannot be.

The two abruptly turn and march back into the jungle, slashing through the branches as they search for their final missing slave.

The vision grows dark. The lamplight returns, as does Pandey's voice, casually discussing the fort:

". . . tribal leaders has complained about the cannons, and though I can understand that it must be unnerving to live with them pointed at you day and night, they've been like that for decades."

Mulaghesh stops and puts her hands on her knees. Nausea coils around and around in her stomach, like an infant snake trying to break out of its egg.

"General? Are you all right?"

The answer, of course, is no, absolutely not. She doesn't understand what's happening to her, but somehow she's catching what seem to be glimpses of past lives and day-to-day proceedings—however ghastly—of how the Voortyashtanis of old lived.

Are they hallucinations? Is she ill? Suddenly Choudhry's bizarre drawings on the walls of her room seem much more understandable.

"Must . . ." She swallows. "Must be an altitude change."

Pandey is silent. When she looks up he is watching her with a queer look on his face.

"What is it, Sergeant Major?" asks Mulaghesh.

"Nothing. Would you like to see more, General?"

She certainly does not, but she knows she needs to. The two of them walk on through the pockmarked tunnels. At one point the lamps run out. "Work ended on this branch a long time ago," Pandey remarks, and he has to lift one lamp off the ceiling to carry. He smiles at her and says, "Try not to sneeze if you can, General. Otherwise we'll have to fumble our way back."

"I had been told," Mulaghesh says, "that you all found some strange materials in the mines here. Signs of tampering—a fire."

"We found signs of someone starting a small fire, yes."

"Where was this, Sergeant Major?"

He nods ahead. He leads her to a small, low tunnel. It's hard to see in the dark, but the bottom and the walls appear scorched and smoked. "This was it, I believe."

Mulaghesh extends a hand. Pandey passes the lantern to her, and she crouches and examines the scorch marks. The placement of the fire doesn't seem to have anything special about it: it's just another tunnel, like the dozens of other ones she's seen down here. There are ashes and crinkled leaves lying in the divots and holes of the tunnel floor, but none of them suggest much to her. *Wrapped in sackcloth, maybe, and set alight . . .*

"And I assume you all conducted a search concerning this?" she asks.

"We did. Checked the fences and all the tunnels, General. No way in or out, except the fort."

Mulaghesh grunts. It's Choudhry for sure, she thinks. She got in here somehow. As a Ministry officer, there's a whole lot of obfuscations and subterfuge Choudhry would have been trained in that Mulaghesh wouldn't know the first thing about. She could've blackmailed a guard, maybe, or perhaps she just knew a way to get through fences without leaving any trace. From the stuff that she saw Shara randomly pull out of her pocket in Bulikov, nothing would surprise Mulaghesh. "Well. Then I'm as stumped as you are. I suppose I've seen all that I can see here."

They start back up through the tunnels. Mulaghesh wasn't aware of how far they'd walked: the tunnels seem to wind and wind and wind around, and soon she's not aware if she's walking up or down, ascending or descending.

"I heard rumors there was a Voortyashtani tomb down here," says Mulaghesh. "No sign of it, I guess?"

"Nooo," says Pandey, suppressing a laugh. "No, General, can't say that I've seen such."

"No stone walls, no arches?"

"No, no. Just rock and more rock. I would imagine that after Bulikov everyone would be very sensitive to mysterious, underground structures. A thing like that would get reported quite quickly, General."

"I'd hope so."

"Besides that little fire we found, we've had few issues, ma'am. The shtanis stay focused on their feuds; they seem to have forgotten us up here."

They walk on in silence.

"So, I understand you're staying with CTO Harkvaldsson, General?" he asks. "At the SDC headquarters?"

"Yes. Why?"

"No reason," he says quickly. "I had to drive her around for a while, when the harbor was first starting. She was qui—"

The oil lamps blink out. Darkness comes rushing in.

No, thinks Mulaghesh. *Get me out.*

The sounds of their footsteps fade away.

Get me out of here. . . .

She expects to see some other grim little scene from Voortyashtani life: perhaps an execution, or some horrifying moonlit rite conducted under the shadows of standing stones. But instead she sees something far more familiar, and far more upsetting.

The bones of a farmhouse, nestled at the foot of a hill. Its roof has fallen in and its walls are blackened and charred. The mortar, which once dammed back drafts of icy air, has turned to powder and crumbled away, revealing the warped ribs of the wide, flat structure. The floor is ashen and still smoking, narrow tendrils coiling across the morning sky.

A young woman kicks through the ruin, poking at the ashes with a slender sword. No, not a woman—a girl. A sixteen-year-old girl, large for her age. She wears a Saypuri uniform—the first generation of Saypuri Military uniforms ever made, in fact.

She stops. Lying before the house's stone chimney, black and raw and half-submerged in the ashes, is a human form. A boy. Maybe not much older than she is.

She looks at it. She reaches forward with the sword point, uses it to lift the blackened hand a few inches. She lets it drop, and it falls back to the blanket of ash with a soft *thump*, sending a cloud dancing up to fill the tattered room.

A young soldier trots up and knocks on the remnants of the door. He calls out, "Lieutenant!"

She doesn't answer, staring at the body.

"Lieutenant Mulaghesh?"

The girl steps away from the shrunken corpse. "Yeah?"

"Captain Biswal is gearing up to move out, Lieutenant. He's requested confirmation regarding whether your team has discovered any supplies."

The young lieutenant sheathes her sword. "No. No supplies, no rations. Everything here has burned to a crisp." She strides out, kicking up clouds of ash. "On to Utusk next, I suppose. They won't know what hit them." She looks at the young soldier. He's not much older than she is, but he still seems younger: there is a softness to his eyes, to his posture, as if always bracing for a blow. "Did you have any casualties?"

"No. No . . . Saypuri casualties, at least." He hesitates, blanches.

"Something the matter, Private?"

"No, Lieutenant."

"You don't look well."

He hesitates. "Sankhar and I . . . There was a farmhouse burning . . ."

"Yes?"

"A man came out. Tried to attack us. And we . . . We cut him down."

"As you should have."

"Yes, but . . . Then I looked up, and I saw a woman watching us from the farmhouse, holding a child. She saw me looking and she ran back inside, and . . ."

"And?"

"And the farmhouse kept burning, Lieutenant, but I never saw anyone come out. I never saw anyone come back out."

Silence. The young girl brushes ash off the toes of her boot.

"You did your duty, Bansa," she says. "Don't forget, it was their choice to get involved in this war. And we are giving every home the opportunity to flee. Some do. Many don't. But that is their choice. Do you understand?"

He nods and whispers, "Yes, Lieutenant."

"Good. Now come on."

The two of them turn and walk around the hill, where the smoldering ruin of a town sends a great column of smoke into the sky.

A string of lights glows through the smoke.

Please take me away, thinks Mulaghesh. *Take me away from all this. . . .*

The darkness of the tunnels floods back in.

"—nough trucks for us to use," Pandey is saying. "Terribly difficult getting around here, as I'm sure you noticed." They round the corner, and the elevator up appears. "Well. Was it everything you expected, General?"

Mulaghesh does not answer. Pandey, a little troubled, flips the switch. The elevator begins grinding away, and they slowly rise.

When they come to the top, she says, "Excuse me for a moment, Sergeant Major."

"Certainly, General."

Mulaghesh walks out, slowly paces around the dock until she finds a spot where no guards can see her, leans up against the wall, and vomits.

***

The ride back to the fortress is quiet and solemn. Pandey is not half so cheerful anymore.

"Did you see Bulikov, General?" asks Pandey after a while.

"Did I what?"

"In the mines," he says. "Did you see the . . . the Battle of Bulikov?"

She is silent for a long while. "No."

"I . . . I see," he says, embarrassed. "Never mi—"

"But I did see . . . *some*thing. Just not . . . that. This happened to you, too, Sergeant Major? You saw the Battle?"

"Y-yes. When I first went into the mines, yes, ma'am. I saw it happening again, like it was happening right in front of me. But I saw it outside of myself. Does that make sense? It was like I was watching myself. And you. You were there. Before the onslaught, and the flying ship . . ."

"I remember. Is this common? Have these . . . I don't know, *flashbacks* happened to anyone else?"

He shakes his head. "Very rarely. I don't think many wish to discuss it. But it only happens, I think, to those who have seen combat. A lot of it."

They drive along in silence. Mulaghesh wishes she knew something of the Divine. Was there something of Voortya's that made this possible, this . . . memory bleed? What is it down there that wakes up these images, these visions, and sends people plummeting down into them, forced to witness (or rewitness) horrors?

She watches as a shrike flits up to the top of the barbed wire fence and hangs the headless remains of a field mouse on one of the spikes. The image of corpses impaled on stakes flashes before her eyes. The thinadeskite in the charcoaler's hut.

What's the connection? What does thinadeskite have to do with all this?

"Mostly all I do here in Voortyashtan, General," says Pandey, "is drive. But, do you know, somehow this is still my oddest assignment yet?"

Though she doesn't say so, Mulaghesh fervently sympathizes.

***

Come 1800 hours that evening, General Turyin Mulaghesh—recipient of the Jade Sash, the Pearl of the Order of the Kaj, the Star of Kodur, and the Verdant Heart of Honor—is quite definitely very drunk, wandering the cliffs north of Voortyashtan with a half-empty bottle of wine and her stomach swilling with several foul concoctions she purchased at some sea shack in the city.

She isn't the only one here: all along the narrow path she spies lovers, grumbling drunks, and tiny campsites crowded with silent, hollow-eyed men. She passes one old man leaning on a walking stick and staring out at the evening sky, and asks him what all these people are doing out here. He simply makes a wide gesture indicating the sea and the hills and returns to his silent watching.

Lonely places draw lonely people, she thinks as she walks farther north, the fort on her right. *They echo inside us, and we cannot help but listen.*

Mulaghesh keeps walking, past the tiny camps, past the couples lounging on their furs, past one man quietly sobbing in the shade of a tiny, leafless tree. She takes a deep sip of wine, tries to convince herself that it makes her feel warm, and keeps walking.

Perhaps I am still plodding on in the Yellow March, she thinks. *Me and Biswal, wearily holding the banner . . .*

She takes another sip of wine. Almost gone now. She doesn't know where it came from, but she wishes she'd brought more.

She almost speaks aloud the familiar refrain: *Woresk, Moatar, Utusk, Tambovohar, Sarashtov, Shoveyn, Dzermir, and finally . . .*

". . . finally Kauzir," she finishes. The little town just outside the gates of Bulikov.

She remembers the names of the towns still. She always will, she knows. They're written on the inside of her skull. She'll go to her grave still knowing them, even though the towns themselves no longer exist. For Yellow Company visited each one of them during the Summer of Black Rivers. And every home, every building, every farm, every single sign of civilization in each of these villages was put to the torch.

She stares out to sea, remembering.

✳✳✳

Biswal told them over and over again it was to be a civilized, strategic procession. "We're here to eliminate resources," he told them. "No more. Burn the farms and the Continental front lines will grow weaker and weaker."

But it quickly became such a hard thing, executing a civilized war. The people in these villages did not evacuate quietly, no matter how much Yellow Company ordered them to. They did not simply watch as Yellow Company burned every last remnant of their lives. Rather, they fought: men, women, and children. And Yellow Company fought back.

She remembers waiting, crouched in a wheatfield, the sights of her bolt-shot trained on a window in the second story of a farmhouse. Just below, on the ground, one of her soldiers lay bleeding, a small arrow sticking from his collarbone, one hand pawing at it, trying to pull it out. She waited, waited, and then in the window a figure appeared with a short bow.

A girl. Maybe thirteen. Mulaghesh didn't see, because her finger was already pulling the trigger, already sending eight inches of steel hurtling at the girl, who just . . .

Dropped. As if she never were.

She can't remember what happened to the wounded soldier. Died, probably. A lot of them died, at first. Until somewhere around the town of Sarashtov, when Yellow Company stopped asking the Continentals to surrender and evacuate, stopped giving them warning at all. Too many of their own soldiers had been lost to a lucky farmer with an axe or a child with a bow and arrow. Yellow Company began simply sneaking in during the night, setting the thatched roofs alight, and rounding up the livestock in the ensuing chaos.

Mulaghesh remembers the sight of a four-year-old child standing alone in a field at night, his face alight with firelight and glistening with tears, screaming for his mother. They marched on and left him there, perhaps to live, perhaps to die. Such a thing did not matter to them.

Figures staggering from burning homes, their nightgowns ablaze, stumbling through the smoke like ravaged puppets. The screams of livestock as Yellow Company herded them through the streets to be slaughtered for their next meal. She remembers the monotonous butchery, killing those they couldn't keep and leaving them to rot, the air so thick with flies. Better to rot than feed Continentals.

An errant memory skitters through her mind: a terrified horse charging into a child's chain swing and hanging itself. This huge, graceful creature thrashing helplessly in the mud. She and the rest of Yellow Company walked on as if this occurrence were nothing of note.

In three weeks they destroyed eight villages, and once word got out that a rogue band of Saypuris was speeding through the heart of the Continent's farmland, all the other villages quickly became abandoned.

By the time Yellow Company reached the gates of Bulikov, the city was slowly realizing that Biswal and Yellow Company had single-handedly destroyed two-thirds of their future food stores in a span of weeks. If a siege began now they could only last a handful of days. Their only hope was that the Continental army would return and crush Yellow Company.

Bulikov's hopes rose when they saw the Continental army on the horizon. But the Continental forces were not returning to deal with Yellow Company: rather, the Continentals were in full flight, General Prandah at their heels. Over the past weeks the Continental troops had seen the columns of smoke north of them and understood that their homes were being destroyed. They'd begun to desert in droves, morale decaying with each passing day. Then General Prandah had pressed the advantage and pushed the wavering forces into a complete rout.

Sandwiched between General Prandah and Yellow Company, the Continental army was utterly destroyed. Within hours, Biswal stood before the gates of Bulikov and demanded that they open. And open they did, creaking and crackling.

But before he could take a single step in, Colonel Adhi Noor arrived, leapt off his horse, and struck Biswal on the chin.

Mulaghesh remembers it like it was only last week: Noor, sweating, stained with smoke and blood, standing over her fallen commanding officer and crying, "What have you done? By all the seas and stars, Biswal, what in all the hells have you *done*?"

***

Like all officers under Biswal, commissioned or otherwise, Mula-ghesh was brought before General Prandah himself and questioned extensively.

"What was Biswal's goal in his expedition?"

"To destroy the Continent's resources, sir."

"And is that why you killed the Continental villagers? Were they a resource too?"

"They were the enemy, sir."

"They were *civilians*, Sergeant." Prandah, of course, did not accept Biswal's promotion of her to lieutenant.

"We felt it made no difference, sir."

"Why do you say that? When was this decided? Who decided this?"

She was silent.

"Who decided this, Sergeant?"

She struggled to recall. The days were a blur, and she could no longer remember which decisions were hers and which ones were an unspoken choice by the whole of the Company.

"What do you mean, it made no difference, Sergeant?"

"I . . . I think I meant that there was no difference between the soldier and the civilian keeping that soldier on their feet, sir."

"There *is* a difference, Sergeant. It is the same difference between a soldier and a raider, a murderer. And neither you nor Biswal have any right to decide otherwise."

She was quiet.

"Did all of the soldiers agree to the March?" asked Prandah. "Did no one resist?"

She was aware of her face trembling. "N-No . . ."

"No? No what?"

"Some . . . some objected."

"And they wouldn't participate?"

She shook her head.

"What did they do, these soldiers who would not participate?"

She did not speak.

"What did they *do*, Sergeant?"

And suddenly she remembered, as if it'd all been a dream or something that had happened so long ago: Sankhar and Bansa, standing before Biswal and saying they would do no more, no more of this, and Biswal slowly looking them up and down, and suddenly calling her name.

And this realization, this bright, brittle memory, formed a tiny crack inside her, and suddenly she understood what she'd done, what they'd all done, and she burst into tears and sank to the ground.

From somewhere she heard Prandah's voice, speaking in horror, "By the seas, she's just a *girl*, isn't she? This soldier is just a *child*."

***

The Saypuri Military chose complete disavowal. Perhaps taking a page from the Worldly Regulations, the Saypuri commanders decided to simply never admit that the March had happened. Yellow Company was far too large to lock up and throw away the key, and Saypur desperately needed manpower to maintain their control of the Continent. In addition, some commanders commended Biswal's accomplishments: he'd won the war, had he not? He'd ended nearly three years of bloody conflict in hardly more than a month.

Biswal was reassigned on the Continent to other, less-glamorous duties. Mulaghesh had no such privilege. She wondered what they would do with her when her service ended. Dishonorably discharge her? Abandon her on the Continent? But in the end their verdict, most likely inadvertently, was the cruelest one possible: they sent her home, with modest honors.

Home. She had never expected to ever see it during the Yellow March. But returning to Ghaladesh proved to be no different than walking the ruined countryside of the Continent: it was strange, intolerable, distant, and muted. She could not adjust to the easy, thoughtless way of living. Her mouth took issue with spices, with salt, with properly cooked food. It took her more than a year to learn to sleep in a bed again, or how to live in rooms with windows.

She tried her hand at jobs, at marriage. She proved to be a miserable failure at all of them. She began to understand, bit by bit, that the devastation she'd wrought did not end on the Continent: perhaps there was some secret place inside her that she'd never known was there, but she'd put it to the torch, too, and only now in civilian life did she realize what she'd lost.

And then one day, drunk in a wine bar in Ghaladesh, she was staring into her cup and thinking about how bitter the idea of tomorrow had become when a voice said over her shoulder, "I was told I'd find you here."

She looked up and saw a Saypuri Military officer standing behind her, dressed in fatigues. She found she recognized him: he was the one who'd punched Biswal, who'd been there when Prandah had interrogated her. Noor, she thought his name was. Colonel Noor.

He sat down next to her and ordered a drink. She asked why he'd found her.

"Because," he said slowly, "I think you, like a lot of veterans, are having trouble adjusting. And I wanted to see if you'd like to reenlist."

"No," she said violently. "*No.*"

"Why not?" he asked, though it seemed he'd expected the question.

"I don't . . . I don't ever want to go back. To go through that again."

"To what? To fight? To kill?"

She nodded.

He smiled sympathetically. He was an unusual soldier, she thought: though there was a sternness in his face, there was something inviting there, too, something often lacking in the commanding officers she'd had. "Soldiers don't just kill, Mulaghesh. Most don't, in fact, these days. We support and maintain and build, and keep the peace."

"So?"

"So . . . I believe you might jump at the opportunity to do some good. You're not even twenty yet, Mulaghesh. You've a lot of years left. I suspect you can find better uses for them than filling your belly with cheap wine."

Mulaghesh was silent.

"Well, if you're interested, we're implementing a new program, a . . . sort of governing system for the Continent. Military stations designed to provide support and keep the peace."

"Like cops, sir?"

"Somewhat. Colonel Malini will be overseeing Bulikov, but he will need assistance. Would you be interested in perhaps returning to the Continent and assisting him? You know a lot about the region. But maybe this time you can put it to some good."

***

Mulaghesh stares over the cliffs of Voortyashtan. Gulls nest in the rocks below, and they flit back and forth over the waves, snapping up moths, ghostly, porcelain flickers in the moonlight. Besides them, she is alone. There's not a single soul for nearly half a mile around her.

The horizon flickers with roiling clouds and lightning. A storm coming—unwise to be out here now.

She wishes she'd grown, that she'd put the March behind her. But seeing those memories in the thinadeskite mine—young Bansa, hardly yet a man, knocking on the wall of the ruined farmhouse, not knowing what would happen to him mere days later—it was as if all the years since the March were just condensation on a pane of glass, wiped away with the flick of a hand, and on the other side was that ruined, scarred countryside, and she could not shut her eyes or look away.

She looks at the label on the bottle of wine. Some putrid Voortya-shtani concoction. She drains it, walks to the edge of the cliff, and drops it over the side.

She watches it plummet, a glittering green teardrop falling to the dark ocean. It turns to dust against the face of the cliff. She never hears the crash.

She stares at the moon's reflection on the face of the waves. She imagines that it's a hole in the world, that perhaps she could dive out and fall through it and find a place where she could rest.

But then it changes, and suddenly the moon's reflection looks like a skull to her.

She blinks. To her bafflement, she watches as the moon's reflection changes, shifts: it's not a giant skull, but a face, a woman's face, still and blank, lying just below the waves.

"What the hells?" she says.

Then the ocean bursts up, something shooting up from its depths. It rises, rises . . .

And Mulaghesh sees her.

She rises up astonishingly fast, like a whale breaking through the surface for a leap, water pouring off her enormous shoulders, pouring off her arms, pouring off her chin: a giant formed of metals, of steel and iron and bronze and rust. When she fully stands the cliffs are just barely at her breast, a vast, glittering creature standing against the frigid moon and stars. Her face is cold and still, an emotionless steel mask, her eyes dark and blank.

It is a helmet, Mulaghesh sees: she is not made of metal but is wearing armor—beautifully wrought, ornate armor, plate overlying mail—and depicted on this armor are a thousand terrifying images of unspeakable violence.

She is magnificent, terrible, beautiful. She is the sea, the moon, the cliffs. Warfare incarnate, violence never-ending.

"Voortya," whispers Mulaghesh.

It is impossible—utterly *impossible*—and yet it is so.

One giant, mailed hand grasps the top of the cliffs, and she hauls her vast bulk up.

No, no, thinks Mulaghesh.

The gulls are shrieking, terrified. The ground trembles beneath Mulaghesh's feet. Her hand fumbles for her carousel.

Voortya towers over Mulaghesh, dark and impossible and lovely and monstrous. With a whine of metal she turns her blank eyes to stare at the fortress. In her right hand is a flicker of light: a sword blade rendered in ghostly, pale luminescence.

I won't let you, thinks Mulaghesh.

Mulaghesh pulls out the carousel and points it up and fires. She sees the muzzle flash reflected on the giant steel greaves, and is vaguely aware of herself screaming: *I won't fucking let you!*

Mulaghesh feels her sanity unraveling—it is all too much, too much to see, to behold—but to her surprise, the Divinity reacts, recoiling as if in pain. Mulaghesh hears a voice in her mind, huge and terrible: "STOP, YOU FOOL! STOP!"

Then the stars wink out and she feels herself falling, and somewhere in the distance is the sound of thunder.

Though no Divinity, from what we have recovered, was ever depicted with much coherence, the Divinity Voortya is interesting in that there was a distinct shift in how she is described in Voortyashtani texts. In the very early days she was depicted as an animal, a veritable monster, a four-armed half-person, half-beast that was wild and savage. This version of Voortya is commonly associated with bones, teeth, tusks, antlers: the natural, biological adornments of combat. These signatures were retained even in her later years.

But somewhere in the sixth century, while the Divine Border Wars were still ongoing and all Divinities and their followers battled for domination, Voortya underwent a distinct change. She stopped presenting herself as a beast and started to commonly manifest as a four-armed woman dressed in armor. The armor is described as being highly advanced for the era: plate on mail on leather, and inscribed on the plate mail were all of her victories, all of the foes she had slaughtered, depicted with graphic detail. It is shortly after this period that she began to wield the famed Sword of Voortya, the blade wrought of moonlight whose hilt and pommel were the severed hand of the son of Saint Zhurgut, her most ardent apostle.

It is interesting that this shift in appearance coincides with three other changes. Firstly, it is after this transformation that we begin to see coherent, consistent recordings of the nature of the Voortyashtani afterlife, as if before this point the Voortyashtani afterlife did not truly or properly exist. Secondly, though Voortya's mostly human, four-armed appearance stayed more or less the same, her top-most left hand now appeared missing, as if severed during her transformation.

And thirdly, and perhaps most notably, after this change, there is no recorded instance of the Divinity Voortya ever speaking again. Either to the other Divinities or her own followers.

— DR. EFREM PANGYUI, "THE NATURE OF
CONTINENTAL ART"

8.

SHE WHO CLOVE THE EARTH IN TWAIN

Somewhere there is screaming. The cough and sputter of engines. The scent of smoke. No gunfire, though: her half-functioning brain makes a note of this, saying only, *Possibly not combat.*

Then a flash, a crash, a bang. She's slapped with rain, and awakes. She is lying on wet earth. Rain patters her back. She remembers, slowly, that she has limbs. She turns herself over, shoulders complaining, and looks up.

Voortya is gone. A driving rain hammers the clifftops, runlets of water carving through the moist grass to go spiraling off into the sea.

She hears more shouting, the groan of machinery. She sits up— her whole body hurts as if she's just fallen out of the sky—and looks behind her.

A thick plume of smoke is rising from the earth a few miles west of Fort Thinadeshi. It takes her no time at all to realize it's the thinadeskite mine.

There are shouts, screams, cries. Automobile lights slash through the swirling dust and smoke. She can see figures sprinting back and forth, pointing, waving their arms. Machinery being set, started, juddering into action. It all has the look of a disaster to her.

She looks around and sees her carousel lying in a mound of bracken. She picks it up, fingers still dull and stupid, and confirms that it's empty: she fired all five rounds. She feels the barrels—still warm—which means she fired them recently.

Though the question remains, she thinks, looking back at the sea, *fired them into* what?

She holsters the carousel, stands, and staggers toward the

thinadeskite mine, her feet sloshing in the wet earth. As she gets closer she sees there's an immense hole in the ground, like a sinkhole after a torrential rain, dozens of feet deep. The wire fences have collapsed, allowing her to cross through. One of the figures running around the rim of the hole is unusually agitated, pointing, screaming orders, darting back and forth with their hands clasped around their head. She doesn't need to get close to know it's Lieutenant Prathda, head boy of the thinadeskite project.

"No, no!" he's crying. "That stone there! It's clearly blocking the aperture! No, not *that* one, the one with the orthoclase striations, on the left!"

One of the soldiers working at the machinery turns to look at Prathda, bewildered.

"The *granite*, Private!" he shrieks at the soldier. "The *granite slab*! Move it, *move it*!"

Mulaghesh wipes rain out of her eyes as she approaches. "What the hells happened here?" It looks like someone's just carved a gigantic trench in the earth. There's no sign at all that this was once a functioning mine.

Prathda does a double take. "Where did *you* come from? The mine's caved in somehow, the whole damnable mine has just *caved in*! In the middle of the night! With no warning!"

"It collapsed?"

"Yes! *Yes!* And damned if I know how! We'd done countless integrity reports, brought in all kinds of mining experts to analyze the density of the soil, and now this! This, when we need it least! It'll flood in *minutes* if the rain keeps up!"

"Was anyone inside?"

"Of course there were! We'd be fools to leave this place unguarded! But . . ." He looks back at the ruined mine.

Mulaghesh understands what he's thinking. "The odds are slim that they're alive."

She steps back to let the emergency crews by and takes stock of her surroundings, doing all she can to defy her whirling head and capture every possible detail. Lightning flickers in the sky, giving her a sliver of illumination. She tries to imagine what could have done this. The only thing she's ever seen in her life create this kind of destruction is an artillery shell.

"I guess that solves it," says a voice over her shoulder.

She looks around to find Biswal sitting on a stone nearby, staring into the chaos.

"What?" asks Mulaghesh.

"The collapse. It answers the question that's weighed so heavily on my mind." Biswal still hasn't made eye contact with her: he just watches as the crews try to haul rubble out of the way. There's something off-putting about his expression, as if he always expected this calamity, or perhaps *some* calamity; and now that he's been proven right, it fills him with a strange energy. "What were the insurgents going to do with all those stolen explosives?"

"You think they bombed the mine?"

"You heard Prathda. He's right. They did countless studies when constructing this thing, took every measure of safety. The only reason it'd collapse is if someone *forced* it to. And all the damage is in a straight line. That's no coincidence, and this is no collapse."

"Why would they attack the mines?"

"Why does a rabid dog attack a bull? Don't give these people too much credit, Turyin. They don't have strategies, they don't have goals. That's why they seem to win." One of his lieutenants waves to him. Biswal watches him for a moment, his eyes heavy-lidded and face inscrutable. Then he stands. "Whatever happened here, it's not over yet." He brushes off his pants and strides away into the chaos.

Mulaghesh watches him go, then turns to look at the collapsed mine. Then she walks away, climbs a nearby hill, and looks down on the damage.

It is all in a line, as Biswal said. But somehow she gets the impression the destructive force did not come from within but rather from *above*, as if a tremendous weight struck the earth above the mine with enough power to crack through yards and yards of soil and stone.

She remembers the sight of Voortya, and the huge sword glinting in her hand.

Did a Divinity climb up on these cliffs, she wonders, *lift her sword high, and bring it down on the mine?*

She jumps down and starts walking toward the cliffs, searching for some sign of a Divinity's passage, or really *any*thing's passage. She finds nothing. And besides, this region is covered with patrols, any one of which would have noticed a ten-story metal woman walking around with a sword, which is the kind of thing you mention to your CO.

She looks back at the mines. If it was indeed Voortya herself who stood here and looked out at all of Voortyashtan, what went through her giant, steel head?

If she did destroy the mines, why? Why bother with them at all? Wouldn't Fort Thinadeshi be a much better target for the Divinity of war, sitting there upon the hill, huge and lit up and covered in cannons?

Was Voortya driven to stop them from mining the thinadeskite? But why would Voortya care about what by all accounts is simply a new type of electromagnetic ore? Are they violating some kind of sacred rule by drilling deep into the earth?

Even if she saw *something,* Mulaghesh reasons, it couldn't have been Voortya. For one thing, the Divinity Voortya had *four* arms. Mulaghesh doesn't know much, but she knows that. In every instance when she presented herself, the Divinity of war had four giant, muscular arms, two to a side. And yet the thing she witnessed here on the cliffs had two. *It also seemed to react in pain when I popped off some rounds at it,* she thinks. Though Saypur's made some striking breakthroughs in weapon technologies, she doesn't think small arms fire would make a Divinity pause. Hells, six-incher cannons only stunned Kolkan and Jukov back in Bulikov, but didn't seem to injure them any.

And last but certainly not least: it couldn't have been Voortya, because Voortya is stone-cold fucking dead. A couple hundred Saypuris witnessed the Kaj blow her head clean off her shoulders in the Night of the Red Sands.

More questions, and no new answers.

Mulaghesh comes to the cliffs where she dropped the bottle off the edge. She sees nothing: no giant finger marks in the rocks, no footsteps, no churning of the earth. There is no sign, save for her empty, warm carousel, that what she experienced was anything more than a dream.

Am I going mad?

The gulls are still shrieking, still wheeling and dipping through the air. They cry to one another in terror, communicating some terrible threat, some passing predator. But Mulaghesh can see no sign of what disturbed them so.

***

Three hours later Mulaghesh, wheezing and gasping, staggers back through the gates of Fort Thinadeshi. She is not at all happy to be parted from the disaster site: though she is ostensibly here as a tourist, she pitched in as much as she could in the recovery effort, trying to locate the bodies of the three guards trapped inside. But then a tremulous Saypuri messenger came up, tapped her on the shoulder, and gave her the request.

When she gets to the main conference room everything's in chaos. Runners—Saypuri and Dreyling, mostly, though there are a few Continental ones—keep darting in to deliver messages. The table is an utter mess, covered in cups, papers, pencils, balled-up napkins. It's clear this has been a point of activity for some time.

Biswal, Captain Nadar, and Signe are all shouting over one another. Rada Smolisk sits quietly in the corner, attempting to take notes. Nadar, unsurprisingly, looks like shit: red-eyed, soaking wet, with a bandage around her right hand. Her face is flushed, which makes the white scar on her forehead glow white. Biswal grips the edges of the table like he's about to break it in half over his knee, and stares straight into it as he issues a steady stream of orders. Signe is pacing along the long side of the table, a frenzy of smoke and ash and frantic gestures, pointing to the wall of maps and describing access points.

For a moment Mulaghesh just watches this scene and drips on the floor. The topic of discussion appears to be throwing up roadblocks, barricades, and traffic stops in order to try to catch whichever perpetrators could be responsible for this.

"... very few weak points at the harbor," Signe is saying indignantly. "The entirety of the harbor works is self-contained."

"Per *your* testimony," says Biswal. "You have not permitted Saypuri officers to tour the harbor works in over four months, so *we* have no way of knowing that for ourselves."

"This is because we are at the *height* of the dredging operations!" says Signe. "We can't stop now to allow a top-to-bottom security assessment!"

"Well, you may have to, CTO Harkvaldsson," growls Biswal. "I have three dead soldiers and a caved-in installation on my hands. I expect your full cooperation."

"And I would expect yours," says Signe. "You tell me that this is an 'installation' or an 'expansion,' but it's clear to everyone that it's some kind of mine! But *what* you're mining you won't say."

"I cannot say," says Biswal. "That is privileged information. And it should not affect how we conduct the search in the harbor works."

Nadar shakes her head. "We can throw up as many dragnets as we'd like, General, but I am convinced the perpetrators are long gone. It cannot be a coincidence that the very day we allow all the tribal leaders into the city is the same day that the mines get bombed. Whoever did this left early today, with the procession out of the city."

"Your suspicions are noted, Captain," says Biswal. "But we still must at least *try*."

So far, Mulaghesh seems to be invisible. She waits, then pulls out a chair and sits. The scrape of the chair leg makes the four of them jump, and they turn to look at her as if she just appeared out of thin air.

"Don't mind me," she says, taking out a cigarillo. "I'd hate to interrupt."

"General Mulaghesh," says Biswal, suddenly formal. "Kind of you to join us. You were with us at the scene just after the cave-in, correct?"

"You saw me, General Biswal," says Mulaghesh. "Unless you've already forgotten."

"I haven't. But your appearance on the scene was quite quick, by my estimation. Word had hardly broken out before you were there. My question is—where were you when the collapse occurred?"

"What, am I a suspect?" says Mulaghesh. She lights her cigarillo. She's suddenly very aware of Rada Smolisk in the corner scribbling down her words.

"We have no witnesses, General," says Nadar. "If you were in the area, ma'am, we'd appreciate hearing anything you have to say."

Mulaghesh sucks on her cigarillo, flooding her mouth and nose with the pungent aroma of tobacco. She swallows, thinking what to say.

She can't tell them what she saw, she decides. Not after Choudhry already went mad up here, painting up the walls with her visions. They'd think her a lunatic and block her out from the investigation. And besides—she herself doesn't know what to make of what she saw.

So what to tell everyone now?

"I was sitting on the cliffs," says Mulaghesh, "watching the storm rolling in, and drinking wine. Probta wine, specifically," she says, remembering the label.

Signe pulls a face. "*Ugh.* You know there's fish oil in that, right?"

"It got me pretty drunk," says Mulaghesh, "so I can't fault it."

"So you were drunk while the mines exploded, General?" says Nadar. She does a good job of keeping some contempt out of her words, but not all of it.

"I figured I'd take a day off," says Mulaghesh. "I wasn't the only one out there, so you can ask them. I fell asleep. I woke up with the rain and thought I heard thunder. It didn't take long to realize what it really was."

"So you did not see anything suspicious in the area after the explosion?" asks Biswal.

"No. I saw what happened and came running. I've been pitching in at the site ever since." She glances around. "So you think insurgents snuck in with the tribal leaders and did this?"

"It's the only theory that makes sense, General," says Nadar.

"How many tribal meetings have you had since the explosives were stolen?"

Biswal frowns as he considers it. "A dozen, maybe. More."

"So they've had a dozen opportunities to pull this off, and only just managed it now?"

"There's a lot of speculation here, ma'am," says Nadar. "If I may say so. The explosives might have been passed throughout the tribes until the right person got ahold of it. Or perhaps they needed the right timing device, or the right access. Or the explosives were only recently stolen from the fortress. There are many reasons why they could have waited so long."

"Are there any reasons why they'd target the mines?" says Mulaghesh. "And not the fortress, or the Galleries, or the harbor? Or any of their enemy tribes?"

"We can't discuss this in front of CTO Harkvaldsson or Governor Smolisk," says Biswal. "The nature and value of the mines is classified."

"So you're telling me that it *was* valuable enough," Signe says languidly, "that the insurgents might know it'd hurt you if they blew it up?"

Biswal glares at her.

"If you're not convinced the insurgents did this, General," says Nadar, "do you have any alternate theories?"

Mulaghesh hesitates. She still has no desire to tell them about her vision. "I'm just saying we might need to keep an open mind he—"

The door bursts open and Sergeant Major Pandey sprints in. Without a word of apology he trots up to Biswal and hands him a note. Biswal, frowning, takes it, opens it, and begins to read. In the time it takes him to do so, two more runners sprint in—one Voortyashtani, one Dreyling—and each hand off messages to Rada and Signe, respectively.

Some big news just came down the pipeline, thinks Mulaghesh.

The room is almost completely still as the messages are opened and read. Pandey glances at Signe, who looks back as she opens her envelope. There's a queer moment of connection between the two: Signe's brow arches, as if asking a question, and Pandey gives the tiniest shake of his head, as if saying, *Not now.*

Mulaghesh frowns. *What the hells was that?*

"What's this?" says Biswal. "This doesn't make sense. Harkvaldsson is already here. She's sitting right there, for the seas' sakes." He nods at Signe.

Pandey coughs a little, leans down, and mutters, "If you'll read the preceding part of the message, sir, it does not concern *CTO* Harkvaldsson. . . ."

Biswal angrily adjusts his tiny spectacles. "Well, then who the hell is supposed to be showing up on our doorstep?"

Rada is reading her own message. "W-Wait," she says, horrified. "Ch-Chancellor je Harkvaldsson is g-going to be *here?* Tomorrow *night?*"

"*Who?*" demands Biswal, furious.

Signe's voice is like an arctic wind: "My father."

Everyone turns to look at her. She's opened her own letter and is reading it with furious eyes, fingers clutching the paper as if imagining a throat. "My *father* is coming."

There's a pause.

"Oh, shit," says Mulaghesh. "Sigrud?"

* * *

Pandemonium ensues. To Mulaghesh's confusion—and terrific amusement—they keep referring to "Chancellor je Harkvaldsson" as a high-level diplomatic personage. The message, Mulaghesh understands, suggests that Sigrud is pulling into Voortyashtan within a matter of hours because his ship took some damage pursuing Dreyling pirates, and is in need of repairs. This is slightly plausible—a damaged ship would be desperate to dock anywhere, including Voortyashtan. But no one seems to believe it. Everyone assumes Sigrud's arrival has something to do with the harbor's construction schedule or the collapse of the thinadeskite mines.

What a minefield this little polis is, Mulaghesh thinks. *So many sensitive subjects.*

It's hard not to laugh: she knew Sigrud took some political office up in the brand-new United Dreyling States, but she hadn't expected him to be walking around with a word like "Chancellor" swinging in front of his name. She tries to imagine him sitting in some bureaucratic office, reading reports. As she has, in her time, seen Sigrud je Harkvaldsson nude, covered in blood, and, on one occasion, both, the idea is downright hilarious.

She watches Signe and Pandey as the discussion mounts. There's something off about them. They don't quite look at each other, but look *toward* each other. They have the air of two people trying very hard not to acknowledge one another.

Something's up, she thinks. *And I don't like it.* She thinks back to what Biswal just said: Signe hasn't let anyone from Fort Thinadeshi tour the harbor works in months. Maybe it's because their schedule's too tight, sure . . . Or maybe it's because Signe doesn't want anyone sniffing around her "test assembly yard," or whatever it really is.

Biswal brings the meeting to a close. Mulaghesh waits for him outside while everyone finishes up and files out. Pandey is one of the first ones out, and he joins her, waiting for Nadar.

Mulaghesh looks at him side-eyed. It's difficult to tell—Pandey's beard is rather prodigious—but his cheeks look a little pink. "You all right, Sergeant Major?"

"I'm sorry, ma'am?" he says, startled.

"You seem somewhat . . . bothered. Are you ill?"

"No, General. I'm weary, as we all are, but I'm perfectly fit and able."

Mulaghesh smiles cheerlessly. "How pleasant to hear."

The door opens again, and she watches closely when Signe charges out. She and Pandey exchange a glance, and Mulaghesh can read the message clearly on her face: *You will not believe this bullshit when I tell you.*

Signe stomps down the hall, her scarf flying like a flag. *CTO*

Harkvaldsson has entirely too many secrets, Mulaghesh thinks. *I may have to remedy that, and soon.*

Next comes Nadar, whom Pandey anxiously follows down the corridor. Then Biswal, slow and grumbling, hauls himself out of the cluttered meeting room. He gives a surly glance to Mulaghesh, as if she's orchestrated this new complication. "This Harkvaldsson fellow . . . The *new* Harkvaldsson, I mean. You knew him, yes?"

"I did. I was stuck in the hospital with him for a couple of weeks after this." She holds up her false hand.

"What's he like?"

She considers it. "Have you ever heard the term 'hard operator,' General?"

"Yes. Referring to troops who specialize in busting heads."

"Well . . . when I knew him"—she stares off into space—"Sigrud was about the hardest operator you could hope to find."

"Is he going to be trouble?"

"Maybe, maybe not. He's a government official now, and he's got family."

"There's a *but* in there, somewhere."

"But, back in the day, he tended to attract trouble like a candle flame does moths."

Biswal sighs. "Fantastic. Will you be there with us when we receive him tomorrow night?"

"I'm afraid I can't," says Mulaghesh. "I've got an appointment then that I can't miss, after all the madness tonight." She holds up her false hand again. "Adjustments."

"Oh. I see. Well, I'd be keen to get your reading on the situation when you get a chance."

"Certainly, Lalith."

She keeps her arm close to her side as she exits the fortress. It's true that it's been hurting all night, ever since she stood in the rain and witnessed the Divinity on the clifftops. But adjusting her prosthetic won't help it any for what she's planning for tomorrow night.

She thinks about the tall, cold walls of Signe's test assembly yard, and the canvas roof. *Now,* she thinks. *How to crack that particular nut?*

***

Mulaghesh isn't alone the next evening when she stands on the sea-wall road, watching the waters. Small clumps of Dreylings dot the path, all watching for the arrival of Sigrud—lost prince to a faded royal line, instigator of the coup that ended the pirate kings' clutch on the Dreyling Republics, and one of the founders of the nascent United Dreyling States. The Dreylings gossip quietly, wondering if the wind will be behind him, if his ship is in a bad state, if he's come to inaugurate the next step of their expansion. They mostly ignore Mulaghesh, who's wearing her black leather greatcoat over her fatigues, hiding the monstrously large electric torch hanging from her shoulder. Saypur has advanced many technologies, but lead acid batteries aren't one of them yet.

There's a collective intake of breath as the ship emerges from the night, a tower of rippling sails on the waves. Some of the sails are rent and tattered, as if the ship's gone through one hell of a fight.

"It's him," whispers one of the Dreylings. "It's him!"

"What has happened to the ship?"

"Are you a *fool*? Have you forgotten that the *dauvkind* swore to drive piracy out of our shores? What else would he be doing?"

Mulaghesh can't help but share their anticipation. Sigrud's one of the few people besides Shara who survived all of Bulikov's madness with her, and he's the one person in the world who might believe that she actually saw a long-dead Divinity last night. But she knows she can't speak to him, not yet. *I have other ugly little deeds to do*, she thinks, and begins walking back toward the harbor works.

As someone who spent the last half decade in the shadow of Shara Komayd, Mulaghesh rarely gets to feel clever. But as she watches the various Dreylings streaming down to the SDC headquarters, she gets to feel a rare flash of brilliance.

Of course the Dreylings are eager to catch the slightest glimpse of their *dauvkind*, their lost (or used-to-be-lost) heir to the throne. Of course that'll make them distracted and reluctant to attend to their duties. And if Mulaghesh ever wanted to sneak behind the iron walls of Signe's test assembly yard, now would be the chance.

Her pulse quickens as she enters the harbor yards. She stands in the shadow of a crane and watches, marking when and where the patrols make their rounds. Moving calmly and smoothly, she dances around the patrols, passing through prep yards, girder yards, cable yards, and finally the pallet yard.

Mulaghesh pauses only once, as she walks beneath the guard tower with the PK-512. She's acquainted enough with that behemoth of a weapon that she checks it out every time, wondering if it might come alive with its hellish chatter. As usual, though, it's unmanned and dormant. She continues on.

The test assembly walls swell up before her. It's quite dark here, as this area is not well lit like the others. She crouches in the shadow of the walls and slowly makes her way down toward the checkpoint. She stops when she sees a Dreyling guard sitting in the booth, smoking anxiously, his rifling slung over his back. He's short for a Dreyling, somewhat rotund, and looks quite irritated.

A second Dreyling approaches, trotting up the path, this one with a closely cropped red-blond beard. "His ship's pulling in now!"

The short Dreyling in the checkpoint booth glowers at him. "Don't tell me that! I don't want to hear about that."

"Surely you can get away for a minute? Löfven and his team are all shutting down for the occasion. They're pulling all their trucks up at the fuel yards." He points northeast, almost right at Mulaghesh. She shrinks up against the wall.

"Would you shut up? You know I cannot leave my post!"

"But certainly yo—"

"You *know* what's in here," says the short Dreyling. "The CTO would drown me if I walked away."

"Ach," says the red-bearded Dreyling, "I suppose that's true. Well. I will see for you, and tell you all about it!" With an excited good-bye, he sprints off for the SDC headquarters.

Mulaghesh thinks, then sneaks back along the walls in the opposite direction. When she hears the roaring of truck engines, she slows.

It's the loading dock of the diesel fuel yard, which happens to back right up into the iron walls. She watches as a dozen large fuel trucks park, their hulking forms lumbering into their spots. It takes nearly twenty minutes for them all to go still. Mulaghesh watches carefully as the drivers hop out and toss their keys into what seems to be a checkout box. Then the supervisor—this Löfven, perhaps—locks the checkout box and follows them down the road.

She looks at the trucks. They're about fifteen, sixteen feet tall. Then she looks at the walls, which are a little more than twenty feet tall.

"Hm," she says.

She waits, then sprints across the loading dock to the checkout box. She never learned to pick locks, and she certainly couldn't do it now, one-handed. So she grabs a nearby prybar, slots it behind the lock's bolt, and gives it a hard shove.

All those one-handed press-ups come in handy, and the lock pops off with a screech. *A lock is only as good,* Mulaghesh thinks, *as whatever it's bolted into.* She grabs a numbered key, finds the right truck, and starts it up.

The fuel truck is a beast to maneuver. She's always hated driving automobiles, especially now that she's one-handed, and she's intensely aware that she's probably now piloting several hundred gallons of highly flammable fluid. But despite all this she slowly, uncertainly backs the truck up to the iron walls. She stops only when the bumper of the truck actually touches the walls themselves.

She jumps out, grabs an oil-stained rope from a trash heap, and clambers up on top of the truck. She runs to the back end where the bumper is up against the wall. The wall is still about seven feet higher than the truck, but she can make it. She ties the rope to a handle on the back of the truck, then hurls it over the wall. It lands on the canvas roof with a *plop.*

She pauses, thinking about how she's going to do this.

"I fucking hate being one-handed," she mutters.

She readies herself, leaps up, and hits the wall high enough to hook her elbows over its top. The canvas is taut but still gives a little, allowing her a good hold. She hangs there for a moment longer, then hitches her right leg up until her ankle can get over the top as well. Then she pulls herself upright, straddling the wall, and breathes for a moment.

She makes sure she's steady, then pops out her combat knife and carves a hole in the canvas wide enough for her to fit through. She glances down into the hole but can see nothing but darkness below. She's glad she brought a torch, even if it does weigh nearly ten pounds.

She throws the rope down. Then she maneuvers the torch around, flicks it on, and shines it down to see if the rope hangs low enough for her to drop down. It does, she sees, but there's . . . something beside it.

Something . . . *wrong*.

"Oh, what in the hells," whispers Mulaghesh.

She grabs the rope with her one hand and slowly, slowly slides down. Once she's inside she flicks the torch back on, turns around, and looks.

"Holy shit," she says.

***

The closest one is fifteen feet tall, a flawless statue of a man seated on the ground, cross-legged. He is perfectly bald and hairless, and his demeanor and posture are calm, relaxed: he sits with his back straight and his palms resting on his knees. Yet there are nine longswords thrust into his sides, back, and stomach, almost to the hilt, their blades poking through in all directions, certainly passing through countless vital organs; but the man stares ahead calmly, serenely, as if holding his breath. He is wrought, she sees, of pale white stone, perhaps marble, but his many crevices have played home to countless crustaceans and barnacles and other sea creatures. His serene face, for example, is marred by a colony of barnacles creeping up his neck and onto his cheekbone, as if he has a skin condition.

In the center of his forehead is a carven insignia: the severed hand grasping the sword blade, the sigil of Voortya.

She stares at this sight, white and ghostly in the light of her torch. He's sitting uneven in the mud, one knee higher than the other, as if dumped here. The mud is covered in track marks, like huge pieces of machinery have been here time and time again.

Mulaghesh gets ahold of herself and looks beyond the statue. The canvas ceiling doesn't allow much light in: the moonlight strikes it and filters through just enough to make it feel like she's in a giant drum, or an animal-skin lantern of some kind, the crisscrossing seams giving it the feeling of veins. As such, she can't see much beyond the light of her torch, but . . . it looks like there are dozens of forms in here with her.

Maybe more than dozens. Maybe hundreds.

Mulaghesh shines the light beyond the white statue of the pierced man to the next object, which appears to be a massive stone table shaped to look like it's made of antlers, bone, and tusks. The table also sits askew in the mud, and its sides are spattered with a thick coating of sand and silt. It's a queerly beautiful sight, and she immediately understands its ritualistic significance: she can see where devotees would kneel before it, the hundreds of tiny stone stanchions intended for tiny candles. There's a basin in its center; maybe someone would wash there, or drink from it.

She walks on, the beam from her torch bouncing over the mud and the other . . . things. Statues, she supposes, but they somehow seem more than statues, as if they are machines or devices with functions hidden to the eye, defying logic.

A column made to look like it's composed of human teeth. A doorway carved to resemble two massive swords leaning together. A throne that seems to have been grown out of coral reef. All of the statues bear clusters of anemones or barnacles or mussels. Many are adorned with drapes and drapes of seaweed, dried and curled against their forms. It gives the statues a queerly somber look, as if in mourning. But nearly all of them are perfectly whole, not a chip or a scratch in them, as far as she can see.

"They're from old Voortyashtan," says Mulaghesh aloud. "They dredged these up from the bottom of the ocean, didn't they?" She remembers Signe saying that the only thing they were dredging up was silt and rubble. Yet these look perfect, as if they were carved just years ago. *Why hasn't anyone heard about this?* Mulaghesh wonders.

She suspects she knows why. As she passes by a sculpture of a black sphere standing, in full defiance of physics, on a narrow column of marble, all the hair on her arms rises up. She can see handprints worn into the sphere, as if it had been gripped in countless places, and some part of her mind irrationally tells her it's *still* being gripped, that whoever held it is *still* holding it, though they're now doing so in some unseen, secret manner.

This all stinks of the Divine, she thinks. And there's nothing that the civilized world would fear more than rumors of the Divine in Voortyashtan.

The next one strikes pure terror into her heart: a white statue of a massive, hulking Voortyashtani sentinel carrying a giant sword. Its back and shoulders are covered in antlers and bones and horns, and its face is the common Voortyashtani sentinel mask, the primitive approximation of human features. The sight of it makes the visions she had in the thinadeskite mines come rushing back to her. She remembers seeing the sentinels' armor, how it seemed queerly organic, intermeshed, and she remembers knowing instantly that their armor fed on blood, that the more they killed the greater their armor became. She takes careful note of this specimen before her, whose armor has grown until it's well out of human proportions, possibly distorting the body within. She hopes its size is an exaggeration: it's nearly four feet taller than a normal man.

She looks at the wide plinth it's standing on. Carved there is the word *Zhurgut.*

She thinks, then takes out her portfolio and looks up the note from Choudhry's room, written by Efrem Pangyui himself.

The blade and hilt of Voortya each had individual meaning to Voortya-shtanis. The blade was attack, assault, aggression, but the hilt, fashioned out of the severed hand of the son of Saint Zhurgut, was a symbol of sacrifice.

"This thing was a saint?" she asks herself. The idea appalls her. This behemoth, bristling with horns and bones and teeth and antlers, is the sort of thing that should haunt dreams. She can't imagine what it would be like to see such a thing in the real world. It would be like glimpsing a . . .

"A nightmare," she whispers.

She remembers Gozha saying, *He cut a fearsome figure, that thing. Like something from a nightmare.*

She switches her torch off, shuts her eyes, lets them adjust, and then opens them.

She looks at Zhurgut's silhouette—a human-like form covered in points.

"A man made of thorns," she says quietly.

Could it be? Could the man Gozha spotted at the charcoal kilns have been dressed like a Voortyashtani sentinel? Mulaghesh herself thought that these murders were part of some ritual, and being dressed like a sentinel could be a part of whatever ritual it might be.

But Gozha also said the man she saw was huge and fearsome, the sort of person one would notice, uncommon in Voortyashtan. People like this don't *exist* anymore. No one gets this big naturally, not without the aid of the Divine.

She thinks about the mutilation of the corpses at the farmhouse, performed in the exact same manner that sentinels did over eighty years ago to Saypuri slaves.

Are you honestly considering, Mulaghesh says to herself, *that a real, live Voortyashtani sentinel committed these atrocities? How could one have possibly survived?*

Mulaghesh jumps as a loud *clank* echoes across the statues. Bright white light comes spilling in from everywhere. She looks around and sees a handful of electric bulbs fluttering to life along the walls. "What the . . . ?"

There's the groan of metal far back behind her. She turns and sees the giant iron door slowly start to swing open.

"Fuck," she mutters. She finds cover behind the sculpture of Saint Zhurgut, shrinks down behind its plinth, and waits, listening.

She can hear voices, footsteps. Two sets, she thinks, squelching in the mud.

She hears Signe's voice saying, ". . . unsure what the material makeup is. It is not conventional stone. Whatever it is, it's clearly different from the statues that line the shore of the Solda. We're presuming for now that the two types of statues had two very different purposes, one utilitarian, one decoration. The ones on the shore of the Solda were decoration, and thus were made of ordinary stone, which hasn't held up well to the change in climate. These are much . . . Well. More durable. Much more dense. Our dredgers didn't even make a dent in them. We can't even chip off a piece for sample. They must have used some kind of craftsmanship that we've never experienced before. We assume it must not have been *Divine,* because if it was then these should have all turned to dust when Voortya died. It seems the Voortyashtanis of old had many secrets, even beyond those of their Divinity."

Mulaghesh pokes her head around the statue of Zhurgut. She sees Signe talking to a richly dressed Dreyling, a man in dark red robes wearing a ceremonial fur hat with lots of gold embroidering. Signe looks very pale, very still, and very awkward, which is unusual, as her ample charisma has always filled any room.

Mulaghesh can't imagine why this man upsets her, in his white fur gloves and white fur boots and white fur belt. He's an absolute fop, if Mulaghesh must say so; but it isn't until he turns to scratch his cheek that she sees the bright gold eye patch covering up one eye.

Oh, by the seas, she thinks. *It's Sigrud.*

She keeps watching, dumbfounded, staring at his rich, ridiculous clothing, the rings on his fingers, the chain dangling from his neck.

Holy hells, she thinks, *he looks like a fucking parade float!*

***

It takes all of her effort not to burst out laughing. She could never have imagined Shara Komayd's most trusted assassin dressed in such a manner in her life.

Then he speaks, and his voice is the same, tremendously low and scratchy, as if it's been marinating in dark ale. "And what," he says slowly, "were they used for?"

"What?" says Signe, irritated. "The statues?"

"Yes," he says. "You said they were utilitarian. What was their use?"

"We have no idea. No idea what they did, or if they're doing anything now." The answer is curt, impatient, even downright rude. Signe seems to realize this, for she continues: "We've noticed a name carved on each of the statues, sometimes in an unobtrusive place. Some of us believe that these are memorials, of a sort—works of art commissioned in honor of the departed. Some are different—we found some that were small chambers, resembling little tombs. You can see one there, a modest little box of a structure—but they contain nothing that appears to have supported a body. Only . . . weaponry."

"Weaponry?"

"Well, one weapon apiece. There is a plinth inside each little tomb that seems designed to hold a sword. But we've found no swords. Perhaps they too vanished in the Blink, or were washed out to sea when old Voortyashtan fell apart."

Sigrud stares around at the statues, quiet. Perhaps provoked by his silence, Signe goes on: "We have used our contact at the fortress to procure a list of Divine tests. Methods that can be used to determine the Divine nature of any . . . phenomenon, or object, or whatever. All the statues tested as negative. That should suffice, shouldn't it?"

He is silent.

"Shouldn't it?" she says again, angrier.

"I heard," he says quietly, "that someone once shot at you."

"What?"

"Someone shot at you. Clipped your hair. Is this true?"

"Oh. That. Yes, that happened some time ago. We've taken extra security measures since."

"And the bombing? The explosives? You considered this a threat as well?" He looks at her, his one eye shining strangely.

"Yes," says Signe, her words harsh and clipped. "But such fears proved unfounded. So. Back to the issue at hand. Our security *here* has thus far been airtight. If it wasn't, the tribal leaders would be all over us to force us to hand the statues over. As it is, my current intent is to use these statues as collateral to force the tribal leaders to give us shipping rights on the harbor. Otherwise we will report their existence to the Ministry, and, this being Voortyashtan, I have no doubt the Ministry would wish to confiscate and review them. Extensively. They'd stay in Saypuri hands indefinitely."

Silence.

"Do you think our current strategy is wise?" she asks. "Or do you wish to . . . correct it for me?"

Sigrud is quiet for a long, long time.

"Well?" says Signe.

Finally he shrugs. "I trust what you are doing."

She stares at him, surprised and suspicious. "You . . . do? You . . . You think this is a good idea?"

"I did not say *that*. If it were me I'd throw all this shit back in the ocean. I hate everything Divine, dead or not. But it is not me. It is *you*. And if you think this is a good idea, then I will let you do as you see fit."

Signe is so taken aback by this that she's lost for words. Then: "Why?"

"Why what?"

"Why are you willing to let me do this, if you think it's a bad idea?"

"Because . . ." He gives a great sigh. "I think you are good at this."

"You don't seem too happy about it."

Sigrud is quiet yet again.

"I get quite sick of your silences," says Signe. "They aren't nearly as clever as you think they are."

"I am not being clever. I just do not know what to say." He pauses.

"I want to ask . . . How . . . How many times has someone tried to kill you here?"

"Why?"

"Because I wish to know."

"I don't think that matters."

"I do."

She snorts, contemptuous.

"More than once, then. Do you think this is worth it?" he asks. "Is it acceptable, to risk your life to build this? If you died here, on the shores of this country, below these cranes, would you feel you spent your life well?"

Signe crosses her arms and looks away. "This is an abrupt change in your disposition."

"Why? Should I not be concerned about my daughter's welfare?"

"Do you have any idea," says Signe, suddenly furious, "how many times someone tried to kill me and mother and Carin when we *lived* here? Do you know how many times we almost *starved* to death? Yet I did not see any sign of your concern then."

A long pause.

"We . . ." Sigrud struggles for words. "We have *had* this conversation. We—"

"We had *your* conversation," says Signe. "The conversation *you* wanted to have with everyone, in front of everyone. How absolutely absurd it is that you—the man who has risked his life for all kinds of murderous, horrible reasons—are suddenly asking if it's wise for me to do the same for somewhat decent ones!"

Sigrud is torn, it seems, between frustration and shock. "I forget how young you are sometimes."

"No," she says. "What you forget is that you don't really know me at all." She checks her watch. "I need to confirm with Biswal and Nadar that they're ready to receive you. You may stay here if you like, and see yourself out as soon as you see fit." Then, without so much as a glance back that Mulaghesh can see, she strides away from her father through the forest of statues and out the iron door, which shuts with a *clang* behind her.

Sigrud gives a great, sad sigh. He stares up at the canvas roof, contemplative and melancholy. Then he says aloud, "All right, Turyin. You can come out now."

***

Mulaghesh pokes her head up. "How long have you known I was here?"

"From the start," says Sigrud. His scarred, battered face is still doleful. "Your boot polish . . . You use too much of it. I'd recognize the smell anywhere."

"It always creeped me out, how you could catch a scent like that." Mulaghesh stands, wipes some of the mud off of her pants, and walks over to him. "Thanks for not ratting me out, I guess."

He shrugs. "It is no affair of mine. I assume Signe did not wish to tell you what was in these walls?"

"Yeah. I chose to come see for myself." She pauses, feeling fiercely awkward. "I'm sorry I overheard all that."

"Yes . . . My adjustment to public life"—he holds out his arms and looks at his clothing—"is not quite as easy as I'd hoped it'd be. For anyone."

"Yeah, you look . . ." She holds back a cringe. "You do look different."

"These damned things . . . *Pah!*" He rips off his fur hat and eye patch and tosses them away. When he turns back his left eye is once again the familiar hooded, empty socket. "I feel more like a human without them."

"That was probably, like, a two-hundred-drekel hat."

"These old specters can have it." He looks up at the giant stone images, leaning over them like predators. "By the seas. Look at them. To imagine my country would one day spend blood and treasure to haul such things from the ocean . . ."

"Your girl's got a pretty cunning idea, though," says Mulaghesh. She walks up to Saint Zhurgut, strikes a match on the statue, and lights a cigarillo. "Blackmailing the tribes might work. And she has some damned brass in her blood, too. Hiding these things right under the nose of Fort Thinadeshi . . . I'd be impressed if I wasn't so pissed."

"She is a very cunning, clever thing. As I said, she is very good at what she does." There's another uncomfortable pause. He looks her over. "You seem to be doing well."

"As do you. You must have done pretty good for yourself during the coup."

"Ah," says Sigrud, waving a hand. "It was hardly a coup for me. I barely struck a blow. It was like a courtly dance, so many pre-arranged steps, and I merely had to move from one to the next. Shara did all the real work, though no one knew."

"As usual."

"As usual, yes. What about you, have you seen any action?"

"Not a jot. They stuck me behind a desk. Then after I quit I stuck myself behind a bottle. So no new scars or limbs lost, or at least not yet. You look like you're all in one piece, or at least what I can see above those kingly robes does."

"Eh. Not quite." He pulls his left lip down, revealing an utter dearth of back molars on the left side of his jaw. Mulaghesh can see extensive scar tissue around the lip, suggesting a broken jawbone.

"Holy hells. Did you try and catch a cannonball with your face?"

"A carpenter's hammer. Makes eating soup difficult these days, and drinking even more so. Three years ago, we boarded the ship of the pirate Lindibier . . . do you know this man? Lindibier?"

"'Fraid not."

"Well." He considers it thoughtfully. "He was a real piece of shit."

"Okay."

"Anyway, we board, we kill, well, almost everyone, and then there's just the cabin boy, hiding down in the aft. I walk over to him, he's, what, fourteen? I take pity on him. I ask him, 'You need food? Water?' And he looks at me, and he leaps at me, and then . . .￼" He taps the side of his head. "He could swing a hammer, for a boy." He looks away, wistful. "I strangled him and threw his body in the ocean. Let the fish turn him to shit as fast as they could. It took time for me to recover. That was when they made me a chancellor. Or my wife did. To save my life, she said."

"Your wife?"

"Hild. Yes. She's . . ." He is quiet for some time. ". . . like Shara. Or Signe. A very, eh, cunning person. She's a chancellor, too. Just a more important one than me—the sort of chancellor that makes other chancellors. Which she did, to me. But I know what I'm good for. I just want to hunt meat and chase pirates. But they've had me behind a desk. Stuck me in a big, nice office where I never see anyone, and no one ever sees me. Though I insisted I come out when Kvarnström attacked a village. Do you know him? The pirate Kvarnström?"

Mulaghesh shakes her head.

"Oh. Well. He is a real piece of shit."

"I'm sensing a theme."

"Yes. We had been so caught up in this harbor thing, our dicks big and hard thinking of money, we had forgotten how to deal with pirates. The pirates took us, what, two years to get under control? Three? And then we forget it all, stumbling all over ourselves to do this job. Anyway, I hopped on a ship and took pursuit. We almost caught him, about sixty miles from here. But he damaged our mast with a chainshot, a cowardly way to fight."

"I heard something about that," she says, suspecting why Sigrud's wife might not want someone who casually uses the phrase "dicks big and hard thinking of money" in the public eye. "So you're actually here because your ship got damaged?"

"Partially. Some months ago Signe sent a signal to the UDS asking if she had approval to move forward with this tactic. I wanted to see what was going on, and a damaged ship is a good excuse. Besides, what are you doing here? This is a strange place for you to be, isn't it?"

"Shara," she says, as if that explains everything.

"Ah. Was you quitting part of her game?"

"No. That was my choice. She just dragged me back in."

"A bad thing, to haul an old warrior back onto the field. What game is she playing now?"

She's relieved Sigrud doesn't ask about the circumstances of her exit, as she's so tired of fielding questions about it. "They discovered some kind of ore or metal or whatever up near the fort. Shara's concerned it might be Divine."

The two of them sit on the plinth of Saint Zhurgut, and she summarizes the generalities of Sumitra Choudhry's investigation and disappearance. He listens intently, smoking his pipe—his *old* pipe, she notices, not a fine little ivory piece but the filthy, scarred, oaken thing he was always carrying around. And suddenly Mulaghesh feels more relaxed and more open than she's felt in weeks. It takes her a moment to realize she might be being more honest with him than she should, but she doesn't care. She and Sigrud passed through fire and death together, and spent weeks recuperating in a hospital outside Bulikov, trapped in their beds. Though she still holds a grudge against him for making a fast and mostly full recovery— which astonished the doctors, who had all written him off as either permanently crippled or, much more likely in their opinions, soon to be dead. Mulaghesh's recuperation was far longer and far more excruciating, fighting infections and trying to keep what was left of her arm.

He thinks for a long while when she's finished. "What kind of ore is this, again?"

"It's an electrical conductor. Like, what they use to make the electric lights work. They think they can use it to . . . I don't know, power more of them, do it easier, faster."

Sigrud stares at her blankly. "Faster? How would they make light . . . faster?"

"Hells, I don't know. It's some engineering shit. I told them they were sending the wrong person, but they squeezed my plums, so to speak."

He shakes his head, staring around at the statues and the form of SDC peeking just over the walls. "Look at this world they shoved us into." He looks up at a bone-white arch. "Maybe they should leave us in here, with this graveyard of relics."

"Hey, it might not all be new. I saw something last night. . . . Something that's probably only familiar to Shara, you, and m—"

Before she can speak further the iron door swings back open. They both look up to see Signe walk through.

Signe sees them and stops in her tracks. Then she gives a savage little nod, as though to say, *As I expected, all along.* She resumes walking toward them. "Well," she says. "Isn't this a delight."

Why is it that, despite us being decades older than her, thinks Mulaghesh, *I feel like we're two children caught causing mischief?* She stands and says, "Evening, CTO Harkvaldsson. Lovely night, isn't it?"

"I will presume it was *you* that broke into the fuel yard checkbox, stole a truck, and vaulted over the walls."

"Is it really stealing if you never take it off the lot?"

"I could have you shot, you know."

Sigrud stands. "Well, n—"

"Try it," says Mulaghesh. "Then try explaining *where* I was shot. Looking around me it seems like you're in a much more vulnerable position than I am, CTO Harkvaldsson."

"As a Saypuri, I would imagine you'd be quite concerned about keeping Divine artifacts like this closely watched."

"True, and as a Saypuri, I think it was damn shitty of you not to tell us you had these. Though I can understand you wouldn't want us taking your trump card. Then what would you play against the tribes?"

Signe's brow creases, wondering how Mulaghesh understood her intent.

"I was hiding over there," Mulaghesh says, gesturing with the cigarillo. "I heard everything."

Signe turns bright pink. "How dare you! That . . . That . . ." She looks to her father. "Aren't you going to say *anything?*"

Sigrud shrugs, bewildered. "What do you wish me to say?"

"Something authoritative and helpful, to start! How ridiculous it is that you must ask *me* what to say when this woman has breached *our* personal privacy!"

"This isn't some family secret," says Mulaghesh. "Or a company trick of the trade. All this shit is a national security threat, CTO Harkvaldsson."

"They're just statues," says Signe indignantly. "We've tested them for any trace of the Divine and found none. If they registered as Divine I would have alerted the fortress immediately."

"Right, if they registered using the tests you *procured* from Thinadeshi," says Mulaghesh. "Do you want me to go sniffing around up there for your source?"

Signe pales a little at that. "This has nothing to do with Sumitra Choudhry."

"Are you so sure? Are you hiding any other secrets from me now, Signe? Or is this the only one? Because a fine way to search your operation top to bottom would be to tug on Biswal's coat about this and have him take the harbor apart out of sheer paranoia."

Signe opens her mouth, aghast, then looks at her father. "This . . . This woman is putting our nation at risk. Everything will fall apart if the harbor project isn't finished. Are you going to idly stand by?"

"You are a cunning creature, Signe," says Sigrud. "Smart enough to know when you're backed into a corner. If you have something to tell her, tell her."

Signe sighs, exasperated. "I have told you *everything* I know about Choudhry. I have always been aboveboard on that subject!"

"Look me in the eye," says Mulaghesh, stepping closer, "and tell me that."

Signe's glacial eyes burn brightly. "I promise. I *promise*, General."

Mulaghesh holds her gaze for a moment, then nods. "All right. I believe you. For now."

"And . . . And the statues . . . Will you, ah . . ."

"Tattle? Maybe. I haven't made up my mind yet. I have fatter lambs to cook at the moment, and doing something like that would just complicate things."

"I suppose I'll have to accept that for the time being. If we are all done threatening one another, can I *please* escort my father to meet with Biswal? And where is your hat?"

Sigrud shrugs. "The wind took it."

"Oh, well. We'll find you a replacement. Come on. Let's go."

The three of them begin to exit the yard. Sigrud coughs and mutters about how after this he'll be happy to return to the headquarters for a night's rest.

"Your rooms are already prepared for you," says Signe curtly. "You will have the lighthouse suite."

"Oh," he says.

"It's the nicest suite in the building," she says. Mulaghesh isn't sure how, but Signe manages to pack a lot of animosity into this statement.

"I do not need that," says Sigrud. "I have slept in far worse pla—"

"I know you have," she says. "That's not the point. The point is that you are the *dauvkind,* and everyone here will expect you to be treated as such. If I stuck you in one of the laborers' quarters they would think I was being disrespectful."

"Then . . . I will tell them not to think these things!" says Sigrud, bristling. "I will tell them to mind their own business!"

"And you can't do that, either! Then it will look as if you're trying to cover for me. You aren't just a nobody anymore! People expect things from you!"

"You sound like your mother," says Sigrud.

"If by that you mean I sound *intelligent,* then yes, I do, and I will take it as a compli—"

Mulaghesh stops listening. She hasn't been to this part of the yard yet, so she hasn't seen the massive, fifteen-foot statue that rests up against the iron wall. The very sight makes her stop where she stands and sends a shard of ice shooting into her heart.

She knows it immediately. Of course she does. Did she not see a much larger version of that carven figure just last night, rising from the sea to place her giant hand upon the cliffs? Weren't every one of

the ghastly illustrations on that plate mail burned into Mulaghesh's
memory, a solid wall of unimaginable violence?

"Voortya," whispers Mulaghesh.

She stares at the statue. It's so pale the light almost seems to filter
through it, like it was made from the purest of snows. The statue
stands on a plinth, but set before it is a wide bowl, almost like a claw-
footed bathtub. Carved into the bottom of the plinth are many titles:

EMPRESS OF GRAVES

MAIDEN OF STEEL

DEVOURER OF CHILDREN

QUEEN OF GRIEF

SHE WHO CLOVE THE EARTH IN TWAIN

She wonders how anyone could ever come to love and worship
such a thing. But then she realizes: *Because they won.* It's as Biswal
once said to her, during the gray, savage days of the Yellow March,
outside Dzermir: "War is a hell beyond anything the Continentals
and their gods could ever dream of. It behooves us to act accordingly.
Those who accept it for what it is will be the victor."

And the Voortyashtanis, perhaps, were all too happy to accept it
for what it was. They embraced it, made a nation out of it, a whole
culture birthed out of the willingness to inflict the unimaginable horrors of war. And, having done so, they won, over and over again.
They survived the Divine Wars and went on to conquer nearly every
piece of territory in the world.

Of course they loved her. No matter how cruel or indifferent, she
helped them win.

Mulaghesh wanders forward, staring into that cold, still face. She
remembers hearing that Voortya never spoke, not to the other Divinities, nor to her followers. *But she wouldn't need to, would she? Just
look into that face, and you'll understand all you need. . . .*

She notices something moving before the statue. It's a tremor in
the air, like a heat haze, like there's a fire on the ground but she can't
see it. She squints at the disturbance, trying to track its source.

But *was* there a fire on the ground once? The mud below the tremor still bears charred sticks and a smattering of gray ashes, as if someone once camped here.

Mulaghesh's brain starts whirring. *Just like in the thinadeskite tunnels. Did Sumitra Choudhry come here to perform her miracle, too?*

She walks over, eager to see if there's any sign of burned rosemary or dried frog eggs.

But as she rushes over, things . . . change.

Mulaghesh stops and looks up into the face of Voortya.

The world goes still.

There is someone in the statue. It's the strangest of sensations, but it's undeniable: there is a mind there, an agency, watching.

"There's someone in there," she whispers.

"What?" says Signe's voice, faraway.

She stares deeper into the empty, vacant gaze. "There's someone behind those eyes. There's someone . . . looking *back*."

The statue of Voortya seems to lean forward to her. And then she sees the sea.

***

Dark waters churn under the light of the yellow moon. She plunges down into the sea, down, down, through the rippling depths and the glimmering spears of moonlight, the swirls of bubbles and the flick of distant fish.

The light changes below her, as if there is a second moon and a second sky at the bottom of the sea, and this moon is not yellow but white, white, the purest white.

She bursts through dark waters, rises up into this second sky, and sees . . .

An island resting on the horizon, surrounded by mists. Strange peaks cut through the clouds gathered about it, like the growths of coral.

There are voices in the night: *Mother, Mother. Why did you leave us?*

The island speeds up to her. Beaches white as bone, delicate as mother-of-pearl, and rising from those strange sands is a mass of enormous structures, massive towers that have the look of chitin and claw. Some of the buildings, she sees, are not buildings at all, but *statues,* bigger than the biggest skyscraper in Ghaladesh, so vast she can hardly see their tops. . . .

Mother. We loved you. We love you. Please, give us what you promised us.

Mulaghesh floats through the white city. The cold white moon fills the dark sky above her. She thinks: *Am I really here? Have I been brought here?* She finds she cannot say. She simply drifts through this strange, bloodless world of bulging structures that rise to become curling, delicate towers, a world of massive, silent giants concealed by the clouds.

Yet then she realizes she is not alone.

The streets and beaches ahead are filled with people. . . . But not normal people. She needs only glance at the hundreds of points on their shoulders and backs to see what they really are.

Thousands and thousands of Voortyashtani sentinels stand perfectly still in the moonlight, shoulder to shoulder in the streets and the city squares and on the distant beaches. Mulaghesh nearly screams, terrified, certain that these monstrous creatures will turn and tear her to pieces. But they do not. Instead they watch the horizon, their thorned hands resting on the pommels of their massive swords, staring at something high up above them.

Please, Mother, they whisper. *Please, speak to us.*

Mulaghesh drifts among these malformed warriors, staring at their skeletal masks and their hideous armor, half antlers and half seashell. Then she slowly follows their gaze.

They are staring at a tall, white tower at the center of the city. At the very peak of the tower is a balcony, and though she knows that in waking life her eyes would never be this clear, she can see someone up there, pacing back and forth.

Mother, they say. *Come to us.*

Then one of the massive statues ahead of her . . . shifts. Just the barest of movements, the tiniest twitch, yet she knows she saw it. The statue is turned away from her, but she recognizes this figure, gleaming in the moonlight—didn't she pour all of her carousel into that very thing no more than two nights ago?

Voortya, she thinks.

Beautiful and terrible and resplendent, cruelty incarnate, Voortya stands up straight in the mist. To see such a massive figure move so silently fills Mulaghesh's heart with pure terror.

Then the goddess slowly turns, twisting her head around as if she heard someone mention her name.

No, no, thinks Mulaghesh. *No, please, no . . .*

The dark, blank eyes turn to face her.

Mother, whisper the sentinels. *Mother, Mother . . .*

Then there's a voice just over Mulaghesh's shoulder: "Are you *supposed* to be here?"

She turns to see something huge standing over her, a towering creature of chrome and metal. Before she can open her mouth to scream she's suddenly plunging into the ocean again.

Up, up, up. Back through the swirling dark waters, rocketing up to the fluttering light of the yellow moon.

She bursts through, and the world spins around her.

***

"Turyin?" says Sigrud's voice. "Turyin!"

She feels cold mud on the back of her neck and realizes that the back of her head hurts. She draws breath into her lungs and is suddenly racked with coughs.

"General Mulaghesh?" says Signe's voice. "Are . . . Are you all right?"

She opens her eyes and sees, to her horror, pale white statues standing over her . . . but they're the ones from the harbor yard, not the massive, terrifying things she glimpsed in the other place.

But what *was* that other place?

I know what it was, she says to herself, terrified. *I know where I just went.*

Sigrud's face appears above her. He kneels to help her. "Turyin? Say something, if you can."

"It's still there," she says, gasping. "It's real. . . ."

"What? What is?"

She feels herself growing weak, as if what she saw bruised her very mind. Before she passes out she tries to shout to them, "The City of Blades! It's still there! *The City of Blades is still there!*"

But before she can, darkness takes her.

Life is but a prelude to death. Other worlds await.

Live your life and choose your path knowing this secret. We shall all find one another past the dark veil at the edge of this land. We shall embrace one another on distant white shores and celebrate our final victory.

—WRITS OF SAINT ZHURGUT, 721

9.
a bLast of siLeNce

She wakes with a start and realizes she's screaming. She sits up and her hand goes to her hip for the carousel, but it's not there. She slowly realizes she's lying on her bed in her room in SDC.

"For the love of . . . ," says Signe's voice from nearby. "What is the *matter* with you?"

Mulaghesh's head snaps to the side to see Signe sitting in a chair in the corner. From the pile of black cigarette butts in the ashtray on the floor beside it she's been there for a while.

"The fuck are you doing?" asks Mulaghesh. She sniffs and rubs her eye. "Keeping vigil?"

"Looking after you. You passed out like you had some episode or something. I chose to keep an eye on you while my father began to make the formal rounds."

"Shit." Mulaghesh sits forward and rubs the center of her forehead. It feels like insects are trying to gnaw their way out of her skull.

"Head hurt?" says Signe.

"Shut the fuck up for a second."

"Mm. Aren't you a pleasant creature in the morning. Though it's closer to noon."

Mulaghesh replays the last thing she saw in her head—or what she *thought* she saw. That moment, that vision, felt like it was beyond seeing, as if she experienced that world with senses beyond the common five.

Her pulse rises immediately. *It's still there. The City of Blades is still out there . . . somehow.*

It's an absurd idea, yet what she saw doesn't leave a trace of doubt in her mind. To say otherwise would be like walking through a rainstorm for the first time in your life and then denying you were ever wet.

There's another world out there, she thinks. *There's a place below this one, floating on an ocean underneath reality.*

She thinks of the sentinels, the dismembered bodies, Gozha whispering about the man made of thorns, and everything starts to suggest a dreadful idea to her.

And maybe the boundaries are beginning to blur.

"Are you all right?" says Signe, worried. "Is it . . . Are you having flashbacks?"

"What?" snaps Mulaghesh.

"Flashbacks. You're a soldier. I know . . . What is it they call it . . . War echoes? Battle echoes?"

"Where's your dad? With Biswal?"

"No," says Signe. "That was canceled. And that's another reason why I'm here. There's been a . . . development."

"Which is?"

"They've . . . found another body. Or *parts* of another body. Much as you found them at the farmhouse, or so I'm told, but these were on the cliffs west of the fortress." Signe sucks at a cigarette hard enough for Mulaghesh to hear the crackle across the room. "It's a Saypuri woman. It was, I mean."

The pulsing in her ears goes silent.

"Choudhry?" she asks quietly.

"I don't know, I'm afraid. They haven't found the head. A patrol discovered it on the cliffs west of the fortress, just where she used to walk. It seems . . . likely."

"Where's the body now?"

"The"—Signe searches for the right word—"parts are with Rada. I suggested to Biswal that this would be wise, as she's the medical expert here, and I thought you'd wish to do a dissection."

"Autopsy."

"Yes. One of those. He consented. The rest of the fortress is quite busy with the collapse of the installation, or so it appears, so he was happy to give this duty to you. He mentioned that there are rather a lot of dead Saypuris for him to worry about these days."

Mulaghesh tries to leap out of bed, but her legs fail and she almost plummets to the floor.

"By the seas . . ." Signe stands and helps her up. Mulaghesh is surprised at how strong she is. "You're not well."

"You're damned right I'm not well! Where's my weapon?"

Signe retrieves the carousel from a drawer and hands it to her. "Off to duel with someone, General?"

"You see your father, you tell him I want to see him," says Mulaghesh, holstering the pistol.

"And what shall I tell him you wish to see him for?"

Mulaghesh tries to think of how to say this without sounding barking mad. "Tell him it's Ministry work. Just tell him that."

***

Two hours later Mulaghesh knocks on the front door of Rada Smolisk's house. It's pouring rain, a bitter thunderstorm suddenly springing on them from offshore, and Mulaghesh is thankful she wore her peaked cap today. Rada's house is nestled in a small forest just below the clifftops on the northwest side of the city, so it's somewhat equidistant between the Galleries and fortress, perhaps as a grand metaphor for Rada's difficult position. The home also overlooks the harbor yards, which lie about five hundred yards below. Mulaghesh can even see the yard of statues, including the tiny hole she carved in its canvas roof last night.

Rada answers her front door wearing a ridiculous and quite ugly fur dress, which she almost completely jumps out of when she sees Mulaghesh standing on her door. "G-General! You're up. I h-heard you w-weren't w—"

"Another body?" says Mulaghesh. "Another one?"

Rada nods solemnly. "I'm afraid so. A woman, this time. A S-Saypuri. Biswal and Nadar did g-g-give me p-permission to perform an a-a-uhhh-autopsy, though they s-said to w-wait for—"

"Show me."

"Certainly. C-Come in."

Mulaghesh brushes rain off her sleeves and steps over the threshold. The front room is dark, messy, and was obviously never intended to receive visitors, as every surface is concealed by tottering towers of books and cups of tea. It's terribly cold inside, a common symptom of a lonely house, in Mulaghesh's experience. But most curiously, Rada's walls are covered in taxidermied animals: sparrows, thrashing fish, the heads of deer and hogs and certain mountain cats. It's as if all the fauna of the hillsides crept down her walls and suddenly found themselves frozen.

Mulaghesh says, "Uh. Do you hunt?"

"No. W-Why? Oh, yes, the a-animals. No. Th-Those I do m-myself."

"You . . . stuff them yourself?"

"Oh, y-yes. It's a hobby of m-mine. There's a lot of hunters here, and they t-tend to d-d-discard much of animals. I f-find a way to use them. I pr-practice in these r-rooms, through here," she says, leading Mulaghesh through a door. On the other side is a much more normal space—a white, plain, medical office one would normally expect to see when looking for a doctor. "N-no one, um, ever actually c-c-comes to the other d-door."

"Oh. I'm, uh, sorry." She coughs. "I didn't realize."

"No, it's qu-quite all right."

Rada's taxidermy skills are still on display here, though in a more restrained capacity: the snarling head of a boar and a duck in mid-flight hang on the walls just beside the entry door. Rada asks Mulaghesh to wait while she changes into something more functional. "The body is qu-kwuhhite, uh, m-messy you see."

"I see." Mulaghesh takes off her rain-slick greatcoat and hangs it in the corner.

Rada withdraws while Mulaghesh sits and thinks. She's more dismayed than she expected: she'd thought for some time that Choudhry was dead, and then after that she thought she was somehow involved in the murders. But to hear she was desecrated so abominably is something Mulaghesh never expected.

Rada returns, now dressed in dark tan clothing with a rubber apron. "She's in the b-back room. If you're r-ready."

"I am."

Rada nods and leads her through the door. On the other side is a small room that looks fit for surgical or perhaps funerary purposes, and in the center is a large stone slab with drainage holes in it. On the slab are . . .

Things. That's all her brain can process them as: items. Objects. Fragments of something. Not a person, certainly not a human being, because she simply can't conceive of such a thing. To see a fellow person cut down to such crude elements is dehumanizing beyond words.

She tries to get ahold of herself. She focuses, and looks.

On the table are two torso halves. Dark-skinned, breasts withered and sagging. The hint of thick pubic hair at the crotch. A woman vivisected carefully and cleanly, her arms and legs pruned away. Only her left thigh remains, but this segment too has been dismembered, placed close to the hip as if to try to give these ravaged pieces of a human the semblance of a whole. It only highlights the monstrousness of all of this.

"It's the s-same as you saw," says Rada. "Yes?"

"Yeah," says Mulaghesh quietly. "Close. But they left the heads and limbs behind the other times."

"We're not wuh-wrong that it's a S-Saypuri woman, th-though?"

Mulaghesh shakes her head. "No. Even though she's bloodless now, the skin's the right tone. They found her on the cliffs?"

"Y-Yes. Where the m-missing M-Ministry officer used t-t-to walk, or so I'm t-told."

She looks at Rada, breathing hard. "And you can do an autopsy?"

"P-partially, yes. Th-the b-body isn't f-fresh, so to suh-speak, but . . . I can t-try. What do you hope t-to find?"

"Anything. Something. I want to find something to use to pin these bastards down."

Rada nods meekly. "Then we'll begin."

Mulaghesh takes a seat on the far wall and pulls up a second chair to prop her feet up. She slouches in the chair, hands resting on her stomach, and watches, much as someone would a spectator sport, as Rada Smolisk carefully and thoughtfully dissects the once-human husk lying on her table. It is not, as Mulaghesh feared, an inhuman, monstrous violation; rather, Rada makes remarks throughout her examination more suggestive of a boat trip through a pleasant and familiar countryside.

"Remarkably clean cuts," she says quietly. "Almost surgical. Yet even surgical cuts, on this large of a scale, would leave . . . how shall I put this . . . sawing marks. It takes work, getting through so much tissue. And yet there's none here. It's as if she's been put through a mill saw." She rummages about for some ghastly instrument to aid her.

She doesn't stutter while she works, Mulaghesh notes. It's as if such close interaction with the corpse transforms her into a completely different person, someone much more confident and focused than she is in waking life.

Mulaghesh herself can hardly focus at all. Through the hours of the autopsy—and it takes far longer than she expected—the echoes of her vision keep screaming in her head. Now that she's faced with yet another corpse—again, mutilated as a Voortyashtani sentinel would do—she feels as if the entire world is about to fall apart, and they shall all go plummeting into the inky dark sea, past columns of glimmering moonlight, to a strange white island on the other side of reality. . . .

Are they coming through? Are the sentinels poking through bit by bit, to attack anyone they can find? And how is this even possible, if Voortya's dead?

"I very rarely have an audience for this," Rada says absently. Her brow is wet with sweat. It must be hard work, Mulaghesh realizes, parsing through all the bone and muscle walls.

Mulaghesh rubs her eyes, trying to focus. "Does an audience make it any better?"

"Perhaps. It's something I feel better having a witness for, this sort of thing. It's remarkable, isn't it?"

"What? The corpse?"

"No. Well, yes, in a way. It's this . . . this opportunity to examine what we are, the many disparate and curious elements that make up our beings." There is a *snap* of breaking bone. "So many systems, so many pieces . . . More complicated than the most complicated of clocks. I wonder, sometimes: are we truly one thing, one being, or many, many different things, simply dreaming they are one?"

"I guess that's a good point," says Mulaghesh, feeling surprised, impressed, and somewhat discomfited. She wonders if Rada always pontificates during such procedures, either to her trapped patients or to the empty walls.

"What do you think, looking at her?" asks Rada.

"That she could have been one of mine."

"Interesting. If I might ask—how does it make you feel?"

"How I feel? Like I want to find out who did this."

"You feel a responsibility to her, then? More than you would any other person?"

"Of course I do."

"Why?"

"We've asked these kids to come all the way across the world to fight and labor for us. Someone has to look after them." *And yet*, a tiny voice says inside of her, *you walked away from the job that could have helped you do that the most.*

Shut up, thinks Mulaghesh.

Does it feel better, being alone? Does it really?

Shut up!

"A thoughtful position," says Rada as she works. "Few possess your capacity for self-reflection, General. We are beautiful, strange creatures of heat and noise, of sudden, inscrutable impulses, of savage passions." She sets down a knife, grabs some kind of miniature saw. "Yet when we consider our own existence, we think ourselves calm, composed, rational, in control. . . . All the while forgetting that we are at the mercy of these rebellious, hidden systems—and the elements, of course. And when the elements have their way, and the tiny fire within us flickers out . . ." An unpleasant cracking sound as Rada separates something from the body that should never be separated. "What then? A blast of silence, probably, and no more."

Mulaghesh can't help but say it, as the subject weighs so heavily on her mind: "You don't believe in an afterlife?"

"No," says Rada. "I do not."

"Sort of strange, a Continental who doesn't believe in an afterlife."

"Perhaps the Divinities made one for us, once," says Rada. "But they are gone now, aren't they?"

Mulaghesh does not voice her extreme concerns about this.

"I wonder how cheated the dead must have felt when that afterlife evaporated around them," says Rada. "It's like it's a game," she says softly. "And no matter how you play it, it ends unfairly."

"The ending's not the point," says Mulaghesh.

"Oh? I thought you were a soldier. Is it not your purpose, to make endings? Is it not your duty to make these"—she taps the corpse—"from the soldiers of the enemy?"

"That's a gross perversion of the idea of soldiering," says Mulaghesh.

"Then please," says Rada, looking up. "Enlighten me."

She is not being sarcastic or combative, Mulaghesh realizes. Rather, she is willing to follow any string of conversation down the path it leads, much like she's willing to follow a damaged vein through a desiccated corpse.

The surgery room is quiet as Mulaghesh thinks, the silence broken only by the tinkle of Rada's utensils and the soft hush of the rain.

"The word everyone forgets," says Mulaghesh, "is 'serve.'"

"Serve?"

"Yes. Serve. This is the service, and we soldiers are servants. Sure, when people think of a soldier, they think of soldiers taking.

They think of us taking territory, taking the enemy, taking a city or a country, taking treasure, or blood. This grand, abstract idea of 'taking,' as if we were pirates, swaggering and brandishing our weapons, bullying and intimidating people. But a soldier, a true soldier, I think, does not take. A soldier gives."

"Gives what?"

"Anything," says Mulaghesh. "Everything, if asked of us. We're servants, as I said. A soldier serves not to take, they don't strive to *have* something, but rather they strive so that others might one day have something. And a blade isn't a happy friend to a soldier, but a burden, a heavy one, to be used scrupulously and carefully. A good soldier does everything they can so they do not *have* to kill. That's what training is for. But if we have to, we will. And when we do that we give up some part of ourselves, as we're asked to do."

"What part do you give up, do you think?" asks Rada.

"Peace, maybe. Killing echoes inside you. It never goes away. Maybe some who have killed don't know that they've lost something, but they have."

"That is so," says Rada quietly. "Deaths of all kinds echo on. And sometimes, it seems, they drown out all of life."

And with those words Mulaghesh suddenly remembers that the woman before her was once trapped in a collapsed building with the corpses of her family, trapped in the dark with them for days and days. And when she does she realizes that, in some way, little Rada Smolisk might still be trapped in that darkness, and trying to free herself. The surgeries, the humanitarianism, the autopsy, even the taxidermy—all of this could be an effort to literally place her hands upon the raw stuff of life and sort through it, seeking some secret that might unlock her dark prison, and bring in light.

Or perhaps, Mulaghesh thinks, Rada Smolisk feels at home only among the dead. She's not stuttering at all now, and is actually bordering on erudition; whereas in the waking hours of life, with Signe and Biswal, she is a trembling, nervous thing, far from her normal surroundings. *If death echoes,* wonders Mulaghesh, *perhaps one could get used to it, or even come to love its noise.* Much like how Choudhry surrounded herself with sketches and images of this hellish country, and its history.

Then she remembers. . . .

The charcoal sketch in Choudhry's room—a landscape depicting a shoreline on which many people kneel, heads bowed, and a tower rising behind them . . .

Mulaghesh sits forward. *She saw it,* she thinks suddenly. *She saw it. She saw the damned City of Blades, just as I did.*

It must have been the Window to the White Shores, she realizes: the miracle Signe described. But it must have *worked.* Choudhry snuck into the statue yard and performed that ancient rite and glimpsed the very island Mulaghesh did; and perhaps the only reason Mulaghesh herself saw the City of Blades last night is because the ritual was still working, like a door left open for anyone to walk through.

So how did she come to die? After all that, how did Sumitra Choudhry come to be murdered just as the other Voortyashtanis?

"I'm s-sorry, General," says Rada finally. "I've l-looked all I could, but I've found n-nothing."

"Nothing?" asks Mulaghesh, dispirited.

"Nothing indicating anything, really. There's j-just not much to g-go on. P-perhaps I am n-not up to the t-task."

Mulaghesh stands and walks to the table, surveying Rada's grisly work. "I hate this so damned much, Rada. I hate it beyond words."

"D-Did you know her, G-General?"

"No. Never saw her. Just heard about her. But to see someone reduced down to this . . ." She shakes her head. "We don't even know it's her, do we. We can't even tell her family that she's really dead. Just that we think so. And it's not like we could have them look to tell us if it's really . . ."

She trails off, thinking.

"G-General?" asks Rada.

Silence.

"Uh. General?"

"She got a Silver Star," says Mulaghesh quietly.

"Um. What?"

"She got a *Silver Star*. For heroism after being injured in the line of duty. She got shot, in the, uh . . ." She snaps her fingers, trying to jog her memory. "In the shoulder. In the *left* shoulder. I read her reports."

"Meaning . . ."

Mulaghesh cranes over the body and gently pushes aside a drooping flap of skin to look at the left shoulder. "It's smooth. It's *smooth*, damn it. No scarring at all!"

"So?"

"So it's *not her*!" says Mulaghesh, feeling relieved and baffled and furious. "It's not her! I don't know who in the hells this might be, but it's not Choudhry!"

"B-Because of a m-missing scar?"

"She got shot in the shoulder, just above the collarbone, and she nearly *died* from it, Governor. It was grisly. They don't give out the Silver Star for nothing. It'd have left a mark." She looks up, thinking furiously. "Someone's fucking with me."

"I'm . . . sorry?"

"Someone must . . . Someone must have *known* I was looking into Choudhry. They must have! Someone wanted me or us to think she was dead. I've got someone out there nervous and they don't like it one bit. They're rattled enough to go through the trouble of mutilating a totally different *body* and staking it out on the cliffs to try and throw me off the trail!"

"Isn't that, uh, a l-little bit p-paranoid, G-General?"

"Maybe. But paranoia usually doesn't harm, and often helps." She only hates herself a little for quoting Signe. "Damn. What time is it?"

"It's 1900, G-General."

"Shit. Dark *already*. I'll have to wait until tomorrow to tell Nadar." She shoves a thread of wet hair out of her face. "Well, Governor. This has been damn educational, I must say."

"Always a p-pleasure to, uh, assist," says Rada, perplexed.

"What will you do with, um, the body?"

"Unfortunately, I am used to d-dealing with c-corpses," she says.

"It will b-be no tr-tr-trouble at all t-to make arrangements w-with the f-fortress."

Mulaghesh thanks Rada for her help, then braces herself for the cold as she exits Rada's house. But, strangely, the shock never hits her. She realizes Rada's house was freezing cold, perhaps inhumanly cold, so she was already accustomed to it. As she crests a wet cliff she looks back and sees Rada standing in the doorway, watching her with her great, sad eyes. Yet up above is her chimney, and from it flows a thick, steady stream of smoke, turned a glowing white by the moonlight.

She wonders who could possibly want to fake Sumitra Choudhry's death. Then she realizes that the most obvious suspect would be Choudhry herself.

***

It's late when she finally fumbles her key into her door and opens it. When she does she freezes, surprised by the roaring fire in her fireplace. Then she sees the mountain of greasy bones and crumbling crusts of bread on her tea table, behind which sits Sigrud je Harkvaldsson, stripped down to his shirtsleeves, his suspenders dangling from his waist, carving up a forearm-sized hunk of white cheese with his giant black knife. The only remnant of his kingly attire is the white glove on his left hand, concealing the injury he bore long ago.

He jerks his chin at her. "I wondered when you would be back."

Mulaghesh stares at the mess and holds her hands out, aggrieved. "What . . . What the fuck?"

"Signe said you wanted to see me."

"How the *hells* did you get in here?"

"I picked the lock?" He picks up a clay jug, uncorks it, and takes a massive pull. "How else?"

"By the seas . . ." She shuts the door and tosses her coat on the bed. "You couldn't find anywhere else in this giant building for you to eat what looks like three *whole* chickens?"

"Not anyplace where I wouldn't get stared at. Or have servants fumbling over me, asking me if I needed things. They treat me like a bomb, waiting to explode. I much prefer your room. No one looks for me in here."

"Hells, I know *I* sure wouldn't! Ah, look, you've gotten chicken fat all over the carpet. . . ."

"What was it you wanted to see me about?" He recorks the jug. "Signe mentioned the Ministry, but, to be honest, I wasn't sure if she was being sarcastic."

She flops into a chair beside the fire. "I'm almost not even sure I want to say it aloud. You might think me a fool, or insane. Or, worse, *I'd* hear it coming out of *my* mouth and *know* I'm insane."

"Shara said that on our first few jobs," says Sigrud, "tangling with the Divine." He looks at her, eyebrow cocked. "Which makes me curious to hear what you are about to say."

There's a silence. Mulaghesh holds up her hand. Sigrud, without a word, tosses her the jug. She catches it, pulls the cork out with her teeth, spits it into the fire, and takes a long pull.

She shuts her eyes as she swallows. "Grain alcohol," she says, her voice now raspy. "That shit's not for the young."

"That shit is often not even for seasoned Dreyling sailors," says Sigrud, watching as she takes a second enormous swig. "This makes me think whatever you say is, ah, very bad news."

"Yes. Yes it is."

There's another silence.

"I'll need you to listen not as a chancellor of a foreign nation," says Mulaghesh, "but as a former operative. And a friend."

"So you are saying, do not use this information against you or your country."

"Yeah, basically. Can you do that?"

He shrugs. "I have always been good at compartmentalization. And, to be frank . . . I am not particularly interested in the work of a chancellor."

So she tells him. She tells him everything, from top to bottom, describing Choudhry, the murders, the mutilation of the bodies, her Divine encounter with that apparition that looked like Voortya, and her glimpse into what she now suspects was the Voortyashtani afterlife. And to her relief, he doesn't look at her like she's crazy, like she's absolutely out of her gourd. Instead he just sits there, one eye blinking slowly, as if he's just heard some rather disappointing gossip.

"So," he says slowly when she finishes.

"So."

"You, ah . . . You believe that the Voortyashtani afterlife—this City of Blades—still exists. Somehow."

"Yes. Do . . . do you believe me?"

He puffs at his pipe, releasing a huge cloud of smoke. "Yes. Why wouldn't I?"

In her relief she chooses not to give him the many, many reasons why a normal person wouldn't. "I saw it, Sigrud. I *saw* it. It's hard to describe what I saw, but . . . it was real, and I know it was real. They're all there, all the Voortyashtanis that have lived and fought and died. . . . It's a . . . a fucking *army*, Sigrud! How it's still around I don't know, but they're still out there."

"And now, you think they are, how shall I put this . . . coming through?"

"That's my suspicion. Just as I was, I don't know, pulled through to them, they can maybe be pulled through to here."

"And it's these sentinels who have committed these murders."

"Yes," says Mulaghesh. "A whole family cleanly massacred, then butchered, and all such perfect cuts. . . . It's not something an ordinary person could do. But a single stroke of a sentinel's blade, they say, was able to part the trunk of an old oak as if it were but a length of straw."

"But how are the sentinels coming through to here?"

"The strange woman spotted at the charcoal kilns," says Mulaghesh. "That's my best guess. She must have found a way to open, I don't know, a door of some kind and let them through. And I think she's the same one who butchered that body to throw me off her trail."

"And though you have not said so," says Sigrud, very slowly, "it sounds like you believe this woman to be Sumitra Choudhry."

Mulaghesh is silent. The wind slaps the windowpanes.

"Yes," she says quietly. "Yes, it seems that way. From the drawings in her room, which seemed so insane, and the way she drew the murder scenes on her very walls . . . She's certainly the one person in Voortyashtan who would know the most about the Divine. And who else would want me to think Choudhry is dead besides Choudhry herself?"

"You think she is mad? That that is why she is doing this?"

"I don't know why she's doing this. But it's the most obvious answer."

"What goal could she have in mind? Why do these things to these families?"

"I don't know what her endgame is. But it's like she's *testing* this process, figuring it out, getting better at it. She's refining her technique, whatever ritual it might be. Something with thinadeskite, though, since we found it at the first murder scene."

"The material from the mines," says Sigrud. "Which you said a Divinity caved in."

"Voortya, yes. Some version or rendition of her, at least, and I *still* don't understand that one tiny fucking bit. And I don't know why the sentinels don't stick around, why they don't last, but . . . Maybe that's why Choudhry keeps trying. She wants to pull them all the way through and keep them here. But damned if I know why."

Sigrud slowly sits back, absently carving at the block of cheese.

"What's your professional opinion?" asks Mulaghesh.

"My professional opinion," says Sigrud, "is that Voortya is dead. That is known. That is undeniable. Shara said Voortya proved the *example* of what happens when a Divinity dies. None of Voortya's miracles work anymore."

"Yet I walked into one last night."

He scratches his eyebrow. "And how this is possible, I do not know. But . . . I have a troubling idea."

"What?"

"Voortya was the Divinity of death, yes?"

"Yeah. So?"

"So, could it be possible for such a Divinity, who aided her own people in defeating death, to do the same for herself?"

"What are you saying? That I saw Voortya's *ghost* on the cliffs?"

"Is it so mad? If you saw all those souls in the City of Blades, if *they* still exist, then why not Voortya? Perhaps whatever mechanisms that allow an army of dead warriors to persist could also do the same for a god. If it is really the afterlife of these lands, then the City of Blades must hold, what, millions of souls? Tens of millions? All the dead warriors from centuries and centuries . . . Many times larger than any standing army in existence today. Keeping them there is no small feat."

Mulaghesh goes still. Something in the fireplace *pops*.

She sits up, feeling the blood drain from her face. Then she slowly turns to look at Sigrud.

"What?" says Sigrud, wary.

"An army," says Mulaghesh. "An *army*, you said. And I said it myself not too long ago."

"Yes?"

"And what do armies do?"

"They, uh . . ."

Mulaghesh stands. "*That's* what this is all about. It must be! It's like what Signe said about the Voortyashtani afterlife!"

He frowns. "What does Signe know about the Voortyashtani afterlife?"

"Like . . . everything? You do realize she was raised here, right?" Sigrud is so disconcerted he appears not to have heard her. She ignores him and continues, "Signe said that when Voortyashtani warriors died, their souls went over the ocean to a white island, the City of Blades. She said the Voortyashtanis believed that one day all the souls would sail back over from the City of Blades . . . and then they'd make war upon all of creation in the Night of the Sea of Swords."

"So?"

"So don't you see? That's what she's trying to do! Sumitra damned Choudhry is trying to trigger *the fucking Voortyashtani apocalypse!*"

***

"We need to tell Shara this right away," says Mulaghesh. "Tell her that her operative hasn't just gone AWOL, she's gone fucking mad and wants to start a damned *war*! A Divine war, the *last* war!"

Sigrud shakes his head. "But there are too many unknowns here, Turyin. Imagine if we go to the Ministry, and tell Shara and her people to start investigating. . . . She will have to make her case before the authorities, convincing them to act. But she has no case, just . . . guesses. Speculation. You must find more; you must find something concrete."

"What's more concrete than *seeing* the damned City of Blades?" says Mulaghesh, frustrated.

"But *I* did not see the city in the statue yard. Nor did my daughter. And one cannot initiate a military action based purely on visions. Especially since much of the government is no longer purely under Shara's control. Many of her powers have been stripped from her in the past year."

"So what now! What do we fucking do now! Wait for another murder?"

"I did not say that," says Sigrud. "And I may be able to be of some use to you. . . . Let me see your notepad. I wish to see these sketches you described."

She hands it to him and he flips through them, examining each mad scrawl.

"What do you think?" asks Mulaghesh.

"I think," he says quietly, "that it was not wise for my people to come here, and unearth the many things that should stay sleeping."

"Don't let your daughter hear that."

His face clouds over. She instantly understands that this was the wrong thing to say. She stays silent rather than fall all over herself apologizing.

The fire crackles and pops. A log gently shifts, sending up a spray of sparks. He flexes his left hand, its white glove rippling. "It still hurts, you know," he says softly. "My hand. I thought it would go away, after Bulikov, after Kolkan. But it came back."

"I'm sorry to hear that."

"Perhaps the past cannot be so easily forgotten. Tell me," he says. "You did not ever have any children, did you?"

"Natural ones, no." She snorts. "Had about a few thousand adopted ones, though."

He looks at her, perplexed, then understands. "Ah. Your soldiers. I see." He turns back to the fire, shaking his head. "I do not understand how to talk to young people." He rethinks his statement. "Or, I suppose, to young people like her." Another pause. "Or, perhaps, I do not know how to speak to her, specifically."

Mulaghesh is quiet.

"She does not like me," he says. "She does not like me coming back into her life."

"She doesn't know you," says Mulaghesh. "And you don't know her. But you will, if you want to."

"Why would she *want* to know me?" he says. "How do I tell my daughter what I've seen, what I've done? How do I tell her that at times, in prison, I . . . I became so furious that my own blood would leap out of me, pouring out of my nose, and I would go mad with anger, a berserk rage, hurting anyone and everyone around me, even myself? Sometimes innocents. Sometimes mere bystanders. I throttled them to death with my bare hands. . . ."

He trails off.

Mulaghesh says, "You're a different person now."

"And so is she," he says. "I thought I knew her. But I was foolish to think so."

"Why?"

"Well." He struggles with the words for a moment. "When I was a young man, and she was just a little girl, long ago, I . . . I used to chase her through the forest near our home. It was a game. She would hide, and I would pretend to chase her. And then she would pretend to chase me. And, later, when I was in prison . . . when I thought I would go mad . . . I held on to this very tightly, this memory of the little blond girl laughing as she ran through the forest. This tiny, perfect creature, darting among these great big trees. When the world grinds you down, you pick a handful of fires to hold close to your heart. And that was one of mine. Perhaps the brightest, the warmest. And after Bulikov, after Shara suggested I come back, and find my family and rebuild my country . . . I suppose I just assumed that she would remember this, too. That she would see me and remember that moment in the trees, laughing as we ran. But she does not remember. And perhaps I was foolish to think she would." He pauses for a long time. "I have been hurt in many ways in my life, Turyin Mulaghesh. But I have never been hurt in this manner before. What should I do? What should I do with this strange young woman who does not care for me?"

"Talk to her, I suppose. Start there. And listen to her. Don't expect her to say things you want to hear, but listen to her. She's lived a life very separate from yours."

"I have tried that. When I try to explain myself, all my words dry up." He shakes his head. "Perhaps it would have been better for me to have died, after reclaiming my country. End on a high note, as they say. Or escape into the wilderness."

"I never figured you as one for self-pity."

"And I never thought I would be a father again," says Sigrud. "Yet here I am."

He stares into her notebook, and she suddenly realizes how intensely lonely Sigrud must feel, forced to play many roles—prince, husband, father—that feel hopelessly beyond him.

Then his eye falls on something: a seven-pointed star Mulaghesh copied in her notes. He sits up and points at it. "Wait. This . . . This star here. Did you copy it exactly?"

"Uh, maybe?"

"Are you *sure*?"

"I think so?"

"And it was found in Choudhry's room?"

"Yes. Why?"

He scratches his beard, anxious. "It's a . . . a signal, a piece of tradecraft. She's telling us what code she's going to use, what language she'll speak to us in. This star means she will be using Old Bulikov rules."

"Uh, what? Old Bulikov rules? I never heard of those, and I was stuck there for twenty years."

"When the Ministry first truly began its intelligence operations," says Sigrud, "most of its work was focused in Bulikov. But they had no technology then, no signals and lights and telephones or whatnot. So they had to use much cruder means—a stroke of chalk, a pin in a wall, a carving in wood, or a splotch of paint. Things like this. It was mostly used to direct operatives to dead drops, often when someone felt they were being pursued."

"As in, they might not survive, but they still wanted to send a message?"

"To leave behind information," says Sigrud. "Yes."

"Can we trust that, though? If all signs point to Choudhry as the suspect, do we really want to believe whatever it is she's trying to tell us?"

"You said she went mad. So perhaps once she was *not* mad. Perhaps she did this when she was still a good agent."

"I wouldn't know what to look for, though. I don't know the first thing about Old Bulikov rules."

"And I cannot go with you. It would be rather difficult to explain away my absence here and my presence there. Even though I would much rather be doing *that* than *this*."

"You'd rather be digging around in the affairs of a madwoman than work here with your daughter?"

Sigrud grumbles to himself. "When you say it like that, I do not sound very reasonable at all." He sighs. "I wish I did not have to do this. I was never a good controller, never a good case officer. I was always the man down in the muck, not the one waiting at home. That was Shara's game."

"What are you talking about?"

"I am saying that you are an operative in need of a case officer," says Sigrud. "You are all alone up here, and maybe this work is so sensitive that Shara could not bring anyone on board. . . . But, you suffer for the lack of one. And I do not exactly see anyone else around who could do the job."

"You don't work for Saypur anymore, you know."

"If what you say is right, then everything happening in Voortyashtan is under threat. Including the harbor, the one thing currently sustaining my whole country's economy. Frankly, I wish Shara had brought me on sooner—but she likely did not know what you would find here."

"So what now?"

He looks at the clock. "So now, I suggest you get comfortable. And put the liquor down."

"Why?"

"Because you are going to have to memorize a lot of tradecraft before morning, if you want to do this right."

***

"So it was *not* Choudhry's body they found, ma'am?" asks Nadar the next morning as they walk through the fortress.

"No, it wasn't," says Mulaghesh. "I don't know whose body it was, but it wasn't hers." She wipes a bead of sweat from her brow and tries not to shiver. She hiked up here rather than be chauffeured, and now her perspiration grows frigid in the cold air of the fortress, like she's being wrapped in bedsheets pulled from an icy lake.

"Fucking shtanis," says Nadar, shaking her head.

"Shtanis?"

"They're mocking us, ma'am. They *must* be. A Saypuri corpse, butchered and put on display just beyond where they blew up the mines? They're showing us how close they can get to us, General. I've increased patrols, but as yet we've spotted nothing. They're talented in moving unseen in this terrain." Nadar shakes out her keys and begins opening the door to Choudhry's rooms.

"Have you . . . considered any alternatives?" asks Mulaghesh, uncertain how to phrase this.

"Alternatives, ma'am?"

"Yes. I had been considering that it was Sumitra Choudhry herself who was involved in the murders, Captain," says Mulaghesh.

"Choudhry?" says Nadar, startled. "Why, General?"

"These murders . . . They're like some kind of old Divine ritual." The door swings open. Both of them stare in at the graffiti-covered room. "And everything here suggests Choudhry was neck-deep in the Divine. To her misfortune."

Mulaghesh walks into the room, watching Nadar over her shoulder. She can't tell Nadar everything, but she needs someone in command here to start thinking in the right direction. If she can get Biswal or Nadar to consider it, then perhaps they can call in more Ministry reinforcements, who might be able to find something solid—something verifiably Divine.

But Nadar's face has gone cold and closed. "It seems unlikely that a Ministry operative could be capable of all that, ma'am."

"You don't know Ministry operatives, Captain."

"And, to be fair, you didn't know Choudhry, General," says Nadar. "Whereas I did."

"What do you mean?"

Nadar hesitates.

"Permission to speak freely, General."

"Granted."

"Choudhry was, like many out of Ghaladesh, a somewhat ineffectual officer."

"Ineffectual."

"Yes, General. Lots of titles, ma'am, lots of certifications, certainly. But no on-the-ground experience in a combat zone. Experience that we here in Voortyashtan have in excess, General." She meets Mulaghesh's eyes very briefly before looking away. "Experience not known in Ghaladesh."

Mulaghesh steps closer. "You wouldn't be doubting *my* combat experience, would you, Captain?" she asks sharply.

"No, ma'am."

"Do you disagree that what we see on these walls are the markings of a madwoman?"

"No, ma'am."

"Do you disagree that the timeline for these murders and the theft of the explosives overlaps with Choudhry's presence here, and disappearance?"

Nadar's face twitches. "No, ma'am. But—"

"But what?"

"But . . . I've been at Fort Thinadeshi for six years now, before the Battle of Bulikov, General. And though Bulikov alerted us to threats of the Divine, here in Voortyashtan we've only ever seen one threat. The one that's just beyond our walls."

"You need to remain mindful of threats beyond the insurgents and the tribes, Captain," says Mulaghesh. "Otherwise you blind yourself."

"I have seen our soldiers killed in the wilderness, ma'am," says Nadar softly. "I've held them in my arms as they died. I've seen the trains sent back to Ahanashtan, loaded up with coffins. I've seen these things time and time again, General. With all due respect, I personally do not believe myself to be blind at all."

* * *

Nadar leaves Mulaghesh alone while she conducts her inspection. Mulaghesh furiously rubs her arm, so angry that it's difficult to focus. *Well, at least I know where Nadar stands. Leaving only Lalith as an option.*

She shakes herself and begins to scan the walls of the room, her eyes tracing over the black scrawls and splashes of paint.

Look for things so simple, Sigrud told her, *that they seem to have no meaning in themselves.*

She asked, *What in the hells does that mean?*

It will not be a curious picture, or a carving in the wall that seems to communicate something, he said. *No riddles or codes, in other words. It will be an ordinary thing that simply does not belong. A stripe of chalk or paint that looks like a painter's error. Something stuck in the walls, like a staple or a pin, or a nick in the walls like someone banged them while moving furniture. Or a slash in a carpet that looks like someone damaged it.*

She looks over the images on the walls, trying not to be disturbed by them. Thousands of swords, stuck in the earth. An arrow piercing the heart of a wave. A face she now knows to be the cold, regal visage of Voortya herself gives her pause—Choudhry did an impressively good job of capturing the Divinity's likeness.

Perhaps she painted over it, thinks Mulaghesh. *Whatever it was. Perhaps her signal's no longer here at all.*

Her eye falls on the window in the far wall. It's long and thin, the barest slit of glass. Mulaghesh recognizes the intent of the design immediately, built to allow in light and air and nothing else.

Yet in the corner of the window frame, almost tucked out of view, is a tiny white dot.

She steps closer. It's a thumbtack, she sees, pushed deep into the wall.

Mulaghesh feels the window, testing the frame for any weaknesses or hollows. She finds none, but it does have a clasp that allows you to open it. With a squeak, she jimmies the window open, wincing at the blast of cold air, and feels the outside of the window.

There's something there, just barely: a piece of string, dangling down. She grabs it and begins to pull it in. It's long, nearly four feet.

Of course, thinks Mulaghesh. *If you're paranoid about room searches, put whatever it is you want to hide outside your room. . . .*

But when she finishes pulling the string all the way in, she's disappointed: at its end is nothing but a small hook, like a clasp from a woman's necklace. Something hung here once, clearly, but it's gone now: maybe she moved it, or maybe it fell.

Tied to the string just above the hook, however, is another white thumbtack.

She remembers what Sigrud said: *Ministry officers are trained to leave behind caches. Dead drops. If they disappear or get killed, they want to tell whoever comes next what they were doing.*

Mulaghesh asked, *So she wouldn't have hidden anything away in the mines or something crazy like that?*

Not if she was following SOP. She will have hidden something in a place accessible to you. And she will tell you what to look for.

Mulaghesh holds the white thumbtack up to the light and begins to understand the message: *I moved it. To find it, look for this.*

"So search all of Fort Thinadeshi," says Mulaghesh. "For one white thumbtack." She bows her head. "Fuck."

***

Mulaghesh wanders the innards of Fort Thinadeshi. She can't help but fight the feeling that she's stepped back in time. The walls are bulky, thick constructions, an architectural design that was abandoned long ago, as it was forced to create alternatingly huge or tiny rooms. She's never sure what she'll find on the other side of any given door: perhaps some dusky, yawning chasm of a room, or a tiny hallway full of cramped offices, like a honeycomb carved in stone. The hallways swim with shadows, for much of Fort Thinadeshi still lacks gas or electric lighting and is forced to use candles and literal torches. All around her are thuds, slams, laughs, and shouts, echoing through the misshapen chambers riddling this vast, crumbling relic.

It's hardly any different from the ruins in the wilderness, thinks Mulaghesh. It suddenly seems unusual that Choudhry was the only one who went mad here.

But more troubling than the atmosphere of the fortress is the amount of firearms and ammunition she sees in motion. The soldiers here are preparing for something. She doesn't want to think the word "mobilization" and all that it implies, but she can't help it.

What is Biswal planning to do in Voortyashtan?

What she hates most, perhaps, is the feeling of distance. She is not truly stationed or in command here, no, and it's true that no one bothers her or even looks twice as she wanders the winding hallways; but with every step Mulaghesh feels like a thief or a liar, sneaking through the shadows and silently watching these boys and girls, most of them hardly more than children.

I am one of you, she wishes to say to them. *I am a soldier just as you. All that has happened to me has not made me any different from you.* But beyond a few salutes, she exchanges little with the rank and file.

Mulaghesh is roving through the medical wing when she nearly abandons her search. She can't imagine a more futile task than this, combing through this ocean of dark stone for a single white dot.

She remembers something Sigrud told her during their hours-long briefing: *Assume she knows you. Assume she believed you would know who she was and what she had been doing when you came to look for her. If she has something to hide, she would hide it in a place you know she has been.*

But Mulaghesh doesn't know a damn thing about Choudhry besides what she's read. All she has are the few communications and requests she sent back to, to . . .

"To Ghaladesh," thinks Mulaghesh suddenly. She stops a passing private and asks, "Soldier—what's the quickest way to your communications department?"

***

The comms desk has the feeling of an ill-kept library, bookshelf after bookshelf of multicolored files. Mulaghesh searches the shelves for the sign of a white thumbtack, yet finds nothing. Dispirited, she's about to ask the young private at the front desk if she perhaps saw Choudhry do something here, months and months ago, when she notices something.

She looks at the front of the desk. Right at the bottom, just above the stone floor, is a white thumbtack pressed deep into the wood.

Mulaghesh stares at the tack. Then she looks up at the young private, who's watching her anxiously.

"Can I . . . help you, General?" asks the private.

"Uh, maybe." She wonders what message the tack is trying to convey. Perhaps Choudhry put it here so that Mulaghesh or whoever would stand in this very spot and speak to the soldier at the front desk. "What can you tell me about your operations here, Private?"

"Is there anything specific you'd like to know, General?"

"I . . . suppose I'm looking for backups or copies of all communications sent out from this station, Private. Specifically sent back to Ghaladesh."

"Well, each communication that goes out has to be copied and placed into storage, ma'am. If the communication isn't received, we have to have some record of what was sent so we can resend it."

"How long do you keep records of the communications?"

"We keep records for up to three years, ma'am, in case of an incident," says the private. "But only those sent or received within the year are readily available." She nods at the bookshelves. "The rest are in deep storage."

"Can you show me the log?"

"Certainly, ma'am. What time period would you be looking for?"

She gives her six weeks on either side of Choudhry's disappearance. This produces a considerable pile of paper, which Mulaghesh promptly sits down and starts poring through.

Two hours later Mulaghesh is still digging through the logs of communications and telegrams. They're all categorized by date, then by the last name of the officer who issued the communication. Choudhry's name is nowhere to be found except for the handful of communications she sent requesting files, which Mulaghesh has already scanned for code, to no avail.

After another hour Mulaghesh is about ready to give it up and try something new when she notices one officer's name is different: ZHURGUT.

Zhurgut, she thinks. *As in* Saint *Zhurgut? The Voortyashtani?*

She looks closer at its log entry. The telegram destination is one she's never seen before. Most of Fort Thinadeshi's telegrams only went to five or six locations: Bulikov, Ahanashtan, and Ghaladesh, as well as the other installations throughout the region. This address is completely different.

"Because it doesn't exist," says Mulaghesh aloud.

"Pardon, ma'am?" asks the private at the front desk.

"N-Nothing. Never mind. Talking aloud."

She looks closer at the line in the log. *The name of a Voortyashtani saint . . . And the telegram's destination doesn't exist. Choudhry put the telegram through but she never intended it to go anywhere . . . so there was never anyone to call the comms desk and tell them they never got it!*

Mulaghesh walks into the shelves, looking for the failed communication. She feels impressed by her own brilliance, but even more so at Choudhry's: the girl was clever enough to use the comms desk backup files as her own cache, duping the attendants here into copying down her message under a fictional officer's name and storing it away. Unless you knew to look for it, you'd never know Choudhry was involved at all.

She finds the file and glances around. The private at the front desk is busy recording something. Mulaghesh slides the file out, pulls out the transcription, and glances at the first line. It reads: "A13F69 12 1IKMN12 . . ."

She sighs. "Ah, for the love of . . ."

It's in code. *But of course it would be,* thinks Mulaghesh. She remembers Shara provided her with a Ministry codex when she first sent her out here. Now it's just a matter of determining exactly which one Choudhry used.

"Well," Mulaghesh says. "I guess I know what I'm doing tonight."

***

She starts the long walk back down to the harbor, wishing she had Pandey here to drive her again. But she's happy to steer clear of Fort Thinadeshi for a while, feeling certain she's increasingly on Captain Nadar's shit list. And it won't do to have someone close to Biswal dislike her quite so much.

She should feel excited, she knows. She just figured out Choudhry's signals and found the one possibly genuine communication that this operative ever made. But everything she saw back there actually makes her more worried.

Because you had to be pretty cunning to think up a scheme like that, and by all appearances Choudhry went the extra mile to make sure whoever came after her would find this. Not exactly the actions of a madwoman, then.

She's approaching the checkpoint down into Voortyashtan when she glances north toward the thinadeskite mines. The machines are still churning away, hauling rock out of the enormous pit. She glances across the cliffs, absently noting how isolated the mines now seem, and reflects on the tremendous amount of damage this region has taken. Cities collapsing, bays dredged, mines carved and then caved in—it's as if all the violence the Voortyashtanis once inflicted on the world has been redirected toward their very lands.

Then her eye falls on a little copse of trees about a quarter mile north of the mines.

She pauses. Cocks her head.

For some reason those tall pine trees suddenly seem familiar to her. Strikingly familiar, even.

She walks around the mines and toward the copse, leaning against the wind. It takes a while to get to them, but the closer the pines get the more familiar they seem. There's something about the way they stand, radiating out in a circle with a gap on one side, like an entrance.

A memory flares inside of her: painting one palm with honey, waiting in the cold and the dark for the wind to carry its scent. . . .

I've been here before, thinks Mulaghesh. *Haven't I? But it was very long ago.* . . .

The trees loom over her. Suddenly they seem just as ominous and strange as the statues in the SDC yard. She hesitates before walking into their shadows, then chides herself for being silly and steps inside.

It's surprisingly dark and still inside the copse of pines, as if their trunks and boughs form a solid wall. The vicious coastal wind doesn't penetrate their perimeter. It's so dark that she almost walks right into the stone before she sees it, despite its size.

The stone sits in the center of the trees, about man-high and rounded, yet running from its top to bottom are countless thin slashes, as if the stone was put through a carpenter's router over and over again. There are hundreds of slashes, even thousands of them, scoring it until it looks like some strange, giant nut with a curious shell. Despite these lacerations the stone is still strong: no matter how she pushes or pulls, no part of it crumbles or falls apart.

She remembers it, she realizes. She remembers this stone, remembers coming here in the night, seeing this ritual. *They'd take us up here,* she thinks. *They'd take us up here and show us what they could do with a sword, slashing through six feet of stone with a single stroke. And so precise was the stroke, so perfect, so smooth, that it never crossed over another slash, never damaged the stone so much it fell apart.*

She walks around it in a slow circle, fingers trailing over the marks on the stone, the gray light dappling its surface.

Once every three years they took us up here, she remembers. *Once every three years they slashed the stones. In gardens like this, all across the cliffs. It was a message to us, to all of us who wished to leave our clans behind: "Do this, and you will no longer be a person. You will be a device. You will be a weapon, perfect and merciless, wielded by Her hand." And we gladly gave ourselves.*

She stops. Steps back from the stone.

She stares around herself, confused and terrified.

This memory she just recovered, she suspects, is over a hundred years old. And it is definitely *not* hers: this is the first time she's ever been here in her life, she knows that.

But she thinks she knows whose memory it is. She glances toward the tall, thick pine at the edge of the copse and thinks, *I remember hiding in branches like those, my palm slick with honey, my knife in the other hand, and waiting for the stag. . . .*

She saw this place when she was in the thinadeskite mines, the vision of the boy with the knife and the white stag, going through some test to prove himself to the sentinels. To imagine that this place is real, still here, and only a few yards away from the mines themselves is dumbfounding to her.

She steps back, aware of her alien reverence for this place and disgusted by it. This awe, this reverence, is not her own. It belongs to some young Voortyashtani boy from hundreds of years ago, and it somehow became trapped inside of her during her short spell in the mines, like some kind of mnemonic transfusion. She wonders what else the mines could have done to her, as well as how they did it, and suddenly she no longer feels too upset that the mines have been obliterated. She keeps backing away, feeling tremendously violated.

But she finds something else isn't right. Her memory is telling her something here is . . . new.

She fights against the feeling—she knows her memories of this place aren't *hers*—but she can't deny the sensation that something has changed here, something that shouldn't have been changed.

It takes her a while, but she finally decides that the small, black boulder about twenty feet to the left of the standing stone is new. It shouldn't be here; they practiced swordwork around the stone—*Not me,* she thinks, *but whoever's memory this is*—all of them pacing back and forth, and they'd never have placed a rock of such size in the area. It would have been dangerous.

She walks over to the boulder. It could have just rolled here, certainly. But it's strangely round and flat, as if it was carven. Maybe someone could have left it here . . . but why would someone do that?

As Mulaghesh steps before it something changes in her footsteps: there's a hollow *thump,* as if she's standing on a wooden platform. Yet this couldn't be, as she's standing on dark green grass.

She lifts up the boulder. To her confusion, underneath it is a loop of rope that rises out of the soft, thick turf. She stares at it a second, then shoves the boulder aside and tugs at the rope.

It takes three tugs before a whole section of sod lifts clean up out of the earth. Underneath it is a large hole, about three feet wide and three feet tall.

She looks at the chunk of sod in her hand, confused. It's a perfect square. She flips it over and sees that it is actually a wooden trapdoor with sod cunningly tied onto the top, and a loop of rope in the center for its handle. It's like a camouflaged sewer cap, in a way.

"What in all the hells?" she says.

She looks into the hole, wondering if this is some Voortyashtani grave site, but she sees it's not a hole at all: it's a tunnel, sloping down sharp and heading south. It's no small feat, either: she sees wooden support beams lining the tunnel, supporting all those tons and tons of earth.

She sits up and looks south, and sees the excavation machines working away on the mines.

"Ah, shit," she says. "The *mines* . . ."

She sprints off toward the closest checkpoint, thankful that she maintained her running exercises in Javrat, and flags down a guard. "Get word to General Biswal at Fort Thinadeshi immediately," she pants. "We've had a security breach at the mines. And have them bring a torch!"

***

Nadar and Pandey shine a torch down the tunnel, craning their heads low to see. "Are we certain it goes to the mines?" asks Biswal, looking over their shoulders.

"Hells, I don't know," says Mulaghesh. "When I encounter a strange hole in the woods my first instinct isn't to jump down it."

Pandey sits back, sighs, and says, "If you would all please give me some room. . . ." Then he stands, shifts the torch around so it's hanging by his shoulder, and does a graceful hop into the tunnel, sliding down it feetfirst.

Mulaghesh, Biswal, and Nadar watch as the luminescence of his torch grows smaller, until he finally reaches a bend and it vanishes entirely.

"Does it go to the mines, Pandey?" Biswal shouts down.

Pandey's voice comes echoing up: "It's . . . It's not necessary to talk *quite* so loud, sir. The tunnel does amplify voices a good bit."

"Oh." Biswal clears his throat. "Apologies."

"But, yes, sir . . . It does seem to run into the remnants of a cave-in down here, sir. So it probably once did go to the mines, sir."

"Damn," mutters Nadar. "Damn it all, damn it *all*! Another breach! Another one!"

"This, I would assume," says Biswal, "is how they managed to bomb the mine."

"It must be, sir," says Nadar. "That's the only possible way. I suppose we didn't find the entrance to the mine down in the tunnels because it must have been as well camouflaged as this damned trapdoor." She kicks the door hard enough to send it pinwheeling through the glen.

"Yes," says Biswal. "How *did* you manage to spot it, Turyin?"

"Sheer chance," says Mulaghesh. "It's a long walk back down to the city, and, ah, no lavatories along the way." She hopes this sounds believable: she's certainly not willing to tell them she miraculously received this memory down in the mines.

"Ah," says Biswal. "I see."

"And you just happened to spot it?" asks Nadar.

"I tripped over it, frankly. Once I was here I came in to look at *that*." She nods at the scarred stone. "Whatever the hells that is."

"Another damned relic," says Nadar.

Nadar and Mulaghesh squat to help Pandey out of the tunnel. He rises, dusts himself off—a useless gesture, considering the amount— and nods at them. "Thank you, Captain, General."

"How long do you think it took to make this thing?" Mulaghesh asks. She squats to peer inside. "Half a year? More? It's no shallow hole in the ground, I'll tell you that."

"True. What are you getting at, Turyin?" asks Biswal.

"I'm just saying this took a long time to make," she says. "And I don't think they made it to be used once, to drop off *one* bomb. You saw those support beams in there, didn't you, Pandey?"

"I did, ma'am."

"This is a serious undertaking. They basically built their own mine, in secret, underneath our noses! And they built it to last." She peers down into the darkness of the tunnel. "Whoever made this wanted frequent access to what we were doing down there, I think."

Nadar can barely suppress her scoff. "Why would they want *that*, General?"

"I don't know. But I wonder if that's why we found thinadeskite at the murder scene in Ghevalyev, which took place months ago. They took it directly from the mines themselves."

"But again, General—why would they want that?"

"Why would they murder those farmers? Why would they blow up the mines, as you suggested? I don't hear anyone proposing any motivations for those two crimes."

"The reason is clear to me, General," says Nadar. "They are savages. They seek to harm everyone that opposes them, ma'am, however they can. They think no more than that."

Mulaghesh stands. "Captain, you've had three serious security breaches in the past months," she says. "Someone stole explosives from you, someone stole extremely sensitive experimental materials from you, and now someone's dug a hole into your mine shaft a quarter mile from your secured site. And you still have no idea who's behind any of it! If anyone here isn't thinking, Captain, it's *not* the Voortyashtanis."

Captain Nadar opens her mouth, furious. Before she can speak, Biswal leaps in. "That's enough, Captain. I will stop you there before you say something insubordinate. You are dismissed."

Nadar looks back and forth between the two of them before giving a ferocious salute, turning on her heel, and marching back to the fortress.

Biswal nods to Pandey and says, "You too, Sergeant Major."

"Yes, sir." Pandey salutes and sprints through the trees after Nadar.

Biswal looks at Mulaghesh with the air of a man who has heard his quota of bullshit for today and is all too unwilling to hear any more. "You, Turyin, are riling up the natives. I wouldn't mind so much if I didn't have to live with them."

"Your captain might be an excellent officer, Biswal, but she's still biased and single-minded. How long has she been rattling her saber in your ear, begging you to go after the shtanis?"

"She's not the only one," says Biswal. "It's the opinion of many of my advisers that we cannot be diplomatic with the insurgents."

Mulaghesh nods at the scarred stone behind them. "But you can't look at that and tell me that isn't the product of something Divine."

A pause.

"You think . . . You think this all has something to do with the Divine?" Biswal looks at her side-eyed, as if waiting for the punchline. "That the Divine is still possible here, in Voortya's backyard, the *one* Divinity we're *sure* is dead?"

Mulaghesh can't tell him the truth, she knows that. But if she can get him to request backup from the Ministry, there's a chance she could get more resources behind her investigation. "I think someone *thinks* they're doing something Divine. Ritually mutilated corpses, with thinadeskite sitting next to them—and now we find a tunnel to the thinadeskite mines, in the shadow of that bizarre totem there. Whoever made this tunnel, I think, did *not* want the mines to collapse. They had free access to the thinadeskite—for unknown purposes, sure, but there's plenty of unknowns when it comes to the Divine. Maybe this stuff was considered miraculous to them once. And even though now we know it's no longer miraculous—you've tested it, after all—maybe they're just choosing to act like it is, going through the motions. But I can't get your captain to consider anything besides the insurgents."

Biswal sighs deeply. He shuts his eyes, and she sees there's something starved to his face now, as if all his worries have scored away layers of his flesh. Then he squats and sits on the ground, groaning as his lower vertebrae rebel. "Come on. Let's take a seat."

"Um. Okay." Mulaghesh sits beside him.

He reaches into his pocket and takes out a flask. "I think I might have actually funded some piracy, buying this," he says. "Rice wine."

"What brand?"

"Cloud Story."

Mulaghesh whistles. "Shit. I only ever drank that twice, and both times it was my birthday."

"Who gave it to you?"

"Same person each time. Me."

He hands her the flask. The rice wine is like milky gold, and it makes her head thrum pleasantly. "Better than I remember."

"It's your palate. You're too used to the shit food and shit drink we get up here. It could be boat fuel and it'd still taste like a prized vintage." He sighs again and looks at her. "Nadar is not alone in mistrusting the shtanis. Other officers have lost friends and comrades here. We're in a war, Turyin. Maybe the first of many, as the Continent grows stronger. Ghaladesh might not want to admit it. The prime minister might not want to admit it. But the shtanis are fine with doing so. And someone in command must have the courage to admit it as well."

"What do you mean?"

"We've seen some movements from the insurgents. Watching us, trying to find weaknesses. They keep withdrawing whenever we respond." He sighs. "But you don't think that this"—he nods to the tunnel—"and the murders have anything to do with the insurgents?"

"Maybe not nothing. But not as much as Nadar wishes."

"I must be insane. But I'm willing to let you keep following this lead, wherever it goes. You've found out a lot of things no one else has, Turyin. I just hope you don't find something that brings ruin down on our heads."

"Me, too."

Biswal looks down at the bottle of wine. "I wonder who they'll replace me with. When I catch my own bullet here."

"If you keep getting melancholy, Lalith, I'll have to take that bottle away."

"I'm not joking, Turyin. They boxed up my predecessor quick as a flash and replaced him—him and a dozen other officers here. It's like the world just forgot them." His eyes have a curious light to them, one Mulaghesh has only seen once here, when Biswal danced around the topic of the Summer of Black Rivers. "The least they can do is remember us. Remember those who took on the sins of our nation to keep it safe. Not all of us get a Battle of Bulikov, Turyin—a battle our people acknowledge and glorify. We're not all so lucky as you. The rest of us are like the cartridge of a bullet, cast away once used. And we are asked to silently bear that burden. Which we, as patriots, do gladly." Then he stands, turns, and walks back to the fortress.

What is a blade but a conduit of death?
What is a life but a conduit of death?

—EXCERPT FROM "OF THE GREAT MOTHER VOORTYA
ATOP THE TEETH OF THE WORLD," CA. 556

10.

tHe cHaff of many wars

Mulaghesh burns with anxiety as she walks back into SDC, but no one looks twice at her while she walks through the halls and up the stairs to her room. She opens the door and begins fumbling with her pockets, reaching for the letter, when she spots the washroom door inching open over her shoulder.

She's not sure how she moves so fast, but suddenly her carousel is in her hand, pointed at the washroom door. Sigrud slowly sticks his head out of the bathroom and cocks an eyebrow at the pistol. "You seem . . . nervous. Was it a success?"

"That depends on your idea of success," says Mulaghesh, sighing with relief. "Fuck, Sigrud. I almost shot you! Why don't you knock or, I don't know, start the evening *outside* of my room."

"Because then my daughter will force me into some other duty: shaking hands, listening to workers."

"I thought you wanted to get closer to her."

"I do. She brings me to the people I need to see, then dumps me there, walks away as they begin talking. It is . . . impolite. But enough of that. You found something of Choudhry's?"

"A message. In code." She slides the paper out of her pocket. Sigrud walks forward—she notes that he seems to move silently, even though he's nearly twice her size—takes it, and moves to the desk in the corner.

"I have laid out the materials we will need," he says, sitting. "Lots of paper. Lots of pen and ink."

"Nice to see you've set up shop. Shara gave me a codex of all the various encryption metho—"

"That will not be necessary." Sigrud sits, pulls out a pen, and unfolds Choudhry's message. "They made me memorize so many codes in my day. . . . This I could do in my sleep. And that is a complaint, not a boast."

He looks over the codes, then begins making small marks on the paper with a pencil, underlining a stray H or I or 3 or an M. He moves with a quiet, thoughtless grace, as if proofreading a letter.

"That's not the only thing I found up there." She groans as she takes off her coat, her back popping and crackling unpleasantly. "Whoever it is we're hunting drilled a damned hole right down to the thinadeskite mines."

Sigrud's brow wrinkles ever so slightly as he mutters numbers to himself. "Mm? What?"

"Someone made a second mine entrance, basically. A little one. Looks like the kind of thing people would carve to escape a prison camp. Biswal and Nadar are convinced the Voortyashtani insurgents used it to bomb the mines, but . . ."

"But you are still convinced it was a Divinity, or something Divine."

"Yeah. There's an ulterior use for thinadeskite besides conducting electricity, or you can have the head off my fucking shoulders."

He purses his lips, continues writing. "Anything on Choudhry? Besides this?"

"I'm no longer so sure she was mad. Or that she's behind this, even. She worked her ass off to get this message to me, or someone from the Ministry. That'll depend on what it says, though . . . which, we're making progress on? Right?"

"Progress, yes. It's a code used for trade delegates in Ahanashtan. Probably the least likely code to be known here. Which is why she used it, to be sure."

"I don't like this. I prefer my madwomen to be absolutely fucking stark mad, thank you very much. This takes thinking."

"There is rice whisky in the washroom," says Sigrud, "if you would like some."

"Mm? What? You hid booze in my room?"

"I have booze hidden all over the place. Dead drop training has its uses beyond espionage."

Mulaghesh finds the jug of whisky—cleverly squirreled away under the sink—and sits and drinks as Sigrud decrypts the message. He shakes his head sometimes, as if what he's writing confuses him, but keeps going. Then, with something like a cringe on his face, he puts his pen down.

"Finished?" says Mulaghesh.

"I . . . do not know."

"How can you not know if you're finished?"

"Because I am not at all sure what I translated. Perhaps it is in code again, but . . . If so, it is one I do not know. Come and see."

Mulaghesh stands and looks over his shoulder, reading:

Listen, listen, little priests
Coming now the bright white shores and all the flock there weeping
Orphans, the disused and forgotten, the chaff of many wars, like snow upon an endless plain
Listen, listen

I've spent too much time there. Put too much of myself through. My mind, my thoughts, some part of me, it's unraveling, and I can't keep the threads straight. I can feel myself losing myself and I don't know what that means
No, I do. I know what it means.
I did not kill enough. One confirmed kill, one measly little murder, not enough, not enough to go there. It only accepts the warriors, you see, those whose hands have spilled oceans of blood, lakes of blood

I am trying, I am so sorry

The ore was strange, so peculiar, so odd, and something was amiss. When I neared it, when I sat in their labs and studied it for hours, I dreamed of things, of awful moments of my own past

the pistol barrel trembling as I raised it, her face dumb with surprise, the jolt as the bolt tip pierced my body and then the crack of my weapon in my hand

So I watched the mines. I did not know why. Something was wrong and I had nothing else to watch. I watched and watched and watched.
Saw a lantern. Then gone. Then a lone figure creeping across the hills, to the trees, to the ancient place. Then gone.
gone
I found the secret entrance, the tunnel. I waited to catch them when they exited. I tried to, at least. Fought them. But they struck me, hard, in the head. Lucky hit, lucky

I almost died
I think I almost died then
did I die

how could one even tell

I could go into the tunnels now but I could find no sign of who it was or what they were doing there, so I tried the ritual, the last one that I thought might work. I had sensed it almost working before, almost almost almost, like a key in a lock, all the tumblers almost falling into place
I could sense it wanted to. I just needed to try it in the right place
The mines

I saw them there, the lost army
They're still there, across the deeps, down in the dark

with Her

someone must stop it, stop what's coming

There is a man I have learned of, an ancient man who knows the ways of this place from long ago
They say he is a man but others say he is not a man but an idea that wears the image of a man
But perhaps
Perhaps, perhaps, perhaps he knows the songs of Voortya's opposite, the songs of sacrifice
He knows the rituals never written, never recorded, he knows the secret ways in and out of this world and the next world
He knows the way things were
The flow of life to death and death to life
Memory, old and withered, waiting upon the isle

I must find him
I must find him and find the ways across, so I can end them all, kill them all, stop what's coming before it starts

Remember
Remember me, remember this
Remember that I tried

Sigrud and Mulaghesh are silent while they reflect on this. The room suddenly feels quite small and dark, the fire in the fireplace a low glimmering that gives off barely any light.

"Um," says Mulaghesh. "Okay. So. Let's try and extract whatever tangibles we can from this."

"Good luck," says Sigrud, standing. He walks to the fireplace and taps his pipe out onto the coals.

Mulaghesh holds up an index finger. "Okay. Um. One—it was *not* Choudhry who made the tunnel to the thinadeskite mines. Someone else made it, and Choudhry got the jump on them, but they got away. That would be how she received the head wound I've been hearing about, and it's how she got into the mines to perform the Window to the White Shores. Unfortunately, odds are that whoever made the tunnel stopped using it the second they were found out, so I don't think I can pull off another stakeout, like Choudhry did."

"What if they left something in the mines to go back for?"

"Then it's crushed flat as a half-drekel coin under all that rock."

"Oh. Good point."

"Second." Mulaghesh sticks out another finger. "It sounds like Choudhry *isn't* the person behind all this. She was hot on the heels of whoever it was, and maybe that's how she came to find out about the murders—though she doesn't mention the murders at all here."

"If her message is true, yes. That is the case."

"Yeah, and let's just assume it's true for now. Because it also suggests that Choudhry left Voortyashtan to go . . . somewhere. To see someone, some old Voortyashtani who might know rituals and rites even the locals would have never heard of—and likely ones that even Shara wouldn't know of."

"Could it even be possible for someone to live that long?" says Sigrud. "The Blink took place almost ninety years ago."

"Eighty-six, to be exact. The Blink and the Plague wiped out tons of people, but not all of them. Perhaps some survived, had children, passed along secrets. But she also makes him sound strange . . . an idea wearing the image of a man? What does *that* mean?"

They sit in silence, each hoping the other will suggest something.

"What we don't know," says Sigrud, "we don't know."

"True enough. Moving on. Third." Mulaghesh sticks out her ring finger. "It sounds like Choudhry experienced the same visions I did down in the thinadeskite mines, visions of the most violent moments of her own past, only she saw it in the thinadeskite labs. She mentions shooting someone with a pistol"—she reaches across her desk and flips through Choudhry's file—"and she did receive a distinguished service award for an 'altercation.' You know what that means."

Sigrud points a finger to the side of his head and drops his thumb, miming the hammer of a gun, and mouths the word *Pow!*

"Right. So somehow . . . Somehow the thinadeskite *reacts* to people who've seen combat, who have been forced to take lethal action, reaching out to them and making them remember those moments. Pandey mentioned it, I saw it, and now Choudhry. None of them mention seeing the violence from other *eras* like I did, though."

"Maybe," he says, "it is because you have killed many more people than they have."

"Mayb—" She stops and looks at him. "Why do you say that?"

"I was a Ministry operative. It was my job to know things. And I mixed with many soldiers."

Mulaghesh watches him clean the bowl of his pipe, stopping briefly to dig something out from between two of his teeth.

"And . . . what did you hear?" she asks.

He examines the chunk of food on his thumb and flicks it into the fire, where it sizzles. He regards her with a cold, steady gaze. "Nothing that would make me blush."

They look at each other for a moment, Mulaghesh concerned and mistrustful, Sigrud blank and indifferent.

"You're an unusual person, Sigrud je Harkvaldsson," she says.

"I feel the same of you," he says nonchalantly.

"I see." She clears her throat. "Well. To return to what's at hand . . . After these experiences, Choudhry grew suspicious just as I did. Which makes me ask, what the *hells* is in thinadeskite that does this? And why isn't it registering as Divine?" She's reminded of what Rada said while operating on the corpse: *Deaths of all kinds echo on. And sometimes, it seems, they drown out all of life.* "None of Voortya's other miracles work, right?"

"No. Voortya's miracles are used as an example of how a Divinity's miracles *stopped* working. That's what I recall Shara saying. Voortya was, how did she say, the textbook example."

"Except I *saw* the damned City of Blades. As well as whatever apparition of Voortya it was that destroyed the mines. And now we know Choudhry saw the city too—which makes me wonder if that's where she disappeared to."

Sigrud stops cleaning his pipe. "You think Sumitra Choudhry is in the Voortyashtani *afterlife*?"

"No one's seen hide nor hair of her," says Mulaghesh. "And besides the person she surprised coming out of the tunnel to the mines, I can't see that she had any real enemies. She explicitly says in the message that she went somewhere. That's the only logical conclusion, illogical as it may be."

"So if she *did* go over to the City of Blades . . . why?"

"She came to the same conclusion I did—the Night of the Sea of Swords, the Voortyashtani apocalypse. She realized it might be coming, that someone might be trying to trigger it. Maybe Choudhry went there to try to stop it. But how she thought she could do that . . . I don't know." She tosses the decoded message back onto the desk. "Fuck. Not for the first time, I wish Shara were here. She'd know what to do."

Sigrud packs his pipe until it is overflowing with what smells like abysmally poor tobacco. "Why don't you just ask her?"

"She's supposed to be hands-off with me. Industry forces looking over her shoulder, that kind of thing. The only means I have of contacting her is routing a telegram through Bulikov to Ahanashtan. It'd take days."

"She didn't tell you about the emergency line?"

"Huh? What do you mean?"

"Her . . . emergency line. For contacting her."

"You're just repeating yourself. No. No, I have no idea what in the hells you're talking about."

He sticks his pipe in his mouth and screws up his face as he thinks about it. "Do you *really* want to talk to her?"

"Well . . . It'd be nice, sure, so—"

"Say no more." He walks to the window and licks his finger. "Now . . . How did this stupid thing start? Ah, yes." He then begins to draw on one pane of the window, his thick finger making delicate, graceful strokes on the glass.

"What are you *doing*?" says Mulaghesh. "Are y . . . Whoa." She watches as his finger appears to dip *into* the glass, like it's not a solid pane but is instead the surface of a puddle, somehow hanging there on the wall.

"It works here," says Sigrud softly. "Good. It's one of Olvos's, who isn't dead, so it should still work."

She shivers. Something in the air changes: it's like the shadows have all turned around, or perhaps the fire has grown larger but is now casting off dimmer light, or light of a hue her eye has trouble catching.

The pane of glass is now dark and opaque: Mulaghesh can see the harbor in the panes on either side of it, but in the one Sigrud touched she can now see nothing but black. She notices she can hear something new, too: a soft clicking, like that of a clock, though there is no clock in the room.

"I . . . *think* that worked," he says slowly, not sounding at all convinced.

There's the sound of someone muttering, "Hmm . . . Hunh?"

Mulaghesh looks around, trying to find its source. "What . . . What did you just do?"

Then the sound of something shifting, but it has a strange quality to it, as if the sound is bouncing up a metal pipe from far away.

"Shara?" says Sigrud. "Are you there?"

And then, somehow, there's a woman's voice saying, "What in the *hells*?"

There's a click and the black pane changes, suddenly filling with golden light, which appears to be coming from a small electric lamp on a bedside table on the other side of the window.

This is, Mulaghesh knows, impossible: what is on the other side of the window is the harbor and the North Seas. Yet it's like the pane of glass is a hole, and by looking through the hole Mulaghesh can see . . .

A bedroom. A woman's bedroom. A very *important* woman's bedroom, judging by the curtained, four-poster bed, the intricately wrought desk, the giant grandfather clock, and the countless paintings of very stern-looking officials wearing sashes and lots of ribbons and medals.

She's seen this place before, she realizes. *This is the prime minister's mansion.* . . .

A face pokes through the curtains of the four-poster bed. It's a familiar face, though it has far more lines and gray hairs than when Mulaghesh last saw it. It is also fixed in an expression of unspeakable, furious outrage.

"What . . . What!" says Shara Komayd. "What in *hells* are you *doing*, Sigrud?"

Mulaghesh says, "Ah, shit."

***

"Turyin?" says Shara. Her voice is distant and wobbly, as if it's not coming from her mouth but is being pulled out of her room, packaged up, transported to this room in the SDC headquarters, and unwrapped beside Mulaghesh's ear. But it's also much, much older and wearier than Mulaghesh remembers, as if Shara has done nothing but talk since they last met. "Turyin, are you *mad*? This is the one thing we absolutely cannot risk right now!"

"Okay," says Mulaghesh. "Whoa. Hold on. I had no idea he was going to do that." She looks at the pane of glass, as if trying to spot any hidden mechanisms. "This . . . This is a miracle, isn't it?"

"Of *course* it's a damnable miracle! It is also three in the morning here! Are there any other obvious matters I need to confirm before you explain why you have interrupted me in a state of . . . of some serious undress? Assuming you *have* a reason, that is?"

Sigrud says, "Turyin thinks your officer has gone to the afterlife." Shara frowns. "What?"

"Um . . . Okay," says Mulaghesh. "Let me start from the beginning here." She tries to rattle off the current state of things—a much more rambling and disjointed version of the very conclusions she just went through with Sigrud.

Shara listens and grows so distracted she lets the curtains drop, revealing that she is wearing a set of bright pink-and-blue button-up pajamas. "But . . . But that's not possible, Turyin," she says when she finishes. "You can't have seen her. Voortya is *dead*."

"I know."

"*Very* dead."

"I know! You don't think I've been thinking that every day since I've been here?"

"Yes, but . . . I mean, *none* of Voortya's miracles work anymore. And I know. I tried them, all over the Continent. It was an easy way to determine if there were any alterations to reality in any given location, certain contortions of physical rules—"

"You're losing me."

"Fine. But the Divinity we know as Voortya is very, very much gone from this world."

"I know that. But I saw what I saw."

Shara sighs, fumbles with her nightstand, and puts on her spectacles. Then she walks to the window and says, "Press your translation of Choudhry's message up against the glass. Hurry now. We can't get caught like this . . ."

Mulaghesh does so. To her surprise, the surface of the pane of glass is quite hard.

She can't see her, but she can hear Shara talk as she reads: "My word . . . Oh, my goodness gracious . . . What did that poor girl go through?"

"So you get the gravity of our situation."

"Yes," says Shara. Her voice sounds like she's just aged ten years. "You may remove the message now, please."

Mulaghesh takes it away. Shara is staring into space, blinking wearily. Then there's a soft sound from the four-poster bed, a quiet *coo*, and Shara comes to life. She rushes back to the bed, sticks her head through the curtains, and shushes something. After a moment longer she returns to the window.

"You have company?" asks Mulaghesh.

"Something like that." Her tone makes it clear that she's not willing to discuss it.

"When's the last time you got sleep?" asks Mulaghesh.

"Sleep?" asks Shara. She attempts to smile. "What's that?"

"I take it things aren't going well."

"Oh, no. Not well at all. I fully expect this term in office will be my last."

"What! But what about all your programs? What about the harbor?"

"Oh, well, they'll be cut. The harbor they'll keep—they're contractually obliged to—but they'll slash it to the bone. Unless whoever inherits the position from me chooses not to, of course, which seems unlikely. Anyway." She rubs her eyes. "That is not the subject at hand. The subject at hand, I think, is one of *sacrifice*."

"Of what?"

"Sacrifice. It grows clearer now. You know the story of Saint Zhurgut? How he fashioned Voortya's sword from the arm of his son?"

"I've heard mention of it."

"His son—his only child—fell in battle against the Jukoshtanis. This was before the Divinities united, of course. Anyway, instead of mourning and weeping, he struck off the hand of his son and presented it as a sacrifice to Voortya. This act of sacrifice was so great that it was transformed into a weapon for her, a tool of slaughter—the sword of Voortya."

"Which is her personal symbol," says Mulaghesh.

"Correct. But what many forget is that that act of sacrifice was done in mimicry of another, much older event—one that took place nearly one hundred years before. Because though it's true Voortya was the first Divinity to create an afterlife, she could not do it alone. She was the Divinity of destruction. She could not build, or create. Such a capacity was beyond her. So she had to reach out to someone who could. Her *opposite*, as Choudhry mentions in her message—Ahanas."

"Ahanas?" says Mulaghesh, confused. "The . . . the Divinity of plants?"

"Of *growth*, Turyin. Of fecundity, fertility, life—and creation. In other words, the very antithesis of Voortya in every way. In the very early days of the Continent, before the Divinities even united, it's recorded that Voortya reached out to her opposite and asked for a truce. And, for a period, Voortya . . . courted her."

"Courted her? Like as in—"

"As in romantically," says Shara. "*Sexually*. Yes."

"So Voortya was . . ."

"She was a Divinity. Which means our terms for whatever actions she might have taken do not have much application. Regardless, it became clear that Voortya had ends beyond romance. She used her relationship with the Divinity Ahanas to create the City of Blades, the ghostly island where her followers would wait for her after their deaths. The most common depiction of its creation has the two Divinities wading out into the sea and the white shores arising under their feet. It was, in some ways, both in accordance with and in complete contradiction to their own natures: life after death, creation beyond destruction. It was a powerfully self-contradictory act, and it required the two Divinities to become so entwined that, on some level, it wasn't easy to tell one apart from the other. But once Voortya had gotten what she wanted—once she had secured an afterlife for her followers—she separated herself from Ahanas. Which was not an easy thing to do, at this point."

Mulaghesh remembers the drawings on the walls of Choudhry's room. "She cut off her own hand, didn't she?" she says softly.

Shara cocks her head. "How did you know that?"

"Choudhry painted it on her walls. Two figures standing on an island, one severing her hand at the wrist. She cut off her own hand while Ahanas held it, didn't she?"

Shara pushes her glasses up her nose. "Yes. Yes, she did. This is an interpretation of what, for we mortals, is an inconceivable act. But it is an apt one. Voortya was forced to mutilate herself in some fashion to strip herself away from Ahanas, to stay true to her nature and remain the Divinity her flock had chosen to follow. It was a tremendously traumatic event for both Divinities, and even after the Continent chose to unite, the two Divinities and two peoples refused to have anything to do with one another. But I suspect it was far more traumatic for Voortya."

"Why?"

"She changed significantly. Before this event, Voortya was always depicted as a four-armed animal, a creature of tusks and horns and teeth. Not unlike a monster. After this, though, she began being depicted as a four-armed human woman dressed in the arraments of battle: armor and sword and spear. And she never spoke again."

"Never?"

"Never. There is a lot of speculation about this transformation. Some wonder if her trauma left her mute. But others suggest that her interactions with Ahanas changed her: she tasted, very briefly, life and love. She tasted an existence beyond one of torment and destruction. As a creature of war, she had never imagined that this could even exist. But then, suddenly, she did. She understood what was possible. And then she had to abandon it, and return to what she was."

"Why did she do that?"

Shara shrugs. "I suspect it was because her people needed her. She had promised them an afterlife, and she was sworn to deliver. These things have a power of their own, you see. Voortya had never been defeated before this moment. She had never lost a battle, nor had her people. But in order to accomplish this victory, in order to win and create this life beyond death for her children, she had to defeat herself, to strike down her own being, to sacrifice herself. Again, the act of self-contradiction: life through death, victory through defeat. And, having done so, I think she never really recovered."

"So what does this have to do with anything?"

"I suspect," says Shara slowly, "that if the Voortyashtani afterlife still exists somewhere, then its persistence can somehow be traced back to this one act. A sacrifice is a promise, in a way, a symbolic exchange of power. Voortya gave up immense power to create the afterlife. I suspect that power escaped the wrath of the Kaj, and can still be found somewhere, anchoring her life beyond death to this world."

"So . . . where is it?" asks Mulaghesh.

"Where is what?"

"This, I don't know, power?"

"Oh, I've no idea," says Shara. "We're far beyond the realm of conventional knowledge here. Voortya's interactions with Ahanas occurred before Bulikov was even founded. I suspect you're dealing with something that took place back in the very early days of existence, before the Divinities understood what they themselves really were."

"Could it be . . . Could it be the thinadeskite?"

"What, the thinadeskite as the physical manifestation of this power?" asks Shara. "That's . . . Well, that's not a *bad* idea, Turyin. But that too leaves a lot to be answered for—this thing you saw, this apparition—if it had anything in common with the original Voortya, why would she destroy the mines, the source of her own power?"

"You yourself said she was traumatized," says Mulaghesh. "Maybe we're dealing with another mad Divinity."

"Perhaps. But it doesn't seem to fit. Voortya never spoke, and in most depictions of her—when she took a comprehensible, humanoid form, that is—she had four arms and one missing hand. None of this matches up with what you saw and heard. And I would need undeniable proof if I were to try to do anything. I am not quite as powerful as when you left me, Turyin."

"So . . . So how does that help me figure out what to do next?" asks Mulaghesh, frustrated. "I don't need stories, I need leads!"

Shara sighs deeply. Mulaghesh is suddenly aware of how frail Shara seems, and she realizes that her demand is likely just one of thousands Shara must hear every single day. "I know. I know it's not what you wanted. But I suspect it's all I can give you. It is known that Voortyashtanis possessed a ritual to glimpse into the life beyond death, into the City of Blades—the Window to the White Shores. If there is a ritual that allowed them to fully cross *over*, I suspect it is a fusion of a Voortyashtani rite and an *Ahanashtani* rite. And, because of this curious quality, I expect it's never been recorded. The one person who might know, it seems, is the old man Choudhry mentioned."

"And he told Choudhry how to cross over. And she went there to . . . to try to stop whatever's happening. But obviously she failed somehow."

"I know," says Shara. "But you will succeed."

"I know I have to! You don't have to tell me that!"

"I did not say you *have* to succeed," says Shara. "I said you *will*. There is not a doubt in my mind, Turyin, that you can resolve this.

You have been through far worse trials and faced far more difficult situations than this. You have a military fortress at your disposal, as well as a massive construction fleet. Though they may be unwilling, they are still potential resources."

"And just how in the hells am I going to *use* them?" snaps Mulaghesh, furious.

"In Bulikov," says Shara, "how did you convince me to collapse the tunnel to the Seat of the World, the greatest discovery in modern history, mere moments after I'd discovered it?"

"I . . . Hells, I can't remember!"

"You did it," says Shara, "by being a very belligerent, obnoxious woman."

Mulaghesh stares at her in disbelief. "Well . . . Well, thank you very fucking much!"

"You have a talent," says Shara, "for valuing what you feel is right over anything else, including, occasionally, the people around you. You do what you feel is right not because it is satisfying, but because you find any other option to be intolerable. This makes you incredibly frustrating to deal with. But it also means you find solutions where many others would simply give up."

"But . . . But this is a fucking Divinity we're talking about! Surely if you went to the Ministry and told them what would happen—"

"We have nothing definitive," says Shara. "No concrete evidence, no proof—only your testimony, and that message of Choudhry's. A half-coherent letter from an agent who went mad and has vanished, and your story, part of a clandestine operation that is occurring completely off the books. If I were to use what little we have here to mobilize our forces under the precept that another Divine event was imminent, there is a not-insignificant chance that it could result in something very similar to a coup."

"A *coup?*" says Mulaghesh, aghast. "In *Saypur?*"

"I'm sure it would begin as an impeachment," says Shara wearily. "Or something wearing much more civilized trappings. But I know there are forces in the military and industry that would be the ones to ramrod it through. I've broken a lot of rules to put you where you are now, Turyin. Without solid evidence, my opponents in Ghaladesh would say I was fabricating the whole thing, trying to drum up support where I have none. And when the dust settled, it would be these figures that would possess much more global power—something that could be terribly bad for Saypur, and the world."

Mulaghesh rubs the center of her forehead. "I thought you were going to toss all those ratfucks out on their ears when you got elected."

Shara smiles weakly. "There are rather a lot of ratfucks, unfortunately."

"So I'm on my own," says Mulaghesh. "Even after this."

"No, no. Not alone. I do not think you are on your own. On the contrary, you have Sig—"

She stops speaking and looks over Mulaghesh's shoulder. Mulaghesh turns and sees that Sigrud has leapt to his feet and is silently stalking toward a blank section of wall. He examines the wall, looking it up and down, then looks at Shara in the windowpane and shakes his head.

Shara mouths, "Good luck," to Mulaghesh, wipes her fingers across the glass, and vanishes. The glass grows transparent yet again.

Sigrud turns to the wall and feels along the crown molding. His finger finds a carving of a whale tooth. He presses it—there's a *click!*—and the wall falls back like a door.

Sigrud dives into the gap. There's a cry of surprise and possibly pain from the other side. Mulaghesh has already grabbed the carousel and is raising it at the secret door, finger close to the trigger but not on it, not yet. She paces to line up along the wall behind the door, holding the carousel just at head-height.

Someone tumbles into the room, stumbling from a hard shove. Mulaghesh's instincts kick in and she puts the carousel's sights right on their head, though it takes her a second to realize this particular head possesses bright blond hair arranged in an urbane coiffure, along with two furious blue eyes watching her from behind a pair of severe-looking glasses.

"Shit," says Mulaghesh. "Signe, between you and your father, I'm wondering if your whole family just doesn't know how to use a door."

***

Sigrud walks back in and shuts the secret door. "How *dare* you!" Signe says to him. "How dare you treat me like that!"

He ignores her and sits back down on the couch with his back to them, and lights his pipe.

Mulaghesh looks at the panel in the wall. "I guess you forgot to tell me you had one of these in my room."

"You didn't ask," Signe says angrily. "You *knew* we had servants' doors all throughout SDC headquarters. Of *course* we'd have one here; this is a vice-presidential suite"—she looks around at the chicken bones and tobacco—"though I see you have treated it with your usual amount of care."

"Why would I want one of these in my room?"

"If you had ordered food it'd have come through that very door. It's all perfectly innocent!"

"I can order food from my room?"

"What else did you think the button in the corner with the sign RING FOR SERVICE is for?" She looks back at Mulaghesh, who has not yet lowered her gun. "Please stop pointing that at me."

"What did you hear?" asks Mulaghesh.

Signe glances around the room. Looking, Mulaghesh realizes, for the third person she heard. "Nothing."

"That's a pretty bold lie."

"I didn't come here to eavesdrop!"

"Maybe. But that's what you wound up doing." Mulaghesh lowers the carousel and sets two chairs up facing one another. She sits in one and gestures to the other. Signe slowly sits. "So. What'd you hear?"

"You can't shoot me, you know," says Signe. "This is my company's property. I could stand up and leave right now."

"Try it," says Mulaghesh. "I might have one hand, but I still know how to restrain someone and not leave a mark."

Signe looks to her father. "Are you going to allow this?"

"I remember today," he says, "when you introduced me to the

welders here, then abandoned me, leaving me with them. It is no fun, being stuck in a difficult spot."

"I . . . I *swear*," says Signe, "you two are the most frustrating, useless people alive! But of course you'd gang up on me; you both *know* each other so well."

Mulaghesh says simply, "The afterlife."

With those two words Signe freezes, just for a second, her pale blue eyes flicking away and then back.

"Yeah," says Mulaghesh. "You heard. I'm betting you heard a lot. Why don't we have a civil conversation about this?"

Signe considers her options. Then she takes out her silver box filled with her tiny black cigarettes. She lights a match with a thumbnail—a trick Mulaghesh feels like she's been sitting on for a while—takes a long drag, and exhales, a seemingly endless river of smoke flowing from somewhere deep inside of her. "All right. I will be direct. You . . . You think Sumitra Choudhry—poor little mad Sumitra Choudhry—has somehow traveled to Voortya's City of Blades?"

"She seems to say that's what she was intending to do," says Mulaghesh.

"And I assume that what is—or *was*—being mined up by the fortress was this . . . thinadeskite you mentioned?"

Mulaghesh grimaces. *So much for state secrets.* "Yes."

"And both you and Choudhry believe this material has some kind of connection to the Voortyashtani afterlife?"

"Jury's still out on that one."

"At the very least," says Signe, "you think it is connected to *Voortya* . . . whom you said you saw. That you . . . you *saw*." Mulaghesh feels Signe's bright, hard gaze poring over her, studying her every feature, and she is suddenly aware of how intensely, furiously bright this young woman is. "Do you really believe that?"

"I don't know what I believe. But I know what I saw."

Mulaghesh doesn't like the condescending, dismissive smile creeping into Signe's face. "You're mad," says Signe. "The two of you, if he believes it. The *three* of you, if Choudhry did too. I'm glad

I heard what I did, because now I *know* I'm dealing with absolute *loonies*, rather than merely suspecting it!"

"I've been there," says Mulaghesh quietly. "I've seen it. Remember when I almost fainted before the statue of Voortya in your yard? It took me there. It showed me something. Sumitra Choudhry had been at that spot before me, performed some rite, and I walked right into its aftereffects."

"But even the Voortyashtanis believe the afterlife's gone!" says Signe. "Everyone accepts that now, when you die, you just rot in the damned ground! If these people don't believe it, why should you?"

"They haven't seen gods before," says Mulaghesh fiercely. "And I have. I almost died facing them. You are young and clever and brash. But I have seen so, so much more of life than you have, child. I have been so close to the Divine before, I could smell it. And I smell it again, right now."

Signe grows sober at this. She looks back and forth between Mulaghesh and Sigrud, who is still facing away. "Do . . . Do you *really* believe what you're saying?"

"I do," says Mulaghesh. She sits back and watches Signe coldly. "And I also believe that if the Voortyashtani afterlife is possible, the Night of the Sea of Swords is possible as well. I also believe that that makes investing in this harbor a damn stupid idea, isn't it? And you *know* there are forces in Saypur just *itching* to rebuke the prime minister, cut her pet project loose, and walk away from it, leaving it to die. I believe they're looking for any excuse to scrap it. And I believe I could tell them the CTO of SDC was hiding Voortyashtani artifacts in order to blackmail the locals. I could tell them anything because frankly, Signe, they're just waiting for an excuse. If one of Shara's own trusted deputies says it's over, then it's over."

Signe stares at her in horror. "You . . . You wouldn't."

"I wouldn't? I just told you what I saw, what I believe. This is my greatest nightmare come to life, Signe Harkvaldsson. Do *not* trifle with me as I try to amend the situation."

"What is it you *want*?" asks Signe, panicked. "To scare me into silence? What would I gain from telling anyone what you believe?"

"I don't want to scare you. I want you to *help*, damn it." She grabs the decoded message and shoves it into Signe's hands. "You're Voortyashtani. You were raised here. Look at this and tell me if you see one damn thing that sounds familiar, that means anything. *Anything.*"

Signe stares at Mulaghesh, confused, then turns to the message. "I have never been told to read something so mad with *quite* so much pressure. It's absolut—"

She trails off. Then all the color slowly leaves her face.

"What?" says Mulaghesh.

"Oh, no," Signe says quietly. "Oh, oh, please no."

Sigrud turns around, now concerned. "Signe? What is wrong?"

Signe sits frozen for nearly half a minute, then shuts her eyes. "I hoped it wasn't there. I hoped it'd just disappeared somehow, swallowed by the seas."

"What are you talking about?" says Mulaghesh.

She says softly, "The Isle of Memory."

"It's real?" says Mulaghesh. "This island is real?"

"Of course it's real," says Signe. She sounds terribly sad and weary. "I know it is. I've been there before."

"Can you take me there?"

Signe bows her head, and it's shocking to see someone who is usually the picture of confidence crumple so thoroughly. Then, very quietly, she says, "Yes."

***

The aluminum roof of the SDC guard booth *plinks* and *plonks* with countless fat raindrops, which sound more like a rain of marbles. Lennart Björck, cursing, maneuvers all his pots and pans so they catch each tiny waterfall. This small armada of crockery is his constant and unwelcome partner during his guard shifts, for though he tries to patch the roof after each torrential downpour, there's always something he missed.

He does a double take as he dumps one of the larger pots out of the booth window. Someone is walking down the road to them, slipping and sliding in the muck. It seems to be a woman, from their size and the tendrils of wet hair peeking out of their heavy cloak, but he can't see much else about them. Not that he would expect to in this weather. You want as much between you and the atmosphere in Voortyashtan as you can manage.

He squints. The woman is carrying something very curious: a very large pine box, about four or five feet long. It's also quite flat, not more than three or four inches thick.

He puts his rifling close, leaning it against the wall. Then he stands at the window and waits for her. She struggles up and maneuvers the pine box around so she can speak to him. It looks like the box is immensely heavy. "Delivery for General Mulaghesh from the fortress!"

"General Mulaghesh?" he says. "The Saypuri?" He looks closer at her. Her face is bound up in a scarf, and he can't make much out about her. "Who is it from?"

"Captain Nadar."

"Oh. Well then. Here, hand it here."

She hesitates. "I'm told it's a very sensitive item."

"I can't allow any items to enter the harbor works without a proper inspection first, miss. We're at a high security alert."

She hesitates some more, then reluctantly hefts up the pine box. "It is a very *old* item, they told me. *Not* to be touched. Especially with the naked skin. Oils, you see."

"Yes, yes," says Björck. He takes the pine box—it easily weighs over fifty pounds—places it on a table, and opens it. He gasps softly. "Oh-hoh."

Inside is a massive, glimmering sword, over four feet long and thick as a butcher's cleaver. Its handle is beautiful yet disturbing, featuring patterns of tusks and teeth and chitin. And the blade shines so strangely, as if it's not a sword but a mirror. He checks the lining—being careful not to touch the sword, following the woman's instructions—but he sees no hint of explosives or hidden detonation devices.

He stares into his reflection in the blade. He likes what he sees, for some reason. His eyes flash handsomely; his shoulders look broader. Somehow he looks stronger in the blade. Fiercer. Powerful.

"It is *not* to be touched, they said," says the woman again.

"Mm?" says Björck, startled. "Oh. Yes, of course." He shuts the box and rehooks the clasp. "Due to the increased security, I'll have to be the one to bring the package to her. Unless you have written approval from the fortress . . ."

"Captain Nadar did not give me any," says the woman. "But . . . provided you do not *touch* it . . . it should be no issue." She bows. "Thank you. And good day," she says, and she turns and walks up the road.

Björck watches her, thinking this all very queer. Then he puts the box under his arm and flags over his supervisor. Upon hearing that it's from the fortress for the general, he's given permission to go ahead.

The rain begins to let up as he walks down the seawall road. With each step the box feels a little heavier and a little heavier, as if begging to be dropped, to taste the glint of moonlight, and be held.

I wonder, Björck thinks, *why it is I think such things?*

***

"Signe . . . ," says Sigrud. "Are . . . Are you sure you—"

"We need to go to my office," Signe says suddenly. She stands, and suddenly all the fear and anxiety is gone from her. "I'll need maps."

"O-Okay," says Mulaghesh.

"Just one moment, first." Signe goes back to the secret door, opens it, and grabs a briefcase that was sitting on the stairs. Mulaghesh pauses to wonder exactly what brought Signe to her room in the first place.

Signe's office lies deep in the recesses of SDC headquarters, which comes as a surprise to Mulaghesh. Someone as high-powered and valuable as Signe Harkvaldsson should surely have an office on the top floor with huge windows. Yet her office is almost in the basement, and resembles a loading dock converted into a loft.

But the room is obscured by what looks like, to Mulaghesh's eye, racks and racks of clothing, each one labeled with numbered tags, starting at 1.0000 and going up to . . . well, the biggest number she sees is 17.1382. As she passes one rack Mulaghesh cranes her head to get a look at it, and she sees that they're not clothes but *blueprints*, thousands and thousands of plans of things that, from what she sees, never got built.

Signe leads them to a large table in the center, an austere block of white stone that's covered in yet more blueprints. At the table's center are square stone cups filled with a variety of drafting materials: pens, pencils, rulers, abacuses, set squares, magnifying glasses, and several types of compasses. Next to these are three ashtrays, all quite full. Signe *tsks* as she approaches. "I'll have to remind my assistant to dump these out."

She makes them wait as she rolls up the blueprints and files them away. "Don't touch anything!" she warns as she paces away through the racks.

Sigrud stares around himself in awe. "My daughter," he says slowly, "lives here?"

"I don't see a bed," says Mulaghesh. "But yeah, I get that impression."

Signe returns with a large, colorful map fluttering in her hands like a flag. "Here we are," she says. She lays the map out. It's a map of the coastline, including the flow of the oceanic currents, though there have been some alterations to where the Solda passes Voortyashtan: dozens of little red blocks are clustered together in a manner that reminds Mulaghesh of a child's strategy game, like Batlan.

"What am I looking for here?" says Mulaghesh.

"This is an SDC map of all the coastlines and currents of the region. But what we're looking for . . ." Then she says, "Ah!" and points to a flicker in the thousands of tiny blue lines a few dozen miles southwest of Voortyashtan. "There."

Mulaghesh peers at where she's pointing. "There's nothing there."

"I know," says Signe. "But that's where it is."

"The Isle of Memory?"

"Yes. It's real. That's where it lies."

"Then why isn't it on the map?"

"Because I removed it."

Mulaghesh and Sigrud slowly turn to look at her.

"Some places aren't worth going to," says Signe quietly. "Some places deserve to be forgotten. And that's one of them."

"What is it?" asks Sigrud. "What is there?"

"It is part of a chain of small islands," she says. "The last, and the largest. It was a place where the highlanders conducted a . . . a rite of passage for adolescents. They'd take children down out of the mountains, along the river, and to the shore, where boats would be waiting. Then we'd sail southwest, along the coast, through the islands, until we found it." Her face is grim and haunted. "They called it the Tooth. At its top was a ruin—an ancient old place made of metal and knives. It was rumored a man lived in it, an old man who remembered everything—a man of *memory*, in other words—but I thought it was just a story, a myth. We saw no man, and no one seemed to expect us to. I thought at the time that it was a place that once had been Divine and held some specific purpose that was lost—but the highlanders, being traditional, kept coming back, kept fulfilling their oath. Those islands . . . they are a very strange place."

"What did they do there?" asks Sigrud. "The highlanders?"

Signe purses her lips and takes out a cigarette. "Bad things."

Mulaghesh clears her throat. "So that's where Choudhry went, yes? Then how exactly am I going to get to this Tooth? I don't know how to sail, and I sure as hells can't swim that far."

"You don't need to know how to sail," says Signe, lighting yet another cigarette. "Because I do."

***

Björck trudges up the muddy pathway to the SDC lighthouse, the seawall tapering off to his left. Someday soon, they say, this will all be paved over and landscaped, a place worthy of being an international embassy, the world's first impression of SDC's accomplishments as they begin to sail up the Solda. But for now, it is—like everything in Voortyashtan, in Björck's opinion—soaking wet and covered with gritty mud.

He hears a shout behind him and awkwardly turns, the heavy pine box slipping down his arm. He frowns when he sees who's running up.

"Ach, Oskarsson," he says to himself, dismayed. "Of all the filthy dogs who had to catch me now . . ."

"Björck!" says the young Dreyling, trotting up. "What in the hells are you doing up here? Why aren't you at the gate?"

He glowers at Jakob Oskarsson, fifteen years his junior and yet several positions his superior. Björck is keenly aware of the rumors that Oskarsson is the son of one of the Dreyling city leaders who helped drive out piracy, and thus was instrumental to the formation of the United Dreyling States; but Björck is also keenly aware of the *other* rumors suggesting Oskarsson's father was in league with the pirates, and only backstabbed them when he saw the writing on the wall. Whatever the cause, Jakob Oskarsson's father was powerful enough to get his son into a good place at SDC, despite Oskarsson having no experience in construction or seafaring, and certainly no personal virtues of his own.

"Delivery for the general," says Björck gruffly. Then he adds, "Sir."

"Delivery?" says Oskarsson. He bites at a fingernail. "How peculiar. Did you check it?"

"Of course I checked it, sir. It is a sword, just a sword."

"A *sword*?" says Oskarsson, agog. "Who is sending the general a sword?"

"It comes from the fortress." Björck shrugs. "I know better than to question that."

Oskarsson leans back on his heels and scratches his chin, thinking. "A special sword then, from the fortress, for the general . . . You know, Björck, perhaps *I* should be the one to deliver this to the general. It would be more befitting of someone of my rank, yes?"

Björck chooses to fix his gaze on a light pole four feet to Oskarsson's right, fearing that if he were to look at this impudent creature's face he wouldn't be able to stop himself from breaking it. "As you wish, sir." He hands it over. "She did say not to touch it."

"Who did?"

"The messenger. That is what she said to me. Do not touch the contents."

Oskarsson thinks about this, then shrugs, laughs, and places the box on the seawall. "Let me at least see what kind of sword this is." He opens it up and, like Björck, gasps at its beauty. "My word . . . What a creation of a thing this is."

"Yes," says Björck dourly.

"Yet who could possibly wield it? It must almost be too heavy to lift."

Oskarsson stares down into the mirrored blade, transfixed. Then something changes in his eyes, and Björck realizes what he's thinking.

"She . . . She *did* say not to touch it, sir," says Björck.

"And this woman, is she deputy security chief? Or better? Is she the CEO of SDC?"

"N-no, sir."

"And if the deputy security chief wishes to place security first, and hold the sword just to see if it is dangerous, is that a bad thing?"

Björck can tell that security is the farthest thing from Oskarsson's mind: he wishes to hold this thing, to feel its heft and power. "I . . . I—"

"No," says Oskarsson. "No it is not. At least, it is not if any sensible guard does not wish to be placed on suspension without pay, at least."

Björck knows that Oskarsson does not make idle threats when it comes to suspension. He shuts his mouth and looks away as Oskarsson laughs. "Always so serious, Björck. That is your problem." He reaches for the sword. "So serious that no one can ever stand to be around y—"

He stops short when his hand touches the sword. Then he just stands there, apparently frozen.

"Uh. Sir?"

Oskarsson stares straight ahead, mouth open, face blank.

"Oskarsson? Sir? Are you all right?"

He does not respond. His throat makes a few low clicks.

"Should I fetch a medic, sir?"

Björck shivers then, not from fear but because it is suddenly bitterly, bitterly cold, as if an icy wind just happened to snake down the shore and through his sleeves. He glances at the sword and pauses, staring at its blade.

Just a few moments ago the blade was facing Oskarsson's face, the young man's arrogant eyes reflected back at him. But now it's different. Now the face in the sword is not human at all.

It is like a *mask*, perhaps made of metal, wrought in the image of a crude, skeletal face, eyes small and far apart, the nose a tiny slit. Strange, monstrous-looking horns and tusks blossom from the back of the mask, like some kind of depraved substitution for hair.

Björck looks at Oskarsson's face. It is still the same face, though his gaze is dead and lifeless. Yet the sword now shows this other, distorted creature standing in his place.

All intelligence slowly dies in Oskarsson's face. A slow exhale escapes from his lips in a hiss. Then the hiss catches voice and becomes a low, loud humming noise—a sustained *om* that grows and grows. The buzzing, moaning sound does not seem to get louder, but instead seems to burrow within Björck's ears and even his body, resonating with his feet, arms, bones, then with the very brick of the seawall road, an endless moan that far exceeds the capacity of any human lung.

"Sir," says Björck. "What is wrong with you? What is *wrong* with you?"

Oskarsson lifts his head to stare at the sky. A waterfall of blood erupts from his eyes and nose and mouth, pouring out of his face to run down his body. Björck watches in horror as the blood twists around Oskarsson's shoulders, congealing and blackening, turning a rainbow of strange and monstrous colors, almost seeming to *harden*. It is as if this rain of gore has its own mind and it is cocooning him, remaking him into . . . something.

Björck shrieks in terror. Perhaps it is out of instinct—or perhaps it is due to his own long-suppressed feelings about Oskarsson himself—but Björck darts forward and shoves Oskarsson, sending the man toppling backward, over the seawall and into the dark waters, still clutching the immensely heavy sword.

There's a quiet *sploosh*. Björck looks at his hands, which are covered in dark blood. Then, screaming, he sprints for the nearest guard.

***

"Hold on," says Mulaghesh.

"Yes," says Sigrud, bristling. "Hold on."

Signe holds her hands up with the air of a schoolteacher asking for silence. "I have already considered your objections. You," she says to Mulaghesh, "don't want me around because you don't trust me. However, I am likely the person who knows the coastline the best, as I've been staring at maps of it for what feels like most of my life. And I'm the one who's been there. And *you*," she says to Sigrud, "don't want me to do it because you think it's dangerous. You would prefer to do it yourself, because you are used to being in danger, and in fact you *prefer* to do this sort of dashing skullduggery rather than do what you *need* to be doing, which is staying here and inspiring the one thousand Dreylings working night and day to keep their national economy afloat. However, having seen morale hugely increase since your arrival, I will *not* allow it to now fall. Your place is here, with the people who are working for you. In the grand scheme of things, I am"—she grits her teeth, and seems to have to dig the final words out of some nasty part of herself—"less important than you."

"Aren't you basically *running* the harbor?" asks Mulaghesh.

"Somewhat," she says. "After a few final large obstructions are cleared, we have multiple strategic plans for mopping up, ones that I designed months ago. I can afford to be missing for a few days, or I can soon."

Sigrud shakes his head. "I do not like this," he says. "I do not like this plan one bit."

Signe rolls her eyes. "You forget I have been to some of the most difficult parts of Voortyashtan. I was *raised* in them."

"And I have no desire to see you go *back* to them!"

"If the general here is correct—and I am reluctantly forced to admit that she, at least, believes it to be true—then everything I've worked for is in peril," says Signe. "Everything I've spent my life preparing could be destroyed!"

"Your *life?*" says Sigrud. "You think five years is a *life?* Five years is no time at all, it is a blink of an eye!"

"Five years for me," says Signe, "but we are talking billions of drekels hanging in the balance here—fortunes for decades to come!"

"Do you think only in money? Is that what you've become?

"Money?" says Signe, furious. "*Money?* You think I'm here to make *money?* No, Father dear, what I'm here to do is put you both out of a *job!*"

Sigrud and Mulaghesh glance at one another.

"Huh?" says Mulaghesh.

"People like you," says Signe. "You think the world's decided in fortresses, atop battlements, from far behind razor wire and fences. It's not, not anymore. The world's decided in *countinghouses*. We don't listen to the march of boots; we listen to type machines and calculation machines pounding out revenues and budgets. This is how civilization progresses—one innovation at the right time, changing the very way the world changes. It just needs one big push to start the momentum. Thinadeshi herself knew that. She tried. And we are left to take up her work."

Sigrud shakes his head. "I . . . I do not doubt you. And I do not doubt what you are doing. I commend you for it."

"Then what?"

"I just . . . I just wish you to know that there is more to life than this. There is more to life than these . . . these great tasks we set for ourselves."

Signe slowly grinds out the cigarette in the ashtray. "You misjudge me."

"I don't think I do."

"You do not know me. If you wanted to, you would."

"If I could have broken down those prison walls, I—"

"I know you were on the Continent for almost a *decade*!" shouts Signe. "I know you were free for years, running about with Komayd, doing her dirty work! You could have come home at any time if you wanted to, you could have known us if you wanted to, but you *didn't*! You just left us up here, in this . . . this *hell*!"

"I did not wish to expose you to what I was!" he says. "The . . . the things I saw in prison . . . the things I did, the things they did to me . . . Your lives were better off without me."

"Until Komayd said it was time for you to run home," says Signe. She laughs bitterly. "Here is the truth of it, Father. You are a brave man when you have a knife in your hand. But when faced with another person who truly needs you, I think you are a cowa—"

She stops as they hear the sirens sounding in the harbor, a low, rising wail.

"What in hells is that?" says Mulaghesh.

Signe looks to the windows. "The alert siren," she says. "Something's wrong. We . . . We must be under attack!"

***

Signe, Sigrud, and Mulaghesh all sprint up toward the first floor of the SDC building, only to find Signe's chief of security Lem sprinting in the opposite direction. "There you are," he says, gasping. "We had some . . . some kind of *attack* happen."

"Where?" demands Signe. "What happened?"

"It's out front. Just in front of the lighthouse, in fact. Should we notify the fortress?"

Signe looks to Mulaghesh, who nods once.

"Yes," says Signe. "Better safe than sorry. Now show me."

As they walk, Lem summarizes the events. ". . . Deputy Chief Oskarsson stopped him just outside to inspect the package, and found it was some kind of . . . sword."

"*Sword?*" says Mulaghesh.

"Yes. A ceremonial sword of some kind." He looks at her side-long. "I take it you don't know about this?"

Mulaghesh grimly shakes her head.

Lem shoves the door open for them as they run outside. "That's not good."

"So what?" says Signe. "Someone tried to give Mulaghesh a sword? Exactly how did this constitute an attack serious enough to sound the alarm?"

"Well . . . Because then *this* happened."

He gestures ahead to the seawall road, where two SDC trucks sit idling in the road. Beside them stands a crowd of armed Dreylings looking at something on the ground. When they see Lem and Signe they part and stand back.

Something dark and thick lies in puddles on the road. Sigrud sniffs the air. "Blood," he says softly.

"Yes," Lem says, leading them over.

"Was someone injured?" asks Mulaghesh.

"That's . . . much less clear, ma'am," says Lem. He points to a group of guards huddled on the other side of the road, then gestures to them. They escort over a tall, jittery Dreyling. The man's face is pale as snow, and his breath has the sour smell of vomit to it.

"Björck," says Signe to the pale Dreyling. "What happened?"

He shakes his head. "Jakob . . . I mean, Deputy Chief Oskarsson . . . He opened the box, and he touched the sword, and then he just . . . changed."

As they listen to his story, Mulaghesh and Sigrud exchange a glance. Mulaghesh cocks an eyebrow—*Divine?*

Sigrud nods once. *Almost certainly.*

Björck shakes his head. "The sound he made was so horrible . . . I panicked. I pushed him. He fell over the wall, into the waters. But the sword did something to him. Before I pushed him, when I looked at his reflection in the blade, he . . . it wasn't him anymore, it was something *else*. Something else standing in his place."

Mulaghesh and Sigrud look over the seawall. The waters are dark and swirling, sloshing up and down a small concrete loading dock just fifteen feet below them. "I assume that would have happened to me if I'd gotten it," says Mulaghesh. "Who gave you the box to deliver? Was it a woman?"

The Dreyling nods.

"And what did she look like?" asks Mulaghesh.

"I could not see her. She wore a cloak, and a scarf. . . . And it was raining then."

Sigrud leans out over the water, frowning, though Mulaghesh can't see what worries him so.

"What did she sound like?" asks Mulaghesh. "Old? Young?"

"She sounded . . . I do not know. Normal. No strong accent, nothing notable. She was short. Wore dark robes. She just went up to the street there." He points.

Sigrud cocks his head, still staring at the waters below the seawall.

"We could do searches in the city," says Signe. "But a fat lot of good that will do. So many people come i—"

Sigrud says, "There is something down there."

"What? Besides the ocean, you mean?" says Signe.

"Yes . . . There is something rising u—"

There's a sudden thrashing sound in the water below them, and something huge goes whirring up into the night sky, bursting from the waters like a startled dove. The crowd of Dreylings gasps and watches its ascent, a spinning, whirring arc of glimmering steel that dances through the air toward one of the SDC cranes—

It's a sword, thinks Mulaghesh, *but who threw it?*

—and slices through the crane's supports like they were made of butter.

There's a pause as physics decides what to do with the several tons of metal suddenly suspended in the sky. Then the crane tips, yaws, and with the groaning sounds of an old man climbing out of bed, begins to slowly tumble to the ground.

"Run!" screams Signe. "Run! *Out of the way, out of the way!*"

It seems to happen in slow motion, like a battleship falling from the sky. The very impact is so great it knocks people off their feet.

Dust and sea spray washes over them, even though it fell several hundred feet away. Mulaghesh watches in mute terror as some of the closer, unluckier Dreylings fall in a shower of deadly shrapnel.

Mulaghesh continues tracking the sword spinning through the sky as the plume of dust pours over them. She watches as it slashes up, up, up, and finally begins to turn, hurtling back down to them, perhaps threatening to cut the very world in half.

But it doesn't. Instead its grip smacks into the open palm of someone's hand, raised up high above the seawater.

She stares at the hand, then at its owner, who is now walking up the dock, water still pouring off their back.

At first the thing seems to be no more than some tangled wreckage washed ashore, a repulsive amalgam of coral and metal and bone. But as the water pours off of it her eyes discern shoulders, arms, and a crude, skeletal face. She sees the back adorned in horns and tusks and blades, the wrists lined with serrated teeth, every inch built to harm, to hurt, to destroy, as if this thing's mere passage through the world could wreak unspeakable destruction.

The sword hums in the figure's hand. It looks at the sword, head cocked, as if beholding a beauty it has not experienced in ages.

It is a Voortyashtani sentinel. But it is far larger than the sentinels she saw in her visions, and its armor is far more ornate, far more terrifying.

The sword vibrates, humming and buzzing, and somewhere in that awful sound is a voice—one that does not speak to their minds as much as directly speak to their souls, crying, *Battle and war! The last war, the last war!*

Suddenly she recognizes the thing standing on the dock, and understands what—or, rather, who—is now striding into Voortyashtan.

"Holy hells," says Mulaghesh. "I don't know how but—it's fucking Saint Zhurgut!"

∗∗∗

"*Who?*" says Sigrud.

"It can't be!" says Signe. "How is that possi—"

She never finishes the sentence: Saint Zhurgut studies his surroundings, raises his sword, and flings it forward once again. Everyone dives to the ground as the massive arc of steel hurtles through the air. It smashes into the SDC trucks, punching through one of them like it's made of paper and clipping another, which then slowly tips over from the blow.

They watch as the sword rips through the air with a low *om* hum that sounds, Mulaghesh realizes, a lot like what Björck described. The sword goes speeding back into the saint's hand, who then turns at the top of the dock and begins to calmly walk toward them.

Mulaghesh takes a deep breath and bellows, "Open fire!"

She's not their commander, but the Dreyling guards quickly oblige, lining up along the seawall and opening up on Zhurgut. The sound that fills the air is a dreadfully familiar one to Mulaghesh: it is the sound of countless bullets uselessly bouncing off of Divine armor. She still hears it in her dreams, echoes of the Battle of Bulikov, and even though the bolt-action riflings are far more advanced they don't seem to do much damage: Saint Zhurgut pauses as if taking a moment to regard this new phenomenon, his masked face swiveling to take in the sparks flying off of his chest and arms. Then he crouches and leaps.

Mulaghesh hears the *om* sound again, and thinks, *The sword's dragging him. It's pulling him through the air.*

The saint comes plummeting down, his sword moaning and shrieking. Again, Mulaghesh hears words in that strange sound, murmuring, *I am battle incarnate. I am a weapon wielded by Her hand.*

When he lands one of the SDC guards dissolves in a spray of blood, vivisected from collarbone to crotch. She watches in horror as the man has a moment to take in his situation—his dangling head craning down, wide-eyed—until the two halves of his body fall away and he topples over. The saint rolls forward—dragged, it seems, by some propulsion emanating from his sword—and the giant blade slashes up, around, and through the crowd of SDC guards. Mulaghesh watches as six stout men seem to dissolve, like cloth puppets having their threads pulled apart.

"Fucking hells!" shouts Mulaghesh. "Take cover!"

Sigrud and Signe sprint in one direction toward a rickety fish shop up the hill, while Mulaghesh, Lem, and the other SDC guards take cover down the street. They find an old slate wall along a vacant lot and immediately take up positions. The guards wheel around and aim at the metal figure slowly stalking up the oystershell street.

"Don't shoot yet!" says Mulaghesh quickly. "Don't attract his atten—"

Too late: there's a series of pops as the riflings go off. Saint Zhurgut swivels his crude face to look at them. Then he raises the sword, there's the droning *om* sound, and then . . .

The slate wall seems to explode. A rain of stones shoves her to the ground. Dust clouds her eyes. Then everything goes dark.

***

Children screaming. Fires dancing beneath the night sky. The bright cold face of the moon and the cold clinging mist.

I always knew I'd come back here, she thinks dreamily. *Back to this place, where we wrought death so gladly . . .*

She watches through puffy eyes as a ragged child totters through the firelit streets, screaming for its mother.

It's good that I'm dying here, she thinks. *I deserved it. I deserve it.*

"General? General?"

Mulaghesh tries to speak. Her mouth is thick and bloody. "Wh-Where am I?"

"Are you all right, General?"

She opens her eyes to see an unfamiliar face standing over her: a young Saypuri officer, apparently a captain, wearing a closely wrapped headcloth and sporting a trim, neat beard. He has the look of a poet about him—something dreamy to his large, dark eyes—and she wonders who he is. Perhaps he's one of her long-forgotten comrades who died in some faded conflict or another.

"Am I dead?" she croaks.

He smiles weakly. "No, General. You're not. I'm Captain Sakthi. I'm here from the fortress."

There's a crash and then a rumbling from somewhere behind them.

"What's going on?" asks Mulaghesh.

"CTO Harkvaldsson sent word up to the fortress of a possible attack. . . . And it seems that the attack is, ah, still ongoing."

Mulaghesh slowly sits up. Her arms and side scream in anguish. No doubt she got banged up by the raining stones—her nose is broken, for the umpteenth time in her life—but she seems to be in one piece. She appears to be in some sort of temporary housing structure, one that no one ever got around to living in. Fourteen other Saypuri soldiers stand at the windows, riflings ready, though they're obviously terrified. She also sees Lem, Signe's security man, sitting at the door, staring out. His face is wildly bruised, and from the feel of it hers isn't much better.

"How long was I out?" she asks.

"I'm not sure, ma'am. You were carried here by Mr. Lem, who flagged us down. We have not attempted to engage the, ah . . . the enemy. He seems remarkably difficult to engage at all, as you'll see."

He helps her stand and walk to the door. He points out, but he doesn't need to.

Voortyashtan is under siege. It's as though it's been through a day's worth of shelling. Fires dance and caper in the tattered ruins of countless yurts and tents. She watches as a slate-roofed house collapses in on itself and goes tumbling down the slopes, raining debris on the homes below.

It takes no time to spot the source of all this damage: Saint Zhurgut stands on the corner of a tall, ragged home, hurling his sword out at the city again and again, carving huge swaths through the buildings and people and structures with each toss. The air seems to vibrate with the constant *om* of his blade's progress, and she watches, horrified, as he successfully levels most of a city block in barely half a minute.

By all the seas, she thinks. *It's like someone's anchored a dreadnought in the bay and it's raining death on us!*

It takes a moment for her ears to discern it, but she realizes Zhurgut is *singing*, chanting through the sword as he flings it across the city:

> *I who gave my life and mind*
> *To be beaten smooth and hard*
> *And shorn of all distraction*
>
> *I who gave the hand of my son*
> *I am Her weapon, I am Her blade*
> *And I shall rend creation asunder*

She watches as the sword slices through one of the malformed statues standing along the Solda. The stone figure—which looks like it was carved to resemble a man drawing the string of an arrow— buckles at the waist and tumbles down the slopes, crushing houses and buildings as if they were no more than toothpicks.

"By the fucking seas," she whispers. "He means to slaughter every last one of us!"

"And it looks like he can do it, too," says Lem.

"I've called up to the fortress for reinforcements," says Sakthi. He pats an enormous lead-acid-battery-powered radio on the floor beside him. It must weigh forty pounds, at least. "They're sending down an entire battalion as fast as they can. Everyone and everything's on full alert."

"And what are *they* supposed to do?" asks Lem. "He shrugged off our fire like it was nothing!"

"I haven't exactly heard any other options!" says Sakthi.

Mulaghesh spits a mouthful of blood out on the floor. "Divine creatures are tough," she says. "But they're not invincible. Do we have anything heavier than riflings?"

"We've got the rock guns up in the truck," says Sakthi. "Could that make any difference?"

"Ponjas?" says Mulaghesh, surprised. "You brought those?"

"Per the general's orders, it's SOP for any squadron exiting the fortress," says Sakthi.

Of course it would be, she thinks. A Ponja rifling would be a pretty standard weapon for this region: firing a half-inch-caliber round, a Ponja can punch through most walls, most light armors, as well as plenty of other obstructions—including stones, which makes it useful when fighting highland insurgents in the upper ranges. After being put to this use by caravans traversing the mountain passes, the Ponja rifling met with great success, earning the nickname "rock gun." So of course Biswal would make sure his soldiers used them.

Now it's just a question of whether a Ponja can punch a hole in Divine armor as well as it can stone.

Another *om*, another rattling crash as a Voortyashtani structure collapses.

"Fuck," says Mulaghesh. "He'll tear through this place like tissue paper if we let him!"

"But the second we open up on him, he'll be on us like a buzz saw," says Lem.

"The Divine warriors you fought in the Battle of Bulikov . . . ," says Sakthi.

"What about them?" says Mulaghesh.

"They couldn't survive artillery fire, could they?"

"No. That they couldn't. What are you getting at?"

Sakthi glances down at the radio in his hand, then up at Fort Thinadeshi and its countless cannons pointed at them.

"Hold on," says Mulaghesh. "Are you seriously suggesting we shell the *city*? With *us* in it?"

"We could evacuate," says Sakthi. "Try and keep him contained. Then pound away at him."

"That would incur the losses of thousands of civilians!" says Mulaghesh angrily. "Not to mention the likely destruction of the harbor, which we've spent billions to build!"

"And if the Ponjas don't work on him?" says Sakthi, with more backbone than she expected. "What then, General?"

Mulaghesh starts thinking. She'll be damned if she sheds more civilian blood in her lifetime without even trying another way.

She remembers, suddenly, Shara's face, suspended in the pane of glass at the SDC headquarters: *You have a military fortress at your disposal, as well as a massive construction fleet. Though they may be unwilling, they are still potential resources.*

An idea starts forming in her mind. *The harbor's basically a factory,* she thinks. *And what's more dangerous than getting stuck in the machinery?*

"Where's Sigrud and Signe?" she asks.

"The *dauvkind* and his daughter?" says Sakthi. "I think they're holed up in the harbor yards. Just down that way." He points down the street.

"And do we have anyone here who's a damned good shot with a Ponja?"

"I would say Sergeant Burdar is a capable shot," says Sakthi, pointing to a short little man with a huge mustache, who gives her a curt nod.

"All right," she says. "I think . . . I think I have another option."

"You do, ma'am?" asks Sakthi.

"Yeah." Then she thinks and adds, "*Maybe.*"

***

Mulaghesh sprints through the streets of Voortyashtan, struggling with the weight of the Ponja gun in her arms. Sergeant Burdar runs alongside her, carrying two Ponja guns as well, one under each arm. When she explained her overall idea to him he seemed to treat the idea of using such a weapon on a saint as no more troubling than dove hunting: "A dancer he isn't," the sergeant said. "He hops about a bit, but he's a slow one. I can plug him pretty ably, marm, if I get a clear shot."

A clear shot, thinks Mulaghesh as they run up to the harbor yard gates. *And the right timing.*

She hears an *om* on her right, up north into the city, and a smattering of screams. The sounds of gunfire are near constant. She keeps waiting for a pause, for Saint Zhurgut to take a breather, but he doesn't: he is an engine of destruction, and he's doing what he knows.

"Sigrud, Signe!" Mulaghesh shouts to the harbor gates. "Are you in there? It's me!"

The gate falls open and she walks in. She sees Signe standing along the wall, pointing a pistol at her. Then Sigrud's face emerges from behind the gate. He jerks his head impatiently, as if to say, *Well, come on.*

"Good," says Mulaghesh. "You're all alive."

"He's paying more attention to the homes and residences," says Sigrud. "He seems to have forgotten the harbor altogether. So we're safe, for now."

"*We* are, but he's destroying the city!" says Signe. "He's killing everyone he can! He's a damned monster! Where did he *come* from?"

"From the sword, I suppose," says Mulaghesh. "You said that in the old days departed sentinels could possess the bodies of the living, yeah? I guess picking up that damned sword was the trick."

"How the hells could a Voortyashtani sword still be . . . be, well, *active?*" asks Signe.

"Beats me," says Mulaghesh. "But someone meant for *me* to pick it up. If it'd worked, that'd be me standing on top of that chimney, trying to kill everyone within a mile."

"Can we stop him?" says Sigrud.

"I have some options," says Mulaghesh. "And we *can* stop him. It's just a matter of simplicity, provided we're all healthy and willing." She looks at Signe. "That PK-512 of yours—is it operational?"

"The what?"

"The *minigun*. The giant fucking cannon you've got set up in front of your yard of statues!"

"Yes, I think so. . . . My predecessor had it installed, but . . . but no one really knew how to use it."

"Well, I do." Mulaghesh squats down and starts drawing a map of the harbor in the mud. "Listen. There's a chance that one of the Ponja guns we've brought can *maybe* penetrate his armor. So there's a chance there's literally a one-shot solution to all this."

"Then why haven't you shot him?" says Signe.

"Because if it doesn't work he's going to know where we are and slaughter us like cattle. If that's the case, we need a backup."

"Which is?" asks Sigrud.

Mulaghesh looks at Signe. "You know how to operate that train of yours?"

"The supply train?" asks Signe. "Yes, of course."

"Good." Then she looks at Sigrud. "And you—are all your limbs in working order?"

"More or less."

"And you think you can use one of these?" She lifts one of the Ponjas, which is like a small cannon.

Sigrud shrugs. "I received training on a prototype, long ago."

"Is that a yes or a no?"

"It's a maybe."

"Maybe will have to do. This isn't Bulikov, Sigrud—I don't think you can get inside Zhurgut's gut and carve your way out of him, not this time." She takes a deep, deep breath. *I hope this sounds smarter when I say it,* she thinks. *Because it sounds damned dumb when I think it.* Then she begins speaking and drawing out her plan in the mud at her feet.

***

Mulaghesh and Signe sprint northwest toward the SDC loading yards, where the supply train runs. Signe hauls Captain Sakthi's radio box, and Mulaghesh has thrown a Ponja over her shoulder. They're not going as fast as Mulaghesh would prefer, because for some damned reason Signe insisted on taking along the damned briefcase she brought to Mulaghesh's room earlier that night.

Mulaghesh tries to ignore how much her feet and arms and back hurt. *You're getting old, girl,* she says to herself. *You can't put yourself through a fight like this anymore.*

"This," says Signe, panting, "is maybe one of . . . of the worst plans I've ever . . . I've ever heard of!"

"Just do your part," says Mulaghesh, "and we'll see how it goes."

"But . . . But the timing of it! The sightlines, the . . . well, the *everything!*"

"You spoke your piece back there," says Mulaghesh, vaulting over a short wall. "Don't waste your precious breath saying it again now."

Finally the supply track appears ahead, along with the watchtower. The spotlight in it is dark, the huge PK-512 beside it crouched and silent. Electric lights run along the track, white and buzzing, giving the area a strangely spectral, antiseptic feeling. The two of them slow to a stop before the track, their breath whistling and chests crackling.

Signe sets the radio box down with a *thump.* "The train's stationed up ahead," she says, pointing uphill.

Mulaghesh looks up at the watchtower standing over the train track. "How long will it take you to fire up the train?"

"I'll make it work," says Signe.

"That wasn't an answer."

"I'll make it work!"

"You'd better. Because you have to." Mulaghesh looks back at the city. Saint Zhurgut stands on his perch, continuing his one-man assault on the entire city. Somewhere, Mulaghesh knows, Captain Sakthi and the other Saypuri troops are escorting all the civilians they can find back up to the fortress.

"There's something else," says Signe, setting down her briefcase and opening it.

"What?" snaps Mulaghesh. "What now?"

"I figure now's the time to give you this. . . . Mostly because I'm not sure if I'll get another chance." She turns the case around.

Inside the case is one of the most intricate creations Mulaghesh has ever seen: a gleaming steel hand, with jointed fingers and a flexible wrist, and some sort of small lock set in the center of the palm. It's a false hand, but it's leagues better than the one she's using now.

"Wh-Where did you get this?" asks Mulaghesh.

"I made it. I have been observing the way you've been trying to compensate. That thing you're using now is an ornamental piece of shit." She lifts the hand out of its case. "Adjustable digits that you can lock into any position. Same goes for the wrist. And there is a latch in the center of the palm. Here's its mate." She takes a small steel ring out of the case. It has a clasp at the top, and at the bottom is what must be the male end of the latch. "You can slide this down a rifle barrel and tighten it on. Then you can lock it to the false hand.

It won't be as good as a normal hand supporting it, but it'll be better than what you're using."

Mulaghesh stares at it, astonished and confused. "I . . . Um."

"I think the words you're looking for," says Signe, "are *thank you*. And also it will make you a better shot, which will be very handy in the next five minutes. Take your shirt off."

"*What?*"

"Take your shirt off! You obviously have that awful prosthetic strapped to your back using some kind of horrible rig. Get it off!"

Mulaghesh reluctantly obliges. Signe takes out a small knife, slices through the many straps, and rips the whole thing off her torso. Then she *tsks*. "It's been beating you to pieces. I'm surprised you can bear it. Here." She applies her new prosthetic to Mulaghesh's arm, does a total of five clasps, and then stands back to admire her work. "There. Much simpler. *Much* sleeker. And it shouldn't bruise you quite so badly."

Mulaghesh looks at the prosthetic, then prods it with her free hand. It's light but firm. She adjusts some of the fingers. "Damn, girl. You're a fucking genius."

Signe blows a thread of hair out of her face. "I know. I hope I survive to keep being one."

"You listen. The second that train starts moving, you run, okay?"

"What about you?"

"Don't worry about me," she says. "You just get out of the city, as fast as you can. And don't look back. Now go. Get her started. You know what to do."

Signe gives her a hesitant look, then starts backing away. "It was nice knowing you, General."

"Likewise." She watches Signe leave, then stands below the watchtower and pulls out her spyglass. It takes her a moment to find Saint Zhurgut—but he's still there, of course, straddling the roof of the house like a monstrous rooster crowing at the dawn. She glasses slightly to the right and spies Sergeant Burdar getting into position in the window of a small, leaning cottage about two hundred yards beyond the saint.

Mulaghesh nods, checks her Ponja gun, and confirms it's ready. She drags the radio box until it sits below the watchtower. Then she pulls out her carousel, draws a bead on one of the electric lights, and fires.

There's a *pop!* and the light dies. Mulaghesh does the same for the remaining lights until the whole area is cloaked in darkness. She trots down the track about fifty yards and starts setting up the Ponja gun, unfolding its bipod. From this angle she has an excellent view down the seawall road running alongside the bay, but she has few other sightlines. Saint Zhurgut is perched atop a roof about two hundred yards north of the seawall road, so she can see him but nothing below him.

She runs back to the watchtower, where it's dark. She faces the city, pulls out her lighter, holds it aloft, and flicks it on and off three times.

She puts the spyglass to her eye and sees Sergeant Burdar peering through a spyglass of his own at her. He takes out his own lighter, flicks it on, and kills it.

Mulaghesh's breath is shaking now, but it has nothing to do with the run. Rather, she knows that if she doesn't call up to the fortress in thirty minutes and tell them that Zhurgut's been put down, those cannons up there are going to open fire and decimate the city— regardless of whether or not anyone in it happens to be alive.

Mulaghesh whispers, "Showtime."

***

She watches as Burdar slowly draws a bead on Saint Zhurgut. She can't see it, but she imagines the sweat running down his temple, the feel of his hand on the grip, his finger resting along the stock above the trigger.

The wind rises, falls.

The *om* fills the air, a low, dreadful howl as the blade returns from another lethal tour across the city.

Saint Zhurgut plucks his whirling sword out of the air once more and swivels on his perch, his face craning about as he finds a new target. Then he rears up, his massive shoulders twisting, and hurls the blade forward again.

She watches as the metal abomination dips forward on one foot like a dancer, putting his whole shoulder and body into the throw.

I sure hope Sigrud saw that.

The sword buzzes out over the city. Mulaghesh hears echoes of eruptions and screams. Saint Zhurgut stands back up, tall and straight, every inch the proud soldier, and holds his hand out, waiting for his sword to return like a faithful hound.

He stands still for one second. Which is when Sergeant Burdar fires.

The retort of the Ponja gun is a low, deep *boom*.

Her eye widens as she focuses on Saint Zhurgut.

There's a loud, hollow *crack!* as the half-inch round strikes his head. It's loud enough that it makes her bones hurt just hearing it, even from here.

The saint's head abruptly tips to the side, like he's been slapped. He stands up a little straighter, and he seems to hang in the air.

She hopes—really desperately hopes—that he'll go limp, plummet off the rooftop, and crash to the street in a heap, dead and done with.

But he doesn't. Instead he slowly, slowly turns to look at Sergeant Burdar's nest in the cottage. She can see the light striking his helmet and, just slightly above his eye, a shallow dent.

"Fuck!" she says.

The sword comes whizzing back into Saint Zhurgut's hand. He raises the blade, maybe a bit creakier and slower than he did previously. She knows Sergeant Burdar should have started scrambling away the second he fired the shot, not even looking to see if it worked. She knows that, ideally, he's about one flight of stairs down in the cottage, maybe one and a half.

She also knows it won't matter. She knows the saint's sword will tear through the cottage like a bolt of lightning.

Saint Zhurgut reaches the apex of his windup. He twists his torso forward, ready to bring his wrist down to fling the sword across the city.

One metal boot lifts up from the rooftop . . .

. . . and Sigrud pops up just three rooftops away, mounts his Ponja gun on the lip of the roof, and shoots out the rooftop from under the saint's foot with a single shot.

Saint Zhurgut topples forward and accidentally hurls the sword down through the very building he's standing on. The building dissolves like it's been expertly demolished. Tumbling awkwardly ass over head, the saint drops down into the rising cloud of dust.

She hopes that hurt him. Maybe twisted his ankle, at least. But if his helmet was able to deflect a half-inch round, she's not holding her breath over it.

And from the way Sigrud reacts, it didn't slow the saint down much: Sigrud throws the Ponja gun over one shoulder, sprints forward, and leaps onto the next rooftop. He scrabbles down the slope of the roof, his boots sliding on the slate tiles, then squats and jumps to the next building.

The *om* sound again, and the sword howls up, shredding the building behind Sigrud. He clatters to the next rooftop in a rain of tiles and debris and dust, briefly using one arm to cover his head. Then he vaults down to the street where she can't see him.

"Fuck, fuck, fuck," Mulaghesh says. She runs down the track to where she set up the Ponja gun.

Time for Plan B.

She lies down behind the Ponja gun, takes out the brace Signe made for her, and slides it down the gun's forestock. She fastens it, then pops the brace into the latch in her false hand. She wriggles it a little and the brace holds fast—though she's not sure if Signe's handiwork can take the recoil of a half-inch round going off.

She puts the stock against her shoulder and aims down the seawall road, remembering that she has never personally fired one of these. She knows the general idea, and she knows its loading procedure. But she also knows that assuming you know the right way around a firearm is a great way to get yourself killed.

Though another good way, she thinks, *is fucking around with a Voortyashtani saint.*

She hears the *om* again and watches as Saint Zhurgut leaps up into the air above a row of houses to the north, sailing fifteen or twenty feet high in the air, raising his sword for a massive, devastating downward stroke at something she can't see—but she knows it has to be Sigrud, perhaps trapped in an alleyway between two buildings. . . .

There's another *boom* of a Ponja gun. Saint Zhurgut jerks back awkwardly as he's struck dead-on in the chest. The impact of the round sends him tipping over, his legs lifting up and his head drifting down, and he caroms off the corner of a roof before crashing into a yurt.

Mulaghesh laughs lowly and shakes her head. "Fucking Sigrud . . ."

The man himself comes dashing out onto the seawall road, his Ponja gun still smoking. He runs toward Mulaghesh, who watches his progression along the sights of her own Ponja.

There's another *om* and the massive blade comes crashing out a few yards behind Sigrud, then turns abruptly to go wheeling toward him. Sigrud dives forward, and the blade arcs through the air he just previously occupied. As he's clambering to his feet Saint Zhurgut bursts through a shop front down the seawall road like a furious bull, bricks and slate tiles clattering over his thorny back. He looks at Sigrud, and though Mulaghesh can't see his face she can tell he's mighty pissed.

The saint holds one hand up in the air, and the sword, droning lowly, comes whirling back to his palm. Sigrud has just now managed to start running again, but he's a slow-moving target in a wide, open space.

Mulaghesh, panicked, tries to get a clear shot at the saint, but Sigrud's between her and her target, blocking her shot.

"Ah, shit," she mutters. "Shit!"

Saint Zhurgut raises his blade, spins around, and hurls the sword forward.

Mulaghesh watches, horrified.

The *om* echoes down the seawall road. The sword rises up, up, fifty feet off the ground, sixty feet off the ground, moving in a wide, graceful arc that will soon collide with Sigrud's path.

Sigrud stops, turns, and raises the Ponja gun.

He is not, to say the least, following standard operating procedure with a Ponja: any weapon firing a .50-caliber round needs to be ground-mounted. As such, when he pulls the trigger, and the deep-throated *boom!* echoes down the seawall road, the recoil is so much that it knocks all two-hundred-and-some-odd pounds of him clear on his back, like he's been hit with a truck.

There's a high-pitched *ping!* sound, and suddenly Saint Zhurgut's sword begins wobbling erratically. The wobbling grows and grows, sending the blade off course, until it flutters into the road nearly half a block short of Sigrud, burying itself in the oystershell pavement.

Her mouth opens. *Did he just shoot that damned sword out of the air?*

Saint Zhurgut stares, outraged. Then he begins running down the road to Sigrud, hand outstretched.

The *om* fills the air again. The sword wriggles in its spot in the pavement.

Sigrud hobbles to his feet, clutching his side—Mulaghesh gets the feeling the Ponja broke a rib, at the very fucking least—then limps to the seawall and dives into the ocean.

The sword extracts itself from the pavement and flies back to Zhurgut's hand like it's magnetized. Zhurgut turns to face the ocean, raising his sword, looking for Sigrud.

Mulaghesh places the sights of her Ponja on Saint Zhurgut. She moves her finger to the trigger, takes a breath, and fires.

The world seems to leap, like the streets around her are all sitting on a blanket and someone just picked up one end and shook it. She's frankly not sure what's worse: being behind the slate wall when it exploded, or firing this big fucking thing.

But she's granted a moment of satisfaction when she sees Saint Zhurgut stagger with the shot. *I might have just broken my clavicle,* she thinks, *but at least I hit you, motherfucker.*

Saint Zhurgut wheels around furiously, looking for the source of

the shot. He must have missed seeing her. Mulaghesh miserably realizes she's going to have to shoot him again.

She waits until he's facing her, and then—wincing and holding her breath like someone about to jump off of a very tall diving
board—pulls the trigger again.

Once more, everything leaps. She groans as her body vocally insists she *not* do that again.

Saint Zhurgut tumbles backward as the bullet hits him in the
lower gut. Then he stares down the street at her, trembling with rage,
and hurls his sword.

But because it's so dark, he can't see that Mulaghesh has already
stood and limped away, up the railway track to the watchtower. The
sword crashes into a stack of crates on the other side of the track, but
otherwise does no real damage at all.

The sword makes its return journey, fluttering through the air, its
grip smacking back into Saint Zhurgut's open palm. He cocks his
head, waiting—maybe for a scream, maybe for another shot—but it
doesn't come.

Mulaghesh quietly, slowly climbs the watchtower.

Zhurgut stalks down the street, sword at the ready, his blank gaze
scanning back and forth, seeking out whoever might still have one
of those damned guns. He moves so carefully, so slowly, that Mulaghesh can hardly bear it.

He comes to the train tracks and looks them up and down. Perhaps he's wondering what they are: he probably hasn't ever seen
something like this before. But he wouldn't care, she realizes. This
thing standing below her is a bottomless pit of rage and hunger, and
all the world is his sustenance.

He looks at the abandoned Ponja gun on the tracks. He peers
at the smashed boxes beyond it. Then he takes one step forward, a
second, and a third.

He now has one foot over the first rail. Mulaghesh has to force
herself to wait until he lifts his other foot and steps forward until he's
fully standing on the track.

Then Mulaghesh, who has had the PK-512 trained on him for some time now, finally opens fire.

***

When Mulaghesh had the PK-512 weapon system explained to her, detailing the firing, loading, and safety mechanisms however many years ago, she noticed how much the officer in charge of the demonstration kept talking about its mounting.

"This is most certainly a fixed system," he kept reiterating. "*Most* certainly. It's possible for us to mount it on a tracked vehicle, and we're researching that currently, but for now, it's best to consider this a fixed system, because of the unusual mounting issues."

"What mounting issues?" Mulaghesh asked.

"Well, General . . . This is a half-ton gun. So the weight of the weapon system itself—especially its barrel motor, fuel tank, and optimal ammunition feed—is extraordinary. We're working to reduce that—engineering makes leaps all the time—but it's not easy. But there's also the issue of propulsion and recoil. The PK features state-of-the-art reduced recoil designs, but we're still talking about six rotating barrels firing about 2,500 rounds a minute. That puts a lot of pressure on its mounting system. We tried one demonstration integrating what we believed to be a heavy enough vehicle to handle the sudden burst of force, but . . . Well. It started tipping over, and nearly crushed the gunner." The officer scratched his chin. "In other words, think of this weapon system as an engine that essentially creates a column of lead in the air, moving at speeds up to two hundred feet per second. That should give you an idea of the physics of this weapon."

The instant Mulaghesh pulls the trigger on the PK-512, her understanding of the weapon's physics grows immensely.

The gun whines softly at first, the barrels rotating up to speed—she sees Saint Zhurgut look up at her, surprised—and then the "column of lead" the officer talked about comes into play.

The barrels flare a bright, blinding white, the air is split with a deafening chatter, and Saint Zhurgut is slammed into the ground like he's had a stack of bricks dropped on him, his body racked with what look like spasms as around fifty bullets strike him every second. But at the same time, the watchtower—which is mostly made out of wood—begins to creak and croak and drift *back*, like a reed bending in the wind, pushed by the sudden explosion of force from this weapon; which means that Mulaghesh has to raise the aim of the massive gun to keep it trained on the spiky bastard probably now wishing he'd stayed dormant.

This setup, she realizes, has some serious mounting issues. The heat from the gun scorches the floor and rails of the watchtower, licking at the wood and turning it a deep black. Every second threatens to tear the whole watchtower apart.

But Mulaghesh doesn't care. She hears herself screaming, *"Motherfucker! Motherfucker!"*

She keeps the massive gun trained on Saint Zhurgut, who is slowly, defiantly trying to stand. It's like his own personal gravity has tripled. His body rattles and shakes and quivers, and she can see myriad dents appearing in his face, his shoulders, his thighs. Yet still he tries to stand.

The train tracks around him are being shredded. The very ground under his feet turns to pulp. An enormous cloud of dust rises up as the PK-512 continues putting hundreds and hundreds of rounds into the skin of the earth, like it's a pressurized water sprayer sawing through limestone. She's aware of the rounds ricocheting off of Zhurgut's Divine armor: a window shatters across the street, a hanging sign is flapping wildly, struck by countless stray rounds. Hot, smoking casings are raining down around her, the legs of the watchtower lost in a pile of broiling brass. The wooden rails of the tower are smoking and, in some places, even on fire. She feels like she's dangling over the lip of a broiling volcano.

But Mulaghesh still doesn't care. She's screaming, shrieking, howling as this terrific, beautiful, monstrous engine of destruction sings, its own low, guttural buzz the perfect countermeasure to Zhurgut's serene *om*. For a moment Mulaghesh delights in this savage victory, and she wishes to scream, *We're better at this than you are! We figured war out in ways you stupid bastards never could!*

But she is very, very aware of Zhurgut's right hand, which is slowly, slowly raising his sword.

She swivels the stream of fire, very slightly, to focus on his sword hand. The PK is about as far from a surgical device as one could ever imagine, but she watches with dismay as even this doesn't stop the sword's slow ascent.

She hears the sword begin to sing—a low, defiant note breaking through the rage of the PK-512's buzz: a quiet *om*. . . .

There is a rumbling to Mulaghesh's left. Zhurgut's focus breaks, and he shifts his head . . .

. . . and watches, helpless, as the eighty-ton supply locomotive comes thundering down the track toward him at top speed.

She can tell he wants to leap out of the way. But Mulaghesh positions her never-ending column of lead so that he doesn't have a chance, pinning him to the ground

Mulaghesh howls in triumph. "*Motherfucker! Motherfucker!*"

She halts the stream of fire as the locomotive slams into Zhurgut like he's a toy soldier. She doesn't even hear the sound of the impact.

But that might be because the instant that the locomotive hits Zhurgut it suddenly *derails,* slowly tilting off the shredded, pulped train tracks around Saint Zhurgut and sliding across the muddy harbor yard with a terrific, deafening grinding and screeching. Somehow it manages to miss grazing the watchtower and instead goes sliding into a stack of steel beams and wire coils, which all tumble onto its roof and boiler with a tremendous clanging. Then the locomotive tilts to the left very slightly, threatening to tip over, but instead it hangs there, its right set of wheels suspended in the air, churning to an arrhythmic beat, like a half-squashed beetle pumping its legs, unaware it's dead.

Mulaghesh watches and realizes the destruction seems somewhat distant to her, and she slowly understands that she's quite deaf from firing the PK-512.

She lets out a breath. She has to force her hand to release the gun's right handle, then undoes Signe's brace holding her false hand to the left handle. She steps back from the weapon. Her whole body is shaking, vibrating, like she's been put in a can and rattled by a giant, and her skin feels like it's cracked and sizzling, furious from being exposed to so much heat.

She tries to tell herself, "Stop. Stop. It's over," but she can't find the voice for it.

I'm in shock, she thinks. *You know this. You've been here before.*

She looks at the locomotive, lying across the harbor yards like a beached whale. If Zhurgut had happened to stand just a little closer to the tower, and she'd damaged the rails *here* instead of *there*, it would have likely pounded through the supports of the watchtower as it derailed like a bullet through a matchstick—a close shave, in other words.

She slowly climbs down the watchtower ladder, then wanders over to the wreckage. The locomotive's firebox door has fallen open, and a handful of embers have spilled across its metal floor. The whole contraption glows with a cheery yet hellish red light.

She stops, twists her finger in one ear, and then listens. Despite the blaring *"eeeee"* in her ears, it doesn't take her long at all to locate Saint Zhurgut—she just has to follow the sputtering *om* sound, which now sounds like it's coming through a bad radio.

He's been cut in two, she sees, vivisected by one of the train's wheels. His intestines have unspooled like rice noodles, and though his arm is obviously broken in several places, it's still reaching for his giant sword, which lies on the ground several feet away.

She cocks her head: the sword is still singing, murmuring, *I am Her brightest blade. I am the distant star of war. I am conquest everlasting. . . .*

"I sure wish you would shut the fuck up," she says.

There's a splash of water from the shore. Sigrud staggers up, one arm folded in close to his chest. He limps over, and his mouth moves.

"*What?*" shouts Mulaghesh.

"Did we get him?" shouts Sigrud back.

"Kind of," says Mulaghesh. She points to the twitching body on the ground. "But *that's* not Saint Zhurgut." Her finger moves to the giant sword lying on the ground. *"That's* Saint Zhurgut."

Sigrud frowns. She can't hear him, but she can tell he says, "What?"

"He said he was Voortya's blade. I think he meant it both meta-phorically *and* literally. His heart and soul and mind are bound up in that metal."

She takes off her coat, walks to the sword, and—pausing as she realizes this might kill her, as it was likely intended to—picks the sword up with it, making sure not one piece of metal touches her skin. To her relief, nothing happens, but the sword is terrifically, burningly cold. She sees the blade is cracked, the barest hairline run-ning from its base to its point.

She begins dragging the sword back toward the locomotive. "Come on. Help me get this big fucking thing up in the train. But *don't* touch your skin to it. Use your coat or something."

The two of them lift the sword up into the locomotive door. It takes Sigrud a minute to find the right position, as he's favoring his left side.

"Broken rib?" asks Mulaghesh.

He nods. "Not a bad one, though."

"There are *good* broken ribs?"

"Sometimes. Also a sprained shoulder, I think. I was lucky. Pull harder on your end."

Once they get it in the locomotive they stand before the firebox, and then—with Mulaghesh muttering, "Ah-one, ah-two, and ah-*three"*—they hurl the giant sword inside.

Instantly the sword's *om* begins to sputter, scream, rise and fall, like a radio frequency oscillating wildly. They watch through the hatch as the cracks in the sword's blade grow, like thin ice under too much pressure, until it finally dissolves, falling away to nothing but the hilt, which slowly begins to melt, like a wax candle set too close to the fireplace.

"Not normal metal," says Sigrud.

"No. Definitely not. I've got to hand it to your daughter. She got this fucking thing hot." She watches as the sword appears to disintegrate, dissolving not into bubbling metal but clumps of something soft and powdery, almost like graphite.

She stares into the boiler, leaning in until it's so hot that her skin can't bear it anymore.

"Holy shit," she says. "Holy *shit*! It's . . . It's damned thinadeskite, isn't it!"

"What?" says Sigrud.

"Thinadeskite!" shouts Mulaghesh. "His fucking *sword* is made out of thinadeskite! That means that . . ." She jumps out of the locomotive and runs to where Saint Zhurgut lay.

But Zhurgut is gone. In his place is a young Dreyling man's body, thickset and red-haired and very dead. His corpse, however, is maimed just as Zhurgut's was, vivisected at the waist.

Sigrud walks to stand beside her. She sees him mouth the words, *What happened to him?*

"That's what happened in the countryside!" shouts Mulaghesh. She's no longer sure if she's shouting because she's deaf or because she's excited. "At the farmhouses, at the charcoal kilns! There were the butchered bodies, but nearby, on the same property, was a man's corpse, dead but uninjured! That's what must have happened!"

"I . . . do not understand," says Sigrud.

"Listen—someone came to these families, gave them a present—a *sword*—then hid nearby and watched! Then, when the man of the house picked up the sword—"

"He transformed into a sentinel," he says slowly. "And killed his own family, just as Zhurgut tried to kill all of us."

"Butchered them just as a sentinel would Saypuris," says Mulaghesh. "Because it *was* a sentinel! A man made of thorns, just as Gozha said!"

"Wasn't the thinadeskite found at only one of the murder scenes?"

"Yeah, the one that didn't go right," says Mulaghesh. "Back when they were sloppy, whoever they are. On this last one, at the farmhouse, they must've been smart enough to clean up after themselves."

"Then why did the sentinels stop?" says Sigrud. "Why did they die? Why did they not keep killing?"

"I don't know! It must have failed somehow. The swords couldn't keep them here, I guess, and their—hell, I don't know, their *hosts*—died from the sheer stress of it. I *said* it seemed like the killer was testing something—maybe some swords work, and others don't." She looks up at the devastation of Voortyashtan. "But it sure fucking worked tonight. They've figured out how to do this right."

"But where are they getting the swords from? How could they have persisted after Voortya died?"

"I don't know that, either. But . . . But thinadeskite must be what the Voortyashtanis made their swords out of! A special ore, just for them to use. We need to tell someone at the fo—"

She looks up to see one of the cannons of Fort Thinadeshi slowly rotating to point at their very location.

"Shit!" she says. "I forgot!" She sprints off toward the watchtower, which is now on fire around the PK-512.

"Where are you going?" Sigrud calls after her.

"I'm keeping us from getting blown to pieces!" she shouts over her shoulder.

She runs up to the radio box, sits, and holds its receiver up to her head. "He's down!" she shouts. "Hold your fire, he's down!"

There's a tinny voice on the other end, but she can't hear it.

"What?" she says into it. "I'm nearly fucking deaf, speak up!"

"Can you confirm, General?" says the tinny voice, much louder. *"Can you confirm that the threat is eliminated?"*

"Confirmed!" shouts Mulaghesh back. "Confirmed! The threat is . . ." She pauses as a piece of flaming timber falls to the ground near her. "Shit! Anyway, yeah, the threat is eliminated!"

There's static. She hears the voice say: "—*econdary assault?*"

"What?" says Mulaghesh.

More static. Then: "—*ssault in progr—*"

Then the static dies. Mulaghesh kicks the big metal box, but the receiver is silent. However gigantic the lead-acid battery in this thing is, it was never meant to last so long.

She sits on the ground, fumbling for a cigarillo. She settles for a half-crushed one found in her inside coat pocket, but she can't find her lighter.

A pigeon alights on a nearby shop rooftop. It coos twice, then sits and watches her with one bemused eye, as if to say, *What was that all about?*

***

Lennart Björck has been hiding in a hole in the ground for nearly two agonizing hours when he hears the crash. It's an enormous, skull-rattling sound, loud enough to knock him down even while standing in a hole, and it makes him wonder if there's some new Divine monstrosity now causing havoc in the city.

He pokes his head up and sees a tremendous column of steam and dust pouring up near the train tracks . . . and just to the west, he can see the very tip of the number three locomotive pointing up past the top of a house, though it seems to be on its side, like a beached whale.

"What in the hells . . . ?" Björck climbs out and begins to run to the crash, wondering what could have caused this new headache. Yet as he runs by the test assembly yard he stops and slowly turns around.

He saw something out of the corner of his eye—a flash of light.

The door to the test assembly yard stands open—something that should normally never, *ever* happen—and someone is lying in the mud before it.

Another victim of that monstrosity? It seems unlikely, as this body is in one piece.

Björck slowly walks toward the test assembly yard. Then there's another flash, illuminating the dark interior of the yard. . . .

Involuntarily, he shouts, "Hey!"

A figure darts from the door of the yard and sprints up the street. Björck gives chase, but finds he's unwilling to go too far into Voortyashtan, much of which is on fire or falling apart.

He looks at the body lying in the mud. It's one of the higher-ranking SDC guards . . . Karl, he thinks the man's name was. A bolt is sticking out of his neck.

Björck walks into the yard. He knows what's in here, and knows not to turn on the light. Yet there's an aroma in the air, a pungent, sulfurous smell he actually finds familiar—he smelled it once, long ago, when he went to a carnival in Jukoshtan with his then-sweetheart, and a man on the pier produced this strange device and said he could capture their images for them for only a few drekels.

"A camera?" says Björck aloud. He scratches his head.

***

After a while the watchtower, still ablaze, begins creaking in a very disturbing fashion. Mulaghesh imagines the PK-512 plummeting to the ground, all of its ammunition spilling into open flame, and decides to seek refuge in the locomotive. Walking, she finds, hurts tremendously. She can't remember where she got all these injuries from.

Sigrud is sitting on the edge of the locomotive door, smoking his pipe, arm held close to his body. "Is this victory?" he asks.

"Harbor's still intact," she says, groaning as she sits beside him.

"Harbor, yes. But . . ." He gestures toward Voortyashtan with the bowl of his pipe. He doesn't need to say anything more. It looks like some impossibly large piece of farming equipment has mown great swaths through the city's crude architecture.

"Where the hells are Biswal's troops?" asks Mulaghesh. "I thought they were sending a whole battalion."

"I don't know. I thought that . . . Wait." He cocks his head. "Do you hear that?"

"I can't hear much, period. I should have worn ear protection, using that thing. What are you hearing?"

"Gunfire. And . . . screaming."

"What? Where?"

He points up the cliffs, at the passage to Fort Thinadeshi.

"But that's *outside* the city," says Mulaghesh. "What could be happening there?"

The two stare up at the cliffs.

Mulaghesh realizes what the voice on the radio said: *Secondary assault.*

"Come on," she says, and the two hop down and begin limping up the cliff paths to the first of the checkpoints.

The city is like a ghost town, a nightmare cityscape, dark and ruined. The only sounds she hears are distant cries and moans and the constant wind. Just an hour ago it was a bustling if unsightly little town: now it is inconceivable that people once lived and worked here.

"I smell gunpowder," says Sigrud suddenly. "And blood."

"Blood?"

"Yes. Blood." He lifts his head, catching the wind. "Lots of it."

They run up to the first checkpoint and find it abandoned, though the door and side are riddled with bullet holes. Then when they rise up to the top of the first hill they stop, look out, and see.

The hills are a cold, dark gray in the moonlight. Mulaghesh sees many still, dark forms lying where the road slashes through the countryside. Figures sprint back and forth atop the hills before the fortress. There is the sporadic flash of gunfire, like distant lightning, and screams—some bellowing orders, others in pain or fear.

"No," whispers Mulaghesh. Suddenly she is running, running toward the group of soldiers she sees gathered ahead.

"Stop!" shouts Sigrud. "Stop, Turyin!"

As she runs her mind takes in all the signs, reading the story written in the countryside: she can see where the Saypuri battalion was marching down the road; she sees where the first volley hit them from the east; she can see where the Saypuris—surprised, terrified—took cover among the dales just west of the road; and she can see where the enemy—whoever it was—took positions north of them, cutting them off from the fortress, leaving them to either stay where they were, retreat to the cliffs, or descend to Voortyashtan, and expose themselves to Saint Zhurgut's hellish assault.

A simple maneuver, really. But a very successful one.

Someone shoves her from behind and falls on top of her. She can tell by the way the impact pains them that it's Sigrud.

"They will shoot you," he croaks.

"Get off me!"

He groans as she pushes against his bad side, but he doesn't budge. "They will shoot you dead on sight."

"Let me go, let me go!" she cries. "I need to help them, I need to—"

"There is nothing to do. The enemy has fled. But the soldiers are wary. They will not take any more chances."

Mulaghesh relents and lies there on the ground, helpless and miserable. He's right, of course: whatever happened here, there's not much for her to do now. She despises feeling so useless.

"Find me a body," she says.

"What?" asks Sigrud.

"There'll be an aid kit on one of the Saypuri soldiers. Yellow rubber thing, waterproof. Inside of that are some flares and a flare gun. Bring it here. You're better at sneaking than I am."

"You ask much of an injured man." But he releases her and withdraws into the darkness. She sits up and stares around herself, mindful now that someone out in the shadows might take a shot at her. She recognizes the movements of the shapes in the distance: infantry securing the perimeter, closing down points of entry and escape.

Sigrud rises up out of the shadows, dragging something behind him. He drops it with a heavy thump. It reeks of sweat and coppery blood. She can see the outline of a cheek and a clutched fist in the darkness.

"That doesn't look like a flare gun," she says.

"No," he says. "I thought you would like to see for yourself."

He takes out a flare gun and hands it to her. She hesitates before pointing into the air and firing.

The flare is bright and brilliant, a festive cherry red, and as its light flickers across the hillsides it touches upon the face of the young man lying on the ground: a Voortyashtani boy of about fifteen, his neck elegantly tattooed, a perfectly round entry point drilled just below his collarbone. Strapped to his chest is a Saypuri pistol. He had to adjust the holster considerably to allow for this slight, boyish frame, perhaps two or three years from truly being a man. Mulaghesh is still staring into his face when the Saypuri troops surround them.

Peace is but the absence of war. War and conflict form the sea through which nation-states swim.

Some who have had the fortune to find clear, calm waters believe otherwise. They have forgotten that war is momentum.

War is natural. And war makes one strong.

—WRITS OF SAINT PETRENKO, 720

11.

a just death

She looks for Biswal in the fortress hospital, though the term feels out of place with what she sees: Fort Thinadeshi's medical wings are dark, primitive, and dirty. Rickety cots and beds line the walls, almost all of them occupied.

As she walks through the hospital she's faintly aware of the bloodstains on the front of her fatigues, none of them hers—she and Sigrud assisted the medical corps as much as they could—and from the deep ache all along her right side she knows she needs to see a medic now. But mostly she hasn't the mind for it: the sight of these young men and women trapped in their beds brings back memories of her hellish recuperation in Bulikov. Her arm aches just to think of it. She pities them.

She stops a nurse and asks, "The general?"

He points to the back of the hospital, to the morgue. Mulaghesh walks to the morgue doors, hesitates, and pushes them open.

The room is larger than she expected. Tall cabinets line the walls, cold and blank. One of them is open, with a table on wheels halfrolled out of its dark, chilly depths.

Lalith Biswal stands in front of the table, looking down on the body on the table. The deceased soldier is short, her clothes dusty, her hands chalky and pale, the queer colors of the dead. The room is quite dim, but Mulaghesh can tell by the gleaming scar on the fore-head that it was once Captain Kiran Nadar.

Biswal looks over his shoulder, nods to Mulaghesh, then turns back to Nadar. Mulaghesh pauses, wondering how to be respectful, then walks to stand beside him.

She was shot three times in the left side. She must have died quickly, as none of her clothes have been removed for operation. Her cheek bears a purple slash, the flesh around it dark. Mulaghesh guesses she fell, likely from her horse.

"They targeted her specifically," says Biswal quietly. "She was rid-ing at the front of the line. Standard shtani behavior, as of late. Kill the officers first."

"What happened?"

"I did tell you we were under surveillance. Shtanis in the hills, watching our movements. They saw us preparing to send a battal-ion down to the city. When the . . . that *horror* began his assault on the city, the passages in and out of Voortyashtan were flooded with civilians escaping the slaughter. Under this cover over seventy insur-gents took positions east along the main passage. They ambushed us, pinned us down, inflicting heavy casualties. They retreated when we mounted a counterattack."

Mulaghesh bows her head, disgusted and furious. "We were try-ing to *help* them."

"Yes. We were trying to help the city. But they do not see it in those terms."

"It feels rude to ask, but . . . Sergeant Major Pandey . . ."

"He's alive, miraculously enough. He was at the front with Nadar, and survived the first volley. He sought shelter in a checkpoint and ably defended a group of civilians that were fleeing the horror in the city. A group that included CTO Harkvaldsson."

Once again, Signe and Pandey are thrown together. It's all too coincidental for her tastes.

Biswal looks at her. "What in the hells happened in that city, Turyin? What in hells was that thing that attacked us?"

Mulaghesh decides that now's the time to lay as many cards on

the table as she can, to try to convince Biswal that *something* Divine
is unfolding here in Voortyashtan. So she summarizes her conclusions about Zhurgut and the sentinels and the murders, aware as she
speaks that she sounds more and more outlandish: magic swords,
possessed bodies, secret mines, ancient ore. She doesn't say anything
about the City of Blades and Voortya, feeling it would be a step too
far in the current circumstances.

Biswal is perfectly still as he listens. When she finishes he says,
"Do you still believe the issues with the insurgents to be wholly separate from the murders and the interference with the mines—as well
as the Divine horror that awoke in the harbor, I suppose?"

"I . . . suspect so. I don't *think* the insurgents were behind any of
this. Their concerns are earthly—they're fighting over land. Whoever is behind this is far more concerned with the spiritual."

Biswal looks down at Nadar and shakes his head. "Thirty-seven
soldiers. The most we've ever lost since the Battle of Bulikov." He
shakes his head again, his neck cracking and popping. "The prime
minister tells me to do one thing. Parliament signals that it wishes me
to do something very different. And now *you*, Turyin, you now come
here and tell me stories of the Divine, of plots and conspiracies taking
place under our very noses."

"Lalith . . ."

"You tell me that these are two very separate things, the insurgents and the Divine. You say this despite the mine collapse taking
place *just after* the tribal leaders came to this city. You say this despite the appearance of that Divine horror coinciding *perfectly* with an
orchestrated insurgent assault. You and the prime minister, Turyin,
you have *some gall*." He whirls on her. "What are you *really* here for,
Turyin? You aren't here on the touring shuffle, are you? Don't lie to
me, Turyin, I'll know."

Mulaghesh decides to tell the truth. Or some of it, at least. "I was
sent here to find Choudhry."

"Why keep that a secret?"

"They weren't sure what had happened to her. They thought
maybe—"

"That one of her own comrades had killed her, one of her fellow soldiers." Biswal laughs bitterly. "The prime minister thinks so poorly of the soldiers in her service. She thinks us cutthroats and brigands."

"She didn't know what had happened. She thought it better to be careful tha—"

"Oh, of course she did, and I am so *tired* of being told to be careful!" snarls Biswal. "I am so tired of being told to draw back, stay firm, appease, and placate! And I am so tired of being told that this is *not* a war. Any fool with eyes in their head can see that these people will never cooperate, never be civilized! They treat us like enemies. And those who treat us as enemies should be treated the same in turn."

"What are you saying, Biswal?" asks Mulaghesh.

Biswal draws himself up to his full height. "I am saying that, in light of recent events, I am reinterpreting my orders," he says. "I *will* defend the harbor. I *will* placate the tribes. And I will do this by pursuing those who dared attack us, and *destroying* them and anyone who might give them shelter."

Mulaghesh stares at him. "You're planning an invasion of the damned highlands?"

"I am saying that Fort Thinadeshi, along with the other installations of Voortyashtan, will be conducting a full-scale counteroffensive against these aggressors."

"Will you just *ignore* the fact that a damned saint appeared in the city outside your gates, and killed what is likely dozens if not hundreds of people?" says Mulaghesh, furious.

"Oh, I've flagged the Ministry," says Biswal. "I've notified them. They'll send their agents here, I've no doubt, and I will let them deal with that. That is their jurisdiction, just as mine is to pursue the insurgents to my full satisfaction. We each have our purposes, don't we, Turyin?"

He walks to the door and places his hand on the handle. Before he can open it, Mulaghesh says, "It's the wrong move, Lalith. They know the terrain, and they've likely had time to prepare. The casualties you'll suffer will be terrible."

He looks over his shoulder at her, his eyes glittering with disdain. "You doubt the effectiveness of my soldiers?"

"What I doubt, General Biswal, is that this will have the same effect as the March," she says. "Times have changed."

He looks at her for a moment longer. Then he says, "You're a coward, Turyin. You fled the military because you couldn't live up to the trials of true leadership. Instead, our gutless prime minister has turned you into a craven spy. Perhaps you've forgotten after the Battle of Bulikov, but this"—he gestures to Nadar's body—"is what *real* combat looks like. Or perhaps you were too busy being commended for bravery to visit the frontlines."

"You sound," she says acidly, "a little *jealous*, General Biswal."

He stares at her coldly. "Do what you need to in the city, Turyin. But if I see you in my fortress again, I'll have you locked up." Then he walks out and slams the door, leaving Mulaghesh alone in the morgue.

***

Mulaghesh limps down the road to Voortyashtan. She borrowed a crutch from the medics at the fortress, but it's not easy to operate a crutch one-handed, even with Signe's prosthetic—especially when your good arm is covered in bruises. She badly, badly needs to see a medic, yet as she approaches the checkpoint she sees a familiar figure standing in the road, smoking and apparently waiting for her.

"Ah, General," says Signe. "I was told you'd passed through here recently. . . . I've something you need to see."

"A bed?" says Mulaghesh miserably. "And opiates?"

"I'm afraid not," says Signe. "Rather, it's something you've seen a lot of recently—a security breach."

Thirty minutes later Mulaghesh slows as they approach the statue yard. It looks much the same to her eye—same high walls, same giant door, same canvas roof—except for two key differences. One is that the door is *open*, just slightly, something Mulaghesh is sure the guards would never allow. The other is the dead body lying in the mud before the door.

"That's the door guard, isn't it?" says Mulaghesh.

"Yes," says Signe. "Ericksson was his name. Shot through the neck with a bolt."

"So while we were dealing with Saint Zhurgut, someone made a beeline for the statue yard, shot the guard, took his keys, and opened the door?"

"It would appear so. We're being carefully watched, I think." She looks up and around them. "But as most of Voortyashtan is uphill from here, it would only take a good vantage point and someone with a high-powered telescope to track us."

Mulaghesh hobbles toward the door. "I assume nothing's stolen? They'd have to use a truck to get any of those damn things out."

"Not as far as we can tell. Nor have any changed in any way—no secret doors opened, no missing trinkets. Again, as far as we can tell."

"So . . . someone knows about your stolen statues," says Mulaghesh. "That's plenty bad as it is. If Biswal gets a whisper of that, he'll come down on you like a monsoon. He's already on the warpath. He's going to *aaaargh!*"

"I'm sorry, he's going to what?"

She grips her side, almost bending double. "Ahh, damn. Starting to get the idea I broke a rib last night . . ."

"Oh. So I'm getting the idea that I *shouldn't* have brought you here first before going to a medic."

"For someone who's so smart," growls Mulaghesh, "you're also pretty damned stupid sometimes."

"Now, now. Why don't I take you to see Rada? That's where I sent my father; he was pretty banged up too. She'll do a much better job of patching you up than our people will."

Mulaghesh sighs. "That's a long way up. But I do need to get the gang together. Someone needs to know what Biswal's about to do."

"I'll have someone drive us." She pauses, suddenly awkward. "I suppose I must say . . . Well." She grimaces, as if trying to remember how to speak a phrase from another language. "The thing I wish to say is . . . thank you."

Mulaghesh looks at her cockeyed. "Come again?"

"Thank you for stopping the bloodshed, for saving the harbor last night. For putting down Saint Zhurgut—which I still frankly can't believe you did. I know I've not been easy. None of this has been easy. But—thank you. Now. Let's get you to Rada."

***

Rada Smolisk's home no longer has the feel of a medical office as much as it does a field hospital. Civilian men, women, and children are packed in in front of her door, almost all of them wounded or tending to the wounded. When they climb out of the SDC auto Mulaghesh shakes her head. "I can't get treated here. I won't take up Rada's time, not when these people so desperately need it." Then she pauses, noticing the many medics in SDC uniforms wading among the civilians. "Wait. What are so many SDC medics doing here?"

"Following orders," says Signe.

"Huh?"

"I consulted with the other SDC senior officers, and we decided to dispatch nearly all of our medical staff to Voortyashtan."

"Don't you have your own injured to look after?"

Signe gives her a grim look. "Do you believe that in hand-to-hand combat, Zhurgut left people merely *injured*?"

"Ah. Ugh."

"Yes. We have all experienced tragedies in the past day." Signe walks to Rada's side door and knocks three times. "Best to focus on the tragedies one can still fix."

The door opens, and the bruised, scowling face of Lem, Signe's security chief, peeks out at them. Then he nods and holds the door open. Mulaghesh and Signe step inside to be greeted by the glassy, terrified stares of the numerous taxidermied animals arranged on Rada's walls.

"Well," sniffs Signe, "she hasn't changed her décor much."

They find Rada in the operating room, performing a grisly procedure on a young Voortyashtani girl with a mangled knee. Sigrud and an SDC medic stand beside her, and though Sigrud is in his shirtsleeves and his arm is in a sling, he seems to be acting as a fairly competent assistant.

"Most of the debris has been removed," Rada mutters—again, Mulaghesh notes, her stutter is gone. "And the wound is clean. I'll close it up now. You'll be turning cartwheels again before the end of the month."

The girl blinks languidly. She's obviously doped to the gills.

Rada sticks out a hand, and Sigrud—his big, rough fingers surprisingly gentle—hands her a needle and thread. As she takes it Rada glances at Mulaghesh and Signe by the door. "If you w-w-will b-be so k-kind as to wait."

After about an hour Sigrud and Rada emerge from the operating room, their hands dripping wet and reeking of alcohol. "I d-do n-not normally pr-protest such things," Rada grumbles, "but I d-do n-n-not relish the idea of p-preferential t-treatment."

"Then we'll make it double duty," Mulaghesh says. "I just spoke with Biswal this morning. You all need to hear this."

As Rada puts her through her paces—making her extend her arms, stretch her ribs, lift her shirt—Mulaghesh recounts her conversation with Biswal mere hours ago.

"He wants to invade the *highlands*?" asks Signe, horrified.

"I don't think 'invade' is the right term," says Mulaghesh. "I expect this will be a much faster, less permanent maneuver. Pursue, engage, eliminate, then retreat. At least, that's what he *thinks* it will be."

"It w-won't be," says Rada. "B-bend your h-hip *this* way, p-please."

Mulaghesh groans as something in her backside insists it's moved as far as it possibly can. "It'll be messy, then?"

"'Messy' doesn't begin to describe it," says Signe. "The highland tribes are always prepared for combat. That's practically all they do. He abandons his duties to go chasing after those who have wounded his pride."

"Thirty-seven soldiers died," says Mulaghesh. "Including the commander of Fort Thinadeshi. A lot more got wounded than his damned pride."

"Fair enough," says Signe. "But would you do the same as he intends, General?"

Mulaghesh hesitates. "No. He has no plan, no exit. He's going to lead his kids out there, but how will they get out?"

"And with so many Saypuri forces allocated to pursuing the insurgents, who will be defending Voortyashtan?" asks Signe. "Who will rebuild? They obviously can't help themselves."

Sigrud, who has so far been sitting in silence in a moldy overstuffed chair in the corner of the room, rumbles to life. "I have been thinking about that. What if *we* did that?"

The three of them stare at him. "We?" says Signe. "We who?"

"We as in us," he says. "SDC."

There's a pause.

"What are you saying?" says Signe. "You want us to rebuild a *city*?"

Sigrud shrugs. "We have lots of resources here. A bunch of workers, builders, construction teams. Surely it cannot be harder than building a harbor."

"But . . . But we don't have the funding for that! If we wanted to do that *and* keep the harbor on schedule, we'd have to apply for much more onerous loans!"

"Well, I was thinking about that, too," says Sigrud, scratching his chin, "and I was thinking that I could just ask them to, ah, *not* make the loans more—what did you say—onerous."

"What!" says Signe.

"Well . . . Am I the *dauvkind* or am I the *dauvkind*? Am I to put this stupid image of me to no good ends at all? If they want, I will put on as many stupid hats as they like if it gets us more workers and more resources."

Signe stares at him, suspicious and mystified. "You really want to do that?"

Sigrud smiles slightly as he stuffs his pipe. "It's as you said the other night," he says, sitting back and readjusting his sling. "One big push."

***

"How am I?" says Mulaghesh.

"N-not twenty years old anymore," says Rada, rifling through a drawer of ointments and salves. "S-so I s-suggest you s-stop acting l-like it."

"Circumstances dictated otherwise."

Rada throws a few tubs of something whitish gray and foul-looking into a box for her. Mulaghesh can hear Sigrud and Signe standing outside, talking in low voices about Sigrud's ostentatious plans. "Then I s-suggest y-you a-uhh-*avoid* those c-circumstances in the f-f-future."

"When Biswal gets back, and finds SDC rebuilding a city under his jurisdiction—what will you do, Polis Governor?"

Hearing her own title evokes a sardonic smile. "I am n-not a true actor in th-this play," she says. "Rather, I d-deal with the *consequences* of the actions. I will c-continue dealing with the w-wounded. More w-will be coming in. People t-trapped under rubble, tr-trapped in their homes . . ."

"Familiar."

"To b-both of us, yes," says Rada. She slumps her shoulders, sighs, and says, "Have y-you ever h-heard of Saint Petrenko?"

"Can't say that I have."

"V-Voortyashtani saint. He is interesting, t-to me at l-least. Pr-Probably the antithesis to Z-Zhurgut. Where Zhurgut was all at-tack and ag-aggression—as you no d-doubt w-witnessed—Petrenko was . . . passive."

"A passive warrior?"

"Yes. He p-preached that to live l-life, one m-must accept that one was already d-d-dead. Every m-morning, one m-must arise and m-make peace with death, accept that it was c-coming." Her words grow stronger as she speaks. "He said, 'Time is a river, and we are but blades of grass floating upon its waves. To fear the end of the river is to fear being on it at all. And though we may look ahead, and see countless forks, when we look back we see only one way things ever could have gone. All is inevitable. To argue with fate is to argue with a river.'"

"Why do you bring this up?"

Rada shuts a cabinet with a harsh *snap.* "I had several deaths on my table last night, and this morning. I will have more today. Some will be children. This, like so many things, is inevitable. I woke up knowing this. And I accepted it. Just as I accept that war is coming here."

"War?"

"Yes." Rada stands and looks her in the eye, and her gaze is not half so fearful now. "I can smell it. I have smelled war before, General. Its smell is q-quite familiar to me. This is only the b-beginning. So what I will *mostly* be d-doing, General," she says, opening the door, "is awaiting the inevitable. G-good day to you."

* * *

Outside, Signe and Sigrud look out at the ravaged cityscape of Voortyashtan, ruby red in the glow of the sunset. Smoke spills out of countless crushed hovels. There is the distant crack of gunfire— looters, probably, Mulaghesh expects. Three of the giant, deformed statues have been sliced in two, one at the waist, one at the knees, then the final at the feet.

Yet despite this, there is a warmth to Signe and Sigrud's discussion that Mulaghesh hasn't ever seen before. They stand close together, shoulders almost touching, and whereas before Signe stood still and rigid around her father, now she's animated, her movements excited, natural, and unself-conscious. *She's found a way to feel at home with him,* thinks Mulaghesh.

Signe seems to remember Mulaghesh standing beside them, leaning on a crutch. "I can't precisely say you look *better*, General, but . . . Are all your various organs in the right place?"

"More or less, though my hip got pretty scrambled. Rada says no fun and play for two weeks." She struggles to light a cigarillo while still leaning on her crutch. "But she's going to have to accept two days."

"Two days? You're only going to rest for two days?"

"Yes," says Mulaghesh. "Because then you're going to take me to the Tooth."

Signe pales at the mention of it. "Even after Zhurgut . . . You're still determined to chase Choudhry?"

"Someone out there has access to Voortyashtani swords," says Mulaghesh, starting the long walk back to the SDC headquarters. "Just *one* of which can wreak devastation in minutes, if activated. They're practically weapons of mass destruction, and someone has been perfecting them, testing them out on innocent, isolated families out in the country—likely, I assume, building up to bring on the Night of the Sea of Swords. And now they've got the process figured out."

"How do they plan to do it, though?" asks Signe.

"I don't know. But Choudhry thought she'd find *something* out on the Tooth. Maybe something that could tell her how this was all supposed to go down." Mulaghesh rubs her eyes. "By the seas, I'm tired. I can't remember the last time I slept. What time is it?"

Signe checks her watch. "Sixteen hundred."

Mulaghesh laughs hollowly. "Almost evening again."

Signe glances over her shoulder, then twitches slightly and grunts. "I think you have the right idea. I have one last piece of business to do, and then I am off to enjoy a giant feather mattress while I can. Good evening." She turns and trots away.

Mulaghesh watches her go, frowning. "That was rather abru—"

"I will go too," says Sigrud. "I need to get very drunk and lie down somewhere very dark."

"Typical Dreyling curative?"

"Something like that." He stands and lumbers away, limping down the steps.

Mulaghesh stands alone on the hillside, wondering what tomorrow will bring. But something troubles her.

Signe saw something, she thinks. *Just now. Didn't she? She saw something that made her want to leave.*

She scans the streets of Voortyashtan with a keen eye. Eventually she notices the short, gray-coated figure standing in the shadow of a tumbled-down house, his peaked cap barely visible in the evening mist.

"Pandey," says Mulaghesh quietly.

She sits perfectly still, waiting for him to move. When he does she follows, carefully.

***

Pandey heads north, climbing up out of the city and across the cliffs. Mulaghesh falls back when he enters the open country, moving from stone to stone and tree to tree, her hip screaming that she is a complete and utter idiot with every step.

Mulaghesh curses herself for not acting on this sooner. *Signe accused* me *of being an industrial spy once,* she thinks, *and here she is with a spy of her own up at the fortress!* She ducks down behind a boulder and watches Pandey hurry over the cliffs. *Oh, Pandey, you stupid boy. What have you gotten yourself into?*

They pass the ruined mines, the copse of trees where she found the tunnel, farther and farther north. She makes careful note of his boot print and begins to read its small, ridged scar in the landscape. It should be almost impossible to lose him now.

Yet she comes to the cliffs, and finds she has. She looks to the left and right, wondering if she could have missed him, or perhaps he dove off into the sea itself. Yet when she looks over the edge, she sees only a smattering of sharp, murderous rocks, and the gray gravelly shore.

She pauses. A small sculling shell rests on the shore with two oars nestled inside. As she leans out to look she sees a small stone staircase has been cunningly hidden in the folds of the cliffs, perhaps carved by someone decades ago.

Mulaghesh gets down on her elbows and knees and watches as Pandey finishes climbing down the narrow staircase and walks over to the sculling shell. He looks around, then looks up.

She moves back, waits, and then looks back out again.

Pandey is now stripping down to his undergarments, carefully folding his clothes and setting them on the gravel. Even though it's evening and cooling off quick, he's naked to the waist now, wearing only a pair of dark gray breeches. He shoves the sculling shell out onto the waves, wading in chest-deep, and then ably lifts himself up and into the shell. She sees his rowing prowess hasn't diminished one jot, for he capably navigates his way through the jagged rocks and out to the sea, where another craft is ponderously making its way north to meet him.

Mulaghesh shields her eyes and squints at the craft. The boat is not half as sleek as Pandey's, a fat washtub of a thing. She takes out her spyglass and places it to her eye, and is not surprised to see it is Signe laboring away at the two oars . . . though she is a little surprised to see that SDC's chief technology officer has also stripped down quite a bit for this jaunt, though she still wears her scarf. Even if she's holding a clandestine meeting with a spy, it's . . . a bit much.

"What the hells?" mutters Mulaghesh.

When Pandey's shell nears Signe he pops the oars out, slides them in, and hops into the open water. Mulaghesh feels cold just watching him. He loops a rope to the prow of his shell, frog-kicks over to Signe's bathtub of a boat, and knots it to the stern, with her assistance. When he grabs onto the edge of the boat Signe leans out over him, and Mulaghesh frowns when she sees the huge, ecstatic grin bloom on the Dreyling girl's face.

Pandey lifts himself out of the water, shoulders rippling and flexing, and places a kiss upon the smile.

Mulaghesh's mouth drops open. "Oh. *Oh*."

Pandey climbs in with Signe and rows to some hidden, rocky inlet along the coast. As the boats slowly leave Mulaghesh's range of vision Signe undoes her ponytail, her bright gold hair rippling down in a shimmering curtain, and then she reaches down and starts to lift her shirt.

"Oh, *shit*," says Mulaghesh. She lowers the spyglass, ashamed.

"Yes," says a voice behind her.

Mulaghesh jumps so much she almost goes tumbling off the cliffs. She turns to see Sigrud about twenty feet down the cliff, sitting with his legs dangling over the edge and watching the waters with a strange look on his face, as if he is both puzzled and pleased by what he just saw.

"Damn it!" says Mulaghesh. "You nearly made me kill myself just then!"

Sigrud is silent.

"You were following her, weren't you?" asks Mulaghesh.

"Yes," he says. "And you were following yours."

"Right. So your daughter . . . Uh, and Pandey . . ." Mulaghesh scratches the back of her head.

"They are lovers," says Sigrud.

"Well, if they weren't already it sure looks like they're going to be."

"No . . . The familiarity of their movements . . . They have done this before, many times."

Mulaghesh holds up her hands. "Okay, please stop. Remember this is your daughter you're talking about."

"Why should this discomfort me, to see my daughter doing this?" He looks into the sunset. "Two young people who nearly died last night, embracing life. That was what I saw."

"With a . . . With a damned sergeant major in the Saypuri *Military*? I thought Signe would be into, I don't know, some astronomically wealthy banker or something. Or at least someone of her own race. A Saypuri courting a Dreyling . . . I can't imagine how such a thing would work. He'd need to tie cans on his feet to dance with her."

"You underestimate her."

"Maybe. Either way, it's dangerous."

"Affairs of the heart often are."

"Don't get sentimental with me. There's a lot that could go wrong here. If either of them is telling the other anything . . ."

Sigrud thinks about it. "I do not care."

"You what?"

"I do not care about espionage, about decorum, about security. I worried my daughter had only work in her life, only success or miserable failure. To see her smile in such a manner makes my heart glad."

"Well, goody for your fucking heart! Pandey was one of *my* soldiers. I can't believe he's . . . fraternizing with a foreign official in such a manner!"

"Didn't you sleep with a member of the Bulikov police department?" asks Sigrud.

"That's beside the point!" snarls Mulaghesh. "The stakes were different then!"

"Were they?" Sigrud scratches his chin. "They are young. Both of them leave soon for uncertain fates. I say let them be humans for as long as circumstances allow. Why is this breach of decorum your concern, when so much else is at risk?"

"And I thought *I* was getting old and soft. You sound like a cheap novel, Chancellor." She sighs. "Come on. Help me get my broken ass back to HQ."

Ask a person what they want most desperately and they will say a child, a home, a fortune, a power, or an influence over their fellow men.

These are all variations on the same thing—a wish for lasting influence, for legacy, for eternity.

We wish to be remembered.

—WRITS OF SAINT PETRENKO, 720

12.

tHe tootH

Two days later, three hours before the break of dawn, Mulaghesh—still stiff, still bruised, still aching—reviews the craft that Signe has bobbing beside a small SDC dock.

"So . . . are we sailing or going on holiday?" she asks.

"I take it you're no sailor," says Signe as she makes her preparations. Despite the impending voyage, she's still dressed the same: same black boots, same scarf, though she is now wearing a life jacket. Mulaghesh tries very hard not to remember the proper young CTO in the state of undress she saw just days ago.

"Maybe not, but I'm not sure how keen I am to get on that thing in the open seas." She walks the length of the craft. It's a forty-foot white yacht labeled *Bjarnadóttir*, which Mulaghesh isn't going to even attempt to pronounce, and it looks to her eye to be more suited for a jaunt across a still lake than navigating the rocky coastlines of Voortyashtan.

"Don't doubt it," says Signe. "I know a Dreyling who sailed one of these fifteen thousand miles single-handedly."

"If you are talking about old Hjörvar," says Sigrud, walking down the dock, "that man sailed slower than a cow gives birth." He's still moving gingerly, his right arm still in a sling. Mulaghesh shakes her head: firing a Ponja from an upright position would be like getting hit by a truck. But never was there a person more born to bear punishment than Sigrud.

"Hjörvar is one of the most accomplished seamen I know of," says Signe, nettled.

"The reason we all thought Hjörvar was so slow," says Sigrud, "is we assumed he kept masturbating in the cockpit instead of sleeping. He was known for that."

"*Anyway*," says Signe, "she is a good vessel, and she'll take us where we need to go."

Mulaghesh looks at Sigrud. "*Is* it a good vessel?"

He holds up a hand and wobbles it back and forth. "It will do."

Signe scoffs as she carries more supplies on board. Mulaghesh eyes the crate as Signe walks past. "Four riflings, ammunition . . . and grenades? Why grenades?"

"You've not been to the Tooth, General," Signe says over her shoulder. "I have. And if you think something Divine is awakening in Voortyashtan . . . I would prefer we be careful." She slips through the hatch.

Sigrud and Mulaghesh stand on the dock, both slightly bent from their injuries. He says, "Take care of her."

"I think she's going to be taking care of *me*. I don't know a damn thing about sailing."

"She may know sailing. But she does not know combat. And she is going to a place that I think could be quite dangerous. We do not even know if Choudhry came back from this Tooth. We do not know what awaits."

"I'll try."

Signe emerges from belowdecks. "We've got more shipments coming in shortly. If we want to depart, now's the time."

"Ah, hells," says Mulaghesh. "Here we go. . . ." She steps on board, her hip still complaining.

Signe shoves a second life jacket in her arms. "Wear this. And keep out of the way."

"Fine, fine," says Mulaghesh. She sits down before the hatch and slips the jacket on.

Signe turns to face her father, and for a moment Mulaghesh sees how their relationship could have been, had the world been different: Sigrud, tall, proud, stern, standing upon the dock with his arms crossed and the haze of early sunrise behind him; and before him his daughter, young and fierce, confidently balanced on the balls of her feet as the craft bobs up and down. They exchange some wordless moment that is inscrutable to Mulaghesh: perhaps each recognizes the competence of the other, and signals their pride; but then each acknowledges that there is work to do, and they must return to it.

"Safe sailing," says Sigrud.

"Safe work," says Signe.

And with that Sigrud bends low, unties the hitch, and throws the line aboard. Signe catches it one-handed, stows it aboard, then walks to the stern and starts the little diesel engine with a single jerk. Then, the engine sputtering and smoking, she guides the little yacht out to the open sea.

She does not look back once at her father. When Mulaghesh looks to shore, Sigrud, too, is walking away without a glance back.

***

For two days and two nights they sail southwest, and most of what Mulaghesh does is stay out of Signe's way. That, and vomit.

She once mocked Shara for her weak stomach, but now that she's on such a small craft on the open seas she regrets it: every bend of every wave is magnified a thousand times on this tiny vessel, and time and time again she feels sure the yacht will capsize, its mainsail plummeting into the dark waters of the North Seas, dragging her and Signe both down to a dark and watery grave.

This never happens, of course. Signe is far too skilled of a sailor. She's a flurry of activity for nearly all of their voyage, scurrying over the bow and the hatch to adjust the tiller or the boom bail, checking the traveler rig or the becket block, or any other piece of nautical anatomy that sounds wholly made up to Mulaghesh. Signe pauses only to mention, "Watch the boom," as the mainsail comes hurtling at her head, or perhaps, "Throw me that there."

As the first night falls Signe says, "We're in a good spot now. And were I a serious sailor, I'd have trained to sleep in twenty-minute shifts, waking up to see the seas ahead. But as I'm not, we'll have to take shifts."

"So what do I do?"

"Sit in the cockpit and shout if you see a damn thing, of course."

"And what does a damn thing look like?"

"It looks like a big damned rock, General," says Signe. "Or a big damned boat, if we stray into the shipping lanes—which we *shouldn't*, if I've set the right course. But you never know."

The first night is terrifying to Mulaghesh, alone in the dark with the sails fluttering gently and the moon shining down on her. The world hasn't ever felt so empty to her before. She supposes she should be glad the weather is clear, but all she can think of is the sight of Voortya's face bursting up through the reflection of the moon on the waves, and rising, rising, water pouring off her vast metal body. . . .

There's the soft click of the hatch opening. Signe silently walks across to sit beside her in the cockpit. For a moment or two, they say nothing.

"You ought to get some sleep, Skipper," says Mulaghesh. "I can't have you passing out on me at the tiller."

"I won't. Just . . . the purpose of our voyage weighs on me."

"Me, too. Do you know anything about what's over there? In the City of Blades itself?"

"Folklore," says Signe. "And rumors. I've heard stories of Voortyashtanis contacting and, yes, passing over into the City of Blades. These instances were always highly controversial, and only done in extreme situations, when departed elders needed to be closely consulted."

"Did those who came back say what was on the other side?"

"There's supposedly a gatekeeper, of some sorts," says Signe. "Some entity or . . . or *something* over there that only allows certain people in. When someone who wasn't suitable arrived in the City of Blades, they were expelled."

"Who's considered suitable?"

"A great warrior. Someone who's shed the blood of many."

"That probably won't be a problem, then," says Mulaghesh grimly. "But if I'm wrong?"

"Depending on their stature or demeanor, frequently the expulsion was . . . lethal."

"But not always?"

Signe shakes her head. "There were ways beyond this ritual to visit the City of Blades. If we had a Voortyashtani sentinel's blade, for example, and if we were trained in the meditative arts of the sentinels, we could hold their sword and project our consciousness there."

"Project your . . . What? I thought picking up a sentinel's sword got you possessed," says Mulaghesh. "That's what happened to that poor guy at the harbor."

"It's a two-way street, in a way," says Signe. "You could use their sword like a telephone, I suppose, directly communing and conversing with them in the City of Blades. It's just that when Oskarsson picked up the blade, well, for one thing, he wasn't skilled in the meditative arts—but more so, Zhurgut clearly had intentions other than education. Either way, back in the ancient days, this gatekeeper was also responsible for blocking or expelling these pilgrims, preventing the unworthy from projecting themselves into the City of Blades."

"So if I can get past this gatekeeper," says Mulaghesh, "then what's after that?" She remembers her brief vision of the City of Blades, and the strange white citadel beyond. "A castle? A tower? The home of Voortya herself?"

"I don't know, General," says Signe. "You know more than I do. You've been there before."

"Great," says Mulaghesh.

Signe looks east, at the ragged gray coast of Voortyashtan. The cliffs look like the folds of a dark, crinkled tablecloth glowing silver in the moonlight. "I forget it can be beautiful, sometimes."

Mulaghesh grunts.

"Vallaicha Thinadeshi's son is buried out there, in that region there. Did you know that?"

"Huh?" says Mulaghesh. It takes her a moment to remember her history. "Oh, right. The baby."

"I believe he was four years old when the plague took him. But yes."

"It was mad for her to try and take her family with her."

"Times were different then, and I don't believe she intended to get pregnant out here. But you're right. Ambition and responsibilities . . . Not very good bedmates."

Mulaghesh looks side-eyed at Signe. She's never seen her look so mournful and contemplative. "What do you see out there?"

"Besides the rocks? It's complicated."

"Try me."

"Fair enough." She points. "I see an excellent site for a hydro-electric dam. Numerous ones, actually. Megamundes', *giga*mundes' worth of power generation. I see fruitful sites for refineries, plants, berths for industries of all types and kinds. Water's the lifeblood of industry, specifically *fresh* water—which Voortyashtan is rich in. Once we crack the river open . . . Oh, what a spark that will be, what a country this will make."

"Sometimes I can't tell if you hate this place or love it."

"I love its potential. I hate its past. And I don't like what it is." She hugs her knees close to her chest. "The way you feel about the place you grew up in is a lot like how you feel about your family."

"How's that?"

She thinks about it for a long time. "Like isn't the same thing as love."

***

Mulaghesh is dozing in the cabin on the second afternoon, lulled to sleep by the rock and roll of the waves, when she hears Signe groan from the cockpit, a sound of deep dismay.

"What?" says Mulaghesh, sitting up. "What is it?"

"We're nearly there."

"Oh. So that's good, yes?" Mulaghesh stands and joins her in the cockpit.

Signe's eye is pressed to her spyglass, which is fixed on some insignificant bump on the distant horizon. "Yes. No. I wanted to come up on it during the *day*. And we won't get there for several hours yet." She lowers the spyglass. "Not at night . . . It's a different place at night. Or it seems that way."

"So what's the move, Skipper? Are we just going to, I don't know, drift and wait until tomorrow's daylight?"

Signe shakes her head. "We can't just drift. It's part of a chain of islands. . . . It's too dangerous. But there is a primitive dock on the Tooth." She grimaces and exits through the hatch. "Hold on."

Mulaghesh sits beside Signe and watches as the islands approach, tiny pinpricks that grow and grow . . .

And grow.

And grow . . .

Her eyes widen. "By the seas . . ."

They are not just simple islands—not the rocky beaches she imagined, perhaps scattered with a few withered trees. Rather, these are huge, towering columns of gray rock, stacks and stacks of it, tottering and leaning like fronds of river grass nudged about by the wind. And on their sides . . .

Mulaghesh grabs the spyglass. "Are those *faces?*"

"Yes," says Signe grimly. "Carvings of Saint Zhurgut, Saint Petrenko, Saint Chovanec, Saint Tok . . . Heroes and warriors with a hundred deaths to their name each." She slightly adjusts the tiller, pointing the bow so that it threads them through the towering islands. "They are called the Teeth of the World. From the poem, you see. And at the very end is the Tooth. What name it originally had is forgotten, or so I am told. But it was the most important of them."

Mulaghesh sits in awed silence as Signe pilots them through the forest of massive columns, their surfaces carved with faces and visages and bas-reliefs, many of them terrifying: images of soldiers, battle, churning tapestries of conquest, of raised blades and torrents of spears, skies black with arrows, horizons blocked out with endless banners, and tangled, twisted piles of the defeated dead.

The islands seem to have once had a purpose beyond decoration, too: a few have windows, or doorways, or stairways running up the sides, as if these were not rock formations but rather towers. Perhaps their interiors are as honeycombed and chamber-filled as the walls of Fort Thinadeshi, dark and cramped and secretive. She wonders what could have gone on in these towers. The thought sets her skin crawling.

Many of the columns are lined with torch sconces, and she imagines how the Teeth of the World must have looked a hundred years ago, covered with glimmering dots of firelight and the windows filled with faces, looking down on them as they sailed by.

"How is this still here?" says Mulaghesh.

"I don't know," says Signe. "Perhaps it doesn't persist with any Divine aid. Perhaps they used Divine abilities to make them, but the rocks and the carvings themselves—they're but simple matter. I can't tell you, General." Then, darkly, "That's the Tooth."

Mulaghesh looks ahead and sees a wide peak emerging from amidst the towering columns. It's not at all like the other islands, which are more or less purely vertical: the Tooth is more akin to a small floating mountain, covered with tall, twisted trees and—though it's hard to see in the dimming light—countless arches of some kind. Its summit is concealed by the tall, warped trees.

She's suddenly aware of Signe breathing hard as they approach the Tooth—not out of exertion, but terror. "Are you going to be okay?"

"Yes," she says defiantly. Then she lowers the sails and starts the little diesel engine, piloting the boat toward the island's south side. She flicks a switch in the cockpit, and the yacht's tiny spotlight stabs out into the growing gloom, its beam bobbing up and down the distant shore.

Mulaghesh spies the dock, though it's not like any dock she's ever seen before. It looks like a massive rib cage made of antlers and horns blooming off the shore of the island, leaving a tiny gap just below what would be its sternum. Beyond the "ribs" she can see distant stone walls, cold and pale. It takes Mulaghesh a moment to realize Signe is aiming the boat toward the gap below the sternum, and she wonders if the yacht will be able to make it through. Then she realizes that the rib cage is much, much larger than she realized, and the boat slips through easily.

She stares up at the carven ribs as they pass underneath them. "Death worship," she says. "What a morbid civilization this was."

"I decided it was a memorial when I came here last," Signe says quietly. "Maybe that's what all of the Teeth of the World are. They are unusually bedecked in the images of death, after all."

They approach the stone dock, its steps stained dark from decades of mold.

"The City of Blades is worse," says Mulaghesh.

Signe expertly steers the boat up to the dock and moors it to an ancient iron ring beside the steps. Then the two women arm themselves, a process Mulaghesh has more guidance for: "Put your ammunition on the left side of your belt. No, your *other* left. You're right-handed; that's easier for you to reach."

"I *did* receive training on this, you know."

"Well, then they did a shit job of it."

Mulaghesh readies herself, then steps onto the dock. She looks back at Signe, and perhaps it's the light, but the Dreyling woman suddenly looks quite pale.

"What?" says Mulaghesh.

"I . . . I was fourteen when I came here last," Signe says.

Mulaghesh just waits and watches.

"I'd hoped it'd all fallen into the seas, frankly. To come here now . . . it feels as if I'm stepping into a memory."

"You haven't stepped into it yet."

Signe nods, then hops up onto the dock with Mulaghesh.

"Now to the ruin at the top?" says Mulaghesh.

"Yes. The dome of shields and knives. It feels like it was something out of a dream . . . but that's what I remember of it."

The stone path winds around and around the Tooth like a corkscrew, and each step is old and well-worn. Countless people must have been here during its life, Mulaghesh thinks—processions of warriors and dignitaries and kings and priests, all threading their way up the hill. About every twenty feet is an arch that stretches over the steps, and carved into each arch are images Mulaghesh doesn't quite understand: a woman, presumably Voortya, firing an arrow into a tidal wave; a sword dicing a mountain as one would an onion; a man disemboweling himself upon a tall, flat rock before the setting sun; a woman hurling a spear at the moon, and showering in the black blood that spills forth.

The bent trees quiver and shake in the steady breeze, making the slopes shift and shudder just as much as the seas below. It's an eerie place, Mulaghesh finds.

"It's all the same as I remember," says Signe quietly.

"The Voortyashtanis brought you here before?"

"Yes. A rite of passage. Twenty children, none older than fourteen. They brought us here and dropped us off with a pitifully small amount of provisions: a few loaves of bread, a few potatoes, some dried fruit. Barely enough for us to last. And then they . . . And then they left us here. Without a word. Without telling us if they'd ever come back. Alone in this miserable place.

"I'm not sure why I came," Signe continues. "My mother didn't want me to. They did not force us to come. I suppose I just wanted to prove myself to them, just like the rest of the children. To show I wasn't just some princess."

Mulaghesh stays silent as Signe talks. Every few steps she sees something odd in the dirt at the edges of the stone staircase: the imprint of a shoe with an intricate tread. A sort of shoe you would see in the modern world, not at all something you'd expect to find in ancient Voortyashtan. The imprint is deep in the mud, deep enough that the rains must not have completely washed it away.

"At first we tried to share," Signe says. "But one of us—the son of some relative of a chieftain—he was bigger than the rest of us, more developed. Stronger. Crueler. He beat one of the other kids terribly badly, in front of everyone, to show us what he could do, I suppose. And he set himself up as the petty king of our little island, monopolizing our food and water, forcing us to do things to survive. Humiliate ourselves. Fight among ourselves, all for his amusement and that of his cronies."

"Sounds like a real charmer."

"Yes. Far from the surveillance and laws of society, not sure if you will live or die . . . Who knows what you will become?"

Mulaghesh does not tell Signe this is a sensation she knows all too well.

"I don't know why I'm telling you this," says Signe. "But this place . . . It brings it all back."

"All of us need confessions sometimes."

Signe glances over her shoulder. "What makes you say this is a confession?"

"The same thing that makes me think I know why you wear scarves."

Signe is silent for a few paces. Then she says, "He took an interest in me. I knew he would. Blond hair . . . it's very rare on the Continent, you see."

"I get it."

"He told me that if I wanted to eat again, ever again . . . I would need to come to him at night. He'd set up something like a throne, behind one of the arches. We would be alone there. I would do as he told me. I agreed, and he was pleased.

"Before I went, I visited an old sparring ground here on the island, and in the earth there I found an arrowhead. And I sharpened it, and sharpened it, until it could cut flesh. I tested it on the back of my wrist. And then I hid it in my mouth.

"He was no fool. He made me strip bare before he took me into his privacy. Made me do it before everyone. I didn't care; Dreylings don't really care about things like that. We don't have such arcane ideas of how the human body should be seen. But he never looked into my mouth.

"He took me behind a tall, flat stone. And then he tried to take me. Tried to pin me down. And as he readied himself, I spit the arrowhead out into my hand . . . and then I rammed it into his eye."

She pauses, perhaps awaiting something, as if she expects Mulaghesh to gasp. When she doesn't, Signe continues. "It was a foolish thing to do. I *should* have jammed it into his throat. He started screaming, shrieking in pain, flailing about. It was not a fatal blow. So I got up, and I took a nearby stone . . . and I hit him on the head. I hit him, and I kept hitting him. I kept hitting him until I could no longer recognize him at all.

"Then I went out. Cleaned myself up. Clothed myself. I went to our rations. I told the other children to come near. And then we ate—sparingly—in silence."

They walk on. The peak is a few hundred feet above them now, the sea a distant, undulating darkness.

"I thought the elders would kill me when they finally returned. I'd killed a boy of serious standing. And I'd done it in cold blood, carefully preparing for it. But they didn't. They were . . . impressed. I'd defeated someone larger and meaner than myself. It didn't matter that I'd done it through deception—to Voortyashtanis, a victory is a victory, and to win through cunning is no small thing. So . . . they made me a full member of the tribe." She uses one finger to pull down the neck of her shirt, revealing the elaborate, delicate, soft yellow tattoo there. It's beautiful, really, artful and strange. "And from then on, when I spoke, they listened. It was a curious thing." She pulls the collar back up. "But I still hated what I'd done. I still hated everything I'd gone through. And I hated, later, that I'd become like . . . him."

"Him who?"

"My father. Who else? He's killed more people than anyone, I think, except perhaps the Kaj and Voortya herself."

Mulaghesh knows that, statistically, this is unlikely: odds are she and Biswal are responsible for many more deaths than Sigrud je Harkvaldsson could ever aspire to.

"I thought I was better than him," says Signe. "More . . . I don't know. Evolved."

"People don't get to choose what the world makes of them," says Mulaghesh.

"And that is what you think this is? The world made him, made us? Or is there some cruelty in us that pushes us into such situations?"

"You aren't born this way. None of us are. We're made this way, over time. But we might be able to unmake some of what was done to us, if we try."

"Do you believe that?"

"I have to," says Mulaghesh.

There's a bird cry somewhere out in the darkness. Signe shivers. They plod on.

"I don't remember what my father looked like," says Mulaghesh. "I thought I'd never forget it, once. We only had each other in the world. Then one night I ran away from home and joined the army. Off to serve my country and find my fortune. It seemed such a fun idea at the time, such a lark. Such a childish thought. When I first landed on Continental shores I wrote him a letter explaining what I'd done and why I did it and what I expected to happen. A bunch of naïve shit, probably. My life seemed like a storybook at the time. I don't know if he ever got it.

"After the war was over I went home and I knocked on the door. I remember waiting in front of it, our red front door. It was so strange to see, it hadn't changed a bit since I was a kid. I had changed, but the door had stayed the same. But then a stranger answered it, a woman. She said she'd been living there for over a year. The previous owner had died some time ago. She didn't even know where he was buried. I still don't know."

They walk on for a moment longer in silence. Then Mulaghesh stops. Signe walks on a few steps, then pauses to look back at her.

"Hundreds would kill to be where you are, Signe Harkvaldsson," says Mulaghesh. "And more still would kill to have what you have now that your father has returned: a chance to undo a wrong done to you long ago. Such things are rare. I suggest you treasure them."

"Perhaps I should. Perhaps you're right. Shall we continue?"

"No."

"No? Why no?"

"Because the tracks I've been following have split off from

the main stairs." Mulaghesh points west, where a stone trail runs through the twisted trees. "That way."

"What tracks? What do you mean?"

"I mean someone's been here before us. Recently, too. I can see their boot imprint in the soil here and there." She points at the ground. "It's a modern shoe type, nothing that the Voortyashtanis would have used. It's been consistent all the way up here. When you didn't step on it and mar the prints, at least."

"You think . . . maybe Choudhry?"

"Maybe." She sniffs. "Let's take a look, eh?"

***

The path is not stone like the staircase, but a rambling dirt trail that winds underneath the crooked trees. Evening is fading into night, and both of them are forced to resort to pulling out torches, which turn the woods into a shifting, spectral nightscape.

Mulaghesh carefully follows the footprints, gingerly taking each next step. "They're old. Months old, perhaps longer. Someone came here a lot."

"Perhaps the tribes are still bringing their children here for their rite of passage."

"Maybe. If so, they brought a damned wheelbarrow." She points at a tire tread running through the soft earth.

"That seems . . . unlikely," says Signe. "I thi . . . Oh, my word."

"What?" Mulaghesh looks up, and sees Signe is shining her torch ahead, its beam falling on . . . something.

It's some sort of tomb or crypt—a tall, arching structure built directly into the cliff behind it, with a set of white stairs leading up to a stone door—or what *would* have been a door, were it not completely destroyed. Chunks of rubble are scattered on the dais before the door.

Mulaghesh walks up and shines her light over the structure before her. It's an elegant, beautiful construction, pale and delicate in the rippling shafts of moonlight, and covered with engravings: whales, fish, swords, porpoises, and endless waves. "I'm guessing they came here for this. But what in hells is it?"

"A burial chamber, I'm guessing. We found a few like this in the silt at the bottom of the bay, but they were much smaller—little more than a box." She walks up to the broken door and shines her light in. "Yes—it's the same. Come look."

Mulaghesh joins her. The interior of the tomb is much smaller than she expected, considerably smaller than the ornate stone dais before it. It's about four feet by five feet, and it's almost completely barren except for a small plinth in the center.

"No place for a body," says Signe. "Just a weapon—a sword."

"Maybe they didn't bury bodies. Their souls were bound up in their blades, weren't they? Why bother with the corpse when you have that? So you just stowed the sword away for safekeeping . . ."

"Until you needed it," says Signe. "Then you made a sacrifice. Someone picked it up, and then . . ." She shudders.

"Maybe the Teeth of the World are a memorial, like you said," says Mulaghesh. "A place to store the weapons and souls of their most revered saints. Only now . . . someone's gone graverobbing." She shines her light back out at the woods. "So maybe this is how someone got their hands on a functional Voortyashtani sword."

"Maybe that was the one your culprit tried to send to you?"

"Maybe. Or maybe they found more."

"That's not comforting."

Mulaghesh walks back out and examines the dais, looking for a name, a carving of a face, anything to identify the owner of the sword that might have been in that tomb. But beyond the ornamentation there are few identifying marks. "Someone so famous, perhaps," she says aloud, "you didn't even need to put their name on their grave. I guess this isn't the tomb Choudhry was looking for back in the city?"

Signe exits the tomb, looking pale and shaken. "The tomb that held all the Voortyashtani warriors, ever? No, I presume not. It'd be a bit cramped in there." She shivers. "I don't especially want to search the rest of the Tooth to see if someone broke into any more tombs."

"I don't, either. Come on. Take me to the summit."

***

The journey up begins to wear on Mulaghesh, but she wonders if it's the path itself that's the culprit: the farther they walk up the wet, gleaming cobblestones, the taller the trees seem, and the darker the air.

"Something doesn't feel right," says Signe.

"No, but it feels familiar. There were places kind of like this in Bulikov," says Mulaghesh. "Places that were here, but . . . *not* here, at the same time. Like scars, I guess."

"Scars in what?" asks Signe.

"In reality."

Finally they come to the top. Massive trees crowd around the summit as if to create a wall, and a wide, perfectly round stone arch marks the end of the steps. Beyond it is some kind of structure.

Mulaghesh slows to a stop as it comes into view. It is like a dome—a broad, brown, curving structure nearly thirty or forty feet wide. But it is made entirely out of beaten and smelted-down blades: sword blades and axe blades, knives, scythes, the tips of spears and arrows, all mashed together and layered on top of one another until they form a brown, rusted tangle of sharp edges. The entryway to the dome is lined with sword blades, all pointed in like teeth in the maw of some great beast. It is the single most hostile thing Mulaghesh has ever seen in her life.

"That's it, huh?" says Mulaghesh.

"That's it," says Signe.

"Did you ever go in there?"

Signe shakes her head. "We came near it, looked at it, but . . . we never stepped off the stairs. It was too *wrong*. One boy was bold enough to shout to it, to call the old man out—we ran away, terrified, and the boy came down later, saying he saw nothing. Do you really think this is the place Choudhry was talking about?"

"I guess."

"And . . . are you going in there?"

Mulaghesh stares at the dome. She can feel it: there is a mind in there, something watching her in the darkness. She imagines a soft sigh from the depths of the dome, a gentle exhalation.

"I am," she says. "I don't like it, but I am. Are you?"

Signe pauses. Then she shakes her head and says, "Not my ship, not my rats."

"That must be a Dreyling turn of phrase, because that doesn't make a damn bit of sense to me."

"I am saying this is your mission, General, not mine. I'll be more than happy to keep watch."

Mulaghesh walks through the gate. "Fair enough. I don't blame you." She stands before the entry to the dome, rifling held ready. "If I don't come out in thirty minutes," she says, "throw a grenade in."

"What?" says Signe, startled. "And kill you?"

"If I'm not out in thirty minutes, then it's likely I'm already dead," she says. "And I don't intend to let this damned place live longer than me." Then she raises her rifling, stoops down low, and steps into the shadows.

***

There's a moment of darkness. Then shafts of light filter through the gloom above. She realizes she's seeing the moonlight shining through the gaps in all the thousands of blades hammered together above, but the color of the light is wrong: it's dull and yellowed, like it's shining from the wrong sky. She remembers how things looked during the Battle of Bulikov, when the Divinity appeared and forced its reality onto the city, changing the very sky: this is much the same, she finds—not true light but a crude approximation of it. It is as if the sky above this dome is different from the one she just left.

The light curls, coils, churns above her head. Then she takes a breath and realizes the dome is full of smoke.

The acrid tang unravels in her lungs and she's overtaken with violent coughing. It's a reek of a sort that she's never smelled before, something oily and woody and putrefied. She blinks tears from her eyes, which are slowly adjusting to the darkness.

The floor of the dome is made of shields hammered flat, just like the blades that form the roof. Across the gloom, at the very end of the dome—she finds herself wondering, *How big is this place?*—she sees there is a human form sitting beside what looks like a pale, silvery shrub.

He's real, thinks Mulaghesh, though she finds it hard to believe it. *He's really real.*

The man is masked in shadow, but he appears to be holding an ornate pipe, long and white like a piece of coral. The pipe curls up from his crossed legs and over his shoulders and around to his mouth, winding around his neck like a noose. She watches as the shadowy figure sucks at it. The bowl in his lap flares a soft orange. Then he exhales an absolute thundercloud of roiling, reeking smoke.

"I take it you're the man atop the Tooth," Mulaghesh calls to him.

If this means anything he doesn't show it. He just takes another huge draw from his pipe, leans back, and sends a stream of smoke up to the ceiling.

Yet this time his face happens to catch one of the rays of light.

She freezes, and thinks: *Holy hells. He's a corpse.*

She watches as he lowers his head, the ray of light sliding across his features. His skin is gnarled and papery, covered with splotches of discolorations like mold blooming in the walls of an old house. His eyes are wide and white and blind, and his eye sockets and cheeks are so sunken and hollow it's like he hasn't eaten in . . . Well. Maybe ever. He is dressed in wraps of thin, wispy rags, and he seems incapable of completely shutting his mouth, so his narrow, blackened teeth are always visible, like the grin of a corpse.

Mulaghesh tightens her grip on her rifling. He doesn't exactly look like a physical powerhouse, but he must be Divine, which means appearances can be deceiving.

She takes a step forward. "Who are you?"

He stares ahead blindly. The only sign that he heard is the slightest twitch of his head. Then a voice rattles up from his skinny chest, a voice like rocks and gravel being washed ashore.

"I," he says slowly, "am not a *who*." Each word he speaks makes a fog of coiling smoke.

"Okay," says Mulaghesh slowly. "Then . . . *what* are you?"

"I am memory," says the man. He sucks at his pipe and exhales again.

"What do you mean, you're memory?"

"I mean," he says, "I am that which remembers."

"Okay. So you just . . . remember things?"

He sucks his pipe but doesn't bother to answer.

"What kind of things?"

"My memory encompasses," he says, "all the things that I remember."

Mulaghesh frowns. His circular answers suggest a lack of basic human intelligence, or maybe she's not asking the right questions. "How . . . How did you come to be here?"

There's a pause. Then he smacks his lips and says in a measured chant, "I am the 374th memory vessel of the Empress of Graves, Maiden of Steel, Devourer of Children, Queen of Grief, She Who Clove the Earth in Twain. Upon this spot I took the place of the 373rd vessel, broke a leaf from the Tree of Memory, and inhaled all the knowledge of what the Great Mother had promised. Within me is the memory of all who have been lost, sacrificed, cut down. I contain villages, armies, generations. I remember the slain and the dead, the victorious and the defeated. I am memory."

Mulaghesh glances at the silvery little shrub beside him. "Tree of Memory?"

"Yes."

"What does that mean? What is the Tree of Memory?"

Again he begins to chant: "In honor of Her people swearing fealty to Her, the Great Mother stabbed a single arrow into the stone, and it flowered and became a great tree, a tree whose roots lie under all the stones of this land." He gestures to the tiny, silvery shrub with one gnarled hand. "The tree is fed by the blood of the people, by their conflict and their sacrifice, and the memory of all that they have done flows through its vessels—and into me," he says, smoke blooming from his lips, "into this thing I am, this creature of flesh and bone.

I am the final vessel of all these memories. I am the pool fed by the many mountain streams."

Mulaghesh looks over his bony wrists, his painfully thin ankles. "How . . . How long have you been here?"

He cocks his head, like he has to think about it. "I have, in my time here, borne witness to ninety-six winters."

"How is that possible?" asks Mulaghesh softly.

"I am memory," he says. Smoke curls up around his head like a ghastly crown. "I need nothing. All I must do is remember. Which I do."

"But this is all . . . miraculous, isn't it?" asks Mulaghesh. "Isn't Voortya dead?"

Silence. Then: "The Great Mother is gone from this world. This I remember."

"Then how are you still here?"

A pause, as if he's accessing some hidden part of himself. "Pass from this world," he says finally, "and your agreements will still exist. Your contracts and oaths and debts will carry on. Promises were made. And some of those promises are being kept. I am here to re-member the dead. When those oaths are fulfilled, I shall fade also." He shudders a bit. "I will finally pass on, out of this room, into the light. Into the light . . . Into the air of the world I once knew . . ." He closes his eyes.

Mulaghesh suppresses a shiver. *Enough of this.* "There was a woman who came before me," she says. "She asked about a ritual. I think it was a ritual to cross over to the afterlife, to the . . . to the City of Blades. Is this so?"

"I remember this."

"I need to know what you told her."

A gray, dry tongue wriggles up from the depths of his mouth and runs over his tiny, discolored teeth. Mulaghesh nearly gags in disgust.

"What did you tell her?" she asks. "How can I get to the City of Blades?"

He reaches over to the tree, and pinches off one thin, silvery leaf. He places it in the bowl of his pipe, and takes a drag—yet then he freezes, as if an idea has struck him. His blank white eyes widen, and he turns to look at her—the first time she feels he's actually looked at her yet, focusing on her with all of his energy.

He stares at her, then softly says, "I . . . I remember you."

"You what?"

"I remember you," he says. He takes another puff from the pipe, and this seems to fuel his memory. "Young and bright and filled with cold anger. I remember you. You swept across the land like a scream-ing storm. In one hand you carried fury and in the other you carried slaughter."

Mulaghesh's skin goes cold. "What are you talking about?"

"War incarnate," he whispers. "Battle made flesh. This is how I remember you. This is how I remember you as you shed blood in the lands east of here. That blood took a long journey to reach the tap-roots of the silver tree. . . . But when it did, you bloomed in my mind like the brightest of stars. How the Great Mother would have loved to have an arrow such as you in her quiver. What a prize you would have been."

Mulaghesh fights the urge to retch. The idea of this *thing*—she can't think of it as a man, by any means—knowing what she did dur-ing the Yellow March, and *approving* of it, is utterly revolting to her. "Shut your mouth! I didn't ask about that!"

He sucks on his pipe and watches her with a strangely critical gaze. "You wish to find the City of Blades," he says. "I remember this. Why?"

"To follow the woman who came here before."

He shakes his head. "No. No, that is not so. I have watched your journey from the west countries. I remember your coming; I remem-ber how you battled your way to me. You have shed blood upon my mountains, upon my country. And when you did, I glimpsed your se-cret heart." He shuts his eyes. "I remember . . . I remember . . ." His eyes snap back open. "You wish to find the Victorious Army there, upon the white shores of the City of Blades. You mean to find them, and stop them, halt their final war."

Mulaghesh does not speak.

"Why?" he asks. His tone is that of someone politely puzzled.

"Wh-*Why?*" says Mulaghesh. "Why would I want to stop an army from destroying the world? *That's* your question?"

"You speak," he says, "as if they were an aberration. A violation. As if warfare was a passing phenomenon."

"I know I don't want it on my damned doorstep!"

He shakes his head. "But this is wrong. Warfare is light. Warfare and conflict are the energies with which this world functions. To claim otherwise is to claim your very veins are not filled with blood, to claim that your heart is still and silent. You knew this once. Once in the hills of this country you understood that to wage war was to be alive, to shed blood was to bask in the light of the sun. Why would you forget this? Why would you fight them and not join them?"

"*Join* them?" says Mulaghesh, appalled. "Join the very soldiers who enslaved my people?"

"Do you not enslave people now?" asks the man. "Chains are forged of many strange metals. Poverty is one. Fear, another. Ritual and custom are yet more. All actions are forms of slavery, methods of forcing people to do what they deeply wish *not* to do. Has not your nation conditioned this world to accept its subservience? When you wear your uniform and walk through these lands, do the people here not feel a terrified urge to bend their knees and bow their heads?"

"We didn't leave any fucking mass graves in our wake!" snarls Mulaghesh. "We didn't torment and slaughter and brutalize people to get what we needed!"

"Are you so sure? You burned down homes in the night, and families perished in the flames. I remember. And now you look back, full of guilt, and say, 'It was war, and I was wrong.'" He leans forward, his ancient face burning with intensity. "But this is a lie. You saw *light*. And now, when you have returned to the darkness, you wish to convince yourself the light was never there at all.

Yet it remains. You cannot erase what is written upon the hearts of humanity. Even if the Great Mother had never walked among us, you would still know this."

Mulaghesh feels tears spilling down her cheeks. "Times," she says furiously, "have *changed*. *I* have changed. Soldiers no longer devote their lives to slaughter and conquest."

"You are wrong," says the man. His voice is low and resonant. The metal walls of the dome, all the knives and swords and spears, all seem to vibrate with each of his words. "Your rulers and their propaganda have sold you this watered-down conceit of war, of a warrior yoked to the whims of civilization. Yet for all their self-professed civility, your rulers will gladly spend a soldier's life to better aid their posturing, to keep the cost of a crude good low. They will send the children of others off to die and only think upon it later to grandly and loudly memorialize them, lauding their great sacrifice. Civilization is but the adoption of this cowardly method of murder."

The smoke is so thick about her it's hard for her to see him. "Only a savage would think of peace that way!"

"No. It is the truth. And you know it. You were so much more honest when you slaughtered your own."

Mulaghesh freezes. The smoke hangs still in the air. The old man slowly blinks his blank white eyes, and sucks at his pipe.

"*What* did you say?" whispers Mulaghesh.

"You know what I said," says the man calmly. "Once those under your command did not wish to obey. And when that happened, you did what was necess—"

The rifling is on her shoulder and she's striding forward, leaping through the smoke. The old man doesn't grunt or make a sound as the muzzle of the rifling strikes his forehead, pushing him back against the wall of knives.

Mulaghesh leans close. "Keep talking," she whispers. "Keep talking to me, old man, and we'll see if I can spill the waters of your memory clean out of your fucking head."

"You see what you are now," he says serenely. "You see where your instincts lead you. Why do you deny what you are?"

"Tell me the damned ritual! Tell me how to get to the City of Blades!"

"The ritual? Why, you know it. You know the Window to the White Shores."

"But that won't let me cross over!"

"But you know the missing element that will augment it," says the old man. "You've spilled so much of it in your time, and it flows through your own veins—the blood of a killer. What else?"

Mulaghesh pushes slightly harder on his head. "What do you mean? And if you speak another riddle then I swear, you will fucking regret it."

"You saw a statue, once," hisses the man. "A statue of the Great Mother, seated before a wide cauldron. Were you to fill this cauldron with seawater and the blood of a killer, enough blood to fill a goat's bladder, and then perform the Window to the White Shores at the base of the cauldron, then you would be able to pass through—through the sea, through the world, and into the lands of the dead."

Mulaghesh thinks back. She remembers that when she saw the City of Blades it was in the yard of statues, before the giant white statue of Voortya . . . and at her feet was what looked like a giant bathtub.

"The living essence of a life of death," she says, "used to push a living person into the land of the dead." She takes a step back, releasing him. "Ironic."

The old man blinks his wide, blind eyes. "You think you are invading. You think you are assaulting enemy grounds. But you are not. You are going *home*. This life beyond death is one you deserve."

"Fuck you," says Mulaghesh. "Tell me about the swords, the sentinels' swords. Someone's found them and learned how to make them—who?"

"This I do not know," he says quietly. "I do not know these things."

"Someone's been on this island robbing your damned sacred graves! They must have come to you!"

"I do not remember them," says the man. "I do not have these memories."

"Someone fucking resurrected Saint Zhurgut! Don't tell me you don't know who was behind that!"

"I remember those who have shed blood," says the man. "I remember the dead. I remember the battle, the victors, the defeated. I remember what matters. All else is trivia."

"Someone is trying to bring about the Night of the Sea of Swords! How is it going to happen? How does it work?"

"Work? As if it were some device, some machine? What you describe is inevitable. Ask why the stars dance in the sky, ask why water flows downhill. Ask the mechanics behind that." He lowers his eyelids. "She promised it will happen. And thus, it will happen. This is the way of the world."

"I'll kill you, damn it!" cries Mulaghesh, raising the rifle. "I'll do it if you don't answer me!"

"If I could die," says the man, "I would let you. I do not fear death. But you are in my world, and this place will not allow me to die."

"I bet I can hurt you th—"

He shakes his head. "You think you have forced the truth from me. But you are wrong—I *wish* for you to see the City of Blades again, for you will see truth there. Truth about the world, and your secret heart. Now go—and see." He opens his mouth wide, and a hot cloud of acrid smoke comes pouring out. It's so much that Mulaghesh has to stumble out, covering her eyes with the crook of her arm. She spies a hint of flickering moonlight, goes reeling toward it, and takes a deep grateful breath when she finds herself in clear air.

***

She collapses onto the mud, reveling in the feel of the cool, damp earth between her fingers, relieved to be free of that awful place.

"Was he there?" says Signe. "What happened? Did you get what you needed?"

Mulaghesh looks up. Signe is watching her with wide eyes, holding a grenade with one finger hooked around the pin. She smiles nervously and stows it away in her pocket. "Well. You *did* say thirty minutes."

Mulaghesh coughs and spits to the side. "Motherfucker," she says hoarsely.

"What's the matter with you?" says Signe. "Are you all right?"

"No. No, I'm not fucking all right." Mulaghesh stands on wobbly legs, then looks back at the dome of blades. "Get back. Get back behind the trees. Now!"

Signe starts backing away. "Why?"

Mulaghesh pulls a grenade from her belt, rips the pin out with her teeth—Signe shouts, "What!" behind her—and lobs it into the entrance in the dome of blades. Then she and Signe start running.

Mulaghesh sprints through the circle gate and slides down into a crouch on the hillside, covering her head. Then she waits. And waits.

Nothing. No blast, no bang.

She waits a little longer. Then she releases her head and looks up, finding Signe flat on her belly in the brush.

"A . . . A dud?" Signe asks.

"No," says Mulaghesh furiously. She stands. "No, it wasn't a dud. It won't let him die, he said. That motherfucker. It won't let him *die*!"

She walks to the circle gate and stares at the dome, trembling with rage. "Fuck you!" she screams at it. "Do you hear me in there? *Fuck you!*"

There is no answer. Just the trees swaying in the wind.

Signe stands up. "General Mulaghesh, I . . . I think we should leave."

Mulaghesh wants to try again, to throw another grenade into that damned dome and hear the echoing crash, to just hurt that bastard a little . . .

"General Mulaghesh?"

"What?" she says dimly. "Huh?"

"We should go," says Signe. "Come on. Let's go. It was a mistake to come here."

As if in a dream, Mulaghesh turns and begins walking down the Tooth with her. She's nearly halfway down when she realizes she's been crying.

* * *

Far out on the open seas, Mulaghesh sits on the deck and stares down at the face of the moon reflected in ocean. Signe's at the tiller, deftly steering the yacht among the dark waves, but neither of them has spoken for over three hours.

Then, finally, Signe says, "You saw him, didn't you?"

Mulaghesh doesn't respond. She imagines how nice it'd be to slip off this deck and into those dark waters and feel herself being tugged downstream to the sea.

"You've looked terrible since you walked out of that place," says Signe. "Like you're ill. You haven't talked about it at all. Did he . . . Did he *do* anything to you? Did he, I don't know, poison you?"

"No. Hells, I don't know. Maybe." Signe slips down to sit beside her on the deck. Mulaghesh doesn't look at her. "Maybe I poisoned myself a long time ago. Only I'm just now realizing it."

She stares into the waters, then down at her false hand. Her elbow aches. Her head feels heavy, her eyes feel heavy. It suddenly feels so difficult to look at anything, to even move.

She starts talking.

She tells Signe about the March, and about Shoveyn, the little town in the middle of nowhere outside of Bulikov, forty years ago. She tells her about the camp the night after, butchering stolen hogs, the night filled with their squeals and the scent of blood. About the smoldering ruins of the town beyond.

She tells her about how she sat there, sharpening her knife outside of Biswal's tent. And then Sankhar and Bansa walked by, entering the captain's tent, and they spoke to him in quiet voices.

Biswal called to her. She came in, and he said, "Lieutenant Mulaghesh, these two young men here have decided they don't wish to continue any farther."

And she said, "Is that so, sir."

"Yes, that's so. They feel that what we're doing here is . . . how did you put it, Bansa? Deeply immoral?"

And Bansa said, "Yes. Yes, sir, I . . . We just don't think it's right to keep doing this. We can't do it anymore. We won't. And I'm sorry, sir, but we simply cannot continue to cooperate with this, sir. You can try to lock us up, but if you do we'll just try to escape."

Biswal said, "That's eloquently put. We don't have the resources to imprison you, and I can't waste the time to have you flogged. So I suppose we don't have any other option than just to let you two go."

How surprised they were. Just shocked. But as they left Biswal looked back at her and said only, "Try not to waste a bolt."

And she understood. She'd known what this would lead to the second she heard Bansa speak.

They walked out, and Biswal stopped them outside the tent. He turned, smiling, and said to them, "Boys, just one more thing . . ."

His voice so chummy, so cheerful. But then he looked at Mulaghesh, his eyes glittering, and her knife was already out.

The night so full of squealing, and the scent of fresh blood.

They watched her do it. The whole camp. They didn't react. Just listened as Biswal told them these two were deserters and cowards, which Yellow Company would not tolerate. Could not and would not tolerate, not at all. "Those who will not make war upon our enemies," he told them, "are *also* our enemies."

She wiped her blade on her sleeve. How bright the blood was.

"And we will treat them as such," said Biswal. He turned around and went back into his tent.

Signe and Mulaghesh sit in silence in the boat.

Signe asks, "How old were you?"

"Sixteen."

"By the seas . . ."

But she tells Signe that that's not an excuse. She knew it was wrong. These children trusted her. But if they'd deserted, and led the Continentals to Yellow Company, then it would have all been for nothing. Every awful thing they'd done would have been for nothing.

Or perhaps . . . Perhaps Mulaghesh simply didn't want for the March to end. It was all she knew by then. If Bansa and Sankhar left, then the spell would break.

But the spell broke anyway, when the Summer ended.

How she wished to die then. Out of the service and adrift in the civilized world, she couldn't tolerate what she'd done. She tried to bait the world to kill her, to do the thing she had no courage for. But it wouldn't. Life went on; it just kept happening.

She tries to tell Signe what a curse that is, to keep living. To have nothing happen to you at all.

But then one day Colonel Adhi Noor was there, offering her a way back into the military in that rundown wine bar, the air full of the stink of smoke and moldering wood. And suddenly she thought she might be able to make it up to everyone. She couldn't erase the past, but maybe she could keep it from happening again. Some young men and women, Continental and Saypuri, never made it home because of her. The least she could do was make sure others didn't fall to the same fate. It'd be a way to make the dead matter. A way to put back some of what she'd broken.

Forty years of training. Forty years of trying. All smashed to pieces in the Battle of Bulikov. And then Shara Komayd whispering in the dark by her hospital bed, telling her about allies and generals and promotions. . . .

Everything was supposed to change then. But it didn't. The higher she went in the world, the more useless she felt. These analysts and officers and politicians described the spending of a life with the cold, clinical language of a banker. So far from the front lines, far from the churning, wet earth and the night full of screams. It all just kept happening, only now she didn't see it in person.

But even though she was now so far away from it, she began to dream of it more and more, awakening in the night wet with sweat, the sounds of the Battle of Bulikov still ringing in her ears. And her arm ached and ached, yet no medicines would dull it. Some of the doctors suggested, somewhat politely, that perhaps the pain was not in her body, but in her mind. In other words, perhaps it hurt because she needed it to hurt.

One day she visited a military hospital—the first time she'd seen front-line troops in some time. And all those young men and women lay in bed, looking like they'd been chewed up by some machine. . . . Yet every single one of them struggled to salute her. She was a general, after all.

And suddenly the pain in her arm was unbearable. As if she had knives in her elbow, sawing into the bone, needles grinding up through her marrow and splintering her humerus like termites. She knelt alone in the staircase of the hospital, white with pain, sweating and gritting her teeth and trying not to scream, not to call to the doctors and say cut it off, cut this thing off of me, cut it out of me now, now, *now*.

She passed out. Some orderly found her there, lying on the stairs, looking like a corpse. When he woke her he asked if something was wrong. She said yes.

Something was wrong. And now she knew what it was.

What a gutless lie it all was. The battles kept happening, and she was just as helpless as she'd always been. For all her medals and for all her power, she wasn't making a lick of difference in the lives of those she commanded. Soldiers and civilians alike were still dying. And she couldn't let herself forget.

"So I ran," says Mulaghesh. "I didn't know what else to do. It hurt to stay. I was lying to myself and to everyone else if I stayed. So I went and hid myself away on a beach."

But it didn't help. Every night she woke up with battle echoing in her ears, and every morning her arm hurt.

Until one day she got a letter from the prime minister. Deadly little Shara Komayd, the woman who brought down countless governments and officials—even those of her own country, in the end. And somehow Shara knew the three words that would bring Mulaghesh crumbling down too, that one wish Mulaghesh had fervently hoped to fulfill for so many years, the words scrawled on a piece of paper and brought to her by a sweat-soaked Pitry Suturashni . . .

"A way out," Mulaghesh says. "She was offering a way to do what I've always meant to. To help make things change. And, by changing, to make everything matter."

"Here? In Voortyashtan?"

Mulaghesh is silent as she stares out at the black waves. "Yes. I think so. If Voortyashtan can change, then anything can change. Right?"

Signe says nothing as she adjusts the tiller.

Nothing is everlasting. Nature has proved this to us again and again. Not even the Divinities were everlasting, for they too fell just as the mountains themselves surely will one day.

If I leave anything behind in this world, I hope it is my work. I hope the streets I helped pave and the water I helped pump and the stone I helped carve speak not my name, but the name of innovation, the name of progress, the name of hope.

The world may not go on forever. But that does not mean we cannot try to make tomorrow better.

—LETTER FROM VALLAICHA THINADESHI TO
UNKNOWN RECIPIENT, 1652

13.

tHe city of bLaðes

Over the years, General Lalith Biswal has developed quite the delicate nose for smoke, an olfactory palette more refined and developed than the tongues of the most accomplished oenophiles. He can tell in one sniff, for example, if the smoke he's smelling is coal smoke, charcoal smoke, or wood smoke; and from there he can determine the wood type, be it teak or oak or ash, as well as if the wood in question has been seasoned properly or if it's green wood.

Right now, as he walks through the smoldering ruins of the insurgents' camp, he smells rather a lot of wood smoke, most of it green—but it would be, as the woods are now alight in the east. But he can smell other aromas in the smoke as well—paper and hot metal, broiling soil and gunpowder.

And flesh. Possibly mutton, as the camp is now flooded with sheep that broke free of their pens—but he doubts it. He knows that somewhere in this camp, a body is burning. Probably more than one.

He surveys the cavalry's work, hand on his sword—a nervous

tic he acquired on the battlefield. They did a clean job of it, riding around the forest to come up on the north side of the encampment, then attacking in the dark, driving the insurgents south, where they were met by the guns of the 112th Infantry.

They'd lost a lot of soldiers by then. Picked off in the woods by the shtanis, little bands of fleeing fighters. So the 112th was eager to make someone pay, at least.

He stares out at the burning tents. An honest war, a real war. A far better thing than the miserable secret wars of spies and diplomats and trade ministers. *I wonder,* he thinks, *if the world will ever see a real, true war again?*

He feels he will. Lalith Biswal believes with all his heart that peace is but the absence of war, and war itself is almost always inevitable. *But when it comes, will our politicians admit it is war?* He steps lightly over a body. *What must I do to wake them?*

How alone he feels, how betrayed. Abandoned by his nation for the second time in his life.

I will not be shamed like this again.

He hears a rustling beside him and stops. There's a twitch from a collapsed tent, just to his right.

He waits and watches. It could be one of his own soldiers, after all, perhaps wounded.

The canvas flies back and a Voortyashtani boy leaps up, pistol pointed at Biswal's chest. The boy hesitates just a little too long, his dark eyes blinking behind his sandy-colored curls.

There's the click of Biswal's sword sliding out of its scabbard. He's trained for this so much that he's hardly aware of what he's doing, his elbow extending and his tricep flexing, wrist rotating just so. . . .

The boy's chest and throat turn into a red flash. A fan of hot blood splashes across Biswal's face. The pistol fires, the round thumping into the soil at the boy's feet, and the boy tumbles backward into the wreckage of the tent.

Biswal stands over him and watches silently as the boy's panicked eyes search the night skies, blood pouring from his neck.

"General Biswal!" cries a voice behind him. "General Biswal, are you all right?"

Captain Sakthi appears at Biswal's elbow, pistol in his hand. He does a double take when he sees the dying Voortyashtani boy, who lies gurgling at his feet.

"Nothing to worry about," says Biswal calmly. He takes out a handkerchief and wipes off his sword. "Just another insurgent. Didn't have the sand to pull the trigger. What are you doing here, Captain? I ordered you to fortify the roadways."

"Yes, sir, but I received a message from Fort Thinadeshi, General. Some . . . strange information about the harbor."

"That damn thing? Has someone finally blown it up, too?"

"Ah, no, sir." Sakthi cringes. "You have a little . . . you have some blood on your face, sir."

"Mm? Oh. Thank you. Such a mess . . ." He wipes his face with the already bloody handkerchief. "Well, if it's not blown up, then what is it?"

"An anonymous tip, sir, sent to the fortress . . . Here, I'll let you see it."

He hands Biswal the envelope, then uses a small torch to illuminate it for him.

Biswal frowns as he reads. Then he reaches into the envelope and pulls out a small stack of black-and-white photographs. He flips through them, looking at each one. Then he stares into space, thinking.

"So . . . someone is claiming that the Dreylings," he says, "have a secret storeroom full of *Divine artifacts*?"

"Yes, and . . . this anonymous source also seems to claim that General Mulaghesh had full knowledge of the situation, and has abstained from informing us. The photographs are . . . Well. They are very convincing. Those statues do *look* Divine."

Biswal's face darkens. He begins slowly folding up the paper. "How did we receive this anonymous tip?"

"It was mailed to Major Hukkeri at the fortress. It might have been a Saypuri, sir, as they certainly knew the correct mailing protocols."

Biswal is silent.

"If we were to do any sort of investigation, sir," says Sakthi nervously, "if we were to take any kind of action, we'd . . . we'd need your approval, sir. But it's an international matter, and the boundaries of authority aren't implicitly clea—"

"Aren't they?" says Biswal. "If the question is what to do about Divine artifacts on the Continent, then we do not need treaties or any diplomatic overtures to establish authority. If I am there, then I am the authority." He stows the message away in his coat. "And I *do* plan to be there."

"You . . . You mean to withdraw from the counterattack, sir?"

"No, no. The work here will continue, Captain, of course it will. But this requires my personal attention." He gets a faraway look in his eyes. "She talked about how worried she was about the Divine. . . ." He looks back at the photos, staring into those cold, white stone faces. "And why would she do that, unless she knew something I didn't?"

✳✳✳

It's late afternoon by the time Signe and Mulaghesh return to the SDC dock, exhausted and sunburned but still alive. Either Signe signaled ahead or they were seen coming, because Sigrud awaits them on the dock, waving to them. "Was it a success?" he asks as he helps Signe moor the yacht.

"That depends on your idea of success," she says, glancing at Mulaghesh, who has dark rings of fatigue under her eyes.

She clears her throat. "Yeah. Yeah, it was a success. It's the next part I'm worried about."

As they leave the dock Mulaghesh describes the ritual as told to her by the old man from the Tooth: the basin, the seawater, the materials from the Window to the White Shores, and the goat's bladder of killer's blood. And with them together, the passageway through to the City of Blades.

"A whole goat's *bladder*?" says Sigrud.

"That's what the man told me," says Mulaghesh. "Why? How much is that? I don't know my goat's biology."

"Two to three pints," says Signe. "At least."

"*That* much?"

Signe nods. "Old Voortyashtanis used them as water bags. They were big enough to keep a man on his feet for days. I suppose that was their standard amount of measurement."

"I guess we don't know any killer's corpses we could drain," says Mulaghesh. "Or any murderous prisoners sentenced to death."

"No," says Sigrud. "Though one wonders how Choudhry got any, in order to perform it herself."

Mulaghesh has been wondering the very same thing during her journey back, but it isn't until she sees Sigrud that she has the idea. "Wait, we talked about this. . . . Choudhry'd been in the military briefly before she joined the Ministry. She'd had to use lethal force once when someone tried to charge through a checkpoint."

"Lethal force?" says Signe. "So . . . you're saying Choudhry was a killer herself?"

"Which means she could have used her own blood," says Sigrud. He pulls a face. "Two or three pints of blood . . . Very difficult for someone to manage that."

"What if she did it over time?" says Mulaghesh. "Bloodletting every couple of weeks?"

"Still quite difficult, I would imagine," says Sigrud. "A lot of recovery time needed. Either way, that doesn't fix *our* problem. How are we to do this? I suppose you and I could do it, Turyin, but that wouldn't be an easy thing to split between us."

"What if you could split it three ways?" says Signe.

"That might work," says Sigrud, "but who would be our third?"

"I would," says Signe.

"You wo . . ." Sigrud slows and comes to a stop as he processes what Signe said. "You . . . *You* would?"

She meets his gaze. "I would. Yes. I would be able to."

Sigrud stares at his daughter for a long time, his face a mix of confusion and anguish as he comes to understand what his daughter is saying. "I did not know."

"I know," she says. "And . . . I know there's a lot I don't know about you." She puts a hand on his shoulder.

Sigrud looks at her hand and then at her, his one eye blinking rapidly. "If the world had been different."

"If it had been, yes. But it wasn't."

"I hate to interrupt, but," says Mulaghesh, coughing awkwardly, "split between three—that should be doable, yes?"

"Maybe," says Signe. "It's still a lot. And you'd still be going through into the City of Blades weakened. You're already exhausted, I can tell. Are you sure you still want to try?"

"No, I definitely fucking *don't* want to try," says Mulaghesh. "But I don't see another way. You'd better swing by the SDC infirmary, because we're going to need some bloodletting tools."

"Why not just get Rada Smolisk to help us?" asks Signe. "She's a doctor."

"Because I don't want anyone else knowing about this beyond us. Doing this would mean taking her to the yard of statues. That's not safe by a long shot. I know some field medicine, so that should be enough—at least, I *hope* it will be enough."

"So do I," says Sigrud.

***

Evening is falling as Sigrud and Mulaghesh wait in the yard of statues. Despite Mulaghesh's recent interactions with the Divine, they've still lost none of their menace: the countless carvings and alien forms disturb her even when she's not looking at them, like they turn to watch her when she's not looking.

The basin to her left is filled with cold seawater, hauled up bucket by bucket by SDC workers. Mulaghesh has already been to the apothecary shop and paid what felt like a few months' salaries for the reeking, shriveled reagents: rosemary, pine needles, dried worms, grave dust, dried frog eggs, and bone powder, not to mention the sackcloth. Mulaghesh is pretty sure the apothecary sensed her desperation and overcharged her.

Voortya's pale white face hangs just over Mulaghesh's shoulder. She tries to ignore it. She especially tries to ignore how the face seems to be looking into the basin of seawater, where Mulaghesh herself will likely be going very shortly, if all goes to plan. She's outfitted herself with her carousel and a rifling, though she's very aware that, if the other sentinels are at all like Zhurgut, these armaments won't make a dent in them. She's packed a decent field medical kit as well, though again, from seeing what Zhurgut did to the Dreylings, she doubts she'd be able to self-apply much after tangling with a sentinel. Her primary strategy is to move as undetected as possible. Though in the situation that she *is* detected, she's also brought four grenades, but she's a little reticent to use them: hand grenades are far easier to operate when the user possesses both hands.

"I'm getting antsy," she says. "Where's your daughter? I don't want to try to bleed myself unless I have the right tools."

"She'll be here. One question on my mind, though, is what do you plan to do once you *get* to this City of Blades?"

"Find Choudhry. Find out how the Night of the Sea of Swords works. Then find out how to stop it."

Sigrud thinks about it, then shakes his head. "You have picked up Shara's ability," he says, "to produce elaborate plans that happen to lack the most important part."

"Well, what the hells do you suggest?"

"Me? Blow it up. Bring explosives over there and mine the place. Then . . . *Ktch*." He mimes pushing down a plunger. "*Boom.*"

"You want me to blow up the afterlife."

Sigrud shrugs. "It worked for me in Bulikov."

The metal door squeaks open and Signe walks in, a small leather satchel hanging from her shoulder. When she sees them she nods and breaks into a run. "Biswal is coming," she says breathlessly.

"Eh?" says Mulaghesh. "Retreating from the highlands already?"

"No, Biswal is coming, and he's on the *warpath*. More so than when he left, I mean. He's making a beeline for here, though I've no idea why—though the rumor has it he's heard about, well . . ." She glances around at the statues. "This."

"He knows about the yard of *statues*?" says Mulaghesh. "How in hells could that have happened?"

"Didn't someone infiltrate this place just days ago?" says Sigrud. "After Zhurgut?"

"Yeah . . . But . . . You think whoever is trying to start the Night of the Sea of Swords is behind the tip-off?" asks Mulaghesh. "Why would they go to Biswal all of the sudden? They haven't exactly be-haved lawfully so far."

"Well, it certainly is fucking us over right now, isn't it?" asks Signe, furious. "If that was their goal, then they are wildly succeed-ing. What are we going to do?"

"The same thing we were going to do before," says Mulaghesh. "Only now we'll need to *hurry*. If Biswal gets here we'll never get the chance to try this again."

"You still want to move ahead with your plan, General?" asks Signe.

"I don't have a choice. Are you with me?"

Signe and Sigrud glance at each other. Then, finally, they nod.

"Good," says Mulaghesh. "Roll up your sleeves."

Mulaghesh does Sigrud first—she knows he probably won't show any pain, so he's a good practice subject before moving on to Signe—and soon she has three needles with three tubes spurting out viscous blood into the basin of seawater.

"So . . . you go over there," says Signe, "wherever there is. And what do we do if you don't come *back*?"

"If I don't come back, then the apocalypse happens," says Mula-ghesh. "And if that happens, you and your dad here need to evacuate everyone in Voortyashtan."

Sigrud nods. "Once you're over there, I will go to the lighthouse and coordinate."

"How's your arm?"

"Painful. But mobile. It will do. Much like your hip. We ask much of our bodies."

They stand around the basin, staring at the muddy red waters.

"So . . . how do we know when it's done?" asks Sigrud, watching the arrhythmic gush of his own blood. "I frankly would like to have this thing out of me as soon as possible."

"You're the Voortyashtani, Signe," says Mulaghesh. "You tell me."

"You forget that I've never seen a miracle performed, General," she says. "Besides the resurrection of Zhurgut. I'm well out of my league."

"We're all out of our league." Mulaghesh kneels—keeping her left arm raised awkwardly so her own blood continues to pour into the basin—and lights the bundle of sackcloth at the foot of the plinth. She blows on it a little to get it going. "The miracles I've seen varied in showiness. Some you didn't notice, some made sure you couldn't help but notice. Are we going to see any rays of light, or chorus of singing, or—"

"—or swirling waters?" says Sigrud.

"Right, or that."

"No," says Signe. "He means the water's swirling. Right *now*."

Mulaghesh stands up. The reddish seawater in the basin is slowly circling, creating a small funnel in the center, like it's draining away—but the level never lowers.

"Huh," says Mulaghesh. "Is this . . . it?"

The more the sackcloth burns, the faster the water swirls, spinning more and more until it begins to make a low rumble as it rushes along the edge of the basin. Finally the sackcloth is just a heap of ash, but the waters keep accelerating.

"Is it done?" asks Signe. "Finished?"

"I believe it is just beginning," says Sigrud.

They watch, forgetting their bloodletting, as the water spins faster and faster until it's a cyclone of bloodstained water, whirling so fast that the very air above it starts to spin with it. Somehow not a drop of it flies out, despite the shallow basin: Mulaghesh and the rest remain as dry as they were when they started.

A cool breeze filters through the yard of statues. Then there's a familiar sound: a soft, droning *om*, much like the sound the whole of Voortyashtan heard whenever Saint Zhurgut hurled his massive blade. And somehow, in some intangible way, there is the unmistakable feeling of a door being opened nearby.

They all shiver. "I think . . . I think that is enough," says Sigrud.

"Yes," says Signe. She looks up and peers around the yard as if she's heard a curious noise. "Something's changed. Something's *different* now, though I can't quite tell what."

Mulaghesh stares down into the roaring tunnel of water. "By the seas . . . I'm going in *there?*"

"That seems to be the case," says Sigrud, removing his syringe and applying a bandage. He walks over to assist Signe. "Are we so sure Sumitra Choudhry wasn't beaten to death by the waters themselves?"

"Thanks for the confidence boost," says Mulaghesh. She winces as she slides the needle out of her arm and wraps her elbow up with bandages.

Signe asks, "Are you going in?"

"I guess." Mulaghesh sits on the edge of the basin, like a deep-sea diver about to drop herself in the ocean. She looks up at them. "Are we all ready?"

"Is it possible for any normal human to be ready for this?" asks Signe.

"Fair point." Mulaghesh grips the edge of the basin, then freezes, suddenly seized with terror. This could be the last moment she has in this world, the last second of genuine waking life. "I didn't think I'd make it to this age," says Mulaghesh. "If . . . If I don't come back . . . Tell them . . . Tell everyone I said I'm sorry. Okay? Just tell them that."

"We will," says Signe. "I'll tell them. I'll tell them that, and I'll tell them the truth."

"You had better," says Mulaghesh. "Someone needs to." Then without another thought, she pitches herself backward into the whirlpool.

***

She expects to fall down a tunnel. That's what it was, after all, when she saw it: a whirlpool of rushing, roaring water, with a narrow tunnel leading straight down into the center of the basin.

But when she falls backward that's not what she experiences at all. Instead it's like she's fallen into the surface of a still lake: the water embraces her all at once, a solid, flat surface rather than a raging whirlpool, and it's not a narrow column of water but a vast, dark ocean with a single hole of light at the top. She's not being whipped around by a cyclone of water; she's just . . . falling. It's like she's fallen through a hole cut in ice, and she can see the rippling faces of her two comrades looking in at her.

Most disconcertingly, though, she's sinking. Fast.

Her instincts kick in: she needs to swim up, back up, *now*. She kicks her feet, trying to gain traction, but she's weighed down by her gear, which itself is strapped to her body very tightly, so she can't let go.

She plummets down into the darkness, feeling the inexorable pressure of all that water gripping her whole body. It's like she's in the hand of a giant, tightening its freezing grip. The hole of light above her is just a pinprick now. She knows she shouldn't—she's been trained on drowning—but she starts panicking, kicking wildly, flailing about in the icy depths. One trickle of water penetrates her lips, and suddenly all the air comes flooding out of her, crystalline bubbles bursting from her nose and mouth and spiraling up to the tiny white pinprick above.

She's drowning. She's drowning and she knows it. She's going to die in this damned big bathtub and there's nothing she can do about it.

But then the world . . . tips.

The pull of gravity spins about her.

Suddenly she's not falling, but *rising*, rising up toward the surface, her legs pointed toward what looks like a pool of stars below her—no, *above* her.

She awkwardly flips herself over and looks up, lungs screaming for air, as she flies up toward the pool of stars. Then she realizes it's not quite a pool, exactly, but a hole, just like the one she fell through . . . except the stars in the sky she's seeing aren't right at all.

She punches through the surface of the water and launches herself up, surging for air, gasping hugely.

Her fingers find stone. She grabs onto it and clings tight like a child first learning to swim. Once she catches her breath she looks around herself.

She stares.

"What the . . . What the fuck," she breathes.

She's in what looks to be a gazing pool set in a courtyard between two giant, towering buildings, each of which resembles a flowering anemone. The ground of the courtyard is covered with white gravel, upon which sit broad, white marble tiles, forming a grid. Golden light flows from nearby doorways, creating honey-colored slashes across the gravel, and standing at odd angles on the tiles are statues of . . .

Wait. Those aren't statues at all.

Her skin crawls as she realizes six Voortyashtani sentinels are standing in the courtyard with her, their massive, hideous armor flexing ever so slightly as they breathe. Mulaghesh tries to stay perfectly still in the water of the gazing pool. She's made a lot of noise so far, but none of them stand or react to her—just like when she had her vision before.

She waits. Nothing happens. Then she stirs up her courage and says, "Hey—*hey!*"

None of them move. Warily, she climbs out of the gazing pool, then scurries over to the wall for shelter. Her breath produces an incredible amount of condensation, even though her skin doesn't feel cold. It's as if there's just something frigid about this place that can't react correctly to the living.

She looks herself over, mostly to make sure her ammunition is still secured to her rig. The cartridges should still work—she's seen these damned things fire underwater before. And Signe's brace has held, so she's still gripping the rifling. It's then that she notices that she's now stained a dark red from head to toe: her clothes, skin, and even her hair are all a dusty crimson. It's like she's been marinating in blood, even though her time in the basin was hardly more than a minute or so.

She licks her fingers and rubs her skin, assuming it will wash off. It doesn't.

"Shit," she mutters. This will make her easy to spot in this colorless place.

She considers what to do now. She looks up at the two massive towers above her, riddled with windows glowing white or gold. The starry sky above is beautiful and strange, featuring some stars that are both the wrong size and the wrong color. Every once in a while a shooting star blazes bright against the dark. It's a hauntingly beautiful place, albeit strange and ghostly.

She looks at one group of sentinels, then walks closer until they're about ten feet from her. She can see variations in their armor now: some feature more aquatic ornamentations, others have more antlers, and some have only teeth of all shapes lining their shoulders and backs. *They're like different uniforms,* she thinks. *Maybe from different military units, different regions of Voortyashtan . . . or different eras in history.*

She walks closer, rifling at the ready. The closest sentinel still faces away from her, but if it was conscious or alert, it'd hear her footfalls. Then she realizes that the sentinel is speaking, mumbling. She leans closer, listening, until she can hear its words:

"I threw down the bridges, threw down the walls, leapt among the fleeing flock and struck them down like wheat before the scythe. I did this for you, Mother, I did this for you. . . ."

She walks to the next two, and hears:

"I stood upon the prow of my vessel and my heart leapt forth and I struck down their ships one by one, dashing them to flotsam and jetsam, and as we sailed by they clutched to the debris and cried out for help and we laughed at them. I did this for you, Mother. We did this for you. . . ."

"We laid siege to the city for three weeks and four days, and when they opened the gates to admit defeat our swords fell upon them like rain upon a

rooftop. They had thought we would be kind, that we would sanction their lives in return for their submission, but oh what fools they were, Mother, what fools they were. . . ."

She listens to them, hearing each brutal story, each horrific victory. They're reliving them over and over, she realizes, reliving their accomplishments, celebrating the deeds that won them their place here in the afterlife. But always they tie each story back to their "mother," and each time they do there is a note of recrimination in it: as if they did these things for her, and secretly they did not *wish* to do them at all, and now she has somehow betrayed them.

She listens to them mumbling, then looks ahead into the gold-lit hallway leading away from the courtyard.

"Now . . . ," she whispers. "Where in hells is Choudhry?"

***

She wanders through the corridors and streets of the City of Blades, trotting over bridges and along canals and through cavernous tunnels. The streets are not all white stone: many of them are battered or rent shields hammered flat, just like in the dome atop the Tooth. She keeps an eye on the horizon, trying to spy that giant tower she saw in her vision, but the buildings and statues are so impossibly tall that it's difficult to see anything behind them. She can only look straight up, really.

The streets are dotted with clumps of sentinels, all of them dormant and muttering like the ones she saw in the courtyard. They barely seem aware of their own presence, let alone Mulaghesh's. But then she notices that no matter where the sentinels are standing, they're all staring in one direction, as if they can see something behind the towering walls and statues.

So—what are they looking at?

Following this hunch—and completely ignoring common sense—she starts to run toward the sentinels, moving from small clumps to large groups and teeming crowds of sentinels, as they all seem to be magnetically drawn to something, clustering around some fixed point deep in the city.

As she dodges between two tall, muttering sentinels standing on a narrow, ivory-colored bridge, she suddenly stops. Then she backs up and looks down the canal.

The City of Blades seems to be riddled with canals, and the one she's currently standing over looks like one of the biggest. As she looks down its length she can see countless other bridges straddling it, bridges of many shapes and sizes.

But on one bridge, about a quarter mile down the canal, she can see something lying on its stairs.

No—not something. Some*one*. A human form, limp and lying there, stained red just as she is.

"Ah, shit," says Mulaghesh quietly.

She navigates through the crowd of sentinels and runs along the canal to the other bridge.

Not like this, she thinks. *It shouldn't end like this.*

But when she emerges from one group of sentinels, and sees the body's dark hair spilling over the white stairs, her shoulders slump.

She knows what this is, who this is.

She slowly walks over to the body.

It's a woman. She's dressed in civilian clothes, but the bandolier, the grenades, and the satchel hanging from her shoulder all suggest access to military supplies. Mulaghesh uses her toe to open the satchel. Inside is a bundle of brown tubes tied together, each capped with metal: TNT.

Packed for one hell of a pop, thinks Mulaghesh.

"So *this* is what happened to Biswal's missing explosives," she says aloud. "The Voortyashtanis never stole them. You did." She almost wants to laugh at the sheer stupidity of it all.

Then she sighs, steels herself, and turns the body over.

She isn't sure what she was expecting. All this time Mulaghesh has only had a picture and a file to go on, an idea of a person more than a person themselves. Yet when she sees the corpse of the young Saypuri woman, stiff and cold, she feels a pang she wasn't expecting.

"Sumitra Choudhry," says Mulaghesh. "Damn it."

She's not terribly decomposed, Mulaghesh notes, which suggests that time doesn't work too well here, as Mulaghesh suspected. There's a scab on her brow, left over from her fight outside the tunnel to the mines, probably. She looks terribly, terribly young to Mulaghesh's eyes, not yet thirty. There's a trace of irritation or discomfort to her large, dark eyes, as if she can't believe this is happening to her, that she should come so far just to die here, alone on a bridge over ghostly waters.

"I'm sorry," says Mulaghesh to her.

The only answer is the trickle of the waters below.

She looks closer at the satchel of TNT, wondering what Choudhry planned to use it on. Probably to blow up the citadel, Mulaghesh thinks, just as Sigrud proposed. Mulaghesh considers taking the TNT herself, but she's never been a fast hand with explosives, and she doesn't want to try now with so much at stake. She definitely doesn't want to run around with a bunch of friction-sensitive explosives on her back as a just-in-case measure, either.

Mulaghesh wonders why it hurts as much as it does to see Choudhry here. But she realizes she's been thinking of Choudhry primarily as a soldier: a soldier operating on her own, trying to stop a threat to her country before it gained momentum, a soldier willing to lay down her life in the line of duty. To see she finally made that ultimate sacrifice is saddening, despite everything that's happened so far.

"For so long I thought you were dead," Mulaghesh says to her. "I don't know why I'm so surprised to find out I was right."

Then a strange, singing voice says over her shoulder, "It's odd she even got here."

Mulaghesh whirls around, rifling at the ready. Then she realizes that the voice came from nearly fourteen feet above her, and slowly looks up.

***

Towering over her is what looks like the figure of an enormous woman, or perhaps a sculpture of a woman made of metal: she is silvery and glimmering, her arms and shoulders smooth like chrome. There is an artfulness to her that is both beautiful and yet repellent—Mulaghesh immediately senses that this thing was *made* by someone—and her limbs are terribly distorted, far too long and thin for a normal human. There's something blade-like about them, the way they narrow and thin at the middle, then expand outward at the ends. Her hands and fingers are nothing but knives, long and curved and thin—so thin it's hard to tell how many fingers she actually has. She wears a ragged skirt that starts high above her waist and then drifts down to coil around her narrow legs. Her feet, Mulaghesh sees, are clawed, like those of a bird, and the woman's face is hidden behind a veil made of woven hair, long and silky and somewhat translucent.

Mulaghesh thinks she can glimpse the features behind that veil, the eyes and the mouth, but . . . but she doesn't *want* to.

The voice comes again, soft and strangely fluting, as if it's not being spoken from a human mouth but rather echoing through many pipes, like a pipe organ: "I know you. You've been here before."

Mulaghesh tries to maintain her composure as she keeps her rifling pointed at this . . . whatever it is. It doesn't seem to be a threat: it just impassively stares down at her. After all, if it wanted her dead it could have just stepped on her. "What?"

"You were here before," says the creature. "Only you fell through. Just a shade of you. A piece of you. Not the whole you." The creature looks back over the canal, its posture wistful, thoughtful. "I would remember. We get visitors so rarely these days. Just the few recent ones, really."

Mulaghesh thinks rapidly. She remembers the voice from her vision: *Are you supposed to be here?*

She asks, "You're the guardian, aren't you?"

The giant head swivels back to look down at her. "I am the Watcher," she says. "I watch and guard these shores."

"Did . . . Did you kill her?"

"Her?" The Watcher cranes her head to the side to survey Choudhry's corpse. "If *I* had killed her, she'd hardly be in one piece." She holds up one hand and flexes her numerous bladed fingers. "Would she?"

"Then what happened?"

"Hm," says the Watcher. Her tone suggests she's intrigued that Mulaghesh would imagine she'd be interested in something so disinteresting. She looks again at Choudhry's corpse, cocks her head, and says, "Dehydration."

"D-Dehydration?"

"Yes," says the Watcher, bored. "She came the same way you did, activating the tribute. But she used only her own blood, and when she came through she was weak and panicked. She ran too hard, too fast. Overexerted herself, poor thing. Not enough blood and fluids in that little body to keep it going, you see. I can tell. I am part of this place, so I know. I saw."

"What do you mean, activating the tribute?"

The Watcher carelessly flicks a finger at the horizon. "You came from the city, didn't you? The flesh place? The place filled with idols, statues, carvings, each attributed to the memory of a great warrior, a great deed? But the carving of the Mother . . . That is carefully linked to here."

"So each one of those white statues memorializes the dead?" asks Mulaghesh.

The Watcher waves her hand, bored: *Of course.* Then she looks at Choudhry and cocks her head again. "That one there did not truly belong here. She had slain but one in her life, and that was a panicked, fretful deed. But *you* . . ." The Watcher bends down to look into Mulaghesh's face—her giant body moves with a horrifying silence—and extends one long, needle-like index finger. Mulaghesh stiffens, terrified, and nearly fires, but the Watcher simply brushes a stray hair away from her face with astonishing delicacy. "*You* belong here. More than most, in my own humble opinion. . . . But you know that already, don't you?"

"What's going on here?" asks Mulaghesh. "How are the dead even still *here*?"

"Because the two worlds are tied together," says the Watcher. "Once they were very, very closely tied." She demonstrates with her massive, bladed hands, folding all the countless serrated fingers together. "One never forgot about the other. Each was impossible *without* the other. The living made war because they knew the City of Blades was waiting for them, and the City of Blades existed because the living made war. But then they broke apart—yet not *completely* apart." Her fingers snap apart with astonishing speed, leaving only two fingers touching. "Some threads remained. This place persisted, a ghost of itself, but still here. But just a bit ago, someone on the *other* side started renewing the bonds." Slowly her fingers extend, until more and more and more begin to touch. "The two worlds grow near again, like a fisherman reeling in a catch. The dead awake, very slowly. And when they wake enough . . . Well. I doubt I'll have much of a job anymore. Because then this city will be empty, won't it?" There's a bored tone of indifference to her words. Mulaghesh is reminded of an employee whose supervisor has left for the day.

"How can someone do that?" asks Mulaghesh. "How can someone just . . . reknit the world like that?"

"How should I know?" says the Watcher. "I simply watch. I refuse access or I grant it. That is my function, my role. It's always been this, since time before time."

"And what have you seen recently? Has there been anything . . . strange?"

"Strange? No. This place is always the same. It always has been this way. Though for so long we had no visitors, no new arrivals, no victorious dead. And then . . ."

"And then?"

She cocks her head again. "And then three came. There's you, of course; you've been here, now and before. And then that one." She flicks her finger at Choudhry's corpse. "She came many times, bursting in through the Window, over and over again. . . . It eroded her mind; I felt it. Each time she came here, she was a little worse, a little stranger. And then there was the acolyte."

"Who?"

"The student of old Petrenko, the ancient smithy."

"Wait," says Mulaghesh. "Did you say smithy?"

"Yes. It was Petrenko who developed the method that the old ones first used to make their swords. He brought an acolyte here, once—I felt their spirit barge into this plane of existence—but because I found them unworthy and unlearned, I banished them and sent them back. Foolish old creature, I've no idea what he was playing at. . . ."

"Their spirit . . . You mean they used a sword to project themselves here?"

"Yes. Of course. How else?"

Mulaghesh's heart feels like it's about to hammer its way out of her rib cage. "Wh-Who was this? Do you know?"

The Watcher looks down at her. "When they project themselves here, I see no face and hear no voice. I only see their thoughts and deeds. And that one was no warrior." She looks down at Mulaghesh. "You belong here. I assent to your presence. You have killed many, and I sense in your heart, in your spirit, that you will yet kill more. Perhaps many more." The Watcher draws a single bladed finger across her smooth stomach, creating a high-pitched squeal that sets Mulaghesh's teeth on edge. "May my mutterings do you well, little warrior. Go and perform your function, as I should do so now. Farewell." The Watcher turns and begins striding back across the beaches, picking her way among the countless Voortyashtani sentinels.

"Wait!" cries Mulaghesh.

The Watcher halts, turning her head very slightly to look back at Mulaghesh.

"Where is Voortya?" she asks. "Where can I find the citadel?"

"The citadel?" asks the Watcher. "Oh. Why it's that way, of course. It always is—isn't it?" She stabs a finger in one direction, then resumes her journey, humming atonally to herself.

***

Mulaghesh heads in the direction the Watcher pointed. She can't even tell if she's going the right way or not: there's no real point of reference for her to use here. But the groups of sentinels grow thicker and larger.

She moves on, and on, and on. Maybe only one mile, maybe forty. She can't tell. Then it emerges from the swamp of white stone and immense structures, which appear to fall away like supplicants parting before their monarch.

The citadel seems to unfold or calcify in the very air, growing on the hill before her like coral forming deep underwater, a great, curving, castellated construction blooming in the moonlight. It is osseous, ivory, an alien amalgamation of bone and frills and strange, aquatic apertures, all building to one tall, slender tower in its center, a shard of white rising into the sky. And there at the tip—a window, perhaps?

Mulaghesh watches the window. Then the light from inside it blinks, blacking out from left to right, as if someone's pacing before it.

"So someone's home after all," says Mulaghesh. "Goody."

But the question remains—who?

She trots off toward the chaotic base of the structure, full of loops and arches and staggered columns. The sand under her feet turns to stone, or perhaps marble. Smooth, hard steps descend into the belly of the structure, then down into a long tunnel. Mulaghesh checks her surroundings before entering, critically aware she is a bright red splotch in this ivory-colored palace. But it seems to be deserted.

She isn't sure what she's looking for here. Choudhry couldn't help her, and the Watcher sure as hells couldn't. But there must be something in here, even if it is Voortya, or perhaps a shadow of Voortya. But what to do when she finds her?

She exits into what looks like a courtyard and finds she's in the center of a tangle of staircases. There are so many stairs up and down and some even to the side that they hurt her eyes. For a second she feels like she's back in Bulikov. More importantly, though, she doesn't see anyone *on* the staircases. Again, she's all alone here.

This isn't right, she thinks. This is a damned palace, after all: Where are the servants, the staff? Who lives here? Who works here?

She screws up her mouth, picks the staircase that seems to go up the highest, and starts off.

Time seems soft here, so she isn't sure if she spends a few minutes or a few hours pacing up staircases, stalking from ivory-colored room to ivory-colored room, pausing before each doorway to check the corners. Her legs begin to ache and throb. She feels like she's climbed up a whole damned mountain.

Finally she comes to a window. It's tall and oblong, and lined with carvings that look very much like some kind of carapace growth. But she still stops and looks out, and sees . . .

"Holy hells," says Mulaghesh.

The whole of the City of Blades lies below her, a forest of towers and statues, the streets tiny and insignificant at their feet. Yet in the streets and the alleys and along the canals are thousands upon thousands of sentinels, perhaps millions of them—more human beings, if they could even be called such, gathered in one place than she's ever witnessed before.

But she can also see the edge of the City of Blades from here, the pale white shores sinking into the dark seas. And on those seas she can see something . . . strange. The surface of the waters are dotted with shapes, long and thin and curiously formed, with one end covered in spears and points, and in their centers a tall, thick pole of some kind.

They're boats, she realizes. Voortyashtani longships, each with a weaponized prow for ramming other boats. Yet they seem somewhat ghostly and unreal, as if they're not quite there, or not quite there *yet:* they seem to flicker, as if they haven't made up their minds as to whether or not they exist.

As such, it's hard to count them. But she would guess the fleet would be larger than twenty thousand vessels. Enough to sink every Saypuri dreadnought five times over.

It's unimaginable. But she doesn't have to imagine it, because they're all right there, right in front of her.

"If those things set sail," she says quietly, "we're doomed."

She steels herself, grips her rifling harder, and turns to the nearest staircase up. Then she begins ascending again.

***

The spiral of stairs narrows, tighter and tighter. She's going up, in smaller and smaller loops. She thinks she's in the center tower now, finally.

About a hundred steps up she spots a tiny splash of color in this endless white place: a splotch of blood, right in the center of one of the stairs. It's crusted over, but she can tell it's fairly recent. She crouches and peers at it, then looks up the stairs.

Divinities don't bleed, she thinks. *Not since the last time I checked.*

She continues up the stairs. The droplets of blood increase. Mulaghesh is perversely reminded of a lover leaving a trail of rose blossoms to their bed.

Finally the stairs end at a large foyer—one that seems far too big for the narrow white tower she saw from the ground. Its ceiling is arched and is covered in what appear to be stone swords, all carved at strange angles, like stalactites dangling from the roof of a cave. Empty, dusty lanterns hang along the wall. She guesses they haven't seen use in years, maybe decades.

She walks in, mindful to move quietly. Then she sees the throne.

It's difficult for Mulaghesh's mind to determine exactly *how* big it is: sometimes it seems to be merely fifteen or twenty feet tall, but then the room will shift and warp, bending at the edges of her vision, and it will seem as if the throne is *hundreds* of feet tall, even *miles* tall—a giant, terrible construction that looms over her like a storm cloud. But no matter the size, its features remain the same: a bright red chair formed of teeth and tusks, all crushed or melted together, sticking out at strange angles. Wide arcs of horns and antlers sprout from the throne's back, curving to form something like a rib cage around the chair. Mulaghesh imagines Voortya taking her place in this terrible seat, her plate mail gleaming and her silent, still face staring out from the cage of antlers like a cold, dark heart.

She shivers. Then she notices something at the feet of the throne: a pair of shoes. Normal ones, women's shoes. They're of a very old fashion, small and brown, featuring a modest heel. She can't help but get the impression that their owner thoughtlessly kicked them off while taking her seat on the throne.

What in the hells?

She takes stock of the room. The door on the opposite side is far, far too large for a person, nearly four times as tall as the tallest man. Still not big enough for the Divinity she glimpsed on the cliffs, but couldn't a Divinity change their size at will? Couldn't they do more or less *anything* at will, really?

Mulaghesh looks down. The trail of blood leads across the receiving room and through the giant door to the chambers beyond.

She looks at it for a long time, thinking. Then she slowly stalks through the columns and through the door, rifling raised. The trail of blood droplets leads through a large door on the other side, then around the corner and down the hall.

She hears someone talking, or rather muttering. They're cursing, it sounds like. And there's a quiet clanking, too, as if they're wearing armor.

Mulaghesh puts her back to the wall and slowly creeps through the doorway, rifling trained on the space ahead.

She reflects that this is possibly an incredibly bad idea. The only thing she knows about anything Divine is to stay away from it, as far away from it as one possibly can. As this person (if it is a person) seems to be occupying Voortya's throne room, or private chambers, or *something* very personal to that Divinity, then all logic suggests she should back away now.

But she doesn't. Something is moving down the hallway. Mulaghesh abandons all protocol and puts her finger right on the trigger: she's willing to abandon trigger discipline in a situation like this.

She thins her eyes, watching. The person paces into view, then back out.

It's a woman, she sees, a *human* woman, or at least she appears to be. The first thing Mulaghesh notices is that she's both wounded and unarmed, clutching her left shoulder. Blood drips from her fingertips in a slow leak. But the second thing Mulaghesh sees is that she's dressed . . . well, like Voortya: she wears the ceremonial plate armor Mulaghesh glimpsed days ago on the cliffs outside of Fort Thinadeshi, covered with horrific images of conquest and sacrifice. It's just that this suit of armor is about one one-hundredth the size of that one, and there appears to be a bullet hole drilled into the left pauldron.

The woman is turned around so that Mulaghesh can't see her face. A tall window is on her opposite side, allowing the pale moonlight to pour in, making it even harder for Mulaghesh to see, but she can make out that the woman's hair is dark, as is her skin.

A Saypuri? How could that be?

What in all the fucking hells, thinks Mulaghesh, *is going* on *in this mad place?*

Whatever this woman's story is she's definitely no god, no Divinity, and certainly no sentinel. And she can bleed, which means Mulaghesh's rifling might be an actual threat.

The next time the woman paces into view, Mulaghesh barks, "Freeze. Hands where I can see them."

The woman nearly jumps out of her skin. She cries out, as this jolt obviously hurts her shoulder.

"Hands where I can see them!" says Mulaghesh again. "And turn around!"

The woman stiffens, then slowly does so, rotating on the spot.

Mulaghesh's mouth opens, and she almost drops the rifling.

The woman's face is familiar, but of course it is: Hasn't Mulaghesh seen that visage in paintings and murals in schools and courtrooms and city halls, staring out with steely eyes on any number of estimable proceedings? Hasn't she seen this woman in countless history books, the face that emblematizes one of the most important periods in the history of Saypur? And, more recently, hasn't Mulaghesh seen this woman's face every single time she paged through Sumitra Choudhry's files?

"Holy hells," says Mulaghesh. "Vallaicha . . . *Thinadeshi?*"

Thinadeshi glares back. It's unmistakably her: the high, aristocratic cheekbones, the sharp nose, the piercing eyes, the face of the woman who in so many ways built Saypur itself, and tamed much of the Continent.

Thinadeshi looks her up and down. "You!" she says angrily. "You're the one who *shot* me!"

The Divine world is largely incomprehensible to us, truly, a world of arbitrary and capricious miracles. But it did have rules, countless ones, all dictated by the Divinities—yet in many cases the Divinities could not break the rules they themselves had created.

What a Divinity said was true, was instantly, irrefutably true. In saying this they overwrote reality—including their own. In some ways the Divinities were slaves of themselves.

—DR. EFREM PANGYUI, "THE SUDDEN HEGEMONY"

14.

a bínðíng contract

Wha . . . What?" says Mulaghesh. "*Shot* you?"

"Yes, by all damned things, shot me!" snarls Thinadeshi. Her voice and accent are unusual: Mulaghesh realizes she's speaking with a dialect and manner that hasn't been used in over fifty years. "I go out of my way and nearly kill myself trying to avoid *unspeakable* catastrophe, only to have some wild woman on a hilltop take out her little cannon and *shoot* me! Of all the madness! Of all the ridiculous nonsense! And what are you here for now? Are you here to finish the job? You're a committed assassin, I'll grant you that! What in damned creation could have happened in the Saypuri Isles to send someone like *you* after me?"

Mulaghesh feels dizzy. It's taking up a lot of her brainpower to accept the idea that not only is she standing here talking to one of the founding figures of Saypur, but this particular founding figure is yelling at her with a lot of vitriol. Eventually Mulaghesh's brain kicks in and she manages to process what Thinadeshi is saying: *Wild woman on a hilltop . . . Does she mean when the mines collapsed?*

"But, uh, I didn't shoot you, ma'am," says Mulaghesh. "If I'm understanding what you're describing, ma'am—and I'm not at all convinced that I am—I shot at Voortya. The, uh, Divinity."

Thinadeshi's stare could punch a hole in the side of a battleship. She holds her arms out—well, one of them, at least, as her left isn't particularly mobile. "Do you not see how I am attired? Does it not look *familiar* to you? I can tell by your egregious accent that it is deeply unlikely that you have had much education, but is putting two and two together *so* far beyond your grasp?"

"Are you . . . Are you saying that *you're* Voortya? The Divinity?"

Thinadeshi sighs and rolls her eyes. "Oh, by all that is . . . *No*. I am saying that when I exercise the powers of this place, it projects an image tha*aaah!*" She trails off as she's racked with pain. Another dribble of blood comes leaking out from under her plate mail. "Damn you!" cries Thinadeshi. "Perhaps you've murdered me already! Am I poisoned?"

"Uh, I don't think so," says Mulaghesh. She undoes the clasp on her rifling and sets it aside. "And listen, I don't understand a thing about what's going on, but I know how to treat a bullet wound. I've brought a med kit, and I can be decent enough with it, even one-handed."

Thinadeshi frowns at her, suspicious. "You're quite sure you're *not* here to kill me?"

"No. I'm here to stop *that* from happening." She points out the tower window to the sea of Voortyashtani sentinels beyond. "By any means necessary. I had no idea you were even here."

Thinadeshi's face softens a bit at that. She swallows. Mulaghesh can tell she's quite weak. "W-Well. You've got quite a task ahead of you, now don't you." Then her eyes dim and she begins to topple over. Mulaghesh darts forward and grabs her before she strikes the ground.

***

Twenty minutes later Mulaghesh has the left arm of Thinadeshi's armor pried off and has cut away her leather sleeve below. "It'll reappear within a few hours," Thinadeshi mutters. "All my vestments return to me, over time. I've tried taking them off, trust me." Mulaghesh ignores her. There's no bed in these chambers, just a giant marble chair about three times too big for a human being, so she has propped her up in that while she goes to work on her shoulder.

There were three opiate shots in her med kit, tiny little syringes not much bigger than your thumbnail, and Mulaghesh dosed Thinadeshi up with one. Thinadeshi hardly makes a peep as Mulaghesh digs in the wound with a pair of tweezers. Mulaghesh can feel the bullet lodged up against Thinadeshi's upper humerus, and it doesn't seem to have shattered or split any, which is good. *So maybe I won't have to go back,* she thinks, *and tell everyone this grand historical figure has died again, and this time I killed her.*

"Who are you?" asks Thinadeshi groggily. "What's your name? You never told me."

Mulaghesh chews her lip as she delicately explores Thinadeshi's wound. "I'm Turyin Mulaghesh, General Fourth Class of the Saypuri Military."

"Military? So the Saypuri Isles still exist as a nation? It's still solvent?" She sounds surprised, but then she would be: her stretch of history was incredibly rocky, with the global economy still in a nascent state.

"Yeah, but they dropped the 'Isles' part a while ago," says Mulaghesh. "Mostly because Saypur kept folding in regions that weren't islands. Or maybe they just wanted a cleaner-looking letterhead."

"I see."

Mulaghesh can feel her tense up, and knows what question she's about to ask.

"So," says Thinadeshi. "What . . . year is it there?"

Mulaghesh glances at her. "Why?"

"Don't humor me, General. When I saw the men in the mines I could tell things were different. I've been gone far longer than I thought, haven't I?"

Men in the mines? "Yeah. Yeah, I'd say so. Hold still."

Then, faintly: "Tell me, and be honest . . . are my children dead?"

Mulaghesh pauses as she works. She can feel the bullet coming loose, but she still feels obligated to answer this question. "I know one of them is still in government. Padwal."

"Padwal?" says Thinadeshi, sounding surprised. "In *government*?"

"Yeah. He's an MP."

"A what?"

"A minister of Parliament."

"Parliament . . . ," says Thinadeshi. "We've kept *that*? Did *no one* read my plans to select a proportionate amount of representatives from each region to vote on each issue?"

"Uh . . . I don't know, ma'am," says Mulaghesh. "I'm a soldier, not a scholar."

"It was a very thorough treatise, I thought," says Thinadeshi, gritting her teeth as Mulaghesh wriggles the bullet. "What about Kristappa? And Rodmal? What about them?"

"I'm afraid I don't know, ma'am."

"You don't know if they're alive?" she asks, heartbroken.

"No. I'm sorry. I don't."

"But how old would they be today? If they are alive, I mean."

Mulaghesh pauses, uncertain how to word this. "You've been gone over sixty years."

Thinadeshi sits up. "Over *sixty*?"

"Um. Yeah. I think the exact number is sixty-four."

"Sixty-four *years*?" She stares out the window, aghast. "Oh, my word . . . I . . . I suppose it's . . . it's fairly unlikely that they are alive, then." Her voice is frail and crushed. "After all, Padwal was one of the youngest. What a curiously dispiriting thing it is, to outlive one's children. If this strange state could even be called living. And I didn't even get to know they died."

Mulaghesh readjusts the tweezers. "Can you hold still? I'm about to get this thing out of you."

"Ah . . . Ah! Please hurry!"

"I'm going!" says Mulaghesh. "I got it, I got it . . ." Then, finally, the chunk of metal comes loose, sliding out of the wound. "There."

She flicks it out the window without a thought, then applies bandages to the wound. "I'm going to need your help to stitch this up, though. I can't manage that one-handed. Think you can assist?"

Thinadeshi's face is wan. "You ask much of an old woman."

"We can wait a bit and then try again."

She sighs. "Oh, no. Don't bother. My shoulder is not the most important thing right now. And besides, I shall be gone quite soon, I imagine."

There's an awkward pause.

"Huh?" says Mulaghesh. "This isn't a fatal wound by any means. Unless you've got a condition or something."

"A condition . . . yes. I have exactly that." She sighs again and shuts her eyes. "I won't perish from any wound to my body, my mortal self. They're killing me out there, don't you see? All those souls out there. They're pulling me apart."

"What do you mean?"

"Here. Look. Help me take off my right glove."

Mulaghesh does so. Then Thinadeshi holds her hand up to the window. "Watch."

"Okay . . ." Mulaghesh crouches beside her, not sure what she's watching: Thinadeshi's hand is small, well-manicured, but otherwise unremarkable.

But then . . .

Mulaghesh sees it, very faintly: the outline of the window frame *through* Thinadeshi's hand, as if her flesh is very slightly translucent.

Mulaghesh says, "What in all the hells . . . ?"

"You see it, then," says Thinadeshi grimly. "My . . . I don't know, my *corporeal* essence is fading. I'm not supposed to be here, so this place is steadily asserting that I'm *not* here. No mortal was ever intended to shoulder the burdens of a Divinity." She puts back on her glove. "I am being rejected, slowly but surely. But I've known I've been losing this battle for some time."

Mulaghesh holds down the bandages on Thinadeshi's shoulder, which is still seeping blood. "Can I ask *how* you came to be here? Or, really . . . what's going on?"

"I suppose in the normal world everyone assumes I just disappeared."

"That's about the cut of it."

"But I didn't, obviously. I have chosen to remain here, in this place, since I left the world I knew."

"You *chose* to come here?"

"Oh, no, I didn't choose to *come*. But I chose to *stay* once I realized the consequences if I left." She sighs and rubs her eyes, exhausted. "What's the last you know about me?"

"I know you vanished in Voortyashtan. That's all anyone knows."

"Yes . . . I was on an exploratory mission, trying to find a rail passage out to the wildernesses, along the Solda to the coast, so we could try to bring it under control. We saw bandit kings and pestilence and warfare and mass rape. There was no leadership, no control after the Blink. And the Blink struck this place quite hard. I remember coming here, seeing the squalor and the vandals, fighting off attackers nearly every day and night. I was brazen, you see. And . . . reckless. I had just lost Shomal."

Mulaghesh remembers this from her history books: Thinadeshi's four-year-old son, lost to plague during her travels on the Continent. "I see."

"I was willing to fight everyone and everything, after that," says Thinadeshi quietly. "I was going to win or die trying, and . . . and I didn't prefer which, honestly. But then one day we made it. We passed through the ranges and came to the ocean. But the question was, what was the easiest route? What was the best way to link the North Seas to Saypur? So we had to survey. And one morning I was walking along the coast, taking measurements of possible passages back through the ranges . . . and then I came upon it."

Thinadeshi's words are growing slurred now: the opiates must be sloshing around in her system. "The Blink did a lot of damage to the Voortyashtani coast. So much of what they built was on the sea, so many miracles worked into the cliffs and the shore, and the Blink was so recent then. It was like chaos, unimaginable devastation. Homes and bridges and rubble all piled up on the bottom of the cliffs. And some of the cliffs had cracked *open*, like an egg. And I came to one of these cracks, and I looked in"—her face fills with an awful dread—"and they saw me, and they *called up* to me."

Thinadeshi's horrified expression sets a chill in Mulaghesh's belly. "Who? Who did?"

"The soldiers," says Thinadeshi softly. "All the Voortyashtani soldiers. *Ever*. They were waiting for me in that cliff. It was a tomb, you see. A massive tomb, bigger than anything I'd ever seen. But the Voortyashtanis had a very strange way of memorializing their dead." She looks at Mulaghesh, wild-eyed. "You know about their swords? That the two bond, with each becoming a vessel for the other, the body carrying the sword and the sword carrying the soul?"

"I'm familiar with it," says Mulaghesh.

"That's what was down there," says Thinadeshi. Her eyes are wide with awe. "All those swords. Thousands of them. *Millions* of them. All with *minds* in them, all with agency, memories of lives and inconceivable bloodshed, and all of them crying out to me."

Mulaghesh remembers the reports of Choudhry searching the hills for a mythical tomb . . . but she never imagined that it was like this. "So the tomb wasn't full of bodies, but full of *swords*?"

"Yes. Voortyashtanis didn't consider there to be a difference between the two. Sentinels fashioned their lives to be weapons, their bodies and minds to be instruments of warfare—their swords were a part of that, perhaps the heart of what they became. That's why they call this place the City of Blades, after all. And when I found them, there were so many of them, exposed to the sky, spilling out into the sea, all of them screaming out to someone to find them, to help them."

"But how were they still alive? How did they still *exist*? They were Divine, right? How could they exist without Voortya?"

"Because Voortya had made a pact with them," says Thinadeshi wearily. "It was an agreement: they would make themselves into weapons, be her warriors and go to war for her, and she would give them eternal life. And this contract was so binding that it *had* to be executed—even if Voortya wasn't there! Her death did not, to use the terminology, render *anything* null and void! The dead were *still* supposed to get their afterlife. They were *still* supposed to reside with Voortya in the City of Blades. And one day, they were *still* supposed to return to where their swords lay in the mortal world and begin the last war, the final war that would consume all of creation. This is what was promised them, and the dead, in essence, intend to see that the bargain is fulfilled. If it was only one or two departed souls, their power might be negligible—but there are *millions* here with me in the City of Blades. With their strength pooled they're able to make sure reality holds up its part of the bargain. They are *insisting* that they be remembered, and any Divine construction created to remember them is therefore forced to persist." Suddenly she looks terribly, terribly weary. "But they needed Voortya herself in order for the agreement to be executed. Some part of her had to reside with them in the City of Blades. Or someone quite similar, I should say."

Mulaghesh slowly realizes what she means. "*You?*" she asks, horrified. "They wanted *you* to stand in for Voortya?"

Thinadeshi smiles weakly. "They needed the Maiden of Steel, Queen of Grief, Empress of Graves, She Who Clove the Earth in Twain, Devourer of Children. Am I not all these things, to some extent? I devoted my life to the railroads, to reconstruction, so I am the Maiden of Steel. I've torn apart mountains to build them, so I am She Who Clove the Earth in Twain. Hundreds of laborers died fulfilling my dangerous dream, so I am the Empress of Graves. And . . . my own children perished in my endeavors. My family suffered unspeakably for everything I wrought. So I am also Queen of Grief, and Devourer of Children. Perhaps it was my punishment to become this thing. Perhaps I deserve this. Whatever the case, they needed someone who matched their *idea* of Voortya—and I came close enough to count. There was a vacuum, and I merely filled it."

"But why did you consent?"

"Because when they spoke to me," says Thinadeshi, "when they reached out to me and begged me to take up the mantle of their mother, I understood that their true hope was that I would allow them their last war. Their final great battle, the one they'd been promised for centuries. And I could not allow that. I could not allow them to make war upon my country, not after it had just been freed.

"So I climbed down to them. And as I did, the world . . . changed. The skies grew dark. The stars changed—they became older, stranger. And the farther I climbed down the broken cliff to them, the more the world shifted and churned until I was walking down a white staircase, and then I was in a grand, white courtyard with many passageways and staircases up—and the voices asked me to climb up, up, and I did. I climbed and I climbed until I came to the top of the tower, and there was the great, awful red throne, and beside it . . . Beside it was this."

Thinadeshi closes her eyes once more, and concentrates. She reaches out with her right hand, appearing to sift through the empty air before her. Then her fingers clench around something, and she pulls out . . .

Suddenly there is a sword in her hand, or rather a sword hilt, as the blade is but a faint flicker of golden light. Mulaghesh can't tell exactly where it came from: it feels as if it's *always* been in her hand, but Thinadeshi simply chose to make it visible now.

The hilt and handle are strange to Mulaghesh's eyes: at first it appears to be made of some dark, viscous black material, like volcanic glass. But then the light shifts, and the hilt isn't dark stone, but a severed hand. Its blackened fingers clutch the bottom of the formless blade, its thumb and forefinger crooked in such a manner that Mulaghesh knows it was not made by any artist.

The more she looks at the sword the more she perceives many things in it, even sensations: the sound of steel on steel, the sight of distant flames, the rumble of horses' hooves. The sword flickers back and forth between being made of stone and fire and steel and lightning before, finally, becoming a human hand once more. And as she looks she knows that this is no mere sculpture: the hand is real, sacrificed by a man long ago to his Divinity, and through the sacrifice of his son she became exceedingly powerful, and this sacrifice was memorialized on stones and books and pieces of armor, the hand clutching the blade, the sacrifice paired with assault.

"The sword of Voortya," says Thinadeshi quietly. "It is with me always now. Just like the sentinels and their own weapons, it is a part of me. It whispers to me, telling me I am Voortya, telling me what I must do, playing with my thoughts. It is damnably hard to resist sometimes. For long stretches, I think I *am* Voortya, sometimes."

"That sounds dangerous," says Mulaghesh.

"You've no idea. I think it is not the true thing, or at least not as it was: like the City of Blades, like everything Divine, it is but a shadow of its former self. But that is still more dangerous and more powerful than any device any mortal has ever wielded. One day I will be rid of it. Perhaps soon." Thinadeshi sits back as if the effort of producing the weapon exhausted her. "When I took up the sword of Voortya, in the eyes of the dead, it was as if I *was* her. And because she'd granted them power, they then bestowed it upon *me*. I was given limited abilities, both within this ghostly realm and beyond. And one of those powers was to enter the land of the living, and destroy. Which I did.

"I crossed over, and I attacked the cliffs with all the power that was granted to me. I brought down the tomb, I pummeled the earth, I hacked at it again and again with the sword of Voortya. The effort exhausted me—in retrospect, it nearly killed me, for I had done something only a Divinity should be able to do—but I did it."

"Why?"

"They wished to return to where their swords lay—but what if there were no swords? What could they do then? The blades act as beacons, you see, tying the land of the dead to the land of the living. By destroying them I cut the strings and set this island adrift, existing in a half-real state. I was marooned here with them, dressed up as their dead god, but at least the world was safe. At least my people were safe. At least my children could finally go on to live happy, safe lives."

"How have you stayed alive all this time?" asks Mulaghesh. "I don't see any food or water around here."

"I've wondered that myself," says Thinadeshi. "But I never get hungry here, or thirsty. My suspicion is that this place is some kind of a limbo, really. When Voortya died, it stopped being completely real . . . and when I destroyed the swords, and destroyed the last final link to mortal life with them, it became even less real than that. Time doesn't work here, or if it does, it doesn't work the way it should."

Thinadeshi is silent for a long, long time. She draws a rattling breath. "But then," she croaks. "But then, but then, but then . . . I felt it. I felt it out there in the land of the living. Somehow we were being pulled back. Someone had found the tomb, or what was left of it. Someone had found the swords. And they began meddling i—"

Mulaghesh sits upright, every muscle in her body clenched to the point of straining. "Son of a bitch! Son of a damned *bitch*!"

Thinadeshi draws away from her, alarmed. "What? What is it? What's wrong with you?"

"It's the thinadeskite!" cries Mulaghesh.

"The what?"

"The thinadeskite! It's not some naturally occurring ore! *It's what's left of their damned swords!*"

***

"Thina . . . deskite?" asks Thinadeshi. "What do you mean?"

"It's this ore," says Mulaghesh. "Or that's what they thought it was, discovered outside of Fort Thin . . ." She pauses as she realizes nearly everything she's about to reference has been named for the ill-looking person sitting before her. "Never mind. But they thought it was this natural resource with some unusual properties, so they started digging it up. But it wasn't natural at all; it was what was left of the swords after you obliterated the tomb, pulverized it beyond recognition! That must have been why Choudhry was so interested in the geomorphological history of the cliffs: she could *tell* that something was wrong! She must have noticed some sign of the damage you did, and known that it couldn't possibly have been some natural effect!"

Thinadeshi looks at her side-eyed. "I won't pretend to know anything about a lick of what you're saying here, but do go on."

Mulaghesh scratches her scalp, excited and anxious. "*And* that must be why the ore never tested as Divine! Because it *isn't* the will of a Divinity that makes it work—it's the will of the dead! If you're right, and anything that memorializes the dead is *forced* to persist, then that would explain everything—why the man atop the Tooth was still alive, why the 'tribute' statues they hauled up from the bottom of the sea are still around, and why any miracle relating to the dead still functions! And that's why I had flashbacks down in the mine's tunnels—I was literally walking through a sea of souls and memories."

"I will assume you are talking about the mine I destroyed," says Thinadeshi.

Mulaghesh stops. "Oh. That's right. That was you, after all."

"Yes," says Thinadeshi, nettled. "This was the incident in which you shot me, if you remember."

"Which was pretty damned justified, if I might say so! From my end you looked a damn sight like the real thing!"

"Of course I did!" snaps Thinadeshi. "When one wields even a shadow of a Divinity's power, that power tends to follow decorum and clothe one correctly!"

"What, it even makes you a hundred sizes bigger?"

"It's all a play of images and perception, a warping of the world! Miracles are apparently very formal things, I'll have you know!" She winces as Mulaghesh tends to her shoulder. "But they do *not* make one invulnerable."

"How was it that no one else saw you?"

"Because I did not wish them to," says Thinadeshi. "I tapped the sword's strength to veil myself from the land of the living. But . . . when I climbed the cliff, the sword *bucked*, like a dowsing rod sensing water. Something was wrong. Perhaps it sensed you—maybe it sensed some quality in you it found familiar, or even desirable. Why hide one's self from a kindred spirit?"

Mulaghesh is silent as she considers the awful implications of this. Finally she asks, "How did you know about the mine?"

"Because someone opened a window into it," says Thinadeshi. "I felt someone trying to open many entryways into this place. I didn't know that was one of the things I could do—sensing such a thing—

but apparently I can. They tried it over and over again. I went to investigate, fearing someone could, I don't know, incite or awaken all the souls here. Then I came across a gap hanging in the air, a mirror or window into . . . somewhere else. A tunnel of some kind, and in that tunnel were some grubby little men. They did not see me, and I listened to them talking, digging down in the dirt and hauling up all the fragments of the very things I'd hoped I'd destroyed long ago. I thought that this might be the reason the City of Blades was being pulled back, reconnecting with the land of the living. So I did what was necessary."

"And you destroyed it," says Mulaghesh. She doesn't bother telling Thinadeshi that she killed three soldiers in the process of doing so. What good would that do?

"But it didn't work," says Thinadeshi miserably. "I can still feel us growing closer and closer. It made me so weak, to do it, but it accomplished nothing. The dead remember more and more of what was promised to them. Something has happened in Voortyashtan, and it acts like a faint light to a blind man, and they are following it, feeling their way back to the land of the living, and what they are owed. What were you people *doing* with that mine, anyway?"

Mulaghesh summarizes what little she understands about the wide-ranging qualities of thinadeskite. Thinadeshi is absolutely horrified. "And they named it after *me?*" she says. "They named this hellish material after the person who tried to *annihilate* it?"

"Well, they didn't know that," says Mulaghesh. "You're well thought of, and they thought it could be world-changing. . . . They said it would revolutionize nearly anything electrical."

"Of course it would!" says Thinadeshi angrily. "If it can store a soul and all of its memories for hundreds of years, then a few photons are no issue at all! Every atom of those things is packed with the fury of millions of people denied what they felt was their due. I've no doubt that's expressing itself in all manner of horrible ways!"

"But they're not doing anything special with it," says Mulaghesh. "They're just making wire and other electrical material out of it. And if you're telling me that destroying the mine didn't stop anything . . . then it must have been something else that started this whole thing."

"Then what?" says Thinadeshi. "What else could possibly be waking the dead?"

Mulaghesh thinks back to that afternoon on the clifftops: tripping over the tunnel, finding Choudhry's letter describing a mysterious person infiltrating the thinadeskite mines . . .

"What if . . . What if it's not just messing around with the ore that does it? You said yourself that the dead wouldn't accept just anyone as Voortya, they needed someone that was . . . I don't know, the right *shape*. The right *clothes*."

"Yes?"

"So the right shape for the thinadeski—"

"*Please* stop calling it that."

"All right! The right shape for the ore . . . would be a sword." She looks at Thinadeshi. "Would it be possible for someone to forge *new* swords out of the ore?"

"I . . . I suppose," says Thinadeshi. "But how would one know how to do it? How would one even know what to make? I made sure no examples of Voortyashtani swords remained in the living world."

"No, you just destroyed that one tomb," says Mulaghesh. "Special saints got tombs of their own. Ones that I guess contained *only* their swords. We found one in the Teeth of the World, one that didn't have a sword in it. Unless someone had already been there and taken it—"

"—so they could use it as an original," says Thinadeshi, "and use it to make copies. But they would need to have extensive smithing knowledge for that to work."

Mulaghesh cocks her head, thinking. Then time seems to slow down for her.

She remembers walking into a house, noting how cold it was . . . but then as she left, turning around and seeing a thick tumble of smoke from the chimney.

A voice in her head: *Have you ever heard of Saint Petrenko?*

And then the words of the Watcher: *It was Petrenko who developed the method that the old ones first used to make their swords.*

"I think I know who it is," says Mulaghesh softly. "But damned if I know why." She looks at Thinadeshi. "Can you leave with me? Do you have enough strength for that?"

Thinadeshi laughs hollowly. "If I leave, they leave." She nods out the window. "I'm the only thing keeping them back. Even as you're talking to me now, I'm fighting a war here." She taps the side of her head. "It's killing me. Destroying the mine weakened me terribly. But I have to keep fighting them, telling them not yet, not yet. . . . So I can't go, General. More so, I won't."

Mulaghesh and Thinadeshi exchange a silent moment then: the two women look at each other, each hard-eyed and determined, and Mulaghesh understands right away that to try to convince Thinadeshi to leave her post would be a waste of time. Her mind's made up, and Mulaghesh can respect that.

"How much time do you have?" asks Mulaghesh.

Thinadeshi looks relieved they're moving on. "Not much. The closer we get to the land of the living, the more the sentinels awake. It's getting harder and harder."

"I *would* propose that I go back to Voortyashtan, find the swords, and destroy them," says Mulaghesh. "But what happens if you die before I do that?"

"Then they invade," says Thinadeshi. "And you die."

"Shit," says Mulaghesh. She rubs her mouth, frustrated. "So there's no Plan B? No backup option?"

Thinadeshi is quiet. Then she slowly looks at the sword in her hand. "There is . . . one option." She holds it out to Mulaghesh, her face grim. "You can take this."

"What? *Me* take the sword of Voortya? What the hells are you talking about? Won't that kill you?"

"I'm already being killed," says Thinadeshi. "This strange device won't keep me alive much longer. And it will take some time for its powers to depart from me: in essence, it will take time for this place to realize I've dropped the act. Probably no longer than the time I have *with* the sword. You can take it, in case you fail."

"And what in the hells am I supposed to do with it?"

"It's a token," says Thinadeshi, "a symbol. It can be unlocked, un-folded, interpreted to be many things. You can do many deeds with it if you use it the right way, if you *think* about it the right way. Voortya was the goddess of warfare, General. And you of all people should know that war is an art requiring decorum and formality. It fever-ishly adheres to rules and traditions—and that can be used against it. Take it!"

Mulaghesh reaches out hesitantly, then takes the black, severed hand from Thinadeshi's grasp. Instantly the faint sword blade van-ishes, and Mulaghesh is left holding a heavy black sword handle with a rather curious crossguard, and nothing more: there is no sugges-tion of fingers or flesh in it, no flash of lightning, no lick of flame. It is just a thing, not a Divine conceit made solid.

"That all sounds like a bunch of variations on 'I don't know' to me," says Mulaghesh.

"It responds to different people in different ways," says Thi-nadeshi. "And the dead still believe me to be Voortya. Once I am gone, it will awaken to you—but I am not sure how. And I would prefer we not have to depend on that at all."

"Me neither," says Mulaghesh. "So how do I get out of this place?"

"I can push you back," says Thinadeshi. "That will not sap my strength much, or so I hope." She shuts her eyes. "I see an entry-way—a doorway in the water. My face looks down on it. No, no . . . It's Voortya's face, of course. There is a young woman there, wait-ing." She opens her eyes. "Is that safe? Should she be there?"

"Was she blond and kind of unbearable-looking?"

"She was blond, yes. And she did have a . . . a *combative* look to her. . . ."

"Then that's fine." She gathers up her gear. "Can you just . . . do it now?"

"I can," says Thinadeshi. She reaches out to Mulaghesh, then hes-itates. "I suppose this would be my last chance to ask how the world has gotten along without me, wouldn't it?"

"Yeah. Is there anything you want me to say or do?" says Mula-ghesh. "Anything you want me to tell your family?"

Since Mulaghesh first saw Thinadeshi she's always had a hard look in her eye, as if her soul is an anvil and she expects the whole of the world to be shaped on it; but at this question the barest crack begins to show, and she trembles a little. "I think . . . I think it would be best to think that I *did* die all those years ago. I did leave the land of the living, after all. Is that not death? But I think I chose this before then. When I chose to travel to the Continent and take my children with me . . . When I chose accomplishment over my responsibilities . . . I look back on all I did, all I got done, and they fill me with nothing at all. Not pride, not joy, not contentment. All I have now is this insatiable hunger."

"Hunger for what?"

She smiles faintly. "To tell my children that, despite everything, I loved them. And I wished I could have loved them more, showed them that more."

"I'll tell them, if I can find them," says Mulaghesh.

Thinadeshi's face hardens. "Then go," she says. "And get it done." She taps Mulaghesh on the forehead, just barely pushing her off balance, and Mulaghesh falls backward, sure to strike the floor. . . .

. . . But she doesn't. The floor isn't there. Instead there are the still, cool, dark waters, and she's plummeting down through them again, sinking faster and faster. The white citadel of the City of Blades shrinks above her, dwindling down until it's a slice of light above her, and then it's gone.

She knows what's going to happen this time, but it doesn't make it any easier: again, the pressure builds and builds until it feels like her head is about to crack like an egg. She swears she can feel her ribs popping and creaking. She doesn't struggle this time, but curls up into a ball. Then she feels gravity swirling around her, like the world can't decide what's up and what's down, and when she opens her eyes she sees a dark black hole opening above her.

She punches through, flailing wildly. Her arms strike the rim of the stone basin. She's still blinking water out of her eyes, but she can see the canvas roof of the yard of statues above her.

"Careful! Careful!" says Signe's voice. Signe grabs her by her arms and hauls her out. She bounces roughly off of a stone edge below before both she and Signe topple over into the mud.

"Good heavens," says Signe. "What happened to you? Did you . . . Did you actually *go* there? And why are you . . . well . . . *red*?"

Mulaghesh coughs up what feels like a liter of seawater again. "I know who it is," she gasps. "I know who it is!"

"Who . . . what is?"

Mulaghesh rolls over and pulls herself up onto all fours. The bone-white faces of the statues stare at her expectantly.

"It's Rada Smolisk," she says quietly. "Rada Smolisk is who's waking up the dead."

He sang to them, "Mother Voortya dances always!
She dances upon the hills, Her blade flickering to and fro!
She dances upon the hearts of men
For battle is our rightful state!

If you were to open up the human heart
And look within,
You would find two figures
Screaming, clutching, wrestling in the mud!"

—EXCERPT FROM "OF THE GREAT MOTHER VOORTYA
ATOP THE TEETH OF THE WORLD," CA. 556

15.

the shadow of oblivion

It won't be easy getting up there," says Signe. "Biswal's forces are returning, and I've had reports they're flooding the harbor works. They'll be here any minute."

Mulaghesh grimaces as she performs a gear check. She's still stained red from head to toe, though it does seem to be sloughing off, a little. She hasn't bothered to tell Signe everything—there isn't enough time to describe how Thinadeshi became the stand-in for the goddess of warfare—but she's given her the details on how the City of Blades is waking up again. "And unfortunately Rada's house is between the Galleries and the fortress," says Mulaghesh. "There'll be lots of exposure between here and there."

"It's in a little copse of trees, though," says Signe. "Perhaps that can give us some cover."

"If we can *get* to the trees, that is. If Biswal's troops are entering the harbor works, that means the roads away from this place are going to be watched."

"Are you *sure* it's her?"

"It must have been. She quoted Petrenko to my face, and the Watcher over there said they'd been visited by a student of his. And Rada would *know* which families were isolated enough for her to test her swords on—one of the dead boys in Poshok had some kind of horrible rash, and they said in Ghevalyev that the man was always fretting over his wife's health. . . . She must have visited each of their homes."

Signe shakes her head, disgusted. "I can't believe this."

"And Petrenko was the saint who invented the method of making Voortyashtani swords," says Mulaghesh. "Rada must have gone to the Teeth of the World, found the tomb . . ."

"Which must have been Petrenko's tomb."

"Right. Petrenko's sword acts as a blueprint for how to make more. And now here we are."

Mulaghesh checks the sword of Voortya, though currently it's still more like a handle. She has it stuffed in the belt of her pants for easy access, though she still has no idea what she'd need it for. Once she's confirmed it's secure, she scans the walls. "You got any rope around here?"

"I'm sure I can find some somewhere, bu—"

"And you're a pretty good climber, right?"

"What are you suggesting?"

"I'm suggesting that that arch over there," she says, pointing at a spectral sculpture designed to look like the bones of a whale, "rises almost to the top of the wall. Meaning we wouldn't have to use the door. Rada's house is just up the slope from this yard, provided we go over the wall."

Signe sighs as she takes in the scale of the arch. "You do have a knack for getting other people to stick their necks out for you."

"Recall, please, that I just plummeted into the afterlife to save the necks of this city."

"Good point, I suppose." Signe fetches a few lengths of rope from a storage area in the statue yard, and the two begin to run over.

"After you get me over the wall," says Mulaghesh, "what next?"

"What next? Why, I'm coming with you, of course. You're making me climb up on a damn wall, I might as well go all the way."

It's the answer Mulaghesh wanted to hear, though she didn't want to ask the direct question: to guilt others into your dirty business is bad sport, in her opinion. "Are you sure?"

"You'll need the backup, won't you?"

"Yes. But I want to make sure that you're sure. You could see some fighting. I can't guarantee that it won't be dangerous."

"General, this woman apparently wishes to destroy everything I've made so far," says Signe. "Though frankly I've no idea why. I intend to stop her, at the very least, and then find out her reasoning." Signe begins to deftly climb up the arch. "She isn't even a true Voortyashtani. She's from Bulikov, for the seas' sakes!"

"Feel like you'd be decent with a rifling tonight?"

Signe vaults up and straddles the edge of the wall. She sighs, bowing her head. "I do despise combat, you know."

"Yeah. I know how you feel."

She begins uncoiling the rope, lowering it down. "But I'm still willing to do it."

"Yeah," says Mulaghesh, grasping the rope. "I know how you feel."

***

As they rappel down the wall Mulaghesh looks out and sees the dark cityscape littered with beams of lights, the roving torches of soldiers on a search. She does a quick count and gauges their number at fifty or so. She can tell by the way the lights are bobbing up and down that they're running, and it looks like a lot of them are running for the statue yard.

"Hurry up and get down!" says Signe.

They slide down the rest of the wall and lurk in its shadows, watching the search beams.

"Oh my," whispers Signe. "There's rather a lot of them, isn't there?"

"On my mark we run to the fence ahead, all right?" Mulaghesh points across the industrial yard to a chain-link fence about ten feet high.

"We're not climbing that, too, are we? There's razor wire at the top."

"I have wire cutters. But it'll take time."

"Why do you have wire cutters?"

"Because every damn soldier worth their salt has wire cutters!" snaps Mulaghesh. "Anything else you want to know?"

Signe cranes her head forward. "I don't think anyone's coming. On the count of three?"

"Works for me." She counts off with her fingers and then they bolt forward. They dart around a stack of rebar, then through piles of soil and pulped wood until finally they come to the chain-link fence.

They squat and look behind them: bright beams of light are slashing through the night air. "Not torches," says Mulaghesh quietly as she pulls out her wire cutters. "Spotlights. They're really looking for us."

Signe takes the wire cutters and goes to work, snipping through the fence. "Will they shoot us?"

"They might if we run. Likely they expect we're armed. And you do have a rifling strapped to your back."

"And what if we succeed tonight? What if we get to Rada and stop what she's doing? Do you think Biswal would forgive us?"

"If we got Rada to tell him the story, maybe," says Mulaghesh.

"Would she do that?"

"She might if I beat the shit out of her a little."

Signe looks at her, shocked. "Would you do that?"

"Hells yeah I'd do that. If it keeps me from ducking a firing line, I'd beat her ass like a drum. Keep cutting."

Mulaghesh keeps watch. The metallic walls of the statue yard reflect the light a little too well for her tastes, bouncing off and sending rays scattered around the yard. Both of them keep ducking down as beams strafe over their heads. Mulaghesh turns and looks up through the fence and up the slope to where Rada Smolisk's house sits in the trees below the cliffs. It's about five hundred yards up, by her guess. She can see one cheery yellow window burning among the trunks, and the chimney, of course, is belching up merry gray smoke. *But it's not your average wood fire, is it?* thinks Mulaghesh.

Then she spots a few sparks of light to the right at the same elevation as Rada's house. She shields her eyes against the other strobe lights to see a band of soldiers, perhaps five or so, walking along the road to the polis governor's house.

"Shit," says Mulaghesh. "We've got company. Soldiers on their way to Rada's house."

"I'm almost done here. How much time?"

"Twenty, ten minutes away. Maybe."

"Then we'll have to book i—"

She's cut short as Mulaghesh drops down and clamps a hand over her mouth. Signe's eyes widen and look at her, surprised. Then Mulaghesh shakes her head and nods backward, behind the mounds of earth.

At first it's quiet. Then they hear it: footsteps, slow and uncertain.

Mulaghesh takes her hand off of Signe's face and pulls out her carousel. She squats down low and readies her aim.

For a moment, nothing. Then a beam of light surges out of the darkness and falls on them.

Mulaghesh almost shoots. It takes a lot of training not to, but she's more worried about giving away her position than anything. She waits for the owner of the light to say something, anything, identifying themselves—but they don't. There's just a long pause.

Then a voice: "Uh . . . CTO Harkvaldsson?"

Signe lets out a breath. "Damn it all, Knordstrom!" she says. "You almost gave me a heart attack!"

The beam lowers. Mulaghesh blinks until she can make out a thickset Dreyling guard with the SDC insignia on his breast standing among the dirt mounds. "Oh. Uh. Sorry, ma'am. I didn't realize you'd be here."

"Well, obviously, I am!"

"I see. Can I ask . . . Uh, what's going on? I'm hearing reports of Saypuri troops storming the harbor. . . ."

"Yes," says Signe grimly. "It seems General Biswal has gone mad with power. He's looking to arrest me. This will be a serious diplomatic incident, I'm afraid. Do *not* report back that you saw us, and I recommend you usher all Saypuri troops away from this part of the yard. Am I clear?"

"Yes, ma'am."

"And one more thing. Find my father and tell him to meet us up at Rada Smolisk's house, up the hill." She points through the chain-link fence.

Knordstrom looks where she's pointing. "The, uh . . . the polis governor's house?"

"Yes. We're to have an emergency rendezvous to discuss the situation. Tell him that. Understand?"

"Yes, ma'am."

"Excellent. Now hop to it."

Knordstrom, despite his ample bulk, hurries away through the piles of dirt.

"That was smartly done," says Mulaghesh. "I hope like hells he gets Sigrud over here."

"Me, too." Signe clips through the last of the chain-link fence, and Mulaghesh kicks it open. The two crawl through, the bits of wire biting at their shoulders and backsides, then stand and sprint away.

The hill stops being a hill and starts being more like a cliff, with Rada's house sitting above. "Why are soldiers coming in the first place?" asks Signe as they begin to climb.

"Standard protocol," says Mulaghesh, breathing hard. "First thing you do during a security threat as regional governor is secure the safety of all other Ministry officials. I just never thought that *I'd* be the threat to the polis governor."

Signe looks up along the cliff. "It's a straight climb up the rest of the way," she says. "Do you need any help?"

"I'll manage," says Mulaghesh. Then, quieter: "Maybe."

They climb, and climb, and climb. Mulaghesh doesn't say so, but it's extraordinarily difficult for her, trying to compensate for her left arm. More than once she's certain she's going to topple over and plummet down to the streets below. She's so focused on not falling that she's shocked when something soft strikes her shoulder. It takes her a moment to realize it's a rope.

She looks up and sees it dangling from Signe's dark form above. "Tie that to your belt," she says. "I've got it tied to mine. I'll steady you."

"So I can pull you to your death, too?"

"I'm bigger than you," says Signe. "I'll be fine."

Tying the rope to her belt on the side of a cliff one-handed is a tall order for Mulaghesh, but after a few minutes of fumbling around in her pants she manages it. She gives Signe a thumbs-up and the two of them start their ascent again. She has to hand it to her: Signe is bigger than her and much better at this than she thought.

Finally they get to the top of the cliff. Signe vaults over it, then turns, lies down, and reaches down to Mulaghesh. "Here. Give me your hand."

Mulaghesh looks up to see a beam of light shoot through the air just above Signe. *They're close,* she thinks. *Too close. We were too damned slow!*

She hurriedly begins untying her end of the rope. "Signe! Get away! Get down, they'll see you!"

"Just jump up and grab my hand!"

"Signe, you—"

"Just do it already!"

Mulaghesh jumps up. Her entire body fills with terror as she's suspended over a precipitous drop for one blistering moment.

Her fingers touch Signe's. At first she's convinced it won't work, that her grip will pass through and she'll go tumbling down the slope. But then Signe's fingers clutch together, seizing Mulaghesh's hand. She then leans down and hooks her elbow into Mulaghesh's left arm, above her false hand.

Then everything goes bright as a beam of light falls on them. "Halt!" cries a voice. "Freeze!"

Neither of them speaks. Signe pulls Mulaghesh up, though their progress feels agonizingly slow.

"I said freeze!" cries the voice. He sounds worried, agitated. Mulaghesh can see that Signe's rifling is very visibly strapped to her back. *That's bad*, thinks Mulaghesh.

Mulaghesh kicks at the cliffside and pushes herself up and over. She tumbles over the edge and rolls away from the light. Signe tries to follow her, but she's still recovering and moves just a little too slow.

A shot. Mulaghesh hears Signe cry out. Mulaghesh rises up onto a knee and draws her carousel.

Even in this moment, when she's being fired on and she's aware her comrade has been hit, she's still painfully aware that these are her own soldiers, her own colleagues and brothers and sisters—and, as an officer, her own responsibility. So she fires three shots up into the trees above them, high but not too high—just enough that they seek cover, fast.

It works: the beams of light go skittering through the trees, fleeing the shots. Mulaghesh hooks one arm around Signe and hauls her up, not bothering to look for where she's hit.

The two of them limp along through the trees, Mulaghesh stumbling and flailing and trying not to fall. Shots ring out, but none of them come close.

"Where did you catch it?" she says as they run.

"My calf," says Signe. "It's . . . It's not too bad. . . ." But she's talking through gritted teeth, suggesting it definitely feels quite bad.

Mulaghesh turns, takes cover behind a tree, and looks for motion. She spies three of them lurching up through the ferns and the bracken toward her. She takes careful aim at the tree above them, then fires. The bark erupts just above their heads, and they dive for cover again.

"They must not be the cream of the crop," says Mulaghesh, hauling Signe up toward Rada's house. "Otherwise you'd be dead."

"Put me down," whispers Signe.

"What?"

"Put me down and leave me here," she says. "I'm just slowing you down!"

"I'm not leaving you, damn it!"

"And you won't make it to Rada's house with me!" says Signe. "They'll catch up to you and either shoot us or arrest us both! Either way, we're dead. If we get arrested and the sentinels invade, we're dead, Turyin. You know that!"

Mulaghesh slows to a stop. She looks around and finds a large clump of bracken underneath one of the pines. "Do you think you can tend to your own wound if I give you the supplies?"

"I can deal with a wounded leg," says Signe, though she's wincing. "Give me the rifling, and I'll give you more cover fire and buy you some time."

"I won't have you killing a Saypuri soldier on account of my dumb ass. Don't use it unless you *have* to." She sets Signe down and sees her face is twisted in pain. She takes a look at the wound and immediately assesses that it was almost a clean shoot, though it looks like it might have nicked the bone a little. She reaches around and pulls out her med kit. "I'd see to you myself if I could."

"I know," says Signe, taking the kit. "Now go! Get out of here and stop her!"

Mulaghesh turns and sprints up through the trees.

***

Mulaghesh darts up the hillside to the other side of the house, to Rada's living quarters entrance. She dives into the bracken and peers through the leaves, watching, waiting. She can hear the soldiers calling out to one another, signaling their positions as they comb the forest. None of them seem to be near her, and she doesn't think any of them can see her.

She starts creeping toward the house. It's dark, but not dark enough for her to feel safe. Finally she comes to the base of the house, where a large bay window spills golden light across the trees. She can see the door, but she'll be plainly visible if she moves toward it. She rises to a squat, reloads the carousel, watches the trees, and, seeing nothing, sprints for the door.

She makes it. There's no sound of a shot or a shout. But she can hear something coming from the base of the house: a soft *ping! ping!* sound, like metal on metal.

I know what that is, she thinks grimly.

She reaches down and tests the knob. It's locked. She feels around for the door frame and confirms that the hinges are on the other side. Then she steps out from the cover of the wall, squares herself with the door, and delivers a powerful kick just beside the knob.

The door cracks open. One of the soldiers out front shouts, "What was that?" But Mulaghesh is already charging into the house, carousel ready.

The lights are on inside, but she doesn't hear movement. She shuts the door and shoves a cabinet in front of it, knowing it won't stop them. Then she quietly begins to move throughout the house, searching from room to room.

Rada Smolisk is not home, or so it seems: no one in the kitchen, the living room, or any of the clinic's quarters. Mulaghesh walks to the fireplace and feels the ashes there. They're quite cold, as are the stones. Yet she just saw smoke pouring out of the chimney, and heard that sound below. . . .

Mulaghesh inspects the chimney and the fireplace. She knows that her time is limited, but Rada must be hiding around here somewhere. She doesn't see any cracks or paneling in the walls around the fireplace, but as she paces over the carpet she suddenly stops, thinks, and looks down.

One corner of the carpet is strangely askew, as if someone tried to pull it into place from an awkward angle.

She grabs a corner of the carpet and hauls it up.

Set in the wooden floor underneath is a wide trapdoor with a metal handle set in its side.

She holsters her carousel and lifts the trapdoor. Below is a set of winding, curving stairs down.

There's a pounding at the door she came in through. She can hear the cabinet she tipped in front of the door creaking and cracking. Mulaghesh glances around, grabs a fire poker from the fireplace, and enters the staircase. She shuts the trapdoor and slides the fire poker through the handle, locking it. She wipes sweat from her brow, draws her carousel, and continues down.

It should be dark here, one would imagine, but it isn't: though there are no lamps, the winding staircase is lit by a faint orange light that filters up through the cracks in the steps. As she descends Mulaghesh can hear that tinny *ping, ping, ping*—the sound of pieces of metal striking one another.

Or a hammer on an anvil, she thinks.

It's only a few steps after that when she starts to hear the voices in her head, whispering and murmuring.

". . . chased them down the shallow river, their arrows singing, and we leapt ashore with our blades and hearts glimmering gladly and struck them down like rag dolls, and how cheered we were by their shrieking flight. . . ."

". . . fought me day and night, for four days, my teacher and I there upon the hills, for she had said she'd show me the primal beast that lurks at the heart of the world, the pet of the Mother, and when I struck her arm from her body and plunged my sword into her throat she died smiling, for she knew she had taught me all there was to know. . . ."

It's familiar, she realizes: this is like the chanting and muttering she heard from the sentinels in the City of Blades.

The stairs level out. She sees the wicked blaze of the forge beyond, and the swords in racks before it.

There are dozens of them. Maybe four dozen, maybe five. Only a few approach the terrible, beautiful weapon wielded by Zhurgut, most not half so large nor half so fine. They are perhaps the products of a prentice smith, one still learning the wend and weft of the metal, still grasping what heat and pliability will allow one to do. But they are still swords, still weapons, and though crude she can see there is a primitive utility to them.

And she can *hear* them. She can hear them talking, whispering.

Inside these weapons, she realizes, are the memories and desires of an entire civilization.

A small figure toils before the forge, adorned in a thick leather apron and a wide, blank metal mask with a tinted glass plate. The sight would almost be comical if the person did not carry themselves with an air of such grimness, pumping the bellows with determination and familiarity, indifferent to the sting of the sparks. This creature knows the forge and knows their work, and intends to do it.

"Little Rada Smolisk," whispers Mulaghesh. "What are you *doing?*"

She watches as Rada holds a blazing chunk of metal in the teeth of a pair of tongs. She sets it on the face of the anvil and gives it a mighty blow, turning it over and over, her movements assured. Mulaghesh can see that the forge is cunningly crafted: Rada has built her own hearth and firepot and tuyere and bellows, with a vent above that must feed into the chimney. It must have taken her months to construct. There are also air vents built into the corners of the basement in order to allow out the heat. There's even a draft in the room as the hot, active air circulates out, bringing the cool, wintry air in.

Mulaghesh glances around at the dozens of swords, and reflects that, not for the first time, Rada Smolisk is trapped down here in the dark with the dead.

Mulaghesh paces forward, mindful of the hammer in Rada's hand. "Stop, Rada."

Rada pauses for a second, then continues hammering away on the lump of metal.

"I said stop it!"

Rada turns the lump over, examines it, then sets it back in the coals. Her voice is small and soft: "No."

"Put the hammer down!"

"No." She takes the piece of metal back out, lays it on the face of the anvil, and pounds away at it again.

"I will shoot you, Rada!"

"Then do so," says Rada quietly. "Shoot me. Kill me." Another ringing blow. "I am indifferent to it."

"I know what you're doing! I've been to the City of Blades, Rada! I've seen it!"

The hammering slows. Then she remarks, "So? What difference does that make? How does that stop anything? So you know. So what?" She looks at the hammer, considering it. "This is the most alive I've ever felt in my life. Did you know that? All the burdens on my soul and on my tongue . . . With each blow of the hammer, they fade away."

Mulaghesh watches as Rada lifts the hammer and begins pounding away again. "The hells with this," mutters Mulaghesh. She holsters her weapon and strides forward. Rada turns, brandishing the hammer, but Mulaghesh can tell that she's not sure what she really wants to do with it: she didn't expect or even really want a confrontation. So Mulaghesh grabs Rada's wrist with her right hand, forcefully spins her around, and delivers a devastating stomp to the back of her right knee.

Something pops wetly in Rada's knee. She screams in agony and falls to the ground, her hammer clanging on the anvil. Mulaghesh ignores her. She walks to the swords and starts grabbing them and hurling them onto the coals.

Rada's shrieks turn into peals of laughter. She lifts her metal mask. Her face is wild and ash-streaked, not at all the timid little thing Mulaghesh has known over the past weeks. "You think *that's* going to do anything? You think you're going to destroy them like *that*? Maybe if you had a few weeks! It's too late, General."

"You went to the Teeth of the World, didn't you, Rada?" says Mulaghesh, pumping the bellows. The swords glow hot, but not hot enough. "Took a boat, maybe hired one of the tribesmen. You found Petrenko's sword. He took you to the City of Blades to learn from him directly, projected you there. But the Watcher there gave you the boot because you didn't deserve to be there."

"I'm not a killer, no," says Rada softly. "But I know death. I know it quite well. It is my constant companion, as you know well, General."

"So what in hells are you doing bringing *more* of it down on the world?" snarls Mulaghesh. "You tested out your swords on those innocent people in the countryside! You sat and watched as people butchered their own loved ones!"

"I had to know if it worked," she says, her voice still soft. "I had to know if the swords were true, if they were really connected to the City of Blades. They took so much work to make. . . ."

"Work? I'll fucking say! *You* made the tunnel to the thinadeskite mines, *you're* the one who's been stealing it to reforge these weapons! You're a damned clever creature, Rada, but are you so damned foolish you don't realize those *things* will kill Continentals and Saypuris alike?"

"Of course I know that," says Rada. "Of course I do."

"Then why are you doing it, for the seas' sakes?"

"Why?" says Rada, her voice rising, torn between amusement and hysteria and outrage. "Why? You want to know *why*?"

"Yes, damn you!"

"Because it is *one thing* to be conquered and lose one's land," screams Rada suddenly, "but it is another to lose *eternity*!"

Mulaghesh pauses, struck by Rada's frenzied outburst.

"Can you imagine it, General?" Rada cries. "Can you imagine being trapped with all the corpses of your family for days and days, the stink of their bodies, the leak of their blood? Feeling them grow cold and clammy in the dark beside you? And imagine growing up fearing that whenever the lights go out, they might come back! Imagine going to bed every night not knowing if you might reach out in the night and feel a cool, wet face beside you, and feeling its mustache and eyebrows and knowing it was once your *father*! Just flesh and bone, and nothing more."

Rada looks up at Mulaghesh, her face contorted with fury. "Then imagine realizing that once there was *more*. Discovering that there *was* an afterlife, a heaven! Once my family could have been safe! Once the dead could have been preserved, loved, respected! When I gripped Petrenko's sword, I saw it. I saw what once waited for these people, and I realized all at once what had truly been taken away from us—that in one stroke all the afterlives that had been lovingly built for us had come crashing down, collapsing, trapping all those souls in the dark. . . . Do you understand what your country *did* to us, General? Do you understand that the Blink didn't merely injure the living, but countless, *countless* souls in the afterlife? And all the people who died in the Battle of Bulikov died *twice*—once in this world, and again when they never passed on to the afterlife intended for them!"

"Well, *we* never got any damned afterlives!" snarls Mulaghesh, pumping the bellows. "When Saypuris were massacred we just rotted in the ground, and if our families knew where we lay then they considered it a blessing! Your tragedy is but a candle flame among a forest fire!"

"I don't care!" screams Rada. "I don't care! Damn the world, damn the Continent, and damn Saypur! If the world gives us no reprieve from life then let them destroy it! When I held the sword, it showed me all its broken kin scattered through the hills—and when they first made the mine, I *knew* what they were digging up, even if *they* didn't! When I made my first sword I knew I brought them a little closer, brought the afterlife denied to me just a little closer to reality. Let them come here. Let them do unto us as we deserve!" She bursts into tears, sobbing hysterically. "We deserve it. We all deserve it."

"Those families you killed, they deserved it? That corpse you butchered to make it look like Choudhry, she deserved it?"

"I don't even know who that was," says Rada softly. "I bought the body from a highland peddler. . . ."

"And all those innocents who died when you resurrected Zhurgut, did they deserve it, too?"

She shrugs. "It was necessary. I had to see if my craftsmanship had gotten good enough to bring a sentinel here and *keep* them here. And you were getting far too close. I thought I could solve two problems at once. But what Zhurgut did will look like a mere bruise in comparison to the Night that is coming. . . . And you can't stop it, General. It took me *years* to make the swords. It'll take far longer than an evening to destroy them, especially by a one-handed old woman with soldiers bearing down on her. I can hear them upstairs—can you?"

Mulaghesh stops pumping the bellows. There's shouting and a hammering from up above—likely the soldiers trying to hack through the trapdoor.

Rada smiles. "Do you know what's funny? *I* brought them here, and they don't even know it. I broke into the yard of statues; I took the photos and sent them along. They think you betrayed your country, General. I'm sure by now every soldier in Voortyashtan wants your head."

"Shut the fuck up." Mulaghesh realizes Rada's right, of course. The swords glow a little, but she's far from smelting them down, let alone all of them. The soldiers will break through long before she makes any headway.

"You're right. I can't do it with this forge," she says quietly.

Then she reaches for her belt and pulls out the hilt of the sword of Voortya.

She stares at it. It is dark and glittering, beautiful in a nasty, savage way, and she imagines how its blade flickered with a pale fire, the barest suggestion of something terrible and powerful.

"But perhaps I can with this," Mulaghesh says softly.

***

Signe Harkvaldsson lies very still under the bracken as she hears the area flood with soldiers. She's given up counting their number: at first there were only the five or six of them, but now there's ten, twenty, even more, all of them surrounding the house. She can hear some of them talking, giving orders, sending signals up to the fort.

". . . know I tagged one of them. I *know* I did. I heard her scream."

". . . blonde, right? The one from the harbor? Or was I imagining things?"

". . . no blood on the door. Could be inside, but I doubt it. She's still here somewhere."

She shifts slightly to the right to look down at her injury. She didn't give it the treatment it deserved, but she didn't have the time for it: she'd hardly applied the tourniquet when she heard Mulaghesh kick in the door, which made all the soldiers come sprinting up. Her calf throbs so much that sometimes it's all she can do to keep from whimpering. She is also disconcertingly aware that she feels quite faint, no doubt from loss of blood: not only has she just been shot, but she also "donated" to Mulaghesh's ritual.

She hears screaming from inside the house. The soldiers go quiet. It takes her a moment to recognize that it's Rada screaming, howling in rage: she only ever heard the woman quietly stutter and stammer through life, so to hear her scream like that is queerly disturbing.

A soldier says, "General Biswal is on his way, correct? Good. But tell him to *hurry*!"

She groans inwardly. If Biswal is coming it's almost certain more troops will be coming too. *And the more troops that come,* she thinks, *the higher my chances are of being discovered.*

She feels faint, and knows that time is running out.

***

"And what," says Rada Smolisk, "is *that* thing?"

"Shut up," barks Mulaghesh. She shuts her eyes and tries to concentrate.

"Is that a sculpture? A piece of a sword?"

"Shut up!" She mentally reaches out to the sword, trying to feel for it. When she saw the sword in Thinadeshi's hand it seemed to speak to her, to become something in her head, a medley of ideas and sensations and histories. Yet now when she needs it most it's just a lump of metal in her hand.

"Is that one of Komayd's trinkets?" says Rada. "I know she had them. Things stolen from the Continent to use against us . . . It won't work. None of this is Divine anymore. None of this is fueled by miracles, General. It's powered by the rage of the dead."

"Will you *shut* your *mouth*?" shouts Mulaghesh.

"No. Why would I? I've nothing to lose. I've never had anything to lose." She laughs miserably, massaging her wounded knee. "Don't you agree with them, General, just a little bit? These forgotten soldiers, furious that their nation and their god didn't give them what was promised? Haven't you and thousands of your comrades been abandoned the exact same way?"

Mulaghesh stuffs the sword hilt in her pocket, draws her carousel, and points it at Rada's head. "By all the damned seas, I'll do it!" she shouts. "I'll shoot you, you damned fool!"

Rada doesn't even blink. Her face is calm and still, eyes watchful and wide. "Do it. I don't care. In a way I'm an even better soldier than you are, aren't I, General? The best soldier doesn't value life, not even their own."

"You're no soldier," says Mulaghesh furiously. "You think yourself a martyr, but you're the world's fool, Rada, fulfilling a prophecy no one even *wants* anymore."

"This world should have never been," says Rada calmly, staring up at her along the carousel. "It is accidental. The first thing we should have done after the Blink was line up and calmly walk into the ocean, entering the oblivion from which we no longer had refuge. What is the point of living if there is nothing beyond life?"

"Do you even hear how foolish you sound?" Mulaghesh holsters the carousel. "I've lived my life in the shadow of oblivion, Rada. I've seen good people go to it and bad. And I've always known I'd go there eventually, one way or another." She looks at Rada. "Maybe I'll go there now and take you with me."

She pulls a grenade from her belt. Rada's eyes grow large as she realizes what she means to do.

"No . . . ," whispers Rada.

"The sword of Voortya won't work," says Mulaghesh calmly. "And the forge won't work. But what if I detonate four grenades here in this basement with you? What about that?"

"You wouldn't."

"I wouldn't?"

"You'd be killing yourself! You *can't*! There'll be *nothing* after this!"

"That's the difference between you and me, Rada," says Mulaghesh. She wedges the grenade between her left arm and her body and puts her finger in the ring. "You think what you're doing is a victory over death, in its own way. But I know there's no beating it. So I'm not afraid."

She closes her eyes.

***

Corporal Udit Raghavan grips his rifling as the auto bounces down the path to the polis governor's house. He listens carefully as General Biswal speaks in the backseat, his voice calm, controlled. Raghavan has been close to Biswal all throughout the excursion into the highlands, and has seen an extraordinary amount of fighting in the past week; but one thing that both calms him and excites him is Biswal's seemingly impenetrable serenity, which appears to stem from an unshakable belief that what they're doing is absolutely, unimpeachably right.

Doubt is not a thing that exists for General Lalith Biswal. And this unspoken belief spreads to his soldiers.

And Raghavan, like many of his comrades, has desperately needed this in the past few days. In the mire of the highland settlements, when civilians were almost indistinguishable from insurgents, when a child of fourteen could somehow produce a pistol from within its rags and point it at your friends and comrades and fire away . . . Raghavan badly needed the shelter of Biswal's confidence not only to pull the trigger when he needed to, but also to forget the bodies left behind: some of which were quite young, or quite old, and, occasionally, unarmed.

The fog of war is an inevitability, he remembers Biswal saying. *We must accept it and move on.*

He listens to Biswal now as the polis governor's house comes into view: ". . . must make sure to take all necessary precautions. General Mulaghesh might be one-handed, but despite this she is one of the most accomplished soldiers I have ever commanded, and it appears she has lost none of her talent. Remain aware of that—but do *not* shoot unless the situation is critical."

"Do we know anything about General Mulaghesh's motives, sir?" asks a lieutenant.

"We do not," says Biswal. "But her collusion with the Dreylings is extraordinarily troubling. She knew of threats to our national security, and she chose not to reveal them to us."

"Are . . . Are you saying she's a traitor, sir?" asks the lieutenant.

Biswal is silent for a very long while. "I find that difficult to believe, even now. But she has lied to us since she first came here. And her lies have endangered the souls of everyone in this city, and in Fort Thinadeshi."

One of the soldiers curses under his breath.

"I am concerned," says Biswal. "I will say that. I am very concerned."

The auto comes to a stop before the polis governor's house. Biswal steps out and discusses the situation with the sergeant who was first on site. Then he says, "I'm going in to talk to her. For now, we need to establish a perimeter. We're extremely close to the harbor, and the Dreylings are well-armed and highly disciplined. Be on alert."

Raghavan watches as Biswal and his lieutenant enter the home. Then he takes a forward post, overlooking the cliff that leads down to the harbor.

It's difficult for Raghavan to come to terms with his disgust, his outrage. He looks back up at the polis governor's house. It's traitorous to think so, but he half hopes Biswal will shoot her. It'd be a terrible incident, but then the press might get involved, and they'd see how suspicious her conduct has been, and then perhaps they'd turn their gaze toward Ghaladesh, and the prime minister, and what she's asking of her soldiers.

Then he frowns. Something's wrong.

He can see Private Mahajan standing in the trees just before the house; but then Mahajan jumps as if startled, and starts to turn, but he hasn't lifted his gun.

Raghavan's mouth falls open as a figure rises out of the bracken. Someone tall with a sheen of gold on their head . . . Blond hair? A Dreyling?

And is that a rifling she has in her hand, using it as a support?

She lifts the rifling up . . .

Raghavan hears himself saying *stop*. He feels himself moving. It's as if he's out of his body, reacting completely by instinct, the stock of the rifling hitting his shoulder, the sights swinging to rest on the figure. . . .

And suddenly all the experiences he's just had out in the highlands come rushing back to him. The children with bolt-shots shooting at them from ditches; the old woman he tried to help stand up trying to cut him with a tiny knife; returning from a patrol to find Private Mishra facedown in the road, a screaming teenage shtani girl stabbing him over and over again, and Raghavan pulled out his pistol and he . . .

Pop.

The rifling leaps in his hands.

The figure falls to the ground among the bracken.

Raghavan blinks as he looks down the sights.

Did I do that?

Even from here he can see Private Mahajan's eyes widen in shock. Mahajan shouts, "No! *No!* Who fired? *Who fired!*"

Raghavan doesn't answer. He lowers his rifling and sprints up the hill to Mahajan. Other soldiers are streaming over as well.

Mahajan is stooped in the bracken, screaming, *"Who fired? Who the fuck was it who fired? We need a medic over here! We need a fucking medic over here!"*

"What happened?" says Raghavan as he nears. "Who was that?"

"She was surrendering!" shouts Mahajan. "I was talking to her! She was surrendering! Who the *fuck* was it who *fired,* damn you!"

Raghavan's stomach goes cold. "They . . . They had a gun. . . ."

Mahajan looks at him. "Was it you? Was it you, Corporal? She was *surrendering,* damn it. She was *giving* me the gun, Corporal! Do you have any idea who you've shot? Do you have any idea what you've *done?*"

Raghavan looks over Mahajan's shoulder at the body on the ground.

His hand flies to his mouth.

"Oh, no," he whispers. "Oh, no, no, no, no, no."

***

Mulaghesh can hear boards splintering above her. Her knuckle around the pin on the grenade is white. Her heart is beating so fast her blood is a roar in her ears.

Just do it, she thinks. *Just pull already! What are you waiting for? Don't think; just do it!*

But her hand doesn't move.

"You don't have the courage for it, do you," says Rada.

"Like hells I don't," says Mulaghesh, sweating.

"Well, if you do . . . I always thought a Saypuri would kill me," says Rada. "It only gives me a slight pleasure to know that you'll die with me."

The faint voices of the sentinels are still echoing in her head:

"*. . . brought the blade down and I grinned and laughed to feel the blood upon my face . . .*"

"*. . . charged forward and our feet ate up the earth and we howled to the sun above us and made it know fear . . .*"

"*. . . abandoned the children to run from us, but it did not matter, young or old they were our foes . . .*"

"Damn you for making me choose to do this, Rada," she says. "And damn my own soldiers for saving you in Bulikov, for doing their *job.*"

"They didn't save me," she says softly. "I died in that building. I just didn't know it then."

There's a tremendous smash from above. Then a rough shout—Biswal's voice—saying, "*Turyin? Turyin, are you down there?*"

"Get the hells out of here, Lalith!" she shouts. "Get away! I'm . . . I'm going to blow this whole damn house up!" Her hand begins trembling.

"*What? Turyin, don't be insane! I'm coming down!*"

"No! No, get the hells out of here! I mean it! I really do!" She shuts her eyes. Tears spill down her cheeks. "It's the only choice! You've got to get your troops out of here!"

"*Don't do anything! Just . . . just wait!*" The tumble of footsteps.

"No!" screams Mulaghesh. "No, don't come down! Get away, get away!"

He doesn't stop. She sees muddy boots, and then Biswal slowly descends the stairs, hands raised.

Even in her state his appearance shocks her: it's clear General Lalith Biswal has just returned from war. His uniform is covered in spattered mud and ash, and there's a splash of what Mulaghesh knows is blood on his right sleeve. His face is gray and haggard, and he looks years older than when she saw him last. She looks into his eyes, which are small and faded with fatigue, lost amidst pendulous bags. She isn't sure who's more haggard and disheartened: the old man on the steps who looks like he just lost a war, or the old woman by the forge with her finger in the ring of a grenade.

"You've got to run, Lalith," she pleads. "You've got to *run!*"

Rada's large, dark eyes flick back and forth between the two of them.

"What are those voices?" says Biswal. He looks around the room, confused. "Who is talking, saying those things?"

"It doesn't matter, Lalith, just get out of here!"

Biswal shakes his head and begins walking forward. "No. I won't. I don't know why you're here, Turyin, or what's going on or why you think you need to do this. But I know Turyin Mulaghesh, and I know she wouldn't do something like this."

"It's the only way!" she says. "These swords she's made . . . Lalith, they're waking up the Voortyashtani dead! The *sentinels*, Lalith! That's who's talking! They were promised an invasion, a war that would end the world, and now they're going to do it! I've got to destroy these swords, Lalith, I've got to!"

Biswal glances around at the swords. "I admit, this . . . is damned suspicious. But we can talk about this, Turyin. You can explain everything to me. Whatever you're trying to do, this isn't the way to do it."

"I can't explain because there's *no time*! I have to destroy them and destroy them now!"

He keeps walking. "I have soldiers here with plenty of firepower.

You *don't* need to destroy yourself in order to do it. If you explain all this to me then I'd be happy to do it for you."

"Lalith . . . Please, you've got to *run*."

"Put the grenade down, Turyin. Just put it down, nice and easy. There are four soldiers upstairs, and if you pull that pin you won't just kill me, you'll kill all of them, too."

Mulaghesh shuts her eyes. "Damn it . . ."

"I know you won't. You'd never kill another soldier. Just drop the grenade. I'm here. This is all over now. Just tell me what's happening."

Mulaghesh lets out a long, slow sigh. Her whole body is taut, trembling. Then—very, very slowly—her crooked finger works itself free of the ring.

There's a *thunk* as the grenade falls to the floor. Mulaghesh follows shortly after, collapsing to the ground. She sits on the floor with her head between her knees, taking in huge, gasping breaths.

Biswal walks over to her and extends a hand. "Your sidearm, too, Turyin."

"What?" she says numbly.

"Your carousel. I'll need it to be sure."

Without thinking, she unholsters the carousel and hands it over to Biswal. "Now," he says. "What's this about these swords?"

"You hear them in your head? Those voices saying those terrible things?"

He nods, his face grim.

"They're sentinels," says Mulaghesh. "The voices of sentinels. The sword and the warrior were one, and that's what 'thinadeskite' is—the pulverized swords of sentinels, with traces of their souls still trapped inside. Rada here realized that by remaking the swords she could awaken the dead, lure them into invading and destroying creation, as they were promised so many years ago."

Biswal stares at her, shocked. "That . . . That can't possibly be true. It's ridiculous! It can't *possibly* be true." He looks at Rada. "Can it?"

Rada's face is serenely triumphant. "Yes," she says. "It's true. And it's over. I've won. You just don't know it yet."

"You . . . You truly believe this?" he asks her.

"I don't need to believe it," says Rada. "It's reality. It's going to happen, and it's going to happen soon. A god manifested in Bulikov five years ago, General—but what's going to happen this evening will make *that* look like a minor skirmish."

He looks back at Mulaghesh. There's a queer light in his eyes. "She . . . She wants to start another Battle of Bulikov?"

"No. Worse. It'll be a massive invasion."

"By sentinels—like Zhurgut?"

"Thousands of them," says Mulaghesh wearily. "More. They'll come by ship. Sailing across the sea from the City of Blades. That's how the stories go, and that's what they were promised."

"You can't fight them," says Rada. "None of you can. You saw what Zhurgut did to the city. They'll shred you like ribbons. Even your most advanced weaponry can't stop them." She smiles beatifically. "I've freed them, you see. Trapped over there in their ruined city . . . I've let them out of the dark."

Biswal is silent. Then, to Mulaghesh: "It'd be a war, then."

"War on a level we've never seen," says Mulaghesh. "We *have* to stop it. We have to."

"It's too late," says Rada. "It's happening. Somewhere out in the sea, two realities are converging. Soon the seas will be dark with longships, and then this entire era will be over."

Biswal looks to Mulaghesh. "Be honest with me, Turyin. Speak to me as a soldier, as my equal. You really, truly believe what she's saying will come to pass?"

"I do," she says. "I've been to the City of Blades; I've seen the army of waiting dead. That's why I'm stained red, Lalith, I . . . I know it doesn't make any sense, and I know it seems impossible, but it's the truth. It'll be battle and war on a scale we've never seen before."

He holds her gaze for a long time, his eyes small and sad, the eyes of a man who has seen much death recently and expects to see more soon. "Battle and war," he says to himself, "on a scale we've never seen before . . ." Then something hardens in his gaze, something cold and furious, and he says quietly, "I believe you."

Then Biswal lifts the carousel, points it at Rada's face, and pulls the trigger.

The gunshot is deafeningly loud in this confined space. The bullet strikes the inside of Rada's right eye, just where the tear gland sits, and her right eye sinks in just slightly, giving her face a strangely fabricated look, as if she were a poorly made mannequin. The back of her head erupts, dark purple viscera spattering over the forge, sizzling furiously where it strikes the coals. Then Rada slumps over, a look of dull surprise forever frozen on her pale, round face.

Mulaghesh stares, shocked. Then she looks up into Biswal's face and sees a stony resolution there that she's glimpsed only once before, years and years ago outside the gates of Bulikov: the intent to see done what he feels should be done, and the expectation that the world will either comply or get out of the way.

"I'd been wondering how we could wake up Saypur," he muses quietly. "And another Battle of Bulikov . . . That is something I would not wish to miss."

"Lalith," asks Mulaghesh. "What . . . What . . ."

"Lieutenant!" he calls out.

"What . . . what did you do, Lalith?" she asks faintly. "What are you doing?"

Biswal nonchalantly unloads the carousel, the rounds tinkling on the floor. There's the rumble of footsteps as someone sprints down the steps. Then Biswal flips the carousel around, grabbing it by its barrels, and swings it toward Mulaghesh. . . .

The world goes bright with pain. Mulaghesh feels herself tumble sideways, the ceiling spinning above her.

A young Saypuri officer trots into the forge, though she slows when she sees Rada's corpse. "General Mulaghesh has just assassinated Polis Governor Rada Smolisk," says Biswal calmly. "I have managed to subdue her. Please take her into custody."

He walks out without glancing back at her. Mulaghesh tries to hold on to consciousness, but then everything goes dark.

I gave my child to this. I gave my child to Her.
I give myself to Her. Now, and forever.
To ask me to release my sword is to ask me to give up the one
   thing I have left.

—WRITS OF SAINT ZHURGUT, 731

16.

QUEEN OF GRIEF

Vallaicha Thinadeshi struggles to breathe. She thought this would be easy; she thought Mulaghesh would destroy the swords and they would all simply begin to drift once more. . . . But rather than drifting, rather than shifting back into the shadows of reality, she feels them all becoming *more* real, *more* themselves, *more* awake.

And as they do, they grow aware that she is not who they thought she was.

This bleeding, terrified woman is not the Empress of Graves. This is not the Divinity of death and warfare. Why is she here? Why were they listening to her? So they continue to reject her.

The process is agonizing. They reject her like flesh slowly pushing out a thorn. She wasn't aware she had become a part of them in so many ways, and for them to abandon her, force her away, is like losing a limb she never knew she had.

She finally accepts what's happened: the strange general has been defeated. She has failed. The swords still persist; they still draw the dead close. And now that Thinadeshi no longer has the sword of Voortya, she's powerless against them.

She's dying now. She can feel it. She can feel herself fade, feel the City of Blades itself push down on her, crushing her mind, removing a person who never should have been here in the first place.

She can still hear the sentinels' thoughts echoing over the beaches:

Mother . . . Mother, we are coming . . . We are coming for you . . . And then she feels them begin to leave, departing for the land of the living.

"No," she whimpers. "Please, no . . ."

It's all too much. She shifts sideways and falls over, unable to support herself. She listens to them pleading for their mother. Their voices intermingle in her head, and suddenly she remembers a day long ago, back in Saypur with her children, when they all held hands and ran down the hillside together, laughing with glee, and some of them tumbled and rolled all the way down. . . .

These are her last thoughts: the hot summer sun; the soft embrace of the grass; the tinkle of children's laughter; and the warm, eager grasp of a tiny hand.

***

Sigrud normally feels at home in the shadows. To be unseen and occupy the dark interstitial parts of the world is second nature to him. But as he squats in the shadows of the trees outside of Rada Smolisk's house, he can't bring himself to feel comfortable.

None of this is right. None of this is what he expected.

He watches as the Saypuri soldiers file out of the house, carrying what appear to be sword racks and then finally two bodies. One of them is Mulaghesh, her hands bound behind her back, with one soldier holding her feet and another holding her by the armpits. *Probably alive*, he thinks. *No one binds the hands of a dead person.* But she's also a deep, dark red color, which is . . . unusual.

The second body is on a stretcher, covered up. The only thing that he can see is that the person is very short, and, from the drip of blood from the side of the stretcher, probably very dead.

He frowns as they load up and drive away. What happened here? Why would Mulaghesh go to the polis governor's office? What could she have discovered in the afterlife to send her here and ask him to come here as well?

And where is his daughter?

Biswal exits the house. He's listening as an officer briefs him on something. Biswal is nodding, though he looks displeased, but not furious: he's being told of something they can deal with, manage, tolerate, not desired by any means but not of chief concern. The lieutenant keeps pointing to a place in the trees just beyond the house, a thick spot of bracken. Biswal looks at it with flat, cold eyes and nods. He says something short—*It is what it is,* perhaps—and then climbs into an auto, which speeds off up the road.

There are only a handful of soldiers left in the area. Sigrud waits for them to disperse, then sneaks through the trees.

There's a guard at the door of the polis governor's office, so he won't bother to try to get inside. But he creeps his way toward the spot of bracken, wondering what could have caused such consternation. . . .

He's ten feet away when he smells it. Blood—a lot of it.

He looks at the area from the shelter of a tree. He can't fully investigate in these circumstances, but he can see where the bracken's been crushed, like someone fell back into it.

And he smells something . . . familiar. The scent of cigarettes. An unusual kind, aromatic and exotic. The exact sort, Sigrud reflects, that his daughter smokes nearly constantly.

Sigrud looks uphill, in the direction of Fort Thinadeshi, and thinks.

***

Mulaghesh wakes and immediately regrets it. Her brain feels like one giant bruise. She groans and lifts her left hand to touch her brow, and remembers only too late that her hand is made of metal. It clunks into her face, causing her injury to flare up furiously. She moans pitifully and shakes her head. The back of her scalp grinds on a stone floor.

She frowns and opens her eyes. She's in a jail cell, lit with an electric light. There's only one place in Voortyashtan she knows of that has electricity. . . .

It all comes back to her like a dream.

The swords.

"Hey!" she says. "Hey, somebody!"

Silence.

She forces herself to sit up. It feels like something in her head is sloshing around uncomfortably, a dense fluid that might break through her skull's fragile walls. She feels her brow—with the correct hand this time—and finds her face is crusty with blood. Biswal must have nearly cracked her head open.

There's not much to see through the bars of her cell door: there's just a blank stone wall on the other side, dark and molded, with a fluttering electric light above it. Mulaghesh stands—this takes a lot longer than she expected—walks to the door, and leans on it.

She checks her pockets. Her holster is gone, of course, as is the rest of her gear. So is the sword of Voortya, she realizes. It could be very bad if someone threw that away, not knowing what it is.

She puts as much of her face as she can through the bars and looks down the hallway. There are just more cells to her left, but to her right about twenty yards down is a private in a dark red beret standing at attention, hands behind her back. She's too far away for Mulaghesh to see her name, but she can see the chevrons on her uniform, so she knows her rank. The door beside her is thick iron with a small glass window in its center. This must be an old part of the fortress, because none of the doors or bars look at all modern to Mulaghesh.

"Hey," says Mulaghesh. Her voice hasn't been used in some time, so she has to clear her throat. "Hey, Private! Listen. Listen, I've . . . Damn, my head hurts . . . I've got to speak to Biswal! I've got to! I don't know what he thinks is going on, but he's wrong, he's . . . he's *wrong!*"

The private is completely still. She barely blinks.

"Listen," says Mulaghesh. "It sounds crazy, Private, but . . . But we're about to be under attack. Another Divine attack is about to happen! I swear it's true, and we've *got* to act now! I wouldn't believe it, either, but . . ."

The private slowly blinks again, staring into space.

Mulaghesh summons up all of her air and bellows, "*Damn it all, Private! I might be in a jail cell but I am still your superior officer, so you had damned well better hop to an order when it's given to you! A critical threat is imminent and it is both my duty and yours to respond!*"

Nothing. It's as if the woman's deaf.

"Ah, hells," says Mulaghesh. "You're not going to listen to me no matter what I say, are you?"

The private blinks again.

"Well, shit," says Mulaghesh, and she sits down on the ground and tries to think.

***

Captain Sakthi sits in the large conference room of Fort Thinadeshi, trying to stay awake. They've been riding nearly all day and all night, so it's a struggle just to sit upright, let alone remain conscious. He glances around at Major Hukkeri and the other senior officers and can tell right away that they feel the same. They're already briefed on the new Dreyling threat. What could General Biswal's meeting possibly be about that could be so important?

The door opens and Biswal walks in, hands thoughtfully clasped behind his back. There is a strange pride and energy to him: his back is a little too straight, his stride a little too jaunty. It's hard to tell if he's pleased or furious.

He takes the podium and turns to his officers. "Thank you for being here with me tonight," he says quietly. "I know the past days have not been easy on you. We do not have much time, so I will cut to the point. We have recently discovered a long-running plot by the Dreylings to conceal Divine Voortyashtani artifacts collected from the ocean floor. My suspicion is that they did so because they feared that we would shut down the harbor project to prevent any unknown side effects. However, their duplicity has had grave effects—for, due to their actions, we are about to witness another Divine attack on our way of life. And it is our duty to defend these shores."

The room is dead silent.

"General Mulaghesh, I have discovered, was part of the Dreylings' conspiracy," says Biswal. "She and CTO Harkvaldsson plotted to assassinate Polis Governor Rada Smolisk, who had deduced their crime. I am grieved now to tell you that General Mulaghesh succeeded in this. And, as there is no honor among thieves or traitors, she also murdered CTO Harkvaldsson in order to cover up her actions. We have apprehended the general, and now have her in holding in the prison.

"Justice will be done. But first, we must fight. The traitorous general confessed that the Divine attack would be coming in by sea, an invasion of Voortyashtan itself. We now have the upper hand, my proud officers of Saypur. We are aware of the attack before it comes. And if we fight, and fight nobly, we will be the victors—and we will be heroes the likes of which will never be forgotten. And all the foolishness our nation has become involved in here on the Continent, all the waste and the stupidity, all of that will end after tonight."

Sakthi glances around at the other officers. Some stare at the general in naked horror, others in teary-eyed admiration.

"Now, go," says Biswal. "Go and man the walls, prepare our defenses, and ready your troops. By morning, we will be legends."

***

Seventy miles south of the city of Voortyashtan, the cargo ship *Heggelund* makes its final leg of the trip to the newborn harbor. Captain Skjelstad has made this trip several times in his career, shipping raw goods back and forth between Voortyashtan and Ahanashtan, but this is the largest shipment he's piloted yet: ten thousand tons of Ahanashtani cement, to be used in the overhaul of the Solda River. By his calculations the *Heggelund* is set to arrive before 0200, just in time for SDC to begin its work.

At least, that's what his calculations say. But tonight, something . . . is not right. As he stands in the bridge, consulting his countless nautical maps and timetables, he tries to prove that the impossible has not happened, even though all of his metrics and equipment says it most definitely has.

He checks the maps again.

Then he checks the barometer and the speed gauges and the fuel supply.

He pushes his hat back and scratches his head. "What in all the *hells* . . ."

They're consuming fuel at an incredibly high rate, but they *shouldn't* be—they should be on the Great Western Current, the oceanic current that not only keeps Voortyashtan's bay warm, but also moves along the coast at a great speed, making it an excellent channel for shipping, meaning they'd use less fuel.

But they aren't. Over the past two hours they've used an absurd amount of fuel, *and* have been going well under speed.

In fact, given the measurements he's looking at, it's almost as if the Great Western Current has completely *vanished,* or at the very least is in a considerable state of disruption.

His first mate runs in, breathless. "I checked again, sir—six knots."

"All right?" says Skjelstad, suspicious. "Then why are we going so damnably slow?"

"You didn't let me finish, sir," says his first mate. "Six knots *south-southeast.*"

"Six knots *south?*" says Skjelstad, boggled. "That can't be! I . . . I mean, it simply shitting *can't!* They call it the damned Great Western because it runs west, you know!"

"I know, sir," says the first mate. "I don't know how it's possible. But it . . . it seems like it is. It's like . . ."

"Like what?" says Skjelstad.

"Like it's . . . been diverted, sir."

"Diverted?"

"Yes, sir. *Blocked,* sir. The whole of the Great Western. Like it's hitting something."

"Hitting *what?*" says Skjelstad, furious.

"I've checked the horizon, sir, but I haven't seen an—"

The first mate's answer is never heard, for at that moment the ship is shook from prow to stern as if they've just plowed into another vessel. Captain Skjelstad and his first mate are knocked off their feet and sent rolling over the floor of the bridge. Skjelstad can feel the ship moving under him, tipping to one side at a speed that should never, ever be achievable on even the roughest of waters. It's like they've run ashore—but there *is* no shore around here, of course, out in the middle of the seas.

The juddering and rocking doesn't stop, but it slows enough for Skjelstad to clamber over to the window and lift himself up to see.

At first glance it appears that the *Heggelund* has plowed into a white shard sticking out of the sea, one protruding about a hundred feet above the water line. "An iceberg?" he wonders aloud. "This far south?"

But as he watches, the shard is *growing:* it's like some giant aquatic spear being shoved up through the surface of the ocean, rising into the air at an astonishing speed.

"What in all the *worlds*," whispers his first mate.

As Skjelstad watches the shard he realizes that it is actually some kind of white *tower*, for a bit farther down on the far side he sees, impossibly, a window and balcony. As it rises the tower also widens, grating up against the port bow of the *Heggelund* with a roaring screech and doing enough damage that the ship will soon be unsailable. Skjelstad is initially terrified that the tower will saw right into the hull and the deck, but then a great bubble of water rises up and shoves the *Heggelund* back, just as the rest of the towers—and there are more, Skjelstad sees, *many* more—penetrate the waters around them.

"What in all the hells is that?" cries the first mate.

The ship groans, moans, bangs, and clangs, miserably protesting this turn of events.

"I am guessing," Skjelstad shouts, "that *that* is what was blocking the Great Western!"

Then there's a discomfiting crunch and the entire ship is shoved *up*. This blow is far more violent than when they struck the tower, so much so that Skjelstad and his mate fly up into the air high enough that they nearly strike the ceiling. Then they slam back down, Skjelstad cracking his head so hard he briefly passes out.

When the world obligingly congeals back into a comprehensible series of sights and sounds, Skjelstad blinks and sees his first mate is staring out the window, pale-faced. "Uh, Captain . . . You'll want to take a look at this."

Captain Skjelstad, groaning, slowly rises to his feet. Then he looks out the window and stares.

An island has appeared in the center of the ocean. Its beaches are bone white, and in its center is an ivory-colored citadel large enough to be a small city, with a tall ivory tower in its middle. The ocean is rushing back from it, the waters drawing back like curtains from a stage, and as they withdraw he sees things standing on the white shores. . . .

Thousands upon thousands of . . . men? People? *Are* they people? To Skjelstad's eyes they look more like monsters, swaying amalgamations of horns and teeth, with enormous blades in their hands, staring out at the moonlit sea. . . . And there in the waters are thousands upon thousands of long, thin ships with pale, silvery sails. They glow very faintly, like a massive school of gigantic jellyfish, manifested here on the ocean waves as if they've always been here.

It's a fleet, he sees. A war fleet, the biggest of its kind he's ever seen.

"Where did it come from, sir?" says his first mate. "Surely all this wasn't sitting on the bottom of the *sea*?"

The monstrous figures begin to wade into the sea, moving to board their spectral vessels and rigging them up to disembark.

Well, most of the figures do. Some of them are turning to face the *Heggelund*.

There is a quiet, low sound, like many voices exhaling at once: a sustained *om*.

The figures on the beach all move, and it appears as if a flock of birds rises up from them, only the birds are glittery and strange. . . .

No, thinks Skjelstad as the shapes hurtle toward him. *Not birds. Swords.*

Then there is a crash and everything goes dark.

***

"Peace," says a voice, "is but the absence of war."

Mulaghesh jumps, sniffs, and realizes she's passed out sitting up against the wall of the jail cell. She looks around. The lights in the prison ward are dim and low, casting coffee-stain luminescence over the grim, dark walls. A figure stands on the other side of the bars of her cell, lost in the shadows of the doorway. She can catch only a glimpse of a craggy forehead and the suggestion of thick, broad shoulders.

"Lalith?" she says groggily.

"The shtanis believe that," he says. Biswal's voice is low and husky. "Here in this polis they preached that for hundreds of years. I read it. 'War and conflict form the sea through which nation-states swim,' or so Saint Petrenko said. 'Some who have had the fortune to find clear, calm waters believe otherwise. They have forgotten that war is momentum. War is natural. And war makes one strong.'"

"Lalith . . . What the hells are you *doing*? Why did you kill Rada? Did you listen to anything I said?"

"I did," says Biswal quietly. "I listened. I believe you."

"And the swords? Did you destroy them?"

He shakes his head. The dull light catches a strange gleam in his eye. Mulaghesh is reminded of a ferocious animal watching sulkily from the shadows of its pen. "I've had them moved up to the fortress for protection."

"You've *what*?"

"You say that if these swords exist then war is coming, Turyin," says Biswal. "And I believe you. But I believe that war has *always* been coming. Saypur has benefited from a substantial imbalance of power over the past seventy years. Its power and hegemony have been uncontested. But that has made it soft and weak."

"What are you talking about?"

"You've seen the people here," says Biswal. "You don't think they'd fight us eventually? They fight us now, with sticks and rocks. Imagine if they ever progress. We haven't fought a real war in forty years, Turyin, and the last one, the one you and I fought and bled in, our country tries to forget. To discuss the reality of our global position is considered *impolite*. Sooner or later, Saypur will have to awaken to reality. We will have to fight again. It can no longer allow other states to simply do as they wish. It can no longer be passive, and it certainly can no longer be *giving*." He bows his head. "And if I must be the one to wake Saypur from its slumber, then so be it."

Mulaghesh stares at him in horror. "You want to . . . to use the Night of the Sea of Swords to start a world *war*?"

"There already *is* a world war, Turyin," says Biswal. "But now it's a quiet one. The Continent is growing more powerful. It struggles against us. It's poor now, but it won't always be that way. We can either act now or pay the price later. I prefer the former option."

"But . . . But . . . This is barking fucking madness!"

"It's the truth," he says calmly. "To be a power is to make constant war upon one's neighbors. We must accept that truth or fail. And tonight will force our nation to make the decision."

"This is madness!" says Mulaghesh, furious. "And more so, it's *stupid*! This will be a fucking slaughter, Lalith, and *we'll* be the ones getting slaughtered! They outnumber us a thousand to one, and each of their soldiers is worth a hundred of ours!"

"You doubt us," says Biswal, with infuriating serenity. "Of course you would. You've been living in the shadow of Komayd, and she's never had much love for the armed services. We have advanced weaponry here, Turyin, and tremendous destructive powers. We have advanced notice. The Voortyashtani army will be drawn to here, where their swords lie, and we will annihilate them. I've already ordered the coastal batteries to prepare. And then after this battle Saypuri attitudes concerning this ruined land will *change*."

"You're a damned fool!" says Mulaghesh. "You're putting the lives of every one of your soldiers in incredible risk due to your own shitting vanity! This isn't about nation-states, or war, or the balance of power, this is about *you*!"

Biswal's huge, gnarled hands grasp the bars of Mulaghesh's jail cell, but he says nothing.

"You just want your time in the spotlight," says Mulaghesh. "You've never forgiven Saypur for refusing to admit that the Yellow March even *happened*. You've never forgiven *me* for being lauded as a damned hero of the Battle of Bulikov. You think yourself a hero, but your superiors act as if you were a monster. And you are, Lalith." Then, quieter, "*We* are. We both are, for what we did."

"For what we did?" hisses Biswal. He grips the bars so hard they rattle. "For what we *did*? Winning the *war*? Is that such a terrible thing? Saving Saypuri lives, ending conflict? Are we fiends for making this possible? Is it at all right that they should *forget* us, forget what we did?"

Mulaghesh stands up and shouts into his face, "We razed towns! Destroyed families! We not only killed civilians, but children, as they slept!"

"Because our nation *asked* it of us! They asked it of us and then they forgot. They forgot those of us who'd thrown our lives away for them! They should have been grateful, but they just *forgot*!"

"Oh, enough!" says Mulaghesh. "Enough of this! May the seas damn you, Lalith Biswal! May fate damn you a thousand times over for not learning what I've learned! We are *servants*. We *serve*. We serve as humanely as we can, and we ask nothing of our country. That is what we agree to when we put on the uniform. And all of your posturing and your dreams of conquest don't belong in this civilized world."

Biswal stares at her, white with rage. "I was going to ask you to join me," he says softly. "To help us defend against this attack. Will you refuse me, and abandon your fellow soldiers?"

"I will refuse your foolish war, yes," says Mulaghesh. "I don't serve *you*. I serve my country. Kill me if you wish, just as I did Bansa and Sankhar. Dying nobly is preferable to living savagely."

He steps back from her cell, breathing hard. He whispers, "You aren't worth the bullet." Then he turns around, hands in fists at his sides, and walks away.

***

Sigrud stands in the doorway of the darkened room in the fortress. He stares at the high metal table on the far end, and the figure lying upon it. It was easy to infiltrate—the fortress is in complete turmoil due to some announcement Biswal made—yet now that he's here he finds he can't go any farther.

He needs to move—he *knows* he will move—but he can't just yet. He can't bring himself to take a step.

The smell of blood and cigarettes is overpowering. His limbs feel faint; his heart is a hum. Sigrud je Harkvaldsson has never felt he wanted many things in his life, not with the fervent desire that some people wish for things, but right now, more than anything, he wishes to disbelieve reality, to defy what lies before him with such ferocity that the world itself is forced to obey, sending this sight scurrying back into its hole like some creeping vermin.

But he cannot. So he is left alone with the dark, empty room, the smell of cigarettes, and the young woman lying on the table.

He walks across the room to her.

He remembers when he first saw her. He was young, too young to be a father. A child, really, and his wife Hild the same. He crept into the dark bedroom, feeling he was infringing upon matters forbidden to him, for up until then only women had entered this room, an endless chain of old women and young serving girls and, of course, Hild's mother, who helped her through her labor. So to open the door to the bedroom was like peeking through to some holy temple, barred to filthy commoners such as he. But instead of any rituals or sacred ceremonies there was just Hild lying in the big bed, wan and sweaty but smiling, and her mother sitting on the side of the bed, and the basket on the table beside them. Hild said, "Come in," her voice creaky and cracked from exhaustion. "Come in and look at her." And Sigrud did so. And though he had fought for his father and sailed across many dangerous seas, he suddenly felt deeply confused and afraid, perhaps sensing, unconsciously, that his world was about to change.

And that was exactly what happened as he came to stand over the basket and the tiny pink person swaddled at its bottom, her face crinkled in displeasure, as if her birth had been an intolerable inconvenience to her. And he remembers now, as he crosses the dark room in the fortress, how he reached down to her, his hands suddenly so big and rough and unwieldy as he stroked one soft, pink cheek with his knuckle and said her name.

Sigrud stands over the body on the table.

She is dirty and mussed, her collar askew in a manner she never would have tolerated in waking life. Bits of ferns and bracken cling to her clothing, and her glasses are missing and strands of hair fall around her face. Yet despite all this she is as beautiful as he remembers her, cool and calm and utterly collected, a creature blessed or perhaps cursed with unimpeachable confidence. Even in death she appears sure of herself.

"Signe," he whispers.

Her left breast is dark with blood. An exit wound—they shot her in the back.

His hands are shaking.

To fight so long to have a thing, and to grasp it so briefly before it is yet again ripped away . . .

The door of the hospital ward bursts open. Three soldiers move in, riflings ready. "Hands up!" shouts one. "Hands *up*! Now!"

Sigrud stares down at the face of his daughter.

"We found your damned rope ladder," says another soldier. "We figured this would be the first place you'd be."

He strokes her cheek with one big, raw knuckle.

The soldiers draw closer. "Hands up, or are you deaf?"

Something falls with a *pat pat* onto the table beside his daughter. Sigrud looks at it and realizes it's blood.

His nose is bleeding. He holds his left hand out and catches three drops in his palm, the white glove turning dark, the scar below throbbing with pain.

He whispers, "I used to chase her through the forest."

"What?" says one of the soldiers. "What the hells did you say?"

More blood falls into his open palm. Sigrud makes a fist and begins to move.

***

Mulaghesh is still stewing in her jail cell when she hears the gunshot. It's muffled by the thick walls of the fortress, but she knows what it is immediately.

"What in hells?" She walks to the bars of her door and looks to the guard. "Hey—what the hells is going on?"

The guard, disconcerted, draws her sidearm. Mulaghesh sees she has lousy trigger discipline, because she puts her finger on the damn thing immediately. The guard takes a step back, looking through the glass window in the door to the prison hallway.

"What the fuck is going on?" says Mulaghesh again.

"Quiet!" says the guard.

There's silence. Then from somewhere nearby comes a bloodcurdling scream, long and loud.

The scream stops short—too short. Then more silence.

"Shit," says Mulaghesh.

"Quiet!" shouts the guard.

An enormous crash from outside the hallway door. Someone is screaming, not in threat or assault, but in sheer terror.

Then there's a face at the door—a young Saypuri soldier, his eyes wide in fright. He pounds on the glass, crying, "Open the door! Open the door, you've got to let me in! Let me in, *let me in!*"

"What?" says the guard. "Pishal, what in hells is happening out there?"

The soldier outside the glass looks over his shoulder at something. "By all the fucking seas, Ananth, let me in!"

The guard glances at Mulaghesh. "This is probably your doing, isn't it? Some damn shtanis sent here to rescue you . . ."

"Do I *look* like I know what's going on?" says Mulaghesh.

The guard hesitates, then raises her pistol and cautiously opens the door. The Saypuri soldier bursts in, terrified. "Thank the seas!" he cries. "Thank all the seas! Now shut it and—"

The soldier never finishes his sentence, as something bright red—a hand, perhaps?—reaches through the gap and rips him back through the door with terrifying speed, as if there were a rope tied to his waist with an auto at the other end. The soldier screams in terror, flailing uselessly at the door and the frame, but within a fraction of a second he's gone, the door slamming shut behind him.

"Son of a bitch!" shouts the guard. She pulls the door back open, pistol raised, and leaps through. Once again the door slams shut, its bang echoing down the hallway.

Silence.

Mulaghesh waits. And waits.

There's a scream from the other side of the door. A fine spray of blood mists over the glass window, and there is a great banging as someone fumbles with the handle. The door flies open, and the guard comes stumbling back through.

Her left arm is bloody and awkwardly twisted, as if it's been caught in some kind of monstrous machinery. She's obviously in shock, but she still has wits enough to slam the door shut with her good shoulder and lock it. She doesn't quite succeed in this last task, leaving the old iron latch just half closed, but she turns and limps down the hall to Mulaghesh.

"What the hells is happening out there, Private?" says Mulaghesh, horrified.

"Help me," whimpers the guard. "You've . . . You've got to *help* me."

"What is going on?"

"He's an animal!" she says, her mouth working to make the words. "He's a *monster*! Please, you've got to help me!"

"Open the jail cell and I will!"

The guard tries to unclip the ring of keys from her belt, but she's in too much shock to manage it.

"Hurry, damn you!" says Mulaghesh.

There's a terrific crash from the door as something on the other side slams into it. The guard stops and stares at it in horror. The door shudders again as another enormous blow strikes it. Then another, and another.

The glass window quivers. There's a tiny creak as the latch she only half closed slowly begins to give way.

"Oh, no," whispers the guard.

With one final crash the door flies open. Mulaghesh can hardly see what's on the other side before there's a soft *thump* and the guard begins screaming, not in terror but in agony. She looks at the guard and realizes that a knife has somehow sprouted from the guard's left side, up under her arm. The knife is huge and thick and black, and is quite familiar to Mulaghesh.

Sigrud je Harkvaldsson walks through the door, his chest heaving with either exertion or wrath. He's covered from head to toe in blood, his face and chest spattered with fans of gore. His face is bruised and there's a slash on his left arm, but besides these tokens it is quite clear that he was the decisive victor of whatever fights he's been in.

"Sigrud, what are you *doing*?" shouts Mulaghesh. Her fury rises as she realizes who Sigrud must have been fighting—and likely killing. "What have you done, you motherfucker, *what have you done!*"

Sigrud ignores her and walks to the guard, who is feebly attempting to crawl away. He grasps her by the head and waist and lifts her into the air, and as he does Mulaghesh sees the steady flow of blood pouring from his nose. . . .

He's in a berserk rage, she realizes. *He's gone mad.*

Though she has no idea what would put him in such a state, she rapidly begins to realize that Sigrud is now likely the most dangerous thing in Fort Thinadeshi.

She watches in horror as Sigrud slams the guard's head into the bars of the jail cell with so much force that the skin on the young girl's forehead pops open like a bag packed too tight. The guard goes silent and her eyes blank, unconscious or worse.

"Stop it!" screams Mulaghesh. "Stop it!"

But he doesn't. He slams the guard's head into the bars over and over again, thrusting forward with one arm, and with each blow her face deforms just a little more, splitting along the temple and the cheek. Blood wells up from around the guard's right eye as Sigrud pounds her head into the bars with a sickening, steady pace.

"You piece of shit!" screams Mulaghesh. "You stupid bastard!"

When the guard is beaten beyond all recognition, Sigrud tosses her aside and lunges at the bars like a wild animal. Mulaghesh is just barely fast enough to escape the grasp of his fingers, which nearly catch her neck. He screams furiously, straining to reach her, kicking and beating at the bars. Then, growling, he steps back, grasps the bars, and begins to pull.

The jail cell should be too strong for him—it really *should*. But Mulaghesh knows that Fort Thinadeshi is quite old, so, like the latch on the hallway door, not everything is built to modern engineering standards. This makes her deeply concerned when something in the doorway begins to creak and moan, and puffs of dust come floating down as if the very stone is about to give way.

Sigrud, growling and snarling, digs his heels in and heaves again. The hinges of the door begin to whine.

She knows that if he gets through that door he'll likely tear her to pieces. Mulaghesh is no slouch at close-quarters combat, but she's seen Sigrud single-handedly kill half a dozen people in combat, and he's got an age, weight, and limb advantage. She eyes the guard's corpse and the knife sticking out of her, which Sigrud has thankfully forgotten, but it's too far away.

"Sigrud!" she shouts. She steps closer. "Fucking snap out of it already—"

His hand snatches out and grabs her prosthetic hand. He rips her forward, and the buckles along her arm begin to give.

"Fucking do it, then!" she screams at him. "Kill me if you have the guts!"

He rips her prosthetic off, which sends them both stumbling back. Sigrud stands, his face furious, gripping the prosthetic like he plans to crush it, his knuckles white and his fingers flexing.

Yet it holds. The metal does not bend.

Sigrud pauses. He blinks and slowly looks down at the metal hand in his grasp. He stares at the hand like he doesn't quite understand what it is. Then he begins blinking rapidly, face trembling, and he cradles the prosthetic in his hands as if it were a child.

"No," he murmurs. "No, no, no . . ."

"What the hell is the matter with you?" snarls Mulaghesh. "You're lucky you're not dead, you stupid bastard! Though you damned well should be! You've *murdered* Saypuri soldiers!"

"She's gone," he whispers. It's like he's speaking to her prosthetic. "She's . . . She's really gone."

"She certainly fucking is," says Mulaghesh. "I hope you're damned well happy! She was a soldier of Saypur, a *soldier of Saypur!* An innocent damned bystander and you fucking beat her to death! Do you understand what that means? If this is your idea of a jail-break, it's a piss-poor one!"

"I thought . . . I thought it was all a dream," says Sigrud. He looks up at Mulaghesh, his one gray eye pale and burning on his bloodied face. "And . . . And Signe? It wasn't a dream, was it? She's . . . She's . . ."

"What are you talking about?"

"I . . . I dreamed I found her here, dead, lying on a table," he whispers. "Shot in the back. I dreamt they shot her in the woods outside of Smolisk's house."

It feels like Mulaghesh has just swallowed a lump of ice. What Sigrud is describing sounds chillingly plausible.

"Wait. Are you saying she's . . . she's *dead?* Signe's *dead?*"

"I thought I dreamed it." His voice is a whimper. "But I . . . I don't think I did. She's dead, isn't she. My daughter is dead. They took her from me just when I got her back." Then his face twists up and, to her shock, Sigrud je Harkvaldsson begins to weep.

Mulaghesh kneels at the door. She's not yet forgiven him for what he's done, but at least now she understands what sent him into a rage. "Biswal had Signe shot?"

"I don't know," he says through his tears. "I don't know. But she is dead. They have her on a table here. They stole her body and hid it away."

"I'm . . . I'm sorry, Sigrud," says Mulaghesh. "I'm truly sorry. I . . . I would never have asked her to come if . . ." She trails off. She knows such comments are useless.

"I wasn't there for her!" he says, sobbing. "I wasn't there! Never when she needed me, not ever!"

"I'm sorry," whispers Mulaghesh. "I'm so sorry. But it wasn't your fault. None of it was your fault, Sigrud. It wasn't."

Sigrud covers his face, beyond words.

She leans her head up against the bars of her jail cell. "Listen, Sigrud . . . Listen, she *chose* to be there. She chose to help me get to Smolisk's house. She did so because she saw a threat was coming and she wanted to do something to stop it. Signe spent her whole life trying to do something remarkable here, trying to make life better for millions of people. And if we don't do anything now, she'll have spent her life in vain." She reaches through the bars and rests a hand on his leg. "Please, Sigrud. Help me. Help me make what she did matter."

Sigrud sits up, still weeping. "I don't . . . I don't even understand what is going *on*."

"Take the keys and unlock my cell," she says, "and I'll tell you."

***

Captain Sakthi paces up and down the coastal walls of Fort Thinadeshi, though he is not at all sure what he and his men are doing here. They're trained for reconnaissance and surveillance, certainly, but not *naval* reconnaissance and surveillance. Almost no one in Fort Thinadeshi is really, thoroughly trained for naval assault, because no other nation has ever *had* a real navy besides Saypur, not since the Blink: the idea of any Continental nation ever being rich enough to fund such a venture is absolutely insane.

"See anything, Sergeant?" he asks, stopping behind Sergeant Burdar.

Burdar is currently nestled down atop the coastal battery with a giant telescope on a tripod glued to his eye. "Not a thing, sir," he says, his cheek crinkled as he watches the horizon. "Though it would help if we knew what we were looking for."

"Ships, Sergeant," says Sakthi. "We are looking for ships."

"That's what the general said, sure," says Burdar. "But what *kind* of ships, I ask you, sir?"

"Continental ones," says Sakthi. "Voortyashtani ones, I suppose."

"And those I don't know the look of," says Burdar, "being as they haven't been seen in nearly a hundred years, sir."

"Well, keep looking. If you see so much as a sole farting swan, I wish to know of it."

Burdar smirks. "Yes, sir."

Sakthi paces back over the walls. He has a few other soldiers monitoring the horizon with binoculars and telescopes, but, as Burdar so accurately put it, without knowing exactly *what* they're looking for, it's a little hard to adequately prepare.

Sakthi doesn't want to admit it—he is, like nearly every Saypur officer, a patriot to the core—but he's been feeling increasingly ambivalent about his service here in Voortyashtan. From the instant Saint Zhurgut surfaced in the Solda Bay, everything has gone to hells. General Biswal seemed so confident when he led the expedition out into the highlands to pursue the insurgents, but what they met was anything but conventional combat: it was ambush after ambush, and when they began to prepare for the ambushers they found it increasingly difficult to separate civilian from insurgent. And when Sakthi returned with Biswal's few elite officers, he found it impossible to determine if they were close to fulfilling their primary objective: Had the people they'd driven out of the highlands *really* been the planners of the attacks? Or had they been just a handful of shepherds with riflings in the wrong place at the wrong time? Either way, Biswal seemed content to treat it as a victory.

But now, to come back and discover some kind of invasion has been brewing on their very doorsteps . . . It's unthinkable.

And if all that wasn't bad enough, what in the *world* is wrong with Sergeant Major Pandey? Ever since the news spread of the polis governor's assassination, the man has been in a melancholy fury. Burdar even reported he'd stumbled across the sergeant sitting on the edge of the coastal walls, weeping.

Burdar speaks up: "Sir? Sir!"

Sakthi paces over to him. "Do you have something, Sergeant?"

"Things, sir," says Burdar, squinting into the telescope.

"What?"

"I have some*things*, sir," says Burdar. "Many, ah . . . *Many* things . . ." He positions the telescope just right, then backs away so Sakthi can take his place.

Captain Sakthi crouches down and puts his eye to the telescope. It takes a minute for the optics to make sense to him. At first he thinks he's seeing a strand of electric lights, dangling out there on the waves, but then he realizes he can see forms in the light.

They're not lights. They're ships. *Glowing* ships, ancient ships with sails and oars and pointed prows, but still ships.

He tries to count their number. His eye flexes in and out of focus. It seems like he's seeing the night sky, with a million twinkling stars before him.

Sakthi clears his throat. "Sound the alarm," he says hoarsely. "*Now*."

***

Mulaghesh flips the dead guard over and strips her of her uniform. It feels deeply dishonest to do such a thing, and the uniform is bloodied, but it's better than running around with her fatigues stained an unearthly red from the City of Blades. And she may have need of the pistol and sword.

Sigrud sits still and placid as Mulaghesh describes what she discovered, what she saw in Rada Smolisk's house, what Biswal did and said. Sigrud is no longer weeping, but an awful, cold stillness has seeped through him, as if he's stepped behind a veil of ice and she can no longer see the man behind it.

"So we must destroy these swords," he says softly.

"Yeah. Biswal has them here, or so he told me. He'll either have them in his quarters, or he'll have them in the thinadeskite labs, down below."

"You're sure?"

"As sure as I can be. We need to split up. I don't like it, but time is of the essence—if we even have any left. I might be able to make this uniform work until I get to him. Do you think you can sneak down to the labs on your own?"

Sigrud nods, not a trace of doubt in his face. "Many of the lower parts of the fortress are deserted. Everyone is on the walls, manning the coastal batteries."

She shakes her head. "By the seas, he's serious about trying to fight them. Let's go. If you don't find the swords, come to Biswal's quarters. If I don't, I'll do the same and come to the labs. Does that work?"

He nods. "Then let's go. The main stairway is this way."

They walk down the hallway. Mulaghesh keeps her carousel up and quietly opens the door.

She stares at what lies beyond, turning pale. "By the seas . . ."

"What?" says Sigrud, behind her. "What is it?"

She looks at him. "You don't know?"

"Should I?"

She grimaces and pushes the door open. There at the foot of the stairs are four corpses, all Saypuri soldiers, all abominably ravaged and mutilated. One man has been disemboweled, another dismembered. One soldier sits in the corner with a rifling bayonet thrust up into his abdomen. On one, a woman, she sees teeth marks on her face and neck.

Sigrud stares at the carnage. "I . . . I did this?"

Mulaghesh doesn't bother answering. *They'll kill him for this,* she thinks. *There must have been witnesses. They'll never forgive him, never let this go. Hells, I'm not even sure if I can.*

Then the sirens start to wail: a low, rising note of alarm that echoes throughout the hallways of the fortress. The very sound of it makes all of Mulaghesh's hair stand up on end.

Sigrud looks up at the ceiling. "What is that?"

Mulaghesh listens as more and more sirens begin to join until it's a shrieking chorus. "Oh, no," she says quietly. "Oh, no, no no."

"What is it?"

"Damn! Damn it all! It means the ships must have been spotted!"

"The . . . Voortyashtani ships?"

"Yes, damn it! It means that even if we *did* destroy the swords, it's too late!"

"What options do we have now?"

Mulaghesh is about to say *nothing:* the invasion is here and there's nothing they can do about it save fight, and lose. But then she recalls one of the last things Thinadeshi said to her: *It's a token, a symbol. It can be unlocked, unfolded, interpreted to be many things. You can do many deeds with it if you use it the right way, if you think about it the right way.*

"Our hand's all played out," she says quietly. "Except for one thing. But I'm not sure what I'm even supposed to *do* with it."

"Do with what?" says Sigrud.

She looks at him, jaw set. "The sword of Voortya." She describes what it looks like to him.

"And what will you do with this sword?"

"I'm not sure—but I know it's a weapon of terrific power. I just don't know how to activate it. . . . Maybe you have to get close to the sentinels for it to work—it's almost *powered* by them, in a way. But if Biswal took it, odds are it's wherever the swords are, too. So, again—the labs and Biswal's quarters."

"The plan hasn't changed, then."

"Oh, hells, *yes* it's changed," says Mulaghesh. "It means we need to book it twice as fast! Come on!"

∗∗∗

Mulaghesh looks behind her as she trots up the stairs to Biswal's quarters. It's hard to sneak about with these sirens wailing all around her, as she can't hear if anyone's ahead of or behind her, but so far these areas are deserted. Everyone's manned the walls, as Sigrud claimed.

She guessed that Biswal wouldn't keep the swords in his makeshift office at the top of the tower. But she knows where the officers' quarters are, and due to the lack of available space in Fort Thinadeshi, odds are Biswal's is there as well.

She knows she's right when she walks down one empty hallway and hears a voice in the back of her head:

"*. . . and our swords will fall like rains . . .*"

She grits her teeth and keeps moving. The awful, babbling sound of the swords intensifies in her mind. The doors get more and more ornate until finally she comes to one thick oaken door with a bronze handle.

She tries the handle. It's unlocked. She pushes it open.

The whisper of voices becomes a blast. The room beyond is wide and spacious, with a large fireplace set in the wall. To her surprise, there's a fire going—but then she sees the room is not unoccupied.

Lalith Biswal looks out of a bay window at the far end, hands clasped behind his back. Between him and Mulaghesh are the racks and racks of Rada's swords, all of them whispering and muttering in Mulaghesh's head.

She stands there for a moment, not sure what to do. She thought he'd be up on the walls with everyone else.

Then Biswal says aloud, "They only speak to people who have killed, don't they."

Mulaghesh hesitates, then walks in, shuts the door, and locks it. She takes the pistol from its holster and turns to face him. "Yeah. That's right."

"I thought as much," he says. "Most of the soldiers here think they're a figment of their imagination." He turns around and looks at her, head cocked, listening to the voices and the rise and fall of the sirens. "It's happening."

"Yes."

"So what are you here for, Turyin? I've started it. The first shot in the war. One that should have been fought long ago. There's no going back now." His words are soft and airy, and his eyes have a glazed-over look to them, as if he's on some drug. He looks at the pistol in her hand. "Are you going to shoot me?"

"Not if I don't have to." She scans the area, looking for the sword of Voortya. His living quarters aren't as sparse as she'd imagined them to be: he has a comfortable-looking couch, a few paintings, a nice table, and a half-full bookshelf.

"Are you looking for this?" he asks quietly. He reaches into his coat pocket and pulls out something small, black, curved, and strange-looking—something that could resemble a human hand clutching at air if you looked at it the right way.

Mulaghesh goes still when she sees the sword.

"What is it?" he asks.

She doesn't answer. She can't tell if he's armed or not: she doesn't see a sidearm on him, which is odd.

"What is this thing you had, Turyin? We found it on you at Smolisk's house."

Mulaghesh slowly begins moving toward him.

"I felt it ask me a question," he says softly. "It spoke to me as I carried it in my pocket, when the sirens started going off, when I knew what was coming. It was so startling I had to walk away."

Mulaghesh's grip on the pistol tightens. "What did it say, Lalith?"

"It asked me something—it asked if I *was* it. It asked if I was this . . . this *thing*, this thing I was holding, or maybe it asked if it was a part of me or if I was a part of it. I wasn't sure. I didn't know how to answer. What is it, Turyin? What is this thing you found?"

"Something that doesn't belong to you. Give it to me. Now. And I'll leave peacefully."

"And if I call for the guards?"

"I know there aren't any. You're alone here."

He considers it. "No," he says. "No, I won't give it to you."

She raises the pistol and points it at him. "I'm not joking, Lalith. I don't have time for this, not while those ships are closing in."

"I know you, Turyin," he says. "To murder one's commanding officer . . . That's something you can never come back from."

"But it wouldn't be the first time that I killed a comrade," she says softly.

"I see," he says. "But I will still not give this to you. Did you think I wasn't willing to die for this?"

"And all your soldiers with you?"

"I remain confident," he says serenely, "of our inevitable victory. We are soldiers of Saypur. We have never lost a war."

"You've gone mad." The pistol trembles in her hand. "Is that why you had Signe killed?"

"Harkvaldsson? It was an accident. An unfortunate casualty."

"You suffer so many of those, it seems." Mulaghesh is breathing heavily. "She was my friend."

"She was a Dreyling. She was in a hostile region. Both you and she were acting against the orders of the Saypuri authority here. But I am attempting to serve the greater good."

"Your idea of the greater good involves far too many innocent deaths, Lalith," says Mulaghesh. "Give me the sword, or I swear I will shoot you dead."

"A sword?" He looks down at it. "Is it a sword? For a second, when it was in my pocket, I got the strangest feeling that it was a human hand. . . . And then when I held it, I looked out on the world, and imagined I saw seas of fire, and thousands of banners in the air. . . ." He looks at her. "It's not *just* a sword, is it. It's more than these things that Rada made. What is it?"

"I'm going to give you one more chance."

"I'll tell you what," says Biswal, suddenly eager. He stows the sword back in his coat. "I remember when you trained under me almost *no* one could beat you in a sword fight. You used those wooden swords, and I could tell when someone had tangled with you. They'd be moving slow and covered in livid bruises. I remember that." He walks to one of the racks and picks up a sword—it must be a crude one, one that didn't work, because he isn't instantly possessed by a sentinel.

Lucky for him, thinks Mulaghesh, *and lucky for me.*

"I never contested you, of course. It would have been unseemly for me to do so, an officer so high above your rank. But I did wish to. To test my mettle against the best fighter under my command . . . We're both creatures of battle, Turyin, here at what might be the greatest battle of our lives. It seems only just for us to fight for the possession of this thing, this strange, whispering trinket."

Mulaghesh keeps the pistol pointed on him but doesn't speak a word.

He smiles and whips his sword through the air. "Rada's workmanship seems quite capable. Will these things break skin?" His smile dims a little. "Will you still be a worthy opponent, despite being one-handed?" He walks to one side of the room and kicks the couch away, clearing some space. Then he turns to face her, a strange light in his eyes. "Come on. Test yourself. Let the art of combat decide who is the righteous one."

Mulaghesh pulls the trigger.

The bullet punches through Biswal's chest and smashes the window behind him. A cold, chilly breeze comes pouring in.

Biswal stares down at himself in astonishment. The wound is bleeding freely, his blood striking the floor below him.

He looks up at her, outraged, shocked. "I can't believe you . . . you . . ."

She shoots again, hitting him again in the chest. He blinks, eyes wide, and the sword in his hand clatters to the floor. He takes one step toward her, then collapses to the ground, pawing limply for the blade that's now just out of reach.

Mulaghesh keeps the pistol trained on him and slowly walks over. "You shot me," he says softly. "I can't believe you *shot* me."

"I'm not quite like you, Lalith," she says. She holsters the pistol, bends down, and reaches into his coat. "You've always believed war to be a grand performance. But to me it's just killing, just the ugliest thing a person can ever do." She pulls out the sword of Voortya. It's covered in Biswal's blood. "So when you need to do it, there's no need to make a show of it."

He stares at her in disbelief. Then he says, "I'm . . . I'm not going to die, am I? I can't. I just *can't*. . . ."

Mulaghesh watches him.

"I wasn't . . . I wasn't supposed to die like this," he says softly. "I was supposed . . . to have a hero's death. I'm *owed* a better death."

"There's no such thing as a good death, Lalith," she says. "It's just a dull, stupid thing we all have to do eventually. To ask meaning of it is to ask meaning of a shadow."

Biswal's trembling face fills with fury. "I hope there *is* an afterlife," he says, his voice shaking. "I hope there *is* a hell. And I hope you go there soon, Turyin Mulaghesh." His head falls back, his neck no longer able to support its weight.

"I've already been living in one, Lalith," she says quietly. "Ever since the March."

She can't quite tell when he dies. She can tell his vision is failing him, and then perhaps he's passed out from blood loss but is still alive . . . and then . . .

Nothing.

There's a *click* from the door. Then it swings open to reveal Sigrud kneeling on the other side, lockpicks in his hand.

He looks at her, then at Biswal's corpse. "Success?"

Mulaghesh walks away without looking back. "Get me to the coast."

***

Captain Sakthi sprints up the steps to the southwest watchtower, his breath hot and burning in his lungs. He can hear the fortress yards behind him, full of soldiers piling in to arm themselves in case of a potential invasion.

Potential, he thinks wildly as he keeps running, *or almost guaranteed?*

He reviews the situation as he runs. No one knows where the hells Biswal is. The general was last seen reviewing the coastal cannons when he abruptly looked up as if someone called his name, excused himself, and walked away. Colonel Mishwal unfortunately took a bullet to the neck in the highlands, Major Owaisi is suffering from acute pneumonia contracted after tumbling into an icy Voortyashtani stream, and Major Hukkeri is frantically preparing her troops to defend the clifftops south of the fortress.

But this all means that no one is entirely sure whose order they're waiting on to fire the coastal cannons. This has never been done in the history of the fortress—who's the authority in such a situation? Yet Captain Sakthi, having seen what is slowly moving across the

North Seas to them, is more than willing to abandon all decorum of
rank if that means they make it out of here alive.

He finally makes it to the top of the watchtower. The walls of the
tower are mostly glass to allow the radio technicians to see into the
bay, so he is instantly confronted with the sight he just left.

"Oh, by the seas," he whimpers. "There's more of them! And
they're *closer*!"

The seas west of the fortress, which are often so dark, are now lit
up with a queer blue-white luminescence, giving their slow, undulating waves a creamy, green color. This curious effect extends for miles,
as if the waters have been invaded by some strange breed of algae.

But the source of the glow is obvious: it comes from the thousands
of spectral ships sailing toward them.

They are the most bizarre and terrifying things Captain Sakthi
has ever seen, splintery creations of bone and horn and metal, long
and thin and positively lethal-looking, as if someone could teach a
knife to float. Their sails are huge and billowing, not at all ragged
but smooth and silvery. And Sakthi can see someone is rowing their
countless oars, hauling at the ocean and driving the ships forward
with furious speed.

He takes out a spyglass and squints through it. He can't quite
make out who is rowing, but . . . but he thinks he can see shadowy,
monstrous figures that couldn't *possibly* be human. . . .

"By the seas . . ." He takes the spyglass away. "By the seas! What
are you *waiting* for?" he cries to the technicians. "Why haven't they
fired yet?"

"We haven't gotten the order yet, Captain," says one of the technicians sitting at a radio. "General Biswal sa—"

"General Biswal is *absent*!" says Sakthi. "Radio the damn positions to the artillery and tell them to fire already!"

The technicians look at one another, crouched in their piles and
piles of bronzed equipment. To do as Sakthi is asking is the most
severe of violations.

Sakthi grimaces, pulls out his sidearm, and points it at them. "Tell them anything afterwards! Tell them I'm culpable! Tell them to hang me! Tell them to put it on my fucking fitness report! Just fire already, *fire, fire!*"

The technicians grab a radio, turn it on, mutter in a jumble of coordinates, and then finish with, "Fire away."

There's a pause.

Then the first cannon fires.

The boom of the cannon is so loud it feels like it will shake Sakthi's bones to the point of dissolution. The coastal batteries light up with the flare as if a spotlight has shone down on them, and three of the technicians put binoculars to their eyes. Sakthi holsters his weapon, fumbles for his own spyglass, and puts it to his eye just in time to see a column of water erupt up from the ocean.

One of the technicians says, "Miss."

The cannons fire again and again, targeting the foremost ship. It feels like it takes an agonizingly long time between each blast. Then finally the Voortyashtani ship erupts in a burst of dark smoke, and it begins to drift on the ocean, a flaming, smoking, directionless hulk that now threatens to crash into the other ships.

The technicians cheer, and Sakthi takes away his spyglass to join them. But as he does he sees things in perspective: the smoking, flaming ship is but a fraction of the flotilla, a tiny candle burning in a sea of glittering, soft light.

We'll have to do that a thousand more times for it to make a difference, he thinks, his stomach sinking. *We're fucked, aren't we? We're so desperately fucked.*

***

Mulaghesh and Sigrud are sprinting across the fortress courtyard when the first cannon goes off. It's incredibly, deafeningly loud, and though the courtyard is full of soldiers preparing for combat it's immediately clear that they've never heard the coastal cannons in use, nor did they ever expect to. They're unnerved, ragged and exhausted from the highlands excursion, and totally unprepared for what might happen.

I have to stop this, thinks Mulaghesh. *Or else those sentinels will cut through these kids like a hot knife through butter.*

"They likely took down my rope ladder," says Sigrud. "So I am not sure how to get out. All gates will surely be watched."

"All but one on the northern side," says Mulaghesh.

"There's a gate on the northern side of the fortress?"

"The loading dock for the thinadeskite mines," says Mulaghesh. "I can almost guarantee no one's bothered to put a body on that exit."

She's right: in all of the confusion and chaos, there are no guards stationed at the loading dock, though it is still penned in with a canyon of tall, forbidding wire fences held up with tall wooden posts.

"No wire cutters this time," says Mulaghesh. "Shit!"

Sigrud grunts, takes off his coat, and wraps his hands in it. Then he walks to one of the posts, grabs three strands of the barbed wire, and heaves.

With the *plunk* sounds of snapping harp strings, the bolts holding the wire to the post pop out. He stomps on the handful of wires with a boot, then grabs another handful of wires, heaves it up, and opens a narrow hole in the fence. Mulaghesh dives through and Sigrud follows, though his hands are now bleeding and the wires manage to score him over his shoulders and back.

They run north and west along the walls of Fort Thinadeshi. These walls are dark and unmanned, as nearly all the fort's focus is on the west and the south. Yet such is the power of the cannons that each time those on the western walls go off, even here on the opposite side of the fortress, it's like a miniature sun has risen, the pale, burning light rippling across the harsh cliffs.

Mulaghesh can't yet see what they're firing at. She's not close enough yet. But she knows. She saw them, after all, in the City of Blades.

Then a voice shouts from the walls: "*You!*"

Mulaghesh looks up and sees the furious face of Sergeant Major Pandey looking down on her. She's not sure why he looks so angry, but she doesn't want to wait to find out. "Damn," she says. "Run."

They move, sprinting over the cliffs with the boom and flare of the cannons just to the left over their shoulders. The western horizon is lit with a queer, unearthly light, and as they near the cliffs she can see the tips of something glowing out on the waters.

She grips the sword of Voortya in her hand. It's sticky with Biswal's blood, but it's still dead, still dormant. She has no idea what to do with it, or even if there is anything to do with it—it might simply be too late.

There's a crash from far behind them. She glances back and sees someone has driven one of the fortress autos through the wire fence and is speeding over the rocks at them in pursuit. The driver must not care for their own well-being or the auto's, as they push the vehicle into terrain most drivers would never attempt. She can hear the tires crunching, the creak of the suspensions, a crack as its bumper dips and smashes into one of the stones. It's obvious that, whoever it is, they're pursuing Mulaghesh and Sigrud and will overtake them soon.

Mulaghesh points ahead at a small gully. "There!" she cries.

She can see the auto's headlights now out of the corner of her eye. Another crunch as it plows over a stone . . .

She and Sigrud dive into the gully, their elbows banging and scraping on the rocks. The car's engine roars once more and it surges over them.

There's an enormous *pop* as the auto hits the gully, dipping forward enough for its wheels to catch the lip just at the wrong angle. Mulaghesh suspects that the axle has snapped upon impact. More concerning, though, is the spray of rocks and rubble from the impact. She can feel small, stinging stones dappling her body, and nearby Sigrud cries out in real pain.

The auto rumbles and rattles a few feet forward past the gully, awkwardly limping into the brush before coming to a grinding halt. Mulaghesh sits up, pulls out her pistol, and takes stock of herself: she's got a few cuts and bruises, but nothing serious. Sigrud, however, has taken a sizeable stone to the left forearm and is cradling his hand in his lap, cursing prolifically. She can tell the second she sees it that his arm is broken.

She brings herself up into a kneel and draws a bead on the auto's passenger door. Someone inside fumbles with the handle, then shoves it open and crawls out. There's another blast from the coastal cannons, washing the cliffs with pale light, and she watches as a battered, furious Sergeant Major Pandey, his eyes red and his cheeks wet with tears, crawls out to stand on the cliffs.

He draws his sword and advances on her. "*You!*" he cries. "*You!*"

"Pandey?" Mulaghesh lowers the pistol. "What the hells are you *doing?*"

"*You're* the reason she died!" he screams at her. "*You're* the one who killed her!"

"What are you talking ab—"

Before she can finish speaking Pandey dives at her, thrusting his sword out in a quick, deadly jab. Mulaghesh rolls away, feeling the stones reverberate as the blade scours over them. She holsters her weapon, stands, and backs away, hands up to show she's no threat. "Pandey! Pandey, what do you think I did?"

"I saw her!" he screams at her. "I saw her on the table! I saw her down there in the dark!" As he screams her nostrils catch the sour tang of alcohol on his breath, and she realizes he's likely drunk. But if so it hasn't dampened his sword work any, for he sweeps his blade at her in a lightning-quick strike that nearly guts her.

Mulaghesh dives away again, but she's forced to use her false hand to help her land, so she falls badly. She can hear him coming at her, his footfalls light and quick, and she draws the sword she took from the guard just in time for its blade to meet his with a ringing *snap*.

"I didn't kill Signe," says Mulaghesh furiously. "I didn't pull the trigger! I wasn't even there!"

"You're a liar!" He disengages, sweeps around, lunging at her exposed breast with a quick thrust. She bats his blade away, rolls backward, and stands, finally assuming a defensive stance.

"You got her mixed up in your conspiracy and then you killed her!" he screams.

"Pandey, damn you, there are more important things happening right now!"

"More important? More *important?*" He rushes at her, a furious blitz of brutally clever attacks that she only barely manages to defend. "She was the only important thing I ever had!"

Again he lunges at her, piling riposte upon riposte as she just barely manages to parry. She knew Pandey was brilliant with a blade, but she never sparred with him when she was stationed in Bulikov. As her forearm and tricep begin to ache, she begins to doubt if she could have managed to take Pandey even in her prime: he fights with liquid grace, his sword seeming to dance weightlessly through the air. Yet he also fights with the fury of the bereaved: as she sees more and more gaps in his defenses, she becomes aware that Pandey is focused wholly on attack, indifferent as to whether or not she can land a blow, indifferent to his own life. She ignores her instincts and refuses to strike. *I've killed enough,* she thinks desperately. *I've harmed enough. I won't do it to you, Pandey, I just won't.*

She's saved only by the uneven ground, which she uses to her advantage, scrambling over the rocks as Pandey flies at her with the speed and poise of a much, much younger person.

"Do you even know what that's *like?*" he cries. "Have you ever had anything in your damnable life besides the service?"

Over Pandey's shoulder she glimpses Sigrud hauling himself out of the gully and limping at them, clutching his broken arm. "Don't, Sigrud!" she shouts. "He'll kill you! I mean it, he wi—"

He forces her into a bind, his blade striking hers with such force that it shakes her all the way up into her shoulder. Again she falls back, and again he pursues.

The cannons boom and shriek, illuminating Pandey from behind with a hellish glow. Behind her the glowing vessels from the City of Blades are less than a quarter mile from the shore, and closing fast. Sometimes the shells strike home and one of the ships explodes, a great fireball laced with black smoke unfurling into the sky, battering them even here with a blast of broiling heat. Yet still Pandey leads his assault, beating down her defenses with seemingly inexhaustible stamina.

She missteps over a slick stone. Pandey jabs at her and her left arm lights up with pain. She can't take the time to see, but she can tell from how much weaker her arm suddenly feels that he's likely slashed open her tricep. *Too slow*, she thinks. *Just too damned slow . . .*

"Pandey, stop!" she shouts. "I didn't mean for this to happen, none of it! Bu—"

"But it happened!" he screams, his face still wet with tears. He slashes forward and she just barely manages to stop his blade.

"I don't want to hurt you, Pandey!"

"Hurt me?" he cries. "*Hurt* me?" He slashes down, and she reacts just in time to deflect his blade. "Am I not hurt!" he roars. "Am I not wounded!"

He thrusts forward again, and she bats the point of his sword away. But it's getting harder and harder each time.

She thinks rapidly. She's seen enough of his technique that she knows what to expect now: another thrust, turning into her and pushing forward and down with his right shoulder. She has an idea, though it's a dangerous one: if she's even slightly wrong about this odds are she'll take his sword right in the gut. But if it works there's a chance she can disable his right arm, putting him out of the fight.

"I loved her more than anything in this world!" he says, still weeping. "I loved her!"

"I know," she says.

"You don't!" he snarls. "You *don't!*"

He attacks, and he does it exactly as she expected: a powerful, deadly thrust down toward her belly.

She uses her own blade to force his sword down to where she's just placed her metal false hand. The point of his sword sinks an inch or two into the hinge at her false hand's wrist, but goes no farther— Signe's metalwork holds fast.

At the same time, Mulaghesh thrusts her own sword up, aiming for Pandey's armpit. . . .

But then Pandey screams in rage, raises himself up, and tries in futility to force his blade down through her hand; yet as he does he lifts himself up and onto the point of her sword.

The blade smoothly enters his rib cage and sinks a half a foot into his chest, up toward his heart.

Pandey freezes with a choke.

Mulaghesh blinks, staring at what she's done.

"No," she whispers.

He coughs faintly. He tugs his sword free of her false hand and steps back, her blade sliding out of him.

Blood spatters onto the stones. His sword clatters to the ground.

"P-Pandey?" says Mulaghesh.

He looks down at himself. Another cannon fires behind them and his features glow with bright white light. All the rage and fury is gone from his face, and instead he looks confused and shocked but also strangely disappointed, as if he'd thought the whole time that this might happen but never quite believed it. He looks at his hand, which is coated in blood as if he'd dipped his fingers in a bucket of it. Then he looks at his side and sees the waterfall of red dribbling out from between his ribs to tumble down his waist to his boots.

His legs go out from under him and he falls to the ground.

"Pandey!" she screams. She throws her sword away and kneels beside him.

Blood is pouring out of his right side. He coughs, and she knows she's badly punctured a lung. He coughs again, more violently, and blood sprays from his mouth and dribbles down his chin.

He's drowning in his own blood. She knows he is, but she has no idea what to do.

"Pandey, no," she says. "No! Keep breathing, Pandey, keep breathing!"

He tries to speak then: he snorts strangely, trying to draw air into himself to form the words, but he only coughs more. Then he mouths six words to her, his eyes shameful and desperate and terrified: *I messed up, ma'am. I'm sorry.*

Mulaghesh realizes she's weeping. "Dammit, Pandey. Oh, damn it, I . . . I didn't mean to, I *didn't*."

He coughs again. The lower half of his face is slick with blood now, and there's a shallow pool of it on his side. He tries to speak again, but the effort is agonizing.

She places her hand on his cheek and says, "No. No, don't talk. Don't. You don't need to. It'll make it worse."

His eyes are red and watery. He stares at her, afraid, his handsome, boyish face marred by the spray of blood from his mouth. She smooths down his hair and whispers, "I'm sorry, I'm so sorry. We owed you so much more than you were given. I'm so sorry."

He seems to lie back a little, to stop struggling to force his lungs clear. He steels himself and shuts his eyes as if preparing for some horrible blow. But then he relaxes, his brow growing smooth, his eyes calm, and Sergeant Major Pandey slowly gains the look of someone who's just fallen into slightly uncomfortable sleep.

The cannons rage behind her. Just ahead, the ships threaten to land. She can see their decks brimming with Voortyashtani sentinels, ancient warriors eager to leap into the fray.

But she has no attention for any of it. She feels the scream begin to build in her.

Again, a child of her nation she was responsible for. Again, someone who once trusted her with all of their heart. Again, blood on her blade and a body cooling underneath foreign skies.

Again, again, again.

The world is afire. The night is filled with the screams of soldiers and civilians, scrambling and scrabbling in the face of incomprehensible war.

She can see Sigrud watching her, bent double, uncertain what to do.

She wishes to scream to him. Perhaps not just to him, but to the fortress, to the ships, to the terrified people at the base of these cliffs, to the night skies and the pale face of the moon turned a muddy brown behind a veil of smoke.

But then there's a voice—a voice in her head that is not her own.

The voice whispers to her, very definitely asking her a question, soft and quiet yet filling the whole of her mind:

Are you a part of me? Am I a part of you?

Something nuzzles at her thoughts, something curious and yet welcoming. It is perhaps the strangest sensation she's ever felt, but she can tell there is some mind or entity reaching out to her—and she has the unshakable feeling that this entity is speaking from her right pocket.

She reaches in and pulls out the sword of Voortya.

The atmosphere in the westernmost watchtower grows grim and desperate as the technicians rattle off positions and coordinates to the coastal cannons, though the ships are now so close and so thick that it would be difficult to miss them. Captain Sakthi watches, gripping his spyglass so hard he's vaguely concerned it may shatter, as the bay of Voortyashtan lights up again and again as shells strike their targets. The bay now appears to be littered with giant prayer lanterns, the seas dotted with flaming, burning wrecks. Ordinarily this would be enough to stave off any coastal attack, but the other Voortyashtani ships simply shove them aside as they plow toward the coast, limitless and indomitable.

The city of Voortyashtan itself is in a complete uproar as citizens stampede up the cliff roads, led by SDC workers. Major Hukkeri's battered, exhausted battalion is taking up positions on the southern cliffs, desperately trying to prepare for the impending invasion, but the flood of citizens out of the city has turned her work into utter chaos.

In his head, Sakthi rifles through all the scenarios that were taught to him during training, all the strategies and cunning feints and clever tactics he might employ in the battlefield to turn situations to his favor.

He considers his options, and realizes with a sinking heart that he has none.

Then one of the technicians says, "Who the hells is that on the western cliffs?"

Captain Sakthi wheels around, frowning. He glasses the cliffs and sees two figures just to the northwest of them, on the very point of the rock. It's hard to make anything out, but one of them has a hand that shines very curiously, as if made of metal.

His mouth opens, surprised. "General Mulaghesh?"

***

Mulaghesh listens to the sword.

It begins to show her things: sensations, concepts, avenues of reality and emotion that were never accessible to her before, aspects of existence hidden to the mortal mind.

The world flickers around her: for one instant she is back in the City of Blades; in another she is on the cold, damp mountains along the Solda; and in yet another she stands at the bottom of a mass grave, watching as a never-ending cascade of bones pours over the lip, indescribable casualties from an endless war.

Not one war, she realizes—*every* war, all wars ever fought by humanity. Never one side prevailing over the other, never separate and disparate groups, but a blazing, monstrous act of self-mutilation, as if humanity itself was cutting open its own belly to send its intestines spilling into its lap.

The sword speaks to her: *Are you these things? Is this you?*

It shows her an image then: a solitary silhouette of a person standing on a hilltop, looking out upon a burning countryside.

She knows, in some wordless, instantaneous fashion, that this figure has not struck every blow in the war it watches, yet it is still responsible for all of them: this person, this entity, has created every battle of this war, caused every scream and every drop of blood. And in its hand the figure holds . . .

A sword. Not a sword, *the* sword: bound up in that blade is the soul of every sword and every weapon that has ever been, every bullet and every bolt and every arrow and every knife. When the first human raised a stone and used it to strike down its kin this sword was there, waiting to be born: not a weapon, but the spirit of all weaponry, harm and cruelty both endless and everlasting.

Do I, the sword asks her, *belong to you?*

The cannons flare around her. Pandey is now pale and cold, just like Signe Harkvaldsson, and long before them Sankhar and Bansa.

Woresk, Moatar, Utusk, Tambovohar, Sarashtov, Shoveyn, Dzermir, and Kauzir.

Weeping, she bends her mind to the sword, and says:

Yes. Yes, you do.

The blade of the sword flickers to life, greedily accepting her, embracing her. And the world begins to change.

***

Sigrud frowns as Mulaghesh stares down at the black handle of the sword, seemingly in a trance. He begins to say, "What are you doing?" when suddenly something is . . . different.

Is he going mad, or does the hilt now have a blade? Faint and luminescent, like the flame of a candle just where it touches the wick?

Then there is a blast as if a shell has struck the coast. Sigrud is thrown back, his broken arm howling in pain. A wave of cold air rushes over him. Once it passes he sits up, blinking, and looks to find Mulaghesh, assuming that she is dead.

But she is not dead. He watches as she tears off her false hand and walks to the very edge of the cliff, stalking forward with a curious, menacing swagger, the movements of someone who intends to do violence and do it soon. The strange blade flickers in her hand, its muddy yellow light spilling over the stones.

Yet as she moves he sees something . . . *behind* her. Or perhaps *over* her, as if she is a drawing in a book and someone has laid down a piece of wax paper with something sketched on it, so both images are separate yet visible at the same time. . . .

A figure, huge and tall, arrayed in darkly glittering plate mail.

Mulaghesh stops at the cliffs just over the thousands upon thousands of ships, looks out upon the fleet, raises the sword, and begins to speak to them.

***

She can feel them now, all of them: her children, her followers, those whom she wrought and yet wrought her in turn. She can feel them on the countless ships: bright, hard diamonds of battle. They are not as they were once, she can tell: they are shadows of themselves, the barest shade of souls. They lost themselves just as the city fell apart in the great cataclysm that brought this nation to its knees. But they are still hers. They are doing what she promised them they would do. And even now they seek her.

She calls to them: *"Children of warfare!"*

The cannons roar and rage. The ships burn and the people scream. They do not hear her over these joyous sounds.

Again: *"Children of warfare!"*

The slap of the oars. The howl of the wind. The shriek of the shells. Still they do not hear her.

She takes in a huge breath, the cold, smoky air reaching every inch of her lungs, and howls to them, *"Children of warfare! Children of Voortya!"*

The call echoes out, out, out, over the seas, through the flames, through the smoke, over the dark waves, until it finally, finally reaches the warriors aboard one single ship.

They stop rowing. They turn to look at the cliffs.

A single thought goes trickling through the vast army below her:

Mother?

They turn their thoughts to her, inspecting her, seeking her out. They parse through her mind, her soul, and slowly, slowly, slowly believe her to be who they wish her to be. And as more and more of them believe, she begins to grow.

The ground falls away below her. She feels the plate mail on her shoulders, the metal boots upon her feet. She feels her neck creak with the weight of the helm upon her brow, and she peers at the world from behind a cold, steel face.

Her face.

***

SDC Security Chief Lem watches, haggard and pale, as the endless line of citizens and SDC workers toil up the mountain paths. The bay beyond is already bright with the queer, spectral light of the warships, and he knows they'll be here soon. Though could there even be a safe place now, with so many ships filled with those monsters?

Then someone screams: "Look! *Look!*"

They look westward, just west of Fort Thinadeshi, and stare as a huge, dark figure swells up against the night sky. The figure is lit from below by the lights of the ships and the flaming wrecks on the waters, but even with these wavering lights one can still see that blank, metal face, dark-eyed and pitiless, and the enormous, terrifying sword in its hand—its one and *only* hand.

"No," whispers Lem. "No, it *can't* be. It simply *can't* be! She's dead! Everyone knows she's dead!"

There is a new sound beyond the cannons and the flames and the screaming civilians: a chanting from the bay as the countless warriors aboard the ships sing one word over and over again, or rather one *name:* a primitive, syncopated chant like the beat of a war drum:

"*Voortya! Voortya! Voortya! Voortya!*"

***

The soldiers in the westernmost watchtower stare in horror as the giant figure swells until it almost completely blocks out their view of the western seas. It seems to have come from nowhere, sprouting out of the rock itself. Its back is covered in broad plate mail, each segment carved with horrific illustrations of violence and depravity. The burning bay beyond makes the sight even more hellish, a Saypuri nightmare come to life.

The goddess of war, the Divinity of death, reborn upon these savage cliffs in Saypur's darkest hour.

"By the seas," whispers Sakthi. "By the seas . . . It simply can't be!"

One of the technicians turns to Captain Sakthi. "Should we . . . ah, fire, sir?"

"We *can't* fire on her!" says another. "She's much too close! We don't have the right angle!"

They all turn to look at Sakthi.

He sighs. "Oh, dear."

* * *

Mulaghesh faces the fleet of warships and the warriors chanting her name—or what the sword *says* is her name. It's hard to tell. . . . The sword says many things to her, whispering to her, urging her to be glad, to be filled with bright, hot, happy fury at this moment, for she is reunited with her army, with those who built her empire.

Yet all Mulaghesh can think of is the body at her feet, and all those she has left in her trail.

She takes a breath and howls out to the sea, *"Children of war! Children of Voortya!"*

The warriors scream and howl in celebration.

She screams, *"Look at me! Look at me and know me!"*

The bay falls silent as the warriors await her words.

She cries out, *"I am the Empress of Graves! I am the one-handed Maiden of Steel! I am the Queen of Grief, I am She Who Clove the Earth in Twain!"*

The world keeps distorting itself around her. She feels huge, gigantic, a titan standing underneath the sky—yet she knows she feels tears on her cheeks, hot and wet and real.

"I am war!" she screams to them. *"I am plague and I am pestilence! In my wake is an ocean of blood! I am death, I am death! Listen to me, look at me and know me, for I am death, I am naught but death!"*

* * *

The Voortyashtani citizens watch in horror as the booming words echo across the waters to them. The figure on the clifftops extends its arms to the sky, as if begging lightning to strike it.

The voice cries: *"I have killed countless soldiers! I have left them rotting in the fields, and their mothers never learned where they came to lie! I struck them down even as they begged me to stay my hand! I have broken open the gates of great cities and listened to the citizens weep! I have done these atrocities. I have! Do you hear me?"*

The crowd of Voortyashtanis is silent, and yet for some reason they begin to weep as they listen to the figure scream to the seas and the skies. Lem himself finds it strange—these words do not have the ring of a declaration of war, but rather they sound like a confession, full of agony and sorrow.

The voice howls, *"I have killed women! I have killed children! Do you hear me? Do you hear me? I have done these things! I have burned down their homes, I have killed them in their beds! I have walked away as they screamed for their loved ones! I have abandoned children to freeze in the dark winter nights! I have done these horrors and countless others!"*

The figure holds its sword high in the air and screams, *"I am war-fare and I am death! I am sorrow never-ending! Look upon me! Look upon me, I beg of you, look upon me!"*

***

Mulaghesh raises the sword. She feels as if it is pulling her, like she is merely its vessel, its instrument. She knows it wants her to turn and bring its edge down upon the fortress, to strike it so hard the very cliffs are sundered beneath it, and then once this is done she shall lead these warriors forward, through Voortyashtan, down the Solda, across the face of the Continent, and from there across the world.

Just as she said she would. Just as she promised them. Just as she swore, just as they are owed.

Yet some part of her resists, thinking only, *I am so very tired of this.*

And as this thought goes skittering through her mind she suddenly understands that she does not hold the sword: rather, it holds *her,* imprisoning her like it is a massive, dark cavern, and she is just a tiny creature lost in its darkness, trapped inside of it.

She feels the destruction gathering in the sword.

No, she says to it.

It wants to fall. It wants to cleave flesh from bone. It wants to split the earth in two.

No, she says to it.

She feels all the thoughts and desires of all of her warriors pulling at it, wishing it into movement, forcing her to be the force they expect her to be.

Her arm trembles as she resists. *No! No, I won't let you!*

Their thoughts rise up to her in a muttering wave: *You must! You must, you must, you must! We did as you asked. We became the warriors you wished us to be! Now give us what we are owed! Give us what you promised!*

Her elbow strains against the sword. It's so heavy it's as if she holds the moon itself in her hand, her will against the will of the countless dead.

Then she thinks, *The warriors I wished them to be . . .*

She remembers Villaicha Thinadeshi in the City of Blades, telling her: *. . . you of all people should know that war is an art requiring decorum and formality. It feverishly adheres to rules and traditions—and that can be used against it.*

Yes, she thinks.

She twists her wrist, points the sword down, and diverts all its power, driving it into the cliff at her feet. The stone parts as if it were made of cotton.

The ground trembles underneath her, threatening to collapse. Yet it holds.

The warriors aboard the ships stare at her, confused. Why does she not do as she promised? Why does she not permit them to wage the last war?

Mulaghesh looks out at the bay, sets her jaw, and rips the sword out of the cliff.

Somehow the sword understands what she wishes to do, and cries to her, *No, no! You cannot, you must not!*

She forces her will upon it, using every measure of her conviction to change it, to unwrap and unfold and redefine and rewrite it and all it stands for—an invisible, agonizing battle that exhausts her, nearly kills her.

The sword cries out: *I was meant for death! I was meant for battle! I was meant for war!*

Mulaghesh's answer has the ring of cold iron: *Times have changed.*

She finishes her work. Then she turns to the warriors below.

She begins to speak, her voice quaking with fury: *"Listen to me, my children! Listen to me! You have slain many and taken many lands! You have won countless battles and waged countless wars!"* Her voice rises until it echoes like thunder. *"Yet I now ask of you—are you marauders or are you servants? Do you give power to others, or do you hoard it? Do you fight not to have something, but rather fight so that others might one day have something? Is your blade a part of your soul, or is it a burden, a tool, to be used with care? Are you soldiers, my children, or are you savages?"*

The bay is silent save for the flicker of flames and the slap of the waters. The sentinels stand upon their ships, staring at her in confusion.

Then one sentinel calls to her, *"Mother, Mother! What is this you speak of? What is this you describe? That is not what a soldier is! A soldier does not give, they take! A soldier does not serve, but forces others to serve! A soldier does not cede power, but wields it, wrests it from the hands of any who dares lay claim to it! A soldier never gives, a soldier never serves! A soldier fights only to kill, to claim, to take, to conquer! That is what we are!"*

The dead murmur their agreement, their low mutterings floating over the waters.

Mulaghesh bows her head. Her disgust and outrage and contempt burn bright within her, and the sword reacts, flaring brighter than the midday sun, a white eruption of purest light, as if she holds in her hand the morning star.

She holds the sword high and screams in fury, *"THEN I FIND YOU WANTING! NO SOLDIERS ARE YOU IN MY EYES! NO TRUE SOLDIERS ARE ANY OF YOU! AND SO I SAY OUR AGREEMENT IS BROKEN!"*

She hurls the blazing sword down.

***

Captain Sakthi stares in disbelief as Voortya swings her hand out and throws the glittering, burning sword down to the waters. It is a bolt of lightning, a comet, a blaze of light so bright it's like the sky has been split open. He raises his hand to shield his eyes, watching through the cracks in his fingers as this fiery, flickering star comes shrieking down to touch the waters at the very center of the fleet.

The horizon erupts. It's like a thousand shells have gone off, like the death of a star, a wall of purest, bright white light flying at them.

Sakthi shuts his eyes. He cries out and crumples to the ground, covering his face with his arms, bracing for the impact. Surely this explosion will send a crushing wave of water roaring up the shores. Surely shrapnel will fall on them like screaming rains, rending them to pieces. Surely they'll dissolve in a wave of hot fire that will set the whole of the countryside alight.

But nothing comes.

He waits. Then he lowers his arms, raises his head, and looks.

His eyes are still adjusting, so the dimly lit world bursts with faint blue-green bubbles. Once this passes he sees the bay is covered with thick, curling smoke. But he can't see a single mast or burning hull in any of it.

The wind picks up. The smoke curls faster, then withdraws like a curtain.

He slowly stands.

The bay is empty. No, not just empty—it's calm and placid, as it has been nearly every night this week. Not a lick of flotsam or jetsam bobs upon its shores, and the figure of Voortya has vanished with it.

"Gone," he says. "They're all gone."

He is still too stunned to react when all of the technicians begin cheering.

***

Sakthi tries to run faster, but his body is rebelling against him now. He's been racing about for nearly four hours, moving at breakneck speeds since Biswal first mentioned this mad night was happening, and now his feet ache and his knees creak and some of his lower vertebrae are complaining terribly. Yet he knows his fellow soldiers must be as exhausted as he is as they sprint over the rocks to where they saw the Divinity, their torches bobbing up and down in the dark, so he pushes himself a little harder, raising the guttering red flare in his hands and crying, "To me, to me! Hurry, my boys and girls, hurry!"

It's all so impossible. He's thinking the same thing everyone else is: Did they really see the Divinity of war tonight? And did she really strike down her own army, wiping them out in a single blow? Or did something . . . *else* happen tonight?

Sergeant Burdar flings out a finger. "There, Captain! Over there!"

There, on the farthest point, the shape of a single person sitting on the cliffs.

Captain Sakthi sprints toward them, crying, "Don't shoot, damn you, don't shoot a damn thing unless you have to! Don't you damned well fire a shot, my boys and girls!"

They drop back, allowing him to be first on the scene. He's not sure what he's expecting: perhaps they'll find the sword of Voortya still buried in the side of the cliffs up to the hilt. Or perhaps they'll find some unearthly, Divine wound in reality, like they have in Bulikov. Or perhaps the cliffs will be sloughing away entirely, unable to support the madness of this evening.

But as his soldiers encircle the people on the cliffs, he finds it is nothing so strange, nothing so surreal. Captain Sakthi is a veteran of combat, so the sight is not unfamiliar: a young soldier, lying on the ground, pale and still with a wound in his side; and there next to him curled over double is a woman, sobbing hysterically, as if it were she, not the soldier, who was mortally wounded.

She says the same words over and over again: "No more, no more. Please, please, no more."

People often ask me what I see when I look at the world. My answer is simple, and true.

> *Possibilities. I see possibilities.*

—LETTER FROM VALLAICHA THINADESHI, 1649

17.

∂efiant Love

Mulaghesh stares at the ceiling of the jail cell.

Everything hurts. Her head, her left arm, her right arm, her knees, both ankles, though one a little more than the other. Even her left hand hurts, her missing hand—a curious, ghostly ache, though perhaps that's because she still doesn't have her prosthesis back. Yet none of it's a real hurt, somehow. It's all far away, muted, as if it's happening to someone on the other side of the world.

It takes her a second to hear the sound of the footsteps. That's unusual: ever since Major Hukkeri had them throw her in here they've mostly left her alone, except for bringing her food or taking out her latrine. They treat her, in many ways, like a bomb that's about to go off, and she can't quite blame them. So who's brave enough to get near her now?

She watches as the visitor comes to the door of her cell, and though it's dark she can tell by the scintillating wall of medals and ribbons on their chest that this is a person of consequence. In fact, there's only one person she knows of who could have ever accrued that many commendations.

She lifts her head a little. "Noor?"

General Adhi Noor leans forward so that a blade of light falls across his face. It's him, though he looks about a thousand years older than when she last saw him.

He smiles. "Hello, Turyin. Mind if I come in?"

"Do I have a choice, sir?"

"You do if you'd like to."

She nods and stands to attention. He unlocks the door and steps in. "There's no need for that. You look like you've had a rough time of it. I'd not put you through any more." He sits down on the cot at the other side of the cell. "Why don't you take a seat."

She does as he asks. She thinks for a moment. "Sir, what are you doing here?"

He smiles again, but there's a bitter touch to it. "When Biswal messaged the Ministry about Zhurgut's attack on the city, that put a lot of things in motion. I happened to be in Taalvashtan at the time. The prime minister recommended I jump on a boat and get here as soon as I could. It was only on the way that she . . . *apprised* me of your operation here. It sounds like a damn tricky one." He gives her a piercing glance. "And from what everyone has said you've either caused quite a bit of commotion or you've walked right into a mess of it."

Mulaghesh is silent. He looks her over, and she knows the look: she herself has given it to soldiers under her command many times.

He takes off his hat and sets it in his lap. "Why don't you tell me what happened, Turyin?" he says quietly.

She hesitates. It seems so much easier to just let it all be walled up inside of her, to pack it away and keep it in the dark, away from her waking life. But before she knows it, she begins to talk.

She tells him everything. She describes it in the only language available to her: the dry, clinical, officious vocabulary of an officer making a report. And he listens throughout, hardly moving.

When she finishes he's silent for a while. Then he says quietly, "That's some story."

She swallows. "It's the truth, sir."

"I know it is. I believe you."

"You . . . You do?"

"Yes. I have never known you to lie, Turyin. I've never known you to stretch the truth one jot—even when I really would have preferred you to. And maybe you forget that I was with you just days after the

Battle of Bulikov. I know what this country is like just as much as you do."

"I wasn't doubting you, sir. It's just that . . . that General Biswal . . ."

Noor purses his lips and nods. "Yes. Biswal. I've been in communication with Major Hukkeri and one officer who has, in my opinion, thoroughly distinguished himself, a Captain Sakthi. Their assessments of Biswal's actions don't quite enter into the realm of the fantastic like yours do, but . . . they're close enough. It appears Biswal told numerous officers numerous different stories about what was happening here, anything to get his men to support his mad endeavor to start a new war. That's reason enough to doubt him. And it is my personal opinion that his command here, while brief, has been nothing short of a catastrophe."

"That doesn't acquit a soldier of killing a superior officer, sir."

"No. No, it doesn't. But being that we did discover fragments of these swords you describe in Biswal's rooms, I am tempted to believe you had reasons for your actions."

"Fragments, sir?"

"Yes. Both the swords and the statues that SDC so carefully hoarded have all more or less disintegrated. If you're right—if these miracles persisted only because the will of the dead insisted they did so, as a way to be remembered—then it seems that power is gone. The thinadeskite no longer registers any extraordinary properties at all. It's simply dust." General Noor rotates the hat in his hands, fingering the brim. "If the swords—damn, I hate discussing this odd stuff—if these swords drew that fleet to these shores, and if Biswal was passively willing to allow them to do so, for whatever reason, then it is an extraordinarily damning piece of evidence. That you managed to defuse the situation—however you managed to do it— is remarkable." He glances at her. "I'll probably regret this—I hate asking about anything miraculous—but how *did* you do it? You just threw the sword at them?"

She shakes her head. "The sword was . . . it was like a symbol, sir, an idea made real, or maybe many ideas made real. It was a symbol of their agreement—they'd be soldiers for Voortya, and she would give them eternal life and their final war. It was a matter of just . . . rewriting the agreement."

"How so?"

There's a glint of steel in her eye. "They didn't qualify as soldiers in my opinion, sir."

"And as such . . . you were no longer obligated to allow them their war," says Noor. "Ah. It seems simple now, but . . . Well, actually, no, it *doesn't* seem simple. I hardly understand a bit of it." He sighs. "I admire the prime minister, but I don't much enjoy having to parse through all of her miraculous nonsense. But I'm glad she put you here. She's foresighted, I'll give you that."

"I didn't do it alone, sir. CTO Harkvaldsson was an enormous asset, and . . . and . . ."

"Yes." Noor's expression darkens. "The *dauvkind*." He is silent for a great while. "Did he really kill those soldiers?"

Mulaghesh nods.

"If he was your friend . . . If he helped you . . . well, why didn't you just lie? Why did you tell me that?"

"Lying about how a soldier died, sir," says Mulaghesh, "is a damned cowardly thing to do. It would dishonor them. Even if it hurts me to admit what happened, I have to tell the truth. He . . . He did it in a blind rage. They'd just killed his daughter. . . ." She trails off.

"And you know that won't matter," says Noor. "Even if he is the *dauvkind*. We cannot let such a thing pass. When we find him, we will have to hold him accountable for his actions, no matter who he is."

"*When* we find him, sir?"

"That's right, I suppose you wouldn't know. The *dauvkind* has not been found anywhere since the night of the attempted invasion. He's a Ministry-trained operative. Those sorts can be hard to find." Noor clears his throat. "He has, however, left a letter behind."

"A letter?"

"Yes. He confesses that the entire plan about the yard of statues—

hiding the Divine here amongst the harbor works—was his idea. His daughter had nothing to do with it, he says. He claims it was an act of patriotism, anything to support his country, and he takes full responsibility for his actions—though that's not quite true, what with him having fled and all." He looks at Mulaghesh. "*Is* this true? Was this his idea?"

Mulaghesh rubs her aching left arm. "Possibly. I don't know."

Noor looks her over again, carefully.

"I do know that the statues had little to do with the situation in Voortyashtan," says Mulaghesh. "Their presence was wholly coincidence—everything that happened here was a consequence of the actions of Rada Smolisk and Lalith Biswal. *That* is the truth."

"And why did you never try to contact me? Why did you never reach out to the military council?"

"The idea of the prime minister running an unofficial operation, investigating the Divine . . ." Mulaghesh shrugs. "What sort of reaction would that have evoked? Even if we had discovered a true threat?"

Noor nods, sighing. "That is probably true. There are some who already think this whole thing was a hoax concocted by the prime minister. I suppose denial is a much more comfortable bed to lie in than the truth."

"And what's to become of me, sir? Will I face a trial?"

"A trial?" he says, surprised. "No, not a trial. Not yet, at least. There'll be a hearing, and likely an inquiry—but I expect they will mostly find your actions commendable, Mulaghesh. There were thousands of witnesses to what you did last night, even if they don't quite understand what they saw. There are dozens of soldiers here who can testify to General Biswal's erratic actions before the invasion."

Mulaghesh feels herself trembling. "But . . . But Pandey, and . . ."

His expression softens. "Yes, the poor sergeant major. You explained to me that was an accident. And we did find part of his sword in your false hand. That is proof enough to me."

"But . . . But someone has to . . . to hold me *accountable*, sir."

"For what?"

She almost says, "For everything," because before this only once in her life has she ever felt responsible for so many ills in this world, so many wounds and so many deaths.

General Noor looks at her for a long, long time. "We need to get you home, Mulaghesh. You've been out here too long, out on the front lines. Both in body and in mind." He stands and pushes the door of the cell ajar. Then he turns and says, "I'm going to leave this open, General Mulaghesh. You come out when you're ready. When you think you deserve it. And you *do* deserve it, Turyin."

She waits until she knows he's out of earshot to finally begin to weep again. It takes her more than an hour to summon the strength to walk out.

***

The next day Mulaghesh walks the cliffs in the morning air, reveling in the sunlight. A front has blown in out of the south, pushing the clouds away and bringing warm air with it. Noor has given her a new uniform and has allowed her time to clean herself up and seek first aid, and all of this makes Voortyashtan feel like a different world to her.

She wanders the copses and woods atop the cliffs, walking north of the fortress and the city. It takes only a few minutes to lose her tails—two of them, both plainclothes Saypuri officers, neither of them very good. Then she turns toward the coast.

She finds it almost immediately: the hidden place where the tiny, terrifying stairs wander down to the shore. She remembers sitting on the cliffs and watching Pandey rowing out to sea, and the girl in the boat who met him.

Mulaghesh climbs down the stairs. It would normally terrify her, but it doesn't anymore. Having been death itself for a little bit, she's no longer much afraid of the idea.

She pauses when she's almost at the bottom. She calls out, "Sigrud? I'm coming down! Don't . . . Don't fucking kill me or anything!"

A silence.

Then, quietly, "Okay."

She climbs down the rest of the way and finds him hiding in a cut-in up under a shallow roof of stone. He looks like shit: he's starved, filthy, and he's set his own broken arm, albeit poorly.

"Gods be damned," she says. "How did you survive the past couple of days?"

"Not well," he admits. He looks at her balefully with one sunken, exhausted eye. "How did you know where to find me?"

She walks over and sits beside him on the gravelly shore. "I thought you would want to come somewhere you could remember her."

He bows his head, but says nothing.

"Is all well?" he says after a while.

"No. I told them the truth," she says. "About what happened. About what you did to those soldiers."

"And the harbor?"

"What, your lie about how it was all your idea? Well . . . That I didn't contradict." She looks at him sadly. "Did you not want to disparage the memory of her?"

"I . . . I wanted to keep one last part of her alive," he says. "The one thing she devoted her life to. But now that you've found me . . . Will you tell them? Will you allow them to arrest me, to cast down all the things my daughter built?"

"No. That I won't do. I'm already arranging meetings with the tribal leaders before I ship out of here about that."

"About what?"

"About how if they fuck up all that Signe did for them, and fail to make a nation out of this place . . . Well. Then I'll come back and kill every single one of them."

He looks at her. "Do . . . Do you think that they'll believe you?"

She thins her eyes. "I was their god the other night, Sigrud. Just a little bit, and just for a little while. But I was still Voortya. They'll fucking listen." She sniffs. "But first I'm going to talk to Lem at SDC."

"About . . . what?"

"About leaving Signe's yacht at this location along the shore," she says, handing him a map. "It'll be there tomorrow morning."

He looks at the map, confused, then slowly takes it. "You . . . You're letting me get away?"

"No. I'm giving you a head start."

"But . . . I killed those soldiers."

"Yeah. And that's a hard thing, and I damned well hate it." She watches as the waves grasp at the stones at her feet, trying but never quite managing to tug them away. "But I did something similar once. And people gave me a second chance. I'd be a shit to deny that to others."

"I don't deserve such kindness."

"Ah, there's that word." She looks out at the ocean. "'Deserve.' How preoccupied we are with that. With what we should have, with what we are owed. I wonder if any word has ever caused more heart-ache." She watches as he folds the map, his fingers trembling, his face pinched like a child not to cry. "I'm sorry about Signe."

He stows the map away. "Will I be able to see her?"

"No, Sigrud. You can't."

"Please, I must. Just . . . give me one thing more. Just this one thing."

"Sigrud . . ."

He looks at her, his face resolute. "I want to see her funeral."

"Her *funeral*? Sigrud, I can't . . ."

"Even if it is far away . . . I must see this. I must see her at rest."

"You don't want her buried at home?"

"Buried? Dreylings do not bury their dead." Then he looks west, along the shore, to where the SDC cranes sit. "And this is her home. She devoted her life to this place, this work. If that doesn't make a home, Turyin Mulaghesh, then nothing does. I was never there for her in life, so please . . . Please just let me be there for her for this."

***

It's a brisk evening, the sun painting the skies with cherry-red swathes. Mulaghesh has pulled out her parade dress uniform for the first time in what feels like ages, and the town below is lit with torch-light as the reconstruction resumes. Yet despite the beauty, Mula-ghesh's heart is dull and leaden.

The rifling is heavy in her hand. She wishes Sigrud hadn't asked this of her. But once he did, she couldn't refuse.

She looks up as the smaller gates to the fortress's west wall open. The litter comes rattling out, pulled by a single big draft horse. Noor walks beside it, also in his parade dress, and he gives Mulaghesh a single nod. There's a small retinue of officers in tow, not large, just enough to be tasteful: this is, after all, not their moment. She waits until the litter draws close before she puts the rifling to her shoulder and walks beside Noor.

She glances up at the litter. It's a hastily prepared thing, nothing like a decent hearse, and she can glimpse inside to the fur-wrapped figure within.

"Seems a damned odd ritual," says Noor as they walk down to the city. "Burning the dead is one thing, but in a *ship?*"

"It's symbolic," says Mulaghesh.

"Seems a waste of a ship," says Noor. "But then I guess the Drey-lings have vessels to spare."

"They feel they owe it to her, I suppose."

It's a long way down to the city, but it's a familiar one now. Mu-laghesh eyes the wooden frames rising along the streets, promises of sturdy Dreyling structures to come, though they've halted work for this. *In three weeks,* she thinks, *I won't even be able to recognize this city.* But the biggest change is what's happening down at the harbor, where the seawall and the lighthouse appear to be glowing a soft, shimmering gold.

"My word," says Noor as they near it. "What is that?"

It takes Mulaghesh a minute to understand it, but then she sees that the seawall and every balcony of the lighthouse is lined with lights, and above each light is a face, grim and sad.

"Lanterns," says Mulaghesh. "It's all the workers. They've come to see. They're holding lanterns, every one."

"For . . . her? I thought she was just an engineer."

The litter turns away from the harbor, south toward the northern shore of the Solda. "She did the impossible," says Mulaghesh. She nods ahead to where the Solda is now flowing somewhat freely. "She freed the waters, she built the harbor. And by doing that, she kept their country afloat. The United Dreyling States can make good on all their loans."

"The *dauvkind*'s daughter did all that, you think?"

"One big push, I suppose."

The little boat lies on the shores ahead. It's a small wooden craft, though perhaps in defiance of Signe's tastes, as it's also of a somewhat ornate design. SDC Security Chief Lem stands beside it, dressed in his SDC uniform, grim and downcast.

Mulaghesh walks up and sees the boat is empty, except for a small layer of kindling, which she didn't expect. Lem gives her a guilty look. "We considered lining it with some of her old blueprints," he says. "The ones she didn't use. But we didn't think she would have wanted that. She would have wished us to make use of them."

"She had no time for creature comforts," says Mulaghesh. "I doubt she drew much comfort from them, really. So . . . how does this work?"

"We set her in the boat," says Lem softly. He lifts a tall, thick glass jar of yellow-orange oil. A candle sits in a small glass cup beside it. "We put the oil in the prow. Then we push it into the water, light the candle, and someone cuts the rope. And when it's out to sea, it's set alight. Traditionally it'd be with a flaming arrow, but . . ." He gives her rifling a guilty look. "Not too many skilled with a bow at the moment."

"I see," says Mulaghesh.

Mulaghesh steps to the side as Lem and another SDC worker gently reach in and lift the body out of the litter. They treat their burden as delicately as if it was a bundle of lily petals.

They gingerly lay her inside the boat. Lem reaches for the knot at the top of the furs, and he plucks at it and it falls apart. As it does the furs slide away to reveal the face beneath.

She looks as Mulaghesh expected: colorless, distorted, slightly swollen. Not like Signe, not like the person Mulaghesh knew in life, so filled with hunger and delight. But Mulaghesh has seen corpses before, so she knew what she'd see.

"Good-bye, Signe," she says softly.

She and Noor turn and slowly make their way down to the seawall beside the Solda. The SDC workers there salute her solemnly, their faces lit with golden light from their lanterns. She salutes back and turns to look upstream.

How many times have I done this before? How many children's funerals have I been to?

She looks upstream. Lem kneels, lights the candle, whispers something, and slashes the rope. The little boat bobs a bit, then slowly wanders downstream, picking up speed in the weak current. It's going at a good clip when it passes Mulaghesh, and she snatches the barest glimpse of the still, pale face within.

I'll wait, she thinks. *I want her to see as much of what she built as I can allow before I do it.*

The little boat passes the seawall, then drifts out beneath the cranes, which sit dark and hunched in the waters. Mulaghesh scans the horizon. Far in the distance, only a half a mile or so past the lighthouse, she thinks she can discern the slightest hint of a boat's sail.

There, she thinks. *Now he can see. . . .*

She kneels, places the rifling on the edge of the seawall—her left arm is still wounded from her duel with Pandey—and draws a bead on the little boat and the glimmering glass jar at the brow.

The rifling jumps. There's a spark and suddenly the boat is alight. Within seconds it's a bright, clean yellow flame, drifting out to sea.

And as the light filters across the bay, a strange sound accompanies it. It sounds like a wave or perhaps a roar, starting low and growing the farther the boat drifts to sea. Slowly Mulaghesh realizes the Dreylings are shouting, starting at the lighthouse and rushing down the seawall until all the men around her are shouting as well, a long, sustained cry.

It's not a cry of grief, she finds, nor one of pain or loss or sorrow;

rather, it's a shout of triumph, of victory, of good-bye and farewell, a shout of love, love, defiant love.

When it's over she and Noor trudge back up to the fortress. "Do you think it will be any different, Turyin?" he asks. "Do you really think the Voortyashtanis can ever truly be civilized?"

She shrugs. "Why only doubt the Voortyashtanis? I'm not even sure if we can civilize ourselves."

***

Sigrud lies in the dark in the hatch of the yacht, unable to sleep. The waves toy with the boat mercilessly, but it took almost no time at all for his head to readjust, learning to move with the waves and the vast ripples of the ocean. He narrowly avoided a storm this morning, which was lucky as he doubted not only his arm but the quality of the ship's jibsail. He's not sure how his daughter managed to pilot this thing out to the Teeth of the World so well.

He does some calculations in his head about the time. Then he rolls over to the tiny porthole beside him, licks his finger, and begins to write upon the glass.

Frost creeps across the window, then recedes, leaving behind the moving image of a woman seated at a desk, staring at a sheet of paper in her hands.

She looks old, worn, and yet blearily noble, the look of a woman prepared to speak but no longer quite capable of believing what she's about to say.

Shara Komayd glances at him, then does a double take. "Sigrud? *Sigrud!* What are you . . . My word, you look *terrible*."

"Hello, Shara," he says hoarsely.

To his surprise she appears to pick up the edges of the image and carry it away with her. He must have wound up appearing in a hand mirror of hers by mistake, rather than a windowpane. "You can't do this, Sigrud. You can't contact me, not now. They're looking for you, all of them! And I can't intervene, not this time!"

"I know," he says. "I . . . I just wanted to talk to you."

She carries him into her bedroom and sets him down on the bedside table. It's evening there. The four-poster bed sits behind her, its curtains drawn. "I'm . . . I'm so sorry about what happened, Sigrud. Your daughter . . . Her presence in the city was wholly incidental to why I sent Mulaghesh in the first place. Are you healthy? Are you safe? Don't tell me where you're going."

"I won't. I am . . . I am all right. I can't tell you where I'm going, because I don't know. But I will take your counsel. Shara . . . what should I do?"

"I'm afraid you must hide, Sigrud. I'm sorry, but . . . I don't have the clout anymore to change the minds of the military. To attempt something like that after what I've done so far—it would cause considerable problems."

"So I must hide," says Sigrud.

"Yes. You must run, and hide. Be someone new. Use an identity you've never used before or never even *had* before. One that you can use for a long time."

"A long time?"

She nods. "I'm afraid it must be so. You killed five soldiers, Sigrud. You killed them brutally during one of the worst assaults in Saypuri history. Those in power—or those who are about to *be* in power—will not be forgiving of that."

"So I am alone," says Sigrud softly. "Again."

"I'm sorry. The United Dreyling States are in no position to shield you. They depend wholly upon Saypur just to stay solvent, and there is an inquiry into what happened at the harbor. I am already in conversation with your wife about . . . about how to distance herself from this incident."

"From me," says Sigrud. "To distance herself from me."

"Yes, from you."

He sighs. "When I first came to Voortyashtan, I wanted nothing more than to make the world leave me alone, to leave the trappings of power behind. But now to actually do it . . ." He shuts his eyes and shakes his head, fighting tears. "I wish to see my family so *much*."

"I know," says Shara. "When it is possible, I will do what I can. I'm so sorry, Sigrud. I'm so sorry."

He sniffs and wipes his nose. "Did . . . Did you know about the swords? About Voortya? About the City of Blades?"

"No, I didn't. I assumed there was malfeasance and corruption taking place at Fort Thinadeshi—but I had no idea it would spiral into something like this."

"In that case, I must ask . . . Why did you send Mulaghesh?"

"Why? What do you mean, why?"

"I mean . . . I know you, Shara. I know you never play the short game. There is always a bigger objective when you do anything. So why Mulaghesh? Why pull a general out of retirement and send her to Voortyashtan if you thought it was just common corruption?"

Shara sighs deeply. "Well. If you really must know . . . You are aware, of course, that my term in this office is not long for this world?"

"It would be hard not to know this."

"Well." She clears her throat and adjusts her glasses. "The incoming party is riding quite high off of a wave of anti-Continental sentiment. They do not like my policies and programs. They wish to see them end. So if they win, then the harbor will likely be much reduced. Financial support will be cut. All aid to the Continent—that will be cut. Any programs encouraging the participation of Continentals in their own politics—those will be cut. Basically anything Saypur sends to the Continent, except for guns and the soldiers to point them, will be cut."

"So . . . what does this have to do with Mulaghesh?"

Before Shara can answer there's a noise from behind her, from the curtains of the bed: "Momma?"

Shara freezes and turns around just as a small, round face pokes through the curtains of the bed. It's the face of a young Continental girl, perhaps no older than five, and she blinks sleepily at Shara and rubs her eyes. "What are you doing?"

"Shhh, my dear," says Shara. "It's nothing. Just talking to myself. Go back to sleep."

"You're talking to that mirror." The girl looks at Sigrud and frowns. "You're talking to that *man* in the mirror." She pouts and holds out her arms to Shara.

Shara sighs, holds out her arms, and the girl jumps into Shara's embrace—perhaps a little too hard for Shara's comfort, judging by her face. Then the girl lays her head on Shara's shoulder and turns just enough to stare at Sigrud quizzically.

"Did she say . . . Did she call you *momma?*" asks Sigrud, astounded.

"Yes," says Shara quietly. She strokes the girl's hair and chin. "Sigrud, this is my daughter—Tatyana." She leans in close to speak into the girl's ear. "Tatyana, this is an old friend of mine."

"How is he in a mirror?" the girl asks.

"It's a special mirror," says Shara.

"Oh." She appears to accept this explanation wholeheartedly.

"You . . . You adopted a Continental?" says Sigrud.

"Yes," says Shara. "When revisiting Bulikov. There was an orphanage. It was"—she glances at the girl—"not in the best of conditions. She asked to come with me. I took her. I've kept it quiet, you see. Maybe because I didn't need to be linked with the Continent any more than I already am—and maybe because I am unwilling to allow the public to know anything of my private life. When I am voted out of office, I will retire with Tatyana to the countryside, and attempt to live a quiet life. The worst thing I can do for my policies is come near them. My very presence is toxic to my own goals, you see. But I must leave *someone* behind to fight for them, and for the Continent."

"So you think . . . Are you saying you think Mulaghesh could do this?"

Shara sits up straight, and suddenly it's quite easy to see how she was elected. "Yes. General Turyin Mulaghesh is a born leader. She has fought for her country numerous times, was subjected to abominable trauma at the age of sixteen, and somehow came out of it a better person. She has defended Saypur's soldiers from Divine forces *twice* now, in full view of the public. She is admired by the public and respected by the military. She is moral and judicious to a fault. She knows a damned sight more about the military than any politician currently holding office. She is, in short, a highly electable candidate."

"You mean to force her into *politics*?" says Sigrud, somewhat horrified.

"I must leave someone behind to fight for my policies, Sigrud," says Shara quietly. "I must have a champion. When Mulaghesh quit, it was quite a blow. But I believed I understood why she left. Turyin Mulaghesh is someone who has chosen to live her life for the safety and betterment of others. She has chosen, in a word, to serve. If she feels she is not serving, she feels she has no worth. I sent her to Voortyashtan to awaken her, to remind her of this, to be with common soldiers again and remember who she is and why she does what she does." Shara bows her head. "I feel Turyin Mulaghesh is very awake now. Perhaps more than she has ever felt in her life. Much more than I intended."

"After what she has been through," says Sigrud, "after what she has seen and done—you wish to force her into leadership?" He shakes his head. "Shara, Shara . . . of all the things you could have said you'd done this for, this is by far the cruelest."

"We all make compromises to try to better the world," she says, her voice small. "This is but one of the many I've had to make. Saypur will soon have to decide what sort of nation it will be. Will it stay the same, and use its force blindly, unaware of the cost it is incurring upon itself and other nations? Or will it try to be something . . . different? Something wiser, perhaps, and more judicious? Mulaghesh is the best possible person to help my nation through this decision, and the wheels are already in motion, Sigrud. When she arrives next week, I will formally ask her."

"And if she says no?"

"I can be convincing," says Shara. "As you know."

"You are very talented," says Sigrud bitterly, "at putting ideas into other people's heads. I wonder if the world will ever forgive us for what we did in our lives, Shara."

"What do you mean?"

"I mean . . . I sometimes wonder if it was fate that took my daughter from me," he says. "I have taken many lives in my life. Many children, perhaps husbands, wives, parents. Perhaps it is only just that this same violation was inflicted upon me. Perhaps it is just that one who lives a life of war becomes a refugee from it." He looks at the little girl in Shara's arms and tries to remember how that felt so long ago—how small she was, how warm, and how her gaze burned so bright. "If you had asked me last week if this fight was worth it, I would have told you yes. But if you asked me today, Shara Komayd, if you asked me right now if this was worth it—I would tell you no, no, a thousand times no. Never, ever, never could this fight be worth what it asks of us." Then he wipes the glass with a finger, and Shara and her daughter are gone.

***

Mulaghesh wakes slowly, listening to the sound of the waves. *Don't forget where you are,* she thinks to herself. *Remember where you are.*

It takes her a moment to realize she's really awake. She opens her eyes and stares at the ceiling of the rundown little shitshack of a hotel. Then she sits up, takes a deep breath, and looks around her.

Sunlight streams in through the stained blinds, strobing as seabirds dip and rise above the docks outside her window. She can hear the longshoremen in the streets below calling to one another, cursing one another's slowness or incompetence, or sharing a filthy joke. Everything smells like sea salt, or diesel, or cigarettes.

It smells and sounds, in other words, like civilization, in all its filthy, raucous splendor. It's been twenty-three days since she shipped out of Voortyashtan to finally stop here on the last leg of her journey back to Ghaladesh. The Ahanashtani docks are no one's idea of a peaceful respite, so she's not sure why she feels so at ease here. But she remembers something Sigrud said to her years ago, in the hospital in Bulikov: *Many people despise ports. They think them filthy, dangerous. And perhaps they are. But sea ports are the staging places of better things.*

She looks at her bedside table, where a gleaming metal hand sits, its fingers extended in a curious position, as if waving farewell. Some mechanism inside was damaged by Pandey's blade, and she can't get some of the knuckles to work right. But she doesn't care. She takes it off her nightstand, affixes it to her left arm, which is still bandaged from her duel with Pandey, and with five simple clicks the prosthetic falls into place.

Not completely broken. Still good. Better than what she had before, certainly.

She packs up, tosses her duffel bag over her shoulder, and heads out to port, scanning her papers for her next ship. As she approaches the dock she looks up and does a double take.

"Ah, shit," she says. "Of all the shitting luck . . ."

The blinding white hull of the luxury ship *Kaypee* stands a few hundred feet before her. She's not looking forward to spending the next three days with a bunch of families and infants and lovers. She's glad she's not wearing her uniform, as that would attract a lot of unwanted attention.

But as she approaches the ship she sees that, though the other passengers are indeed very young, they aren't who she expected.

About thirty young privates, all in fatigues, stand on the dock with their bags in piles around their feet, waiting nervously for permission to board. She glances at their uniforms and sees they're from the 7th Infantry, which last she heard was stationed somewhere inland—Bulikov or Jukoshtan, she can't remember which. Probably being sent back to Ghaladesh to prep for new deployment, new assignments. They have a brittle sort of nervousness to them, and Mulaghesh guesses that her nation must be making some bold military moves if they're willing to pull these troops out and buy up the *Kaypee* for it. But they would have to be bold, considering what happened. Saypur must posture, and prove it's not vulnerable.

She's not surprised no one told her. Her country likely has no idea what to do with her right now.

She gets in line behind the young soldiers and drops her duffel bag. It makes the boards quake, causing a few of the soldiers to glance back at her, watching as she lights a cigarillo. One of them takes in her bruises, bandages, scars, her prosthetic left hand. He gives a nod to her, a gesture between equals. But of course it would be. If she were senior rank, she'd be in uniform. She nods back.

She looks closer at their uniforms. "Seventh Infantry, huh?" she says.

The soldiers look back. "That's right," says one, a young woman.

"Last I heard you were in . . . Jukoshtan, right?"

"Right."

"That's an exciting assignment."

She smirks. "Not hardly."

"Yes, a great station to work on your Batlan game, they told me. Any of you serve under Major Avshram?"

"Uh. Yes, actually. I did," says the young woman.

"He still got that fucking mustache?"

The soldiers grin. "That he does," says the young woman. "Despite any sense of common decency." She looks her over. "You in the service?"

"Used to be. Might be still. Won't know until we get home."

They nod sympathetically. To be a soldier is to no longer own your life.

"Where were you stationed?" asks the young woman.

"Well, technically," says Mulaghesh, "I was on vacation."

She laughs in disbelief. "That must've been some vacation."

"You're telling me."

They chat and joke and share cigarettes as they wait to board. One bold young private tries one of Mulaghesh's cigarillos, one of the foul things she purchased at the docks. He turns a dull green a few puffs in, inciting peals of laughter and raucous ridicule. Mulaghesh smiles, watching them, drinking in their adolescence, their optimism, their naiveté, their mannered cynicisms. She knows such youth is far behind her, but she has always felt that to foster it, protect it, and watch it grow is still a fine thing. Perhaps one of the finest things.

She thinks about what could have happened to these children if she hadn't picked up the sword, if she hadn't listened to it speak, and then spoke to the sentinels in turn. She wonders what would have happened if she'd figured it all out earlier, if she'd listened and watched Rada a little closer. A contained disaster, she thinks, is still a disaster. Hundreds of people died deaths that could have been avoided. And Nadar, and Biswal, and Pandey and Signe . . .

She watches light bounce off the waves and dance along the hull of the ship. *Gone,* she thinks. *All gone. And yet again, I survive.*

Her arm aches. Less than it used to. But it's still there. Maybe it'll always be there.

The young soldier who tried her cigarillo is now trying to feed it to a seagull, much to the amusement of his comrades. Mulaghesh smiles. *I don't know if I'm ever going to wear a uniform again,* she thinks, watching the soldiers, *but I will still fight for you.*

The line starts moving. They throw their bags over their shoulders, lean forward, and start up to the plank to the *Kaypee.*

The young soldier looks back at her, and says, "Well. No matter what's waiting for you in Ghaladesh, I hope you find some rest, and peace."

"Peace?" says Mulaghesh, a touch surprised. "Well, maybe. Maybe."

They climb aboard and ready themselves for the short journey home.

ACKNOWLEDGMENTS

Thanks to Brent Weeks, who read *City of Stairs* and gave me some very foresighted advice about the state of Sigrud's health.

Thanks to my editor, Julian Pavia, for helping me cut one whole book out of the middle of this one, much to the improvement of everything.

Thanks to Deanna Hoak and Justin Landon, whose observations about these books have fueled ideas for future ones. Innovation sometimes arises from the simplest mistakes.

Much thanks to Myke Cole, for taking time out of his busy schedule to educate me on all things military for this novel. I now know the difference between a clandestine and a covert operation.

Many thanks to Ashlee and Jackson, who continue to tolerate me for reasons unknown.

And many, many thanks to those who read *City of Stairs,* without whose support this book would surely not exist.

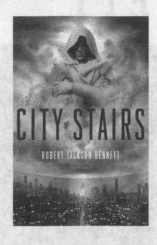

A dazzling new series, which finds a secret war brewing
in a city that runs on industrialized magic, from author

ROBERT JACKSON
BENNETT

COMING
SOON

"Complex characters, magic that is tech and vice versa,
a world bound by warring trade dynasties . . . Bennett will
leave you in awe once you remember to breathe!"

—TAMORA PIERCE

"An absolutely riveting secondary world fantasy . . . I went
to bed late reading it and woke up early to finish it. . . .
A magnificent, mind-blowing start to a series I'm hungry for."

—AMAL EL-MOHTAR,
The New York Times Book Review